LOVESICK BLOSSOMS

LOVESICK BLOSSOMS

a novel

Julia Watts

THREE ROOMS PRESS
New York, NY

Lovesick Blossoms
A Novel by Julia Watts

ISBN 978-1-953103-42-0 (trade paperback)
ISBN 978-1-953103-43-7 (Epub)
Library of Congress Control Number: 2023934221

TRP-109

Publication Date: October 24, 2023
First Edition

BISAC Coding:
FIC018000 Fiction / LGBTQ+ / Lesbian
FIC014080 Fiction / Historical / 20th Century / General
FIC082000 Fiction / Small Town & Rural

COVER DESIGN:
KG Design International: www.katgeorges.com
with design assistance from Arden Paterson

BOOK DESIGN:
KG Design International: www.katgeorges.com

DISTRIBUTED IN THE U.S. AND INTERNATIONALLY BY:
Publishers Group West: www.pgw.com

Three Rooms Press | New York, NY
www.threeroomspress.com | info@threeroomspress.com

For those who cleared the path for us

LOVESICK BLOSSOMS

1953

CHAPTER 1

"Boots," Miz Elizabeth said, "tell that wife of yours she's got to let me do something with her eyebrows."

Boots gestured in Samuel's direction with his gin and tonic. "She's sitting right there, Mama. You tell her."

Miz Elizabeth pursed her fuchsia lipsticked lips, the print of which now decorated the rim of her cocktail glass. "You're the one who should tell her. You're her husband. She'll do what you say."

Boots smiled, a little moue. "That's a logical fallacy if I ever heard one, Mama. B does not follow from A, not any more than it did with you and Daddy."

"The difference is," Miz Elizabeth said, taking a cigarette out of a silver case and waiting for Boots to light it, "your daddy always *thought* I did what he said." She leaned toward her son's proffered Zippo. "You young people are different."

More different than you know, Samuel thought. And in Boots's case, not even that young, but Miz Elizabeth had reached the age where anybody under the age of sixty might as well be riding a tricycle and licking an all-day sucker.

Boots was fifty-two but still his mama's baby. Sitting there at five o'clock, in what still got called the parlor, halfway through her first gin and tonic, Samuel tried to imagine how she and Boots must look through Miz Elizabeth's eyes.

Boots was what Miz Elizabeth had made him, wearing the same seersucker suits (Today's had stripes the color of orange sherbet) along with the cowboy boots that had given him the nickname he'd had since childhood. But Samuel knew that she herself was a puzzle to Miz Elizabeth, a confusing assortment of choices that would make no sense to a woman who prided herself on being a lady, who wore high heels and stockings in her own house. Why would Samuel choose to use her mother's maiden name instead of the perfectly lovely first name she'd been given (Katherine)? Why did Samuel insist on wearing her hair in the same straight bob she had worn as a child? Why the boys jeans, the baggy button-down shirts, and the penny loafers? Samuel knew if she tried to explain herself to Miz Elizabeth, it would only confuse her more.

"What do you want me to do with my eyebrows, Mama Liz?" Samuel asked, shaking a cigarette from the pack on the coffee table. "Dye them? Give them a curly permanent?"

"Oh, now you're just being silly," Miz Elizabeth said, smoothing out the skirt of her rose-colored dress. Impeccable. Miz Elizabeth always looked impeccable. "You know I want to pluck them."

"Just like a chicken," Boots said. Miz Elizabeth rolled her eyes at her son's comment.

"I tell you what, Mama Liz," Samuel said, draining her cocktail and holding out her empty glass for Boots to refill.

"Why don't you have another gin and tonic? The more you drink, the better I'll look."

Boots hooted with laughter. "It's a tried and true beauty secret!"

"Well, all the same, I believe I'll pass," Miz Elizabeth said. "If I didn't know better, I'd think you children were trying to get me tiddly. Besides, I need to keep a steady hand in case you change your mind about me taking the tweezers to you, missy."

Supper was always at six. Before Priscilla left at five to fix supper for her own family, she always made sure their food was ready and kept warm on the stove or in the oven. Tonight, was smothered pork chops, mashed potatoes, turnip greens, and cornbread. Jars of pickles and chowchow and preserves sat on the table beside a sweating glass pitcher of iced tea. Miz Elizabeth always switched to tea at dinner. Samuel and Boots often worked in a third cocktail but drank iced tea, too. It was two-fisted drinking, with one hand temperate and one hand tipsy, that Boots had once compared to those rough boys who have *good* tattooed on the knuckles of one hand and *evil* on the other.

Miz Elizabeth had to know that Boots and Samuel did not have a typical marriage. The twenty-eight-year age difference between them was just the start; however, Samuel figured that Miz Elizabeth was so relieved that Boots had finally found a wife—any kind of wife—that she wasn't going to ask too many questions.

Boots had been Samuel's English professor at Millwood College for Women, which was just up the street from the home he and Samuel and Mama Liz now shared. Samuel had grown up two towns over, the daughter of a mill worker and a housewife, and had come to Millwood on a full academic scholarship. She was the first member of her family to enroll in college. Boots had been her freshman English teacher, and she thought he was the most glamorous person she had ever met. Unlike the men in her hometown, he took pains with his appearance. His hands were soft, and his nails were clean and neatly trimmed. The color of his bowtie always matched the stripes in his seersucker suit.

Boots was the author of a novel, *This Quiescence of Dust,* which had received a glowing review in *The New York Times* and had landed him on several lists of promising young writers. He dropped names in class like *Miss Flannery* and *Miss Eudora,* which always made the hair on Samuel's forearms prickle with excitement.

After Samuel turned in her first paper in Boots's class, he had asked her to come see him in his office. She went there in a cold sweat, afraid she was in trouble because the essay she had written—about the horrific beating of a shy, bookish boy in her hometown—was too frank, too brutal to write about for a class. But instead, once she had accepted Boots's invitation to sit down across from his huge, polished walnut desk, he picked up her paper and said, "This is good. Remarkably so for someone of your limited age and experience. Have you ever thought about becoming a writer?"

Samuel feared she might embarrass herself by crying. "It's all I've ever wanted to be," she said. She spilled all of it: the stories she had started writing when she was seven, the dozens of composition books she had filled with stories (some pretty good), poems (none any good), and ideas.

Boots had looked her up and down, then looked back down at her paper. "Well, between the two of us, I think we can make that happen."

Samuel had felt a pleasant inflating sensation, like she was a balloon being filled with helium so it could float up into the clouds. She had never received admiration from someone she admired, had never had a knowledgeable teacher so generous in sharing that knowledge with her. It was new and exciting, a kind of love.

It was a kind of love, too, she felt now, living with Boots and Miz Elizabeth in their family home in the row of Fine Old Homes that lined Main Street. The three of them eating supper together at the kitchen table was cozy, especially with the gin making Samuel feel convivial, and Priscilla's cooking was good and plentiful, a contrast to the meals when Samuel was growing up when there had been just enough to eat but no more. Having meat at every meal still felt like a luxury.

After supper, they went back to the parlor where Boots poured them each a sherry and put a record on the turntable. It was always opera. Tonight was Maria Callas in *Aida.* Silence was the rule when listening; there was no talking, even when Boots got up to flip the record from Side A to Side B.

Miz Elizabeth sat in the crimson wing-backed chair, sipping her sherry. Boots stretched out on the camelback sofa, closing his eyes as he listened, and Samuel sat in the rocking chair, listening too, but also watching her husband and mother-in-law as they listened. Sometimes when Callas hit a high note, Boots's hand would fly up to his heart as though such beauty would be the death of him.

Miz Elizabeth retired to her room after the sherry and the record were finished. Samuel and Boots waited until Miz Elizabeth had made her way up the stairs and closed the bedroom door behind her before speaking.

"It's Friday night, missy," Boots said. "What kind of trouble do you reckon we should get into?"

"You want to call Carlyle?" Samuel asked. Carlyle Cox was a librarian at the college and a wicked-witted drinking buddy of theirs.

"Oh, Carlyle's in Lexington this weekend, getting into way worse trouble than we could in this little old town. You've got to watch those librarians. The reason they're so quiet is they're always plotting something."

Samuel considered. "Anything good on at the Hippodrome?"

Boots crinkled his nose like he was smelling something unpleasant. "A Western."

Samuel didn't mind Westerns—she had played cowboy a lot as a kid—but she knew that if a movie didn't feature glamorous people in beautiful clothes, Boots wouldn't sit through it. "You wanna grab the gin and go out to the guest house?"

"The gin and the tonic and the ice, you heathen," Boots said. "If it weren't for me, you would descend to utter savagery."

"I'm pretty sure your mama thinks I already have."

She grabbed the gin bottle from the cabinet and headed toward the kitchen with Boots following.

"Honey, she made up her mind you were a savage when she found out your family didn't have a china pattern."

Stepping out on the back porch, the wet summer heat smacked Samuel in the face. They walked down the pebble path lined with azalea bushes to the guest house. Since Miz Elizabeth rarely had overnight guests, Samuel and Boots used the small outbuilding for late night drinking sessions. Miz Elizabeth thought they went there when they wanted privacy. Which they did, but not in the way she thought.

Once they were in the guesthouse, which was basically a free-standing bedroom with adjoining bath, Samuel slipped off her shoes, propped up on some pillows against the headboard, and patted the spot beside her.

"Are you beckoning me to bed, my comely wife?" Boots said, pulling off his namesake footwear.

"After a fashion, my darling husband," Samuel said.

Boots set his drink on the nightstand, took off his jacket, and undid his bowtie. "Aren't you afraid I might ravish you?"

"Not at all, actually," Samuel said, and they both laughed.

Boots McAdoo wasn't the first professor at Millwood College to marry one of his students. A few of them had even impregnated students, then married them. Though Samuel and Boots's matrimonial status was the same as these other couples, the reason for their marriage was quite different.

Her name was Peggy, but since her chosen name in the intermediate French class where Samuel had met her was Claire, Samuel preferred to think of her as Claire. Even though she was from Richmond, Virginia, instead of Paris, there was something about Peggy/Claire that seemed European and sophisticated to Samuel, especially compared to the other girls at Millwood. Peggy/Claire wore her hair in a sleek chignon instead of the de rigeur ponytail. She wore fitted skirts instead of poodle skirts, and her startlingly green eyes were traced in black liner that curled at the creases like the markings on a tabby cat. She smoked cigarettes and wore ballet flats and wrote poetry.

Peggy/Claire lived on the same hall of the girls dorm as Samuel, and it had been exquisite torture to have her so close yet so separate. One night, Samuel had walked down the hall to the shared bathroom to brush her teeth and found Peggy/Claire standing at one of the sinks wearing only a fluffy white towel. Samuel had turned tail and run back to her room before Peggy/Claire could see her.

But then there had been the night when there was a knock on Samuel's door and she opened it to find Peggy/Claire, fully clothed this time. She had missed French class that day, she told Samuel, for personal reasons, and she wondered if she could get the assignment. Samuel invited her in, and as they sat on the narrow bed together, Samuel's heart beat so loudly she was sure Peggy/Claire could hear it as they pored over their French verbs. Samuel kept her eyes on her textbook, but when she finally got up the nerve to steal a glance at Peggy/Claire, she saw she was crying.

"What's the matter?" Samuel asked.

Peggy/Claire rubbed her fingers under her eyes, smearing her kitty-cat eyeliner. "It's stupid. I'm a living, breathing cliché. I just found out my boyfriend is cheating on me."

"Who would cheat on you? You're the prettiest girl at Millwood," Samuel blurted out.

"He would, apparently. But thank you."

Samuel had never been one of those nurturing girls who seemed to automatically know what to say to comfort the suffering, so what came out of her mouth was, "Want a drink?"

"Yes," Peggy said, giving her eyes one more wipe. "That's exactly what I want."

Samuel retrieved a contraband bottle of bourbon ("No alcohol on campus" was one of Millwood's most cited and most ignored rules) and poured a generous amount in a water glass she held out to Peggy.

"Aren't you having one, too?" Peggy asked.

Samuel grinned sheepishly. "I've only got one glass."

"Then we'll just have to share, won't we?" Peggy accepted the glass from Samuel's embarrassingly shaky hand. "Alcohol kills germs anyway, right?" She took a sip and grinned. "Not that I think you're germy or anything."

They passed the glass back and forth until a refill was necessary. After that round was finished, Peggy said, "You know, it's not that I was even in love with Chuck. It's just that the rejection hurts so much. The not being wanted."

Samuel had to bite her lower lip hard to stop herself from saying, "I want you." Instead, she said, "Chuck is an idiot." She had never even met Chuck, but she was still confident in her opinion.

Peggy laughed. "He really is. You know, he wouldn't even be passing American lit if I wasn't writing his papers for him. When I gave him the paper on unreliable narration in 'The

Cask of Amontillado' that I wrote for him, I told him about my family going to the Poe House back in Richmond. He thought I was saying my family was poor."

Samuel laughed as hard as she'd laughed in a long time. "Alms for the Poe!" she said, refilling their glasses with the last of the bourbon.

"Sometimes I get so tired of dating boys," Peggy said. "The way you have to pick out outfits and fuss with your hair and makeup. And you have to worry about what you say and what you eat. I wish it could be more like this, just two people being relaxed and natural."

It was probably just Dutch courage, but Peggy's words felt like an invitation. "It can be," Samuel said. She leaned over and kissed Peggy lightly and—she thought—sweetly on the lips.

Peggy sprang from the bed. "Oh, no!" she said, backing to the door as if she feared Samuel would pounce on her if she turned her back. "That's not what I meant. That's not what I meant at all!"

Even as Samuel sputtered her apology, she was aware of the irony, that she, an English major and budding writer, had been rejected with words made famous by J. Alfred Prufrock.

Two days later, Samuel found herself sitting in the office of the Dean of Women. Dean Walker was so butch that the skirt she was wearing was her only concession to femininity. She barked at Samuel, "You have been accused of making homosexual advances toward another student. This behavior is in violation of the Millwood College Student Code of Conduct."

"I'm sorry," Samuel's voice came out small and scared. "It was a misunderstanding." She looked at Dean Walker's short haircut, broad shoulders, and lack of a wedding ring. Deep down, could she really be that unsympathetic?

"Given your excellent academic record and the fact that the semester is almost over, you will be allowed to complete your current coursework," she said. "But you will not be returning to Millwood next term."

"You're kicking me out—because of a kiss?"

The Dean of Women winced as if the word "kiss" were repulsive. "Don't pretend it was something innocent, Miss Boatman. A classmate came to you in distress, and you chose to take advantage of her—to prey on her in her weakened state. We expect our students to have strong morals, to serve as positive reflections of the school and fine examples of Christian womanhood. You, Miss Boatman, are not Millwood material."

"But I have a straight A average, and I only need one more semester to graduate."

"And you will be completing that semester at another institution. If you can find another school which will have you, given your disciplinary record."

"But this is the only time I've ever been in trouble." Samuel seemed to be incapable of producing a sentence that did not start with the word *but.*

Dean Walker narrowed her eyes. "One major offense is more serious than a dozen minor ones."

Samuel ran from the Dean of Women's office straight to Boots's. She sat down across from him, crying and out of breath.

"What's all this, Miss Boatman?" Boots said. "You look like your best hound dog just died."

Samuel unspooled the whole story: Peggy, the kiss, the expulsion by the Dean of Women.

"She's a mean old dyke, is what she is," Boots said. "She thinks if she's celibate and goes to church every time the door's open, it'll save her from her nature. But all that repression just makes her meaner than a striped snake." He sighed. "I know what you're feeling right now, Miss Boatman. I know we've never talked about it, but my struggles are your struggles, too."

Boots stood and closed his office door. "I never talked to you about these things because what I saw in you . . . I didn't know if you'd seen it in yourself yet. And if you try to talk to a young person about these things before they're ready, it can explode right in your face. Can I offer you a cup of tea?"

"Bourbon would be better," Samuel said.

"Well, as luck would have it, I just happen to have some of that, too. And it saves me the trouble of boiling water." Boots opened is desk drawer and pulled out a pint bottle of Kentucky straight which he proceeded to pour generously into two china teacups. "There. Very civilized, don't you think?"

"I'll stick out my pinkie when I drink it," Samuel said, accepting the fancy cup.

Boots sat back down, took a healthy slug of whiskey, and then said, "I must tell you, in utmost confidence, that I, too, am a homosexual."

In retrospect, Samuel had wondered if it would have been polite of her to act shocked at this revelation. Instead, she had just nodded.

"Because I share your predilections," Boots continued, holding his teacup in both hands, "it puts me in a delicate situation. I will help you, but I must do so in a way that will not cast suspicion on me. I have had some close calls here. Very close. But fortunately, I am protected by the fact that my family's name means a great deal in this community—and that my grandfather was one of the major donors to this institution. You do not have this kind of protection. We need to figure out how to change that. Tell me, does your family have any money?"

Samuel laughed. "Not a red cent. My daddy's a coalminer, and I grew up in a two-room shack. I'm here on a full academic scholarship. If I hadn't been good in school, I'd probably be washing dishes at the Sundown Diner."

"I see the gravity of your situation," Boots said, refilling their teacups.

Two drinks later, Boots asked, "Miss Boatman, would you be willing to marry me?"

Samuel spat bourbon all over Boots's polished oak desk. "What?" Laughter bubbled up in her throat, and soon she was laughing so hard she couldn't control herself.

"No, no," Boots said, holding up his hands in a "stop" gesture. "Hear me out. It's perfect! It'll put me in a position to advocate for you with the administration, seeing as how you're my intended, and it'll also protect me against certain allegations that pop up from time to time. We'd take care of each other."

"But Professor McAdoo—"

"Boots."

"But Boots," Samuel said. "Look at us." She was dressed straight out of the Sears and Roebuck boys department in trousers and a button-down shirt, and Boots was wearing seersucker in the unlikely shade of lemon yellow. "Would we really fool anybody?"

Boots smiled a teacherly smile. "Well, you see, this is where you fail to understand the mindset of the garden variety heterosexual. The garden variety heterosexual longs so for normality, longs so for people to be easily comprehensible and like himself that when he sees someone trying to be thought of as normal, he is immediately reassured, confident that the person must be 'okay.' It doesn't matter how ham-handed and inept the deviant's attempt at normality is." Boots smiled. "The heterosexual sees what he wants to see."

Their marriage, which had been quickly conducted at the courthouse a few weeks later, seemed to confirm Boots's theory, as the entire courthouse staff expressed delight that "old Dr. Boots is finally tying the knot." After Boots had a few meetings with key Millwood administrators, Samuel's expulsion from school went away, and some of the girls who had never been friendly with her before now expressed admiration that she had managed to snag a professor—and such a handsome and well turned out one, too.

Three years later, here they were in bed together, just not in *that* way. "Did you get much work done today?" Boots asked.

"About five pages." She let her head rest for a moment on Boots's shoulder.

"That's not much for you. Usually, it pours from you like water from a bucket."

"Wrote myself into a corner today. Couldn't figure out what happens next."

"Well, don't think about it too much. Take the weekend and let your subconscious work it out. You'll have it when you sit down at your desk on Monday morning."

He was probably right. He usually was. Even though she had graduated three years ago, he was still her teacher. Her teacher and her benefactor, as he insisted that no wife of his with as much talent as she had should do anything with her days other than write. Plus being home all day, Samuel could take care of Miz Elizabeth if she needed anything, even though she rarely did and didn't seem to enjoy Samuel's company. And if occasionally Samuel had to put on the one dress she owned—a funereal black sheath—to accompany Boots to some excruciating faculty party, so the garden variety heterosexuals could see them as a happy couple, that was a fair trade, too. Just like Boots had said when he proposed to her, they helped each other.

CHAPTER 2

"SUSAN, EAT YOUR PEAS," FRANCES SAID.

Susan was forking up individual peas and arranging them around the pool of gravy in her mashed potatoes as if they were swim-suited dancers surrounding a sparkling blue pool in an Esther Williams musical number.

"Say *eat your peas, Dorothy,*" Susan said.

Frances knew it was best to pick her battles. "Eat your peas, *Dorothy,*" she obliged. Frances didn't want to be the kind of mother she had growing up, the type who finds her daughter's flights of fancy annoying and is always trying to bring her back to the dull reality of pea eating and table manners.

"I will eat my peas, Auntie Em," Susan said, depositing another pea onto her mashed potatoes. "But right now, the peas are frogs, and the mashed potatoes and gravy are a pond."

"Well, then maybe we should tell you to eat your frogs," Henry said, looking up from his plate.

"Eat your frogs!" Susan giggled. "You're silly, Uncle Henry!"

Susan's *Wizard of Oz* phase was a little confusing in its nomenclature because Susan insisted on calling her father, whose real name was Henry, Uncle Henry. Frances always found it discombobulating to hear Susan call her father by his Christian name.

"You're the one who's silly," Danny said to his sister. He had already vacuumed up all the food on his plate and was waiting squirmily for everyone else to finish so he could go outside and play baseball with the other neighborhood boys.

"You don't get to call me silly because you're Toto the dog and all you can say is *arf, arf*," Susan said.

"I never agreed to be the dog," Danny said, folding his arms against his chest.

"Nor did I agree to be Uncle Henry," Henry said, dragging a forkful of meatloaf through his mashed potatoes. "But Susan's like a Hollywood casting agent. She chooses our parts."

"Well, she could at least give me the part of a human," Danny said.

"*Arf, arf*," Susan coached him.

Danny pushed his plate away theatrically. "Jeez, how long does it take for people to eat a meal in this house? I know the guys are already out there waiting for me."

"Let me finish these last two bites," Frances said, "and I'll bring out the chocolate pudding. I'm guessing you can deign to stay in your family's presence for five more minutes if chocolate pudding is involved."

Danny brightened considerably. "I didn't know you made pudding."

"But doggies can't eat chocolate pudding," Susan said. "They can only eat doggy chow."

"Dorothy," Henry said, "I wouldn't stand between a growing boy and his dessert." He patted his round belly. "Or a growing man and his dessert either."

Frances got up to go to the refrigerator. "I should probably pass on the pudding myself," Frances said, knowing she wouldn't do it. "I need to get rid of this baby weight."

"Nonsense," Henry said, grinning at her. His grin, appearing from the depths of his wild beard, always made her think of the Cheshire cat. "You are a voluptuous goddess, full of life-giving energy."

"And you're full of something yourself," Frances said, setting down a large bowl of chocolate pudding and a smaller bowl of whipped cream. Henry was the new Classics professor at Millwood College. As the wife of a classicist, Frances often found herself being compared to a goddess. Goddesses, though, could be voluptuous because they had the luxury of wearing flowing robes or nothing at all. Frances had to wear earthly garments, and it was getting increasingly hard to button the waistbands of her skirts.

"What does *voluptuous* mean?" Danny asked.

"You take that one, Uncle Henry," Frances said, spooning pudding into dessert dishes.

"If you look it up in the dictionary after dessert, I'll give you a dime toward that new ball glove you're saving for," Henry said.

"Okay!" Danny said.

"Well played, Uncle Henry," Frances said. She and Henry had often speculated where Danny's athleticism had come from. Not from either one of his bookish, sedentary parents, that was for sure. Henry had suggested that the gods had decided to give them Danny as some kind of cosmic joke.

After a silent vow to restrict herself to dry toast for breakfast and cottage cheese for lunch the next day, Frances sat down with a heaping dish of chocolate pudding. A loud "*WAAH!*" sounded from down the hall. "I think I hear the source of all that baby weight," she said.

She abandoned her pudding and dashed down the hall to find Robert sitting up in his crib with that *Where am I and who put me in this cage?* look common to infants. Frances had often thought about how strange it must be to be a baby, falling asleep in one place and waking up in another, being carried around like a little suitcase.

Robert regarded her with big, blue eyes.

"Do we need a new diaper, sir?" Frances lifted him up and laid him on the changing table. He did need a new diaper, and for a reason which robbed Frances of her appetite for chocolate pudding. Well, one step toward weight loss, anyway.

After a cleaning, powdering, and changing, she carried Robert into the dining room where he was greeted like a dignitary.

"We're honored that you joined us, sir," Henry said, and Danny got up from his chair to shake Robert's tiny hand. It was a running joke in the family, talking to Robert like he was a distinguished middle-aged businessman instead of a baby. It seemed to amuse Robert as much as it amused the rest of them. The more seriously they talked to him, the wider his toothless grin.

"Su—I mean, Dorothy, why don't you hold this gentleman while I heat up his bottle?" Frances said.

Susan opened her arms. "Come here, sir. Actually, he's not a 'sir' at all. He's a Munchkin baby."

"It's time for my bottle, too," Henry said. "And a little Thelonious Monk, I think."

After dinner, Henry always retired to his study to sip Scotch and listen to jazz while Frances fed the baby and washed the dishes. She set the bottle of formula in a pan of boiling water on the stove. Sometimes she could talk Susan into feeding Robert so she could get started on the dishes sooner, but she had to be careful how she phrased her request. "Dorothy," she tried, "do you think you could give this hungry little Munchkin baby his bottle?"

Susan looked thoughtful for a moment, then said, "Okay, Mrs. Munchkin."

"Thank you, Dorothy." Frances tested a drop of formula on her forearm to make sure it wasn't too hot, then passed the bottle to Susan.

The meatloaf pan was hopeless and would have to soak for at least half an hour. Everything else should come clean fairly easily, provided that the water was nearly scalding. As she scrubbed and rinsed, scrubbed and rinsed, she listened to Susan make up a song that began: *Who's the cutest baby in Munchkin Land?*

"He's all done, Mrs. Munchkin," Susan said.

"Thank you, Dorothy. Let me dry my hands, and I'll come get him."

She took Robert from Susan, who said, "Now I really need to be getting back on the yellow brick road."

"Of course. Bon voyage!" Frances said, even though she didn't think Munchkins spoke French. Susan ran outside, no doubt to skip on the stone walkway leading up to the house, which she had spent the morning coloring with yellow chalk.

Frances draped Robert over her shoulder and patted his back. When the burp came, she felt a warm gush on her sleeve. With the first baby, she always changed her blouse when this happened. Now she didn't even bother.

She set him in his playpen and handed him a rattle, which he shook joylessly and with great concentration, as though it were a job he had been paid to do. After she finished the dishes, she filled a glass halfway with ice and club soda and knocked softly on the door of Henry's study. "It's an adult!" she called, then pushed the door open.

"I figured it was. Children knock louder. When they bother to knock at all." Henry was sitting in his favorite bedraggled armchair with a Scotch in his hand, his shoeless feet propped on an ottoman. His right sock had a hole that his big toe protruded through, and Frances made a note to herself to do some darning.

"Where are you hiding the booze?" she asked.

"Bottom right drawer of my desk."

Frances usually tried to stay away from Henry's desk. It was piled with books and papers in an order that only made sense to Henry. Moving something from one pile to another or neatening a pile into a stack would send him into a panic. She found the Scotch, filled her glass, and settled into the room's other armchair.

Truth be told, she preferred Broadway show tunes to jazz any day, but she did like the way the free-flowing instrumental music let her mind wander.

"Cigarette?" Henry asked.

"Please." Henry didn't like to talk while his music was playing, so she made sure to keep her communication brief.

He lit two cigarettes, Paul Henreid style, and passed one to her.

She smoked and sipped and sighed with contentment. The scotch was smoky in a way that complemented the cigarette. Why were smoky things so comforting? She gazed at the overflowing bookcases that lined the walls, the same bookcases and books they'd had back in Vermont, and felt at least a little at home.

Kentucky didn't feel like home yet. She wondered if it ever would. Henry seemed to have settled right in, but he had a job and therefore, daily contact with other adults. Some days Frances didn't talk to anyone who had shed all their baby teeth until Henry came home in the evening. Other days she'd find herself listening to the chit-chat of one of the other mothers in the neighborhood that was so inane she would have much rather listened to Susan chatter about *The Wizard of Oz*.

Frances had met Henry in a poetry class at Matthews College in Vermont. They had fallen in love with each other's poems and then with each other, although looking back at their earnest college scribblings, Frances was glad they had found a more solid foundation than their poetry to build a relationship on. The war interrupted Henry's education, though thankfully his eyesight was so bad that his military service was at an office in D.C. Frances waited for him for two years and finished her degree. When he returned to finish his, they married in a perfunctory courthouse ceremony, and Frances took a job in the Matthews College library. After one more year of college for Henry, they moved to Connecticut so he could start graduate school, and Frances worked in the university library for a year until she got pregnant with Danny. After Henry finished his degree, he accepted a teaching position back at Matthews, and they moved into a cute little rental house which they proceeded to fill with books and babies.

Frances thought they would stay there forever, but then there was a departmental shake-up and Henry was denied tenure. Since institutions weren't exactly clamoring for classicists, even one like Henry whose dissertation, *Under the Gorgon's Stare,* had been published to some acclaim, the only job he could come by was at modest Millwood College in a Podunk town in Kentucky, of all places. It was a step down—well, more than one step, really—in academic prestige, but Henry put a good face on it, saying that a move south of the Mason-Dixon line would be an adventure.

With a new baby plus two young children, Frances hadn't been sure she was up for an adventure. Raised in Illinois and educated in New England, she had never been further south than Washington, D.C., which she had visited on her high school senior trip. All she knew about Kentucky was horses and bourbon, and she was more of a house cat and Scotch girl herself. Otherwise, her knowledge of the South was straight out of Margaret Mitchell. For all she had known, the region was full of vain young women flouncing about in hoop skirts and saying, "Fiddle-de-dee!"

She was relieved when they arrived to see that Collinsville was a fairly ordinary-looking small town and that the Southern belle look seemed to have gone with the wind. There was a reasonably modern supermarket, a drugstore with a soda fountain, a dime store full of cheap merchandise, a small movie theatre, and a tiny public library. However, there were discoveries that unsettled her: the churches on every corner; the dumpy, college-provided bungalow that was too small for a family of five; the signs in public facilities that read *white* and *colored.*

When the record ended, Frances was halfway through her second scotch and soda. "Tomorrow," she promised Henry and herself, "I will unpack three boxes."

"Good girl," Henry said. "I know I've abandoned you to all this unpacking."

"It's all right. I should have it all done by now. But it's not easy with constant interruptions from Mr. Robert and Dorothy of Oz." The truth was, sometimes she just couldn't face unpacking. She'd stare at a box labeled *dishes* or *mystery novels* or *kids winter clothes* knowing what she needed to do but finding herself unable to do it. Instead, she'd promise herself she would unpack the box after one more cigarette, one more cup of coffee. She'd find herself at the kitchen table smoking and sipping, and if Danny was at school and the baby was quiet and Susan was outside playing, she'd take out a composition book and tell herself she'd write for just ten minutes, just until her cigarette was smoked and her cup was empty. And then she'd write furiously for at least an hour, until Robert cried, or Susan came inside asking for lunch.

Writing was like falling into a hole where time didn't exist. She filled composition book after composition book, but she never showed them to anybody, just shoved them in a box she kept in her bedroom closet. Writing wasn't what she was supposed to be doing.

From the living room, wailing. "Well, there goes Mr. Robert," Frances said, rising to her feet.

"No, sit. Have another drink," Henry said. "Let him cry it out. It's good for him." Henry stood, took the glass from her hand, and went to his desk to refill it.

"That's what all the experts say," Frances said. "But he sounds so miserable."

"He's just exercising his lungs," Henry said, handing her a glass and refilling his own. "No different than a dog barking."

After a while, Robert tired himself out and was quiet. It was nearly full dark, so Frances, feeling a little tipsy, went out onto the front porch and called Danny and Susan in from playing. It was time for them to wash up, brush their teeth, grab their books, and go to bed. Since there were only two bedrooms, Danny and Susan were forced to share a room with a sheet hanging between the twin beds to create an illusion of privacy.

Danny was of the opinion that he was much too old to be read to, so he settled down to entertain himself with *The Book of Astounding Baseball Facts.* Susan had woken up one morning at the age of three with the ability to read fluently, and though Frances missed reading to her at bedtime, Susan now insisted on reading "to herself," working her way through the books in the Oz series.

When Frances left the children's bedroom, Henry took her hand and said, "I thought we might turn in early ourselves."

"Is Robert sleeping?" Frances asked. The crib was in their bedroom, and she refused any hanky-panky if Robert was awake and staring at them with those guileless blue eyes.

"Like a baby," Henry said, "which makes sense, given that he is one."

"I might just take a quick bath first," Frances said, catching a sour whiff of the spit-up on her shoulder.

"If you like," Henry said. "Or we could play Napoleon and Josephine." This was a running joke based on a something Frances had come across in a book of little-known historical facts. Apparently, Napoleon didn't like his wife to wash.

"Yuck," Frances said. "I'll be quick. Don't wake the baby."

The bathtub was the best thing about the dumpy little bungalow. It was big and old with clawed feet like some kind of medieval monster. She ran the water steamy hot and wished she had another drink to sip as she soaked, but she had promised Henry she would be quick, so she washed her face and soaped up her legs and ran a razor over them, then did the same with her underarms. She looked down at her still pregnant-looking belly. Nothing she could do about that, though. The best she could manage was to make sure she wasn't stinky or stubbly.

Bathing quickly was no problem. It was the part after the bath that always posed the challenge.

The plastic box was in the medicine cabinet next to the tube of jelly. She took the little rubber dome out of the box and squirted it with jelly, toothpaste-style. This was the easy part.

Now came the part where she stood naked with one foot on the toilet seat, spread out like a French whore in a Toulouse Lautrec painting, and tried to put the damned thing in. She pinched the slippery dome between her thumb and forefinger but did it too forcefully, making it fly from her fingers like a rock shot from a slingshot. It splatted against the bathroom door, leaving a blob of spermicidal jelly, and fell to the floor. She cursed, picked it up, washed it off, squeezed more jelly, and reassumed the position. This time it was at least in, but not far enough and at the wrong angle. She shoved it in further, but it still didn't slip into place.

There was a soft knock on the door. "Honey? Are you okay?"

So much for being quick. "Yes. Just having trouble with . . . the thing."

"Do you want me to help?"

"No," she said, more forcefully than she had intended. "I'll be out in a minute."

It was strange. Even though she and Henry had been intimate for over a decade, she couldn't bring herself to say the word "diaphragm" to him, and letting him help insert it—even though it was in an area he probably knew better than she did—was unthinkable.

Finally, she felt it slip into place, or at least she thought it was. "No more babies," she said to herself like a magic spell. At least not for a couple of years. She put on her nightgown. Plain white cotton. Henry didn't expect her to look like a pinup.

The actual lovemaking didn't last as long as the diaphragm insertion. It was fine. Frances enjoyed the closeness and cuddling of marriage—the running jokes, the long conversations, and shared meals of a life together—but was largely indifferent to sex.

Sex was like macaroni salad. She wasn't repelled by it, and if it was placed in front of her, she would have some. But she didn't crave it, and she didn't long for it when there wasn't any.

She knew, though, from her mother's talk before her wedding, that this feeling was perfectly normal. When it came to sex, men had to have it, but women could take it or leave it. What her mother hadn't known during "the talk" was that Frances and Henry had already been sleeping together for nearly a year, so her words provided more relief to Frances than her mom could know.

After he rolled off her, Henry closed his eyes and immediately fell asleep. Frances reached over to the nightstand for the book she was reading, Carson McCullers's *The Heart Is a Lonely Hunter.* She was trying to read books set in the South in hopes of feeling more at home, but tonight for some reason, she just kept staring at the strange and lovely title on the cover, her eyes tracing the shapes of the letters in the word *lonely.*

CHAPTER 3

Samuel plopped herself down into a kitchen chair with a dramatic sigh. "I can't write anymore," she said.

Priscilla was standing at the counter, stirring mayonnaise into a bowl of diced potatoes. "Well, you've been in there scribbling for about three hours. Maybe you just ran out of things to say." Priscilla was a tall, solidly built woman, what a flowery writer might describe as statuesque. She always wore a floral-print dress she had made herself, which she covered with an apron while she worked. Unlike most of the white ladies of means in town, Miz Elizabeth didn't insist on her maid wearing a uniform. "You want some coffee?" Priscilla asked.

"Sure, thanks," Samuel said. She was fighting a headache and hoped the caffeine would help. "God, I'm consumed with dread."

"Over what?" Priscilla set a cup down in front of Samuel. She knew how each member of the family took their coffee—and their most frequent houseguests, too.

"This party tonight."

"Well, that don't seem like something to dread," Priscilla said, adding pickle relish to the potato salad bowl. "I love a good party."

"Ah, there's the rub," Samuel said. "I love a good party, too, but this isn't going to be a good party. It's at the chair of Languages and Literature's house, supposedly to welcome the new faculty and welcome back the old ones. It'll be a bunch of professors trying to impress each other while their wives cheer them on from the sidelines."

"Hm. Sounds like one of those white people parties where everybody's really working while they're pretending to be playing."

"That's exactly it," Samuel said, sipping her coffee. "Which is why it won't be a good party."

"I've served at parties like that before," Priscilla said, putting the bowl of potato salad in the refrigerator. "They never feel like anybody's having fun, and the food—if they even bother to have any—is no count at all. Potato chips and peanuts if you're lucky. But lots and lots of liquor. You and Dr. Boots make sure you eat some ham and potato salad before you go. That way you won't be drinking on an empty stomach." Samuel knew she'd end up drinking too much at the party. She always did at events like this because it was something to do.

"We will, Priscilla. Thank you." Truly, Samuel thought, Priscilla had the best sense of anybody in the household.

"You want me to iron your dress for tonight?" Priscilla asked.

"No, it's fine. It's hanging in the closet right where I put it the last time I went to one of these things. I didn't have it on long enough to wrinkle it."

Priscilla shook her head and said, "Hm."

"What?" Samuel had known Priscilla long enough to understand that the sound meant that she had a strong opinion and was holding it back.

"Nothing. I just think it's peculiar for a married lady like yourself to only have one dress. Me, I've got the dresses I wear to work, then the dresses I wear to church. I've even got a party dress stuck in the back of my closet but it don't get much wear these days. And you with that one sad little black dress that makes it look like you're going to your best friend's funeral."

"Your mouth to God's ear," Miz Elizabeth said, coming into the kitchen fresh from her three o'clock nap. "I believe I'll take a cup of that coffee, Priscilla."

"Yes, ma'am." Priscilla busied herself fixing coffee, then looked up and said, "Miss Samuel, what you ought to do is pick out some material and let my mama run you up a few dresses. She just made me two new ones for church, and they're prettier than anything you could buy in a store."

"Oh, that's a fine idea!" Miz Elizabeth said, sitting down at the kitchen table. She was wearing a light blue shirtwaist dress that was nice enough to wear to a party even though she hadn't been out of the house all day. "And you should let Boots pick out the material. He has exquisite taste, you know." She let her gaze rest on Samuel for a moment. "Well, mostly."

"Why, Mama Liz, I can't imagine what you're implying," Samuel said. She wondered if Miz Elizabeth would have been happier if Boots had brought home a more conventional wife—maybe one closer to his age with classic feminine good looks and style. But why would a woman like that agree to marry Boots and live with him and his mama?

"Thanks for the coffee, Priscilla. I'll think about the dresses," Samuel said, getting up from the table. But she knew the dresses would leave her mind the second she left the presence of the other women.

* * *

DR. WELLS, THE CHAIR OF THE Languages and Literature department, also lived in one of the Fine Old Houses that lined Main Street. However, as Boots pointed out to anyone who would listen, Dr. Wells had bought his house after being named department chair, while the McAdoo house had been in Boots's family since it was built in 1865; it was unthinkable that anyone without the name McAdoo would live there.

Unlike the antique-filled parlor of the McAdoo home, Dr. Wells's living room was sparsely furnished with modern store-bought furniture, all straight lines and sharp angles. Men in jackets and ties stood in the living room, talking animatedly with cocktails in their hands. The wives clustered around the periphery and chatted amongst themselves.

Samuel took a deep breath and tried to will herself to be sociable. She was sure Mama Liz had never fought back terror when walking into a party. Mama Liz was a social butterfly, not a cocooned caterpillar like Samuel.

Then again, Mama Elizabeth had been born into a family where she was taught social niceties. The daughter of an on-again, off-again miner father and a mother who had dropped out of high school at sixteen to marry, Samuel grew up in a home where "keep your elbows off the table" was the only etiquette advice she could recall hearing. And it wasn't much help at a cocktail party.

It was the women at the party who filled her with anxiety. With their shampooed and set hair and their strings of pearls, they were the grown-up versions of the girls who had terrorized her throughout school. It was like she was back in the changing room in junior high P.E. class and the girls were laughing at her for wearing a too-small undershirt when they all had bras.

"Shall we go into the fray?" Boots asked, taking her arm.

She nodded. She wished she could stay with Boots. The men were always jockeying for position and territorially pissing, but at least there was some talk of books or ideas. The wives had only three topics: people Samuel didn't know, their children, and illness (their children's, their own, or those of people Samuel didn't know). She knew, though, that if she tried to stay and talk to the men, it would be scandalous, a ripping off of the masks she and Boots were supposed to wear to make people comfortable.

"What are you drinking, McAdoos?" Dr. Wells, a squat and balding man, waddled up to them and slapped Boots on the back.

"Oh, I suppose I could be persuaded to have a wee nip of bourbon," Boots said. "How about you, dear?"

"Also a bourbon, please," Samuel managed. She was always amazed by how sparkling Boots was in social situations. People had to wonder how such a sparkling man could have such a dull wife.

Bourbon in hand, Samuel steeled herself and walked toward the women clustered on the couch and armchairs. They were laughing uproariously about something, many of them with their hands covering their mouths to be ladylike. Samuel felt like they were laughing at her, but she knew this was her schoolgirl-self talking. She took a large gulp of bourbon and waited to be acknowledged. It didn't take long.

"Why, good evening, Katherine," Marjorie Wells, the department chair's wife, said. Her honey blond hair had been freshly set, and her lipstick was unsmeared even though she was sipping some kind of cocktail that looked to have lemonade in it. "And how is Millwood's answer to Jane Austen?"

"Present and accounted for," Samuel said, taking a slug of bourbon. Mrs. Wells was always comparing her to famous lady writers. Not favorably.

Samuel could never remember any of the other wives's names. She thought of them collectively as the Mrs.-es but couldn't keep straight which male faculty members they matched up with. Was the one with pink lipstick on her rabbit teeth Dr. Jameson's wife? What about the one with the little cap of dark curls and the three-strand pearl necklace? She went with Dr. Carter, the French professor, right? She would never get it straight. The other wives were as pretty and indistinguishable from each other as daffodils in a field. She sipped her drink, pasted what she hoped was a pleasant expression on her face, and let the little cluster of women surrounding her resume their chatter.

"Some of the children, especially the ones from the country, come from such unhygienic homes," Rabbity Teeth was saying. "When little Arthur told me the boy who sat in front of him got sent home for head lice, you should have seen me going at his hair with a fine-toothed comb. He didn't have them, of course, but still, my head itches just thinking about it!"

"I never even heard of head lice until we moved down South," Curly Cap said. "Or chiggers or ringworm."

Samuel wondered if she should regale the wives with tales of all the parasites that had colonized her during childhood: head lice and chiggers and once—because of an ill-fated swim in a cow pond—a couple of leeches. She was sure these ladies would say her upbringing had been unhygienic, but what child wanted to be sealed up in a spotless house all day? Samuel had always wanted to be outside in the sunshine, so close to nature that it sometimes took a bite out of her or burrowed right into her skin.

"I know!" exclaimed a wife with a tiny hat perched atop her head like a funny bird. "When we moved here, I couldn't believe the size of the mosquitos. I told Bill we might as well have moved to darkest Africa!"

"Well, I don't know about darkest Africa," said an older wife with a great shelf of a bosom. "At least here we have the sense to keep the colored children separate from the white children. Can you imagine all the lice and worms if the coloreds were allowed to go to school with our children?"

"Unlike humans, I don't think parasites discriminate on the basis of race." These words came from a wife Samuel had never seen before. She wore thick glasses and simple clothes, a white blouse, a navy-blue A-line skirt, and flat shoes. Instead of being shampooed and set into submission, her hair fell in soft, natural waves over her shoulders. "Actually," she continued, "historically lots of African tribes had very advanced hygiene techniques for the prevention of head lice and parasites. It's really white people who were historically filthy. Did you know that the tradition of the June wedding actually came from the fact that many medieval Europeans took their one bath a year in June?"

Samuel found herself laughing for the first time at one of these awful parties. "No fooling? Is that last part true?"

"It is," the new woman said. "Kind of takes the romance out of things, doesn't it?" She took a cigarette out of her purse and put it between her lips.

"You'll have to do that outside, dear," Mrs. Wells said.

"Oh, I'm sorry. Excuse me, then." The new woman got up.

Before Samuel fully knew what she was doing, she was on her feet, too. "I'll join you," she said. They wove their way through the crowded living room into the kitchen where a uniformed maid was filling bowls with potato chips and peanuts.

"Hello," the new woman said to the maid. "We're going outside to smoke."

"I don't blame you," the maid said, not looking up from her work.

Once they were out in the backyard, Samuel said, "Mrs. Wells is real peculiar about people smoking in the house. She has some notion that it'll hurt the baby."

"I can't imagine how it could, unless you burned the baby with your cigarette," the woman said. "I'm Frances Harmon, by the way. I gather you're not much for this kind of party either."

"I'd rather be fed to starving hogs than come to one of these things. Well . . . almost rather. I'm Samuel McAdoo." She held out her cigarette-free hand to shake.

Frances's face lit up. "Oh, you must be Dr. Boots McAdoo's wife! Henry—that's my husband—met Dr. Boots the other day, and when he came home, he was all 'Dr. Boots' this and 'Dr. Boots' that. He just couldn't stop talking about what a colorful character your husband is." She covered her hand with her mouth. "But maybe you don't like hearing him described that way—as a colorful character?"

"It fits him perfectly," Samuel said. "I mean, Jesus, did you see that suit he has on tonight? Talk about colorful!

They both laughed.

"I liked what you said in there," Samuel said, "about hygiene and all."

"Well, socially it was probably the exact wrong thing to say." Frances ground out the stub of her cigarette in a potted plant. "But I've never excelled at being appropriate in groups of ladies."

"Me neither," Samuel said. She couldn't stop smiling.

"And I'm even more inept with these Southern gals," Frances said, sitting on the porch steps and slipping her feet out of her shoes. "They're all so mannered, I always feel like they're speaking in some kind of code." She looked up at Samuel. Behind her glasses, her eyes were a silvery blue. "But you're different, aren't you?"

"I am that. And you're looking at the most socially acceptable version of me, too. This is the only dress I own, and I only drag it out when I have to come to one of these things."

"You wear slacks the rest of the time?" Frances drained her drink which, Samuel noticed, looked to be straight whiskey instead of the sweet concoction the rest of the women were drinking.

"Boys jeans, mostly."

Frances smiled. "You look like you'd be more at home in Greenwich Village than here."

"That's in New York, right? Where all the beatniks are?" Samuel had never been to New York, though Boots had promised to take her someday.

Frances nodded. "It's quite a place."

"Is New York where you're from?" Samuel wasn't good at placing Yankee accents.

"Illinois, originally. Vermont for college, then Connecticut, then Vermont again. And now here. It's . . . an adjustment. But the kids are little. It's not as hard on them as it would be if they were older." She took another cigarette out of her purse. "One more before we rejoin the ladies, I think. Sometimes I think I just use smoking as a stalling tactic." She lit up, then asked, "Do you and Boots have kids?"

"Lord, no," Samuel said. She couldn't help laughing. For her and Boots to have children, they would have to have sex, which was an image she couldn't capture despite her vivid imagination. But she couldn't tell Frances this. "We're not grown-ups ourselves," she said, which was her and Boots's standard line when questioned about procreation, "so how could we possibly have children?"

"Oh, you'd just fake it like the rest of us," Frances said. "Hope that at least the kids think you know what you're doing."

Samuel smiled. Frances was easy to talk to, which was something you couldn't say for most people.

"Oh, Lord," a voice called theatrically from the back door. "Heaven knows what kind of troublemaking is going on out here!"

Boots stepped out on the back stoop with a tall, round-bellied man with a dark beard and horn-rimmed glasses. "I thought I might find you out here," the man said.

"Yes, we flew away from the hen party," Frances said.

"Too much squawking about nothing," Samuel said, ashing her cigarette.

"Your wife's funny, too," the bearded man said to Boots.

Boots gave Samuel a gallant nod. "To be married to me, one must be in full possession of a sense of humor."

"And maybe not much more sense of any kind," Samuel said, sticking her tongue out at Boots.

"Samuel, you impertinent creature, this is Henry, our new Classics scholar."

Henry already strode over to envelop Samuel's small hand in his enormous one. "Delighted," he said. "And I see you've already met my co-conspirator here. Boots, this is my wife, Frances. Frances, Dr. Boots McAdoo."

Boots took Frances's hand and kissed it. Samuel did her best not to roll her eyes. "Charmed," he said.

"Likewise," Frances said. Once her hand was free, she held it under her nose. "I was washing dishes before I came here. I'm afraid my hand smells like dish detergent."

"It smells," Boots said, "of ambrosia."

Frances laughed. "Well, I thought Henry might be exaggerating your Southern charm when he told me about you, but I see he wasn't."

"Well, my mama raised me to know how to treat a lady," Boots said, taking out his silver cigarette case.

"Show 'em what your mama gave you for your fifth birthday," Samuel said, enacting her role in one of their standard set pieces.

"Of course." Boots reached into the same pocket and pulled out a silver cigarette lighter. He held it out so they could read the engraving: *To my precious Boots from Mother.*

"This was for your *fifth* birthday?" Frances asked.

"Yes, ma'am," Boots said, flipping the lighter open. "So I could light my mama's cigarettes. And there's not been a day since—when I've been in my mama's presence—that she's had to light her own cigarette."

"But five years old," Frances said. "Wasn't she afraid you'd burn yourself?"

"Well," Boots said, "she figured—and quite rightly, I might add—that a little burn was nothing compared to knowing how to treat a lady."

Henry laughed. "Our oldest son is eight, and if we gave him a lighter, he'd have the house burned down faster than you could say 'call the fire department.'"

Boots nudged Frances. "Well, Mama, there's still time to train him."

Frances laughed. "So is your mother still living, Dr. McAdoo?"

"Boots, please. And yes, Mama's still going strong."

"She lives with us," Samuel said. "Or rather, we live with her."

"I couldn't imagine it any other way," Boots said.

"I could," Samuel said so softly she hoped only Frances would hear.

Frances let out a laugh, then turned into a cough and said, "Pardon me."

Henry looked over at Boots. "Well, while the company here is much more pleasant, we should probably return to the land of masculine machinations."

"I suppose so," Boots said. "They're all in there sniffing each other out, marking their territory. Why, one associate professor sidled right up to me and hiked his leg. If I hadn't growled at him, he would've piddled all over my seersucker!"

Once Henry and Boots were inside, Frances said, "Well, our husbands seem to be hitting it off."

"They do. It's nice. Men don't always like Boots. Women love him. But some men . . . I think they find him too much."

Frances nodded. "Henry can be a handful, too. He can come off as arrogant, but it's just that he's so brilliant. It's okay to act like a know-it-all when you really do know it all." Frances looked back at the house. "Well, I suppose it's our wifely duty to return to the party."

Samuel sighed. She much preferred being outside with Frances. "What do you suppose they're talking about in there? Needlework? Casserole recipes?"

Frances grinned. "They're probably talking about those two peculiar wives smoking cigarettes outside."

"I hope they are." Samuel wanted another drink but hated that going inside was the price she had to pay for it. It wasn't just a desire to escape the inane prattle, though. It was also that she found Frances interesting. It had been a long time since she had met someone interesting. "Hey, I've liked talking to you," she said, then immediately felt stupid.

"I like talking to you, too," Frances looked at Samuel with her clear blue eyes, magnified by her thick glasses. "You ought to come around to our house for lunch. With two little ones at home, by mid-day I'm starved for adult conversation."

"I usually write during the day, but I reckon I could knock off for lunch."

"Oh, you're a writer?" Frances sounded excited, though Samuel couldn't figure out why she would be.

"Well, yes. Not one you've heard of, but I've had a few short stories published." They weren't huge publications—not *The New Yorker* or anything, but the kind of regional literary magazines Boots referred to as respectable: *Tulip Poplar, The Southern Quarterly*. Boots was friends with the editor of *The Southern Quarterly*, and in her more insecure moments, Samuel worried that this friendship was the only reason her story had been accepted. But Boots had said, "Pish-posh. Everybody uses what connections they have, and if the story hadn't been good, Ed wouldn't have published it."

"That's wonderful," Frances said. "I . . . my husband writes. Nonfiction, scholarly stuff. He wrote a book, *Under the Gorgon's Glare*."

"Boots has a book, too—a novel—*This Quintessence of Dust*." Boots's first novel had come out shortly before his thirtieth birthday, and he was hailed as a young novelist to watch. That had been over twenty years ago, and people had stopped watching. One of the first lessons Samuel had learned in her and Boots's marriage was that he could ask her about her writing, but she couldn't ask him about his.

"I know," Frances said. "It's on my nightstand right now, waiting to be read. I checked it out of the college library."

"You won't be disappointed," Samuel said. The sentences in that book could still make her swoon.

"Now if I were to invite you to lunch," Frances said, "is there anything you won't eat?"

Samuel thought. "I don't care for beets or chicken livers."

"Well, so much for my famous beet and chicken liver casserole." Frances cocked an eyebrow. "As you can imagine, my children can't get enough of it. Actually, you'll be lucky if I do better than peanut butter and jelly. That's the most frequently served luncheon at Chez Harmon."

"I'm partial to peanut butter and jelly," Samuel said, smiling back at Frances.

CHAPTER 4

SITTING ON THE GROCERY CART'S BABY seat, looking fat and pleased with himself, Robert made Frances think of a child emperor in some faraway land being carried on a palanquin by his servants. All he was missing was a jeweled turban.

Susan walked alongside the cart, dragging her feet so her Mary Janes would be even more scuffed, looking at the boxes of cereal and cans of soup as if they were strange items she had never seen before. "In Oz we don't have to go to the grocery store," she said. "Lunch pails grow on trees, so you can reach up and pick one when you're hungry."

"Well, that would certainly be convenient," Frances said, tossing a box of cornflakes into the cart. "No dishes to wash either."

"And everybody can choose whatever sandwich they like," Susan said. "Ham, roast chicken, tongue. Except I don't like tongue."

"I know you don't," Frances said, grabbing a couple of cans of tomato soup which, unlike tongue, Susan would reliably eat.

"I always feel like it's tasting me back," Susan said.

Frances laughed. "Well, that's certainly a valid reason not to like it."

Samuel was coming for lunch tomorrow, and Frances was trying to decide what to serve. She supposed she could make aspic or dainty little finger sandwiches or some other fussy, ladylike food. But Samuel seemed neither fussy nor ladylike, which came as a huge relief. "I'm having a new friend over for lunch tomorrow, Dorothy," Frances said. "What do you think I should serve?"

"Sandwiches and potato chips," Susan said without hesitation. Susan was mad for potato chips, so Frances suspected an ulterior motive.

"Hmm . . . what kind of sandwiches? Tuna fish salad? Chicken salad?"

Susan crinkled her brow in thought. "Not everybody likes tuna fish, but most people like chicken."

"You're wise beyond your years, Dorothy." So chicken salad sandwiches, potato chips, and maybe a relish tray with celery and carrot sticks and some pickles and olives it was.

It was amazing how much of Frances's time was spent planning what the people around her would eat. Henry never had to think about such things. When he got hungry, food was set before him, and he ate it heartily. It was just like when he needed a fresh shirt, there was generally one hanging in the closet; there was no need for him to reflect on how the garment had gone from dirty to clean.

It wasn't his fault, really. When he was growing up, his mother had taken care of him so well that her efforts seemed invisible, as if little elves cleaned up after him and washed his clothes while he slept. Now, it was Frances's turn.

As Frances walked to the butcher section in hopes of finding a nice hen to boil for chicken salad, a well put together dark-haired woman holding the hand of a tow-headed little boy approached her.

"Hello," the woman said. She was wearing a floral print dress and white high heels. She looked like she was going to a garden party instead of the grocery store. "Aren't you the new classicist's wife?"

"That's me," Frances said. "It's what I always said I wanted to be when I grew up. A classicist's wife." When the woman didn't laugh, she covered the silence by saying, "My name is Frances."

"Nice to meet you, Frances," the woman said. "I'm Maude Sellers. My husband teaches English." Her accent was different than other people around here. It was Southern, yes, but more of a drawl than a twang. "You were at the party last night," she said. It sounded like an accusation.

Blurrily in her mind's eye, Frances could see Maude sitting in the clump of faculty wives. "Yes, I was. Nice to see you again."

Maude looked her up and down, and Frances could see how sloppy and indifferent she must've been in Maude's eyes: her makeup-free face and her hair snatched back in a ponytail; the loose-fitting, untucked blouse and plain gray skirt; the penny loafers with white ankle socks.

"You don't strike me as much of a party person," Maude said. "You're the quiet type, aren't you? Wouldn't say boo to a goose."

Wouldn't say boo to a goose? What did that even mean? Did people around here generally go around frightening geese for no reason? "Well, I guess it takes a while for me to get comf—"

"Auntie Em! Auntie Em!" Susan was tugging frantically on Frances's shirt tail. "Look!" She pointed at the blond toddler holding Maude's hand. "It's a flying monkey!"

"I not a monkey!" the little boy said, then burst into tears.

Maude raised a perfectly tweezed eyebrow. "Frances, did your little girl just call my Harold a name?"

"And that"—Susan pointed at Maude—"is the Wicked Witch of the West!" Susan turned to a woman passing by them with her shopping cart and yelled, "That witch is trying to steal my shoes!"

Before Frances could collect her thoughts to explain Susan's behavior, Maude, whose artfully applied rouge had disappeared into the redness of her face, said, "Well, I don't know what you teach your children where you come from, but down here we have manners!" She turned on her heel and stomped off in the direction of the dairy aisle, dragging her flying monkey with her.

Frances wanted to scold Susan, to explain to her that not all people were willing to enter her fantasy world, but unfortunately, she couldn't stop laughing. She managed to keep a straight face long enough to pay for her groceries, but as soon as she was in the relative privacy of her car, she started laughing again so hard that she had to wipe tears from her eyes.

"What's so funny, Auntie Em?' Susan said.

"You are. Dorothy," Frances said, gasping to catch her breath. "You are an absolute hoot."

After their shopping trip, Frances had planned that she and the children would surprise Henry at work with a picnic lunch. And now she would have a good story to tell him, too.

Millwood College was a picturesque little campus with red brick buildings and big shady trees under which students lounged, talking and laughing. Seeing the girls in their pert sweater sets with their slender, pre-motherhood figures made Frances feel frumpy, but seeing them engaged in intense, earnest discussion made her nostalgic for her own college days. It also made her feel old even though she was just a few months shy of her thirty-fifth birthday. Still, that gave her well over a decade on these coeds.

"Uncle Henry's office is this way," Susan said. "We just have to follow the yellow brick road." Susan started to skip. "You should skip, too, Auntie Em."

"Not on your life," Frances muttered. She wasn't going to give these fresh-faced college students the treat of seeing a frowsy faculty wife skipping across the quad.

"What was that, Auntie Em?" Susan asked.

"I said you skip on ahead. I have to push Robert in his stroller."

Susan skipped with gusto, drawing smiles from students, as opposed to the derisive laughter Frances's skipping would have no doubt caused.

Henry's office was in the damp bottom floor of Riggs Hall, which housed the classrooms for humanities courses.

Henry joked that he "labored away like Hades, in the bowels of the earth."

Once they were in the building and reached the stairwell, Frances had to leave the stroller near the door and carry Robert down the stairs. It wasn't easy balancing a baby with one arm and a picnic basket with the other. But wasn't balancing what being a wife and a mother was all about?

The hallway, as always, was dimly lit and smelled of mildew. They passed a janitorial closet, then came to Henry's office. The door was decorated with a line drawing of Medusa one of his students had made for him.

Frances knocked on the door. "Persephone here to see Hades!" she called.

"Oh. Ah, just a minute," Henry called back.

Frances took his distraction in stride. When he was working on something, he became so immersed that the return to reality was disorienting. She felt the same way when her writing was interrupted, though because these interruptions often came in the form of her children, she was quicker to snap out of her trance.

Frances heard Henry shuffling about, then the click of the lock.

He opened the door. "Well, look, the gang's all here!" he said, smiling.

"We decided to surprise you with a picnic, Uncle Henry," Susan said.

"What an excellent idea," Henry said, ruffling Susan's hair. "Just give me a moment to finish up here, and we'll find a nice shady tree."

It was then that Frances noticed that Henry wasn't alone in his office.

The young woman sitting in the chair across from Henry's desk had shoulder length honey blond hair and a trim figure. She was wearing a tight baby blue sweater stretched over one of those bras favored by young women which made their tits look like torpedoes. Frances had a feeling that these torpedoes were aimed directly at her husband.

The young woman walked out of the office, followed by Henry.

"Miss Long, this is my wife Frances and two out of three of my brood of children. We have released our eldest into the American educational system."

"Nice to meet you, Mrs. Harmon," the blond said in a syrupy Southern accent. *"Nice"* came out as *"nahce."* She didn't make eye contact with Frances.

"You as well," Frances said frostily.

Miss Long gave a little wave and departed down the hall with a gait that showed off her tiny waist and curvy hips. Frances was sure these attributes hadn't escaped Henry's attention. They never did.

"Shall I take the basket?" Henry asked. "You already have quite an armful there." He reached out to stroke Robert's fuzzy baby hair.

It was, to all appearances, a nice picnic. They ate the food Frances had packed that morning: ham and cheese sandwiches, hard boiled eggs, apples and bananas, Henry's favorite homemade chocolate chip cookies. They passed around a chilled jar of lemonade which Henry joked made them look like they were drinking Kentucky moonshine. Periodically, Robert would crawl off the picnic blanket, and one of them would have to grab him.

But for the whole meal, Frances felt distracted and irritable, with one question looping in her mind. *Why had Henry's door been locked?* Closing the door was understandable such that the teacher and student could have some privacy during an advising session. But why did it need to be locked?

By the time she and the children got home, Frances convinced herself that she had been overreacting. Sure, Henry had had a wandering eye in the past, but he had assured her that those days were over, that he could be a classicist without being a satyr. Besides, it was easy to get paranoid staying home alone with the kids all day while your husband was out in the world having grown-up conversations and doing grown-up things. And it was natural for Henry to have a student in his office. If it had been a boy or a plainer looking girl, she wouldn't have thought a thing of it.

Probably the girl locked the door because she wanted to sob in private over some small schoolgirl problem that she found terribly serious.

Feeling better, Frances sent Susan out to play and put Robert down for his nap. Then she reheated a cup of this morning's coffee, sat down at the kitchen table, and wrote furiously until Danny came home from school, claiming starvation and demanding a cheese sandwich.

CHAPTER 5

BREAKFAST WAS THE ONLY MEAL PRISCILLA didn't cook for the McAdoo family. Its preparation was a cooperative affair. Boots made the coffee and filled the juice glasses. Samuel toasted the bread, burning the first batch about half the time, and Miz Elizabeth presided over the eggs, her only concession to cooking. During the process, there was a great deal of bumping into each other and saying "excuse me" and under the breath cursing when the toast was too dark or a yolk broke.

By the time the three of them sat down for their meal, there was a shared sense of accomplishment. They had pulled it off once again. They left the breakfast dishes for Priscilla to take care of when she came in at ten.

"So what's in the hopper for today?" Boots said, buttering his toast. He was already dressed for work and had tucked a napkin into his collar to make sure he didn't drip egg onto his white shirt and light blue bow tie.

"I'm going to spend the morning trying to whip my short story into submission," Samuel said, dragging her toast through some runny egg. "Then I'm having lunch with Frances."

"Yes, that's today, isn't it?" Boots said. "Henry was just saying yesterday how glad he was that Frances had met you. He said she needed another smart woman to talk to."

Samuel found herself smiling unexpectedly. "That was nice of him."

"What, to say you're smart?" Boots said. "Because you are. It's not like I would marry some little idiot. Because Lord knows the opportunities to do so have been ample."

"That's the truth," Miz Elizabeth said. As always, she was paying more attention to her coffee than her food. "All those dim-witted little coeds throwing themselves at you over the years."

"And missing every time." Boots chuckled.

"I guess," Samuel said. "I meant it was nice of Henry to notice that I'm smart. It seems like most smart men are so busy showing off how smart they are that they don't notice other people's intelligence. Especially if the other person happens to be female."

"Well, there are advantages to not letting a man know how smart you are," Miz Elizabeth said, taking out a cigarette and waiting for Boots's prompt attention with the lighter. "If they don't expect much of you, it gives you the upper hand."

Samuel was always astounded that even at Miz Elizabeth's present age, she still relied on the "feminine wiles" school of womanhood. Perhaps it was because she had always been extraordinarily beautiful, and men were unlikely to think that beauty and brains could coexist in the same person.

Samuel didn't have a feminine wile to her name. Her way of dealing with both men and women had always been plain and straightforward, like her looks.

"And what kind of trouble are you getting yourself into today, Mama?" Boots asked, shoving his plate away and taking out a cigarette of his own.

Miz Elizabeth gave a world-weary sigh. "Garden Club this afternoon."

"Oh, and will you be discussing *gardening*?" Boots asked, giving Samuel a sidelong glance. It was a running joke that Miz Elizabeth was a member of all kinds of clubs devoted to activities that the club members never performed or discussed. The Sewing Club, for example, had originally been founded to sew handkerchiefs for soldiers during the war. The club still met monthly, but no one had sewed a stitch since before V-Day.

"Lord, no," Miz Elizabeth said. "It'll be the Gossip Club as usual. We're meeting at Thelma Warren's house, so the refreshments will be abysmal. Last time we met there, she tried to pass off store-bought cookies as homemade. She went on and on about how much work she put into making them when the damn things had 'Lorna Doone' stamped right on them."

Samuel laughed. "Why, Mama Liz, I'm sure it took a lot of work to stamp those letters on all that cookie dough."

"A lot of work for somebody at the Nabisco factory," Miz Elizabeth said.

"Speaking, however tangentially, of gardening," Boots said, untucking the napkin from his collar, "I have a potential gardener coming in for an interview before I leave for work. He should be here any minute."

"That's good," Miz Elizabeth said. "Lord knows it's looking pretty shaggy out there. I never understood what happened with the fellow we had before."

Samuel noticed that Boots didn't make eye contact with her.

"Why, Mama, I just didn't think he was treating your roses with the respect and care they deserved."

Samuel knew it wasn't about the roses. In the McAdoo household, the position of gardener was multifaceted.

The doorbell rang.

"Oh, he's punctual. That's a good sign," Boots said, rising. "If you ladies would excuse me from the table."

Samuel followed Boots but hung back a little. She wanted to get a look at the new candidate.

This one was tall and broad-shouldered with sleepy eyes and a shock of black hair. His plain white t-shirt clung to a v-shaped torso. "Hey," he said.

"Good morning!" Boots crowed. "You must be A.J."

The young man nodded.

"Well, permit me to show you around the grounds."

Samuel slipped out onto the porch but stopped short of joining Boots and A.J. for the tour. She knew Boots needed to explain his expectations in private. Still, she wanted to be nearby in case there was a misunderstanding.

After ten minutes of walking around the yard and speaking in hushed tones, Boots and A.J. returned to the porch.

"I believe we've come to an agreement," Boots said, smiling. "Samuel, allow me to present our new gardener."

"Welcome," Samuel said. Boots had run through at least a dozen gardeners since their marriage. She had begun to think it might be a waste of mental energy to learn their names.

"Thank you, ma'am," A.J. mumbled.

As the new gardener was walking away and safely out of earshot, Samuel regarded Boots's pleased expression. "Well, don't you look like a kitten full of cream?"

"Me-ow," Boots said. "He is handsome, isn't he?"

"Very. Even I noticed. He's got a Robert Mitchum kind of quality. How did you find him?"

Boots's lips formed a delicate moue. "Word of mouth."

* * *

BAREFOOT, HUNCHED OVER HER DESK, HER third cup of coffee going cold, Samuel suddenly understood the problem with her short story. It didn't want to *be* a short story. No matter how hard she tried to contain it, it kept straining at the seams like a growing child forced into too-small clothes. It wanted to be a novel. The thought both thrilled and terrified her.

Nothing to do but keep writing. She let the words spill from the pen, flipping the page after page of her composition book. A lot of her words were the wrong ones, but she couldn't worry about that now. She just had to let them all come from whatever mysterious source—her subconscious? her muse?—produced them.

She had written this way, in an almost ecstatic trance state, since she had started keeping a diary at the age of thirteen. The diary had started out as a typical log of daily activities, but that got dull fast. When she started writing about other people, though, she found she couldn't stop. She wrote about the girls at school who were pretty on the outside but ugly on the inside, about how her mother often did her housework while tears streamed from her eyes, a fact which she never acknowledged, or how her daddy tended to come home drunk and was equally likely to be full of love or hate.

When Samuel was fifteen, her mother had found one of her diaries when she was changing the bedclothes. After she read it, she slapped Samuel's face and threw the notebook into the fire in the wood stove. From then on, Samuel kept her diaries in her locker at school. She always finished her lessons before the other kids, so there was plenty of free time to write during class.

The alarm clock gave a loud *brrrring!* that made Samuel feel like someone had reached into her body, grabbed her spine, and shaken it. But the noise was necessary. She knew that if she hadn't set the alarm for 11:30, she would have lost track of time and written right through her lunch date with Frances.

She shut off the alarm and closed her composition book. Usually coming back to reality after writing was a little sad, like sobering up after being pleasantly tipsy. But today she felt nervous and excited. She couldn't remember the last time she'd had a social invitation that was just for her.

When she carried her coffee cup to the kitchen, Priscilla was peeling potatoes. "Am I right that you won't be having lunch here today, Miss Samuel?" Priscilla asked, not looking up from her work. A growing ribbon of potato peel unspooled beneath her knife.

"That's right, Priscilla. I'm going over to a friend's house. Heading there right now, actually."

Priscilla set down the peeled potato and regarded Samuel. "You gonna put some shoes on?"

Samuel had forgotten her feet were bare. She grinned. "Shoes. Good idea."

CHAPTER 6

FRANCES HAD NO IDEA WHY SHE was so nervous. She'd made the chicken salad plus a fruit salad hours ago, so that took care of the food. She had fretted briefly over the drinks. Southerners liked iced tea, but Frances had neither drunk it or made it much, and she was sure that whatever version of it she approximated wouldn't satisfy a connoisseur of the beverage. Finally, she decided Samuel could just choose from what was in the refrigerator: club soda, ginger ale, orange juice, milk, or beer.

"Lunch is going to be so fancy!" Susan said. Frances had tasked her with setting the silverware on the table.

Frances smiled. With the plain white plates, chipped from being jostled around during the move, the tables hardly looked fancy, but Frances supposed it was fancier than the lunches Susan was used to when Frances just handed her a peanut butter sandwich and a cup of milk. Most days they didn't even use plates. "Well, I figured we should at least make a little effort since I have a new friend coming over."

"Is she Ozma, the beautiful girl princess of Oz?" Susan asked, straightening a fork to line up with a plate. She wasn't dressed up, but Frances had made her wash her face and put on clean play clothes.

"Well, I'm sure she wouldn't mind if you pretended she's Ozma of Oz," Frances said, lighting a cigarette. "But her name is Samuel McAdoo, so you'll call her Mrs. McAdoo."

"Samuel is not a girl's name."

Frances took an ashtray to the kitchen table and sat down. "Well, not usually, but in this case it is because she's a girl and it's her name."

Susan looked thoughtful. "Can I ask her why she has a boy's name?"

"Not today. Mrs. McAdoo is a new friend, and this is her first visit. We shouldn't bombard her with questions, or this might also be her last visit." Frances and Henry had joked that Susan was going to be a private eye when she grew up, shining a bright light into suspects's eyes and interrogating them brutally. Henry's nickname for her was The Little Inquisitor.

Susan nodded. "Okay. I will call her Mrs. McAdoo and pretend that I don't know she has a boy's name."

"That seems a sensible approach." It was interesting, the differences in her children's personalities. Susan was a thinker and a planner. Danny was impulsive and bursting with physical energy. It would be interesting to see if Robert would fall into one of these two camps or if he would have quirks all his own.

Susan smiled. "But I'll call her Ozma if she'll let me."

"If she'll let you indeed," Frances said. She didn't know how accustomed Samuel was to childish exuberance and hoped Susan would not overwhelm her.

Frances wondered briefly if she should freshen up. She had on her sloppiest skirt and one of Henry's old shirts, and her hair, as usual, was pulled back in a ponytail. But before she could even decide to do an overhaul, the doorbell rang.

Samuel hadn't dressed up for the occasion either. She was wearing what looked like boys jeans and a plaid shirt. "There's a baby on your porch," Samuel said, as if this might be news to Frances.

An hour or so before, Frances had rolled Robert out in his pram to nap on the porch and soak up some Vitamin D. "Mailman must've brought him," she said.

Of the available drink options, Samuel chose beer, so Frances decided to have one to keep her company. In the kitchen, she opened two cans of Schlitz with a church key and handed one to Samuel, who took a long swig.

"That's good and cold," Samuel said. "Boots and his mama won't have beer in the house. Boots doesn't like the taste of it, and his mama says she doesn't even know what it tastes like because drinking beer is common and unladylike." She took another big gulp. "That's probably why I like it."

"I like it, too." Frances tapped her can to Samuel's. "Here's to being unladylike."

Susan came tearing into the kitchen, being rather unladylike herself. "Is this your friend Mrs. McAdoo?"

"It is." Frances was taking the bowl of chicken salad out of the refrigerator. "Why don't you introduce yourself instead of talking about like she's not in the room?"

"I'm Dorothy." Susan gave a little curtsy. "How do you do, Mrs. McAdoo?" She giggled at the sound of her words.

Samuel grinned at her. "I McAdoo very well, thank you. And I hope you McAdoo, too."

"McAdoo, too!" Susan said, collapsing in giggles.

Once they sat down to lunch, Susan speared a strawberry with her fork and used it to gesture toward Samuel. "I think you are Ozma, but before she knows she's Ozma, when the witch Mombi has enchanted her and disguised her as a boy."

"The boy's named Tip, right?" Samuel said. "He's in the book with Jack Pumpkinhead and the Sawhorse and the chicken with the name I can't remember—"

Susan's mouth hung open, but she recovered enough to say, "Billina. The chicken's name is Billina. And that's the second book, *The Land of Oz*."

"Billina! That's right!" Samuel smiled. "I read all the books in my school library when I was a kid, but I especially loved the Oz books."

"Well, you've made a friend for life," Frances said to Samuel. "She eats and sleeps Oz."

"Would it be all right if I called you Tip?" Susan asked.

"I'd like that," Samuel said.

"After you finish your lunch, Dorothy, you may be excused to go outside and play," Frances said.

Susan nodded. "Is that because you want to talk about grown-up things?"

"That's right."

Once Susan had run outside, Samuel looked intently at Frances. "So, what grown-up things do you want to talk about?"

Samuel's eyes were an unusual shade of green, and for some reason, the unexpected eye contact made Frances feel shy. "How about another grown-up drink for starters?"

"Sure."

Frances opened two beers and sat back down at the kitchen table. "I hope Susan wasn't too much for you. She's a very exuberant child."

"Susan? I thought she said her name was Dorothy."

"Think why," Frances said, shaking a cigarette out of the pack.

"Oh!" Samuel laughed. "Of course. I guess it would be too convenient if her name really was Dorothy." She reached into her shirt pocket and pulled out a book of matches and a pack of cigarettes. "Here, allow me," she said. She struck a match, leaned over and lit Frances's cigarette, then her own. It was an elegant gesture, almost gentlemanly.

"Thank you." Frances felt like she might be blushing.

"When I was a kid, I went around saying I was Tom Sawyer," Samuel said.

Frances scooted the ashtray so it sat between them on the table. "I was Anne of Green Gables, which must have been exhausting for everybody."

Samuel smiled. "I was probably more like Huck than Tom. At least my family was more like Huck's. My daddy was bad to drink. Probably still is. I don't go back there much."

"And your mother?" Frances asked. Maybe Samuel didn't have a mother. That could explain her relative lack of femininity.

Samuel shrugged. "She was there. Physically anyway. I know she was unhappy. She probably still is. But she just kind of accepted unhappiness as her lot. She kept my brother and me fed, even if it was just a cold biscuit and a glass of buttermilk a lot of the time, and she made sure we had a few changes of clothes for school and kept them clean. But she never seemed to take any joy in us or in anything else much. My brother joined the army as soon as he was old enough, and I got a scholarship to Millwood and moved here. I reckon we were both itching to get the hell out of there." She was quiet for a moment with a faraway look in her eyes before she focused again on Frances. "How about you? What's your sad story?"

Frances had a feeling her upbringing had been a lot easier than Samuel's. There had been no alcoholism in her family, no true poverty. Sure, they had tightened their belts during the Depression, but there was always food on the table, most often meat and potatoes and a vegetable. But she had been a lonely child, both at home and at school, always waiting for some kind of understanding that never came—well, not until she met Henry in college.

"Oh, it's not that sad," Frances said, grinding out her cigarette in the ashtray. "Let's see . . . little town in Illinois that you've never heard of, insurance man dad, housewife mom, and two daughters, a pretty one and a smart one. Guess which one I was."

Samuel looked at her with those intense green eyes. "I think you're pretty and smart."

Frances's face heated up. She wasn't used to being complimented on her looks, especially by another woman. "Have you had your eyesight checked lately?" She felt the urge to get up, to busy herself with something to distract from the awkwardness. "I'd better get these dishes cleared."

"No." Samuel touched her forearm. Her hand was small but strong. "Tell me your story."

It was as if Samuel's touch had glued her to the spot. "If you insist."

Samuel smiled. "I do."

"Okay. So, the pretty sister gets married right out of high school, stays in our hometown, and starts having babies. The smart sister—that's me, by the way—went off to college in Vermont, read a lot of books and learned a lot of stuff, met the smartest guy she'd ever encountered, then married him and started having babies."

"And now you're here," Samuel said.

"Yep. I'm here, along with dozens of boxes I should've unpacked ages ago."

"I can help you unpack some if you want me to," Samuel said. "I don't have any place I have to be this afternoon."

"Nonsense," Frances said, though she was struck by the kindness of the offer. "I invited you here for lunch, not to put you to work."

"It would be my pleasure," Samuel said. "And I'm not kidding. I'm real nosy about other people's stuff."

An afternoon of unpacking with Samuel was a much cheerier prospect than an afternoon of unpacking—or, more likely, procrastinating unpacking—on her own. "All right. I'll take you up on it. Maybe we should drink the last two beers while we work?"

"We should," Samuel said. "Unless your husband will be mad that we've drunk up all the beer."

"Henry's more of a Scotch man than a beer man." Frances got up to clear the table. "The only time he drinks a beer is after he mows the lawn, and god knows he doesn't do that any oftener than he has to."

"Boots hires a gardener to do ours," Samuel said. "I've offered to do it myself, but Miz Elizabeth says it would be the talk of the town if a McAdoo woman were seen doing something as common as pushing a lawnmower."

"The town must not have much to talk about," Frances said, smiling.

"You've got that right. They sure can make a lot out of a little, though."

Frances opened the last two beers, and they took them into the study, which was lined with boxes of books. They sat on the floor to unpack them. Samuel took off her shoes, so Frances did, too.

"You sure have a lot of stuff to fit into this little house," Samuel said.

"Too much. One of the things they don't tell you when you get married is you're not just marrying a man, you're also marrying his stuff. It's your responsibility to take care of it in addition to any stuff you may have. And when the children start coming, each of them brings their own stuff, too—clothes and books and baseballs. Shoes and dolls and blocks and toy trains. It's overwhelming."

Samuel was inspecting each book she took out of the box. "I've never had much stuff—just enough clothes to get by, a comb, a toothbrush. When I moved into the McAdoo family home, I used the stuff in the house, especially Boots's impressive library of books and records. But none of it's mine. Everything I truly own would fit in one little old suitcase."

Frances wondered what that would be like, for life to be stripped down to its barest essentials. "That sounds pretty good, actually. Free. Like the hoboes riding the rails with just a knapsack."

Samuel laughed. "I used to say I wanted to be a hobo when I grew up until my mama told me little girls couldn't live that way. She was probably right, but not for the reason she thought. She just thought it was trashy. But really, for a woman, it wouldn't be safe."

"I don't know that it's safe for anyone," Frances said. But she knew what Samuel meant. There were certain kinds of dangers that women were particularly susceptible to. "But it's interesting, isn't it, how men can just go whenever they feel like it? Women get tied down. First to men, then to the little ones tied to our apron strings."

"Well, there won't be any of that for me," Samuel said, taking a copy of *Sons and Lovers* out of a box and examining it. "No little ones. No apron either."

Frances was taken aback by the certainty in her voice. "Oh, you don't know that yet. You're still awfully young."

"No," Samuel said, taking out more books. "I know."

Frances wanted desperately to know why, but she hadn't known Samuel long enough to ask such a personal question, so she just said, "Okay."

"Boots and I—we're not compatible that way. To make babies, I mean."

"Oh. I see." Frances feigned a great deal of interest in the mystery novels she was unpacking. So, one of them was sterile—either Samuel or Boots. She suspected Boots because he was old enough to be Samuel's father—though apparently, he wouldn't be anyone's real father.

"I've told you more than you wanted to know, haven't I?" Samuel said, smiling. "I'm sorry. It's just because you're easy to talk to."

"There's nothing to apologize for," Frances said. The truth was she found Samuel easy to talk to, too. She was the first person in town Frances could say that about. "I'm very sorry you and Boots can't have children."

Samuel grinned and shrugged. "Never wanted 'em anyway. I like kids—your daughter is a hoot—but when I look at somebody else's kids, it's like when I look at flowers somebody else has planted. I think how beautiful they are, and then I think if those were my responsibility, they'd be dead in no time."

Frances laughed. "I'm sure you wouldn't be as bad as that. I can kill plants practically on sight, but I've managed to keep all my children alive, knock on wood."

"You have probably guessed," Samuel said, "that I do not excel in the domestic arts. Like right now, I know if I was unpacking these boxes by myself, I'd end up reading one of the books cover to cover and not get any work done."

Frances laughed. "Why do you think I've not gotten more unpacking done than I have?" One morning she had unpacked a total of one book, *Jane Eyre*, then spent the whole day rereading it. "If there are any books you want to borrow, feel free."

"Thanks." Samuel held up *Sons and Lovers*. "I might take this one. Boots has a good collection, but there are some gaps I'd like to fill in. And none of those gaps are going to be filled in by the Collinsville library. I'm pretty sure they've still got a ban on D. H. Lawrence."

"Wait till they get a load of Henry Miller," Frances said.

"Oh, it'll be a couple of decades before they hear of him. But when they do, it won't be pretty."

Frances and Samuel talked and worked, and then somehow a dozen boxes were empty and three whole bookcases were filled. Robert woke up from his afternoon nap, and Danny came home from school. But somehow it felt as if no time had passed at all.

CHAPTER 7

IT WAS AFTER SUPPER, TIME TO sip sherry and listen to an opera record—*La Bohème* tonight. Boots was leaned back on the couch, his eyes closed in ecstasy. Miz Elizabeth sat smoking, her expression far away. Samuel couldn't tell if she was immersed in the opera or thinking about something else entirely. She could be the chattering belle of the ball or a silent sphinx depending on her mood.

Samuel's own thoughts were flitting about like a hummingbird flying from flower to flower. She thought about the story she was working on. The novel. She had to own up and start calling it a novel. Then her mind wandered over to Frances and what she was doing now. Maybe she had finished the dishes and was curled up in the big squashy armchair she liked with a book and a drink. She liked to imagine her like that, enjoying a hard-earned hour of quiet.

Tonight, after Miz Elizabeth retired for the evening, Samuel and Boots were hosting what Boots always called a *salon* in the guesthouse. Their friend Carlisle was attending, as were Trish and Marj, a lesbian couple Boots had known for more than two decades. Boots had also expressed hope that A.J. might stop by.

On a whim, Samuel had jokingly asked if they should invite Frances and Henry, but Boots's refusal had been immediate. "Absolutely not. They are lovely, charming people, but their heterosexuality and fecundity disqualify them from membership in our club. We're like the Masons. We cannot let the uninitiated be privy to our secrets."

Once Miz Elizabeth had made her way up the stairs to her room, Samuel and Boots began the process of hauling provisions to the guest house: a bucket of ice, half a dozen glasses, a bottle of gin, two bottles of tonic water, a six-pack of beer in case A.J. showed up. Samuel arranged the gin and tonic station on the coffee table in front of the floral print loveseat. Boots arranged the bottles of beer in the bathroom sink, then emptied half the ice bucket onto them.

Samuel remembered how easily that six-pack of beer she'd split with Frances had gone down. "I might have one of those beers, actually," she said, sitting down on the bed and taking off her shoes.

"My darling wife," Boots said moving around ashtrays to be in easy reach of guests, "the beer is not for you."

"So all the beer is for A.J.?" Samuel lay back on the bed. "Why, my sweet husband, if I didn't know better, I'd think you were betraying me . . . with the gardener!"

Boots hooted. "Honey, I'm betraying you with the gardener six ways to Sunday! You can just call me Lady Chatterley."

Samuel laughed. "Funny you should mention Lady Chatterley. I borrowed *Sons and Lovers* from Frances the other day."

Boots switched to full professorial mode. "That was a good choice. It's a better novel than *Lady Chatterley* actually—"

There was a soft knock at the door.

"That's definitely Carlisle's knock," Boots said. "Soft as a kitty cat." He hopped up and opened the door.

Carlisle was a tall, gentle man with bright blue eyes and ash blond hair turning to silver. "Is this speakeasy open?" he asked.

"It is if you say the password." Boots stage whispered, "*Fellatio.*"

Carlisle's cheeks pinkened. "Boots McAdoo, you are one nasty queen. Talking like that in front of your lovely bride!"

Samuel had risen to greet Carlisle. "I'm glad somebody around here has some manners," she said, accepting the kiss on the cheek Carlisle always gave in greeting.

Samuel liked Carlisle. She didn't know if his quiet, calm manner was the result of working in a library for years, or if his subdued nature was what had drawn him to be a librarian in the first place. Either way, she always found his presence soothing.

"Can I interest you in a G and T?" Boots asked.

"My two favorite letters of the alphabet," Carlisle said sitting next to Samuel on the edge of the bed. "So, who are we expecting tonight?"

"Trish and Marj said they'd come," Samuel said. Trish taught history at the college. Her lover Marj was an English teacher at the high school. They had lived together for more than twenty years, a fact which seemed like it should scandalize the town. But the official local opinion was that Trish and Marj were old maid schoolteachers sharing a house to economize. As Boots was fond of saying, heterosexuals saw what they wanted to see.

"Always a pleasure to see our Sapphic sisters," Carlisle said, giving Samuel a pat on the knee for good measure. "And is there any chance that The New One will be joining us?"

Boots smiled as he mixed the drinks. "He said he might. I bought some beer just in case he decides to grace us with his presence. He can't abide gin. Says it tastes like drinking a Christmas tree."

"Forgive me," Carlisle said, "But can you remind me of this one's name?"

"A.J.," Boots purred. He brought Carlisle and Samuel their drinks. "G and T may be your two favorite letters of the alphabet, but right now mine are A and J."

Samuel nudged Carlisle. "He gets silly when there's a new boy."

Carlisle smiled. "I know! He always has. As giddy as a schoolgirl. I wouldn't be surprised if he was going around carving his and the boy's initials into trees with his pocketknife."

"I'm the one who carries the pocketknife in this family," Samuel said.

"It's true." Boots pulled up a chair next to the bed. "My daddy gave me a pocketknife for my tenth birthday, and I nearly mortally injured myself trying to impress some boy playing mumblety-peg. I've not carried one since." He sipped his drink. "Of course, that's just one of the reasons I don't go around carving my initials into things. When your initials are B.M., it doesn't look very nice."

They were all laughing uproariously now, which was typical of these salons in the guesthouse. Sometimes Samuel found herself laughing hard at something she would normally find only mildly amusing. It felt good to let her guard down and be her natural self.

There was another knock on the door, this one more assertive. "That's Trish," Samuel said. "I'll get it."

"Hey, ladies, come in," Samuel said.

Trish made a big show of looking around. "What ladies? I don't see any ladies here." Trish was dressed in a white button-down shirt, pleated pants, and penny loafers. Samuel knew she wore skirts to work but found them a misery.

"I beg your pardon," Marj said. She was wearing a butter yellow summer dress and big earrings that looked like daisies. "I'm present, and so are Boots and Carlisle." She flounced through the door ahead of Trish.

Trish laughed and clapped Samuel on the back. "I guess she got us there," she said.

"She sure did," Samuel said, resisting the urge to rub her stinging shoulder blade. Trish was a big, strong woman.

Boots made a great deal of fuss over getting the ladies settled with chairs and drinks and an ashtray to share. He was quick with the lighter to ignite Marj's cigarette but deferred to Trish's desire to light her own.

"So, Trish, when I saw you earlier on campus, you hinted there might be gossip," Boots said. "I'm all ears." He put his hands on top of his head, approximating bunny ears.

Trish shrugged. "Well, it's nothing too spicy. Just that a certain new coed has developed a crush on a certain dashing butch history professor and isn't being subtle about it."

"And as a result, a certain new coed is in danger of getting her eyes scratched out." Marj displayed her red-polished claws.

Boots chuckled. "So, if I see some poor girl in dark glasses, making her way across campus with a cane, I'll know she's the one."

"Boots, you're awful!" Marj said. "Seriously, though, the girl needs to back off. Not just because I'm the jealous type, but because it's not safe for a college girl to be indiscreet like that."

"I certainly learned that the hard way," Samuel said, getting up to mix a second drink. "It would've been even harder if my knight in seersucker armor over there hadn't saved my ass."

"Yes, but at least your crush was on another student," Trish said. "You weren't putting a professor in a dangerous situation, too."

There was another knock at the door.

"Boots," Carlisle crooned, "do you think that could be your two favorite letters of the alphabet?"

"It could be," Boots said, getting up. "Or it could be Mama telling us to pipe down. I hope it's the former, not the latter."

It was the former.

A.J. stood silently in the doorframe. His shock of black hair was perfectly pomaded, and a cigarette dangled from his pouting lips. He was wearing the only clothes Samuel had ever seen him in—jeans and a body-hugging white T-shirt.

"I'm so happy you could make it!" Boots said. "Just delighted. Come in, come in."

A.J. sauntered in and glanced around the room.

"A.J.," Boots said. "You have of course met my charming wife. This is Carlisle and Trish and Marj. Everyone, this is A.J., the new gardener."

Samuel knew that everyone in the room understood what the word "gardener" meant in the McAdoo household. They had met other gardeners before.

A.J. finally took the cigarette from between his lips for long enough to say "hey," and everyone greeted him in return, Carlisle giving him a long, appreciative looking-over.

"You got any beer?" A.J. asked.

"I have a cold six-pack with your name on it," Boots said, patting A.J. on the arm. "Let me show you to it." Boots escorted A.J. to the bathroom and closed the door behind them.

It was always awkward when Boots invited one of the gardeners. While everybody knew what was going on, there was also a silent understanding that acknowledging the nature of the relationship would be embarrassing for the gardener. Men like A.J. and the others that had come before him were often not homosexual in their personal lives; they were simply willing to be accommodating to someone else's desires if the right amount of money was proffered.

A.J. returned from the bathroom with a beer in each hand. He didn't sit but leaned back against the wall, propping up one foot. Samuel knew that shoe was going to leave a mark on the wall that would drive Boots crazy.

A.J. drank the first beer straight down, his Adam's apple bobbing as he swallowed again and again. He swigged the next one with a little more leisure, looking at Boots and

Carlisle, then at Trish and Marj the way a lion in a cage regards the humans who have come to gawk at it.

"Can I offer anyone another gin and tonic?" Boots asked.

Only Carlisle was ready for another drink. A.J.'s presence seemed to have an inhibiting effect on the conversation. No one talked as freely as they had before his arrival. Finally, Trish said, "Lord, I wish y'all could've tried the pecan pie Marj made the other day."

Marj smiled shyly at the compliment. "Maybe next time we get together I can bring a pie over."

Something about this exchange irritated Samuel. "Are we gonna start swapping recipes like the ladies in the Garden Club?"

"No, but I don't see that there'd be anything wrong with that," Marj said, sounding a little hurt. "People have got to eat, right?"

"Yeah," Trish said, putting a protective arm around Marj. "And who doesn't like pie?"

"Oh, don't pay any attention to Samuel," Boots said. "She always gets a little morose on the third drink. The fourth one usually sets her right, though!"

Samuel was feeling morose all of a sudden, and the amount of booze she'd consumed was only partly to blame. She liked Trish and Marj—they were the only real lesbian couple she knew—but sometimes she was annoyed by how much they cast themselves in the role of husband and wife. She could easily imagine Marj bringing Trish her pipe and slippers at the end of a long day. There was a rigidity in their relationship. Maybe it was because they were both old enough to be Samuel's mother, but except for the fact that they were working with the same equipment sexually, their relationship didn't seem that different from a lot of heterosexual marriages.

And then there was how the boys did it. The boys she knew, anyway. Boots with his "paid help," Carlisle with his monthly trips to a bar in Lexington where he could have quick trysts with strangers. Samuel didn't want that kind of thing either.

But desire flowed through her even if she wasn't quite sure what shape that desire would take, except a feminine one. She planned to keep her virginity where men were concerned, but she wore her virginity with women like an albatross around her neck, "The Rime of the Lesbian Mariner." She suppressed a giggle. It was time for her fourth drink. Time to emerge from her emotional funk.

Counting the empty bottles lined up on the floor, Samuel saw that A.J. was working on his sixth beer. He drained it and set the bottle down with its fellows and gave a small salute before heading toward the door.

"Leaving so soon?" Boots said, trailing him. "I'm so glad you could join us even if it was just for a short while."

There was a murmur of hushed conversation in the doorway, and then A.J. was gone.

Boots closed the door and pantomimed swooning. "Carlisle? What did you think?" he asked.

"Gorgeous," Carlisle said. "Absolutely dreamy. Not much for conversation, though."

Boots put his hands on his hips. "Well, I didn't hire him to *talk*!"

Everybody laughed, and the uninhibited feeling was back in the room again.

Boots turned on the radio—he only listened to popular music when he was drunk—and soon Trish and Marj were slow dancing, their bodies pressed together. Carlisle got up and took Boots's hand, and after some laughter and protesting, the two of them were dancing a companionable waltz.

"You know what our problem is?" Boots said, laughing. "Neither of us wants to lead."

Samuel sat on the bed and watched the dance. The heat between Trish and Marj seemed sufficient to melt the ice in her drink. And even though there wasn't sexual chemistry between Boots and Carlisle, there was an ease to the way they moved together. Samuel was the odd girl out.

When a new song began, Boots disengaged from Carlisle and said, "I saved this dance for my better half." He swooped over to the bed and dramatically held out his arm. Samuel rose to take it.

She knew that lavender marriages like hers were often described as "living a lie." But that wasn't wholly accurate. Boots was not her lover, but he was her mentor and best friend. There was love between them, just not the kind heterosexuals thought of when they saw a man and a woman together.

In many ways, Samuel adored Boots. But he wasn't who she wanted to dance with.

CHAPTER 8

IT FELT STRANGE TO BE OUT alone in the middle of the afternoon, and even though the reason was a dental appointment to get an aching tooth attended to, Frances still experienced a little thrill at her temporary freedom with the children safely ensconced at home with a sitter.

Or maybe the thrill was a lingering effect of the drugs the dentist had administered while filling her tooth. Either way, it was nice to feel giddy while walking solo down Main Street.

Not that there was a whole lot on Main Street to inspire giddiness. All the businesses were straightforward and practical: the dentist's office she had just visited and the doctor's office where she supposed she needed to transfer the children's medical records. There was the drugstore, a hardware store, a barber shop with a twirling striped pole, and Lovins' Discount, which everybody called the dimestore. But there was no bookstore, no sit-down restaurant, nothing extra for intellectual stimulation or pleasure. The motto for downtown seemed to be *just enough to meet your needs, but no more.*

That said, it was always worth a walk-through of Lovins' to take in their cornucopia of cheap merchandise: sewing notions, soaps and cosmetics, and toys and candy. The dimestore kingdom was guarded by Charlie, a shrieking mynah bird who fascinated Danny and Susan, but terrified Robert. Frances had just decided to take a quick tour and maybe pick up some coloring books as a surprise for the older children when she heard a voice behind her say, "Frances?"

She turned to face Samuel, whom she hadn't seen since their lunch together the week before. "Samuel!" she said, genuinely glad to see her. "Isn't this usually the time of day when you write?"

"I'll get back to it shortly," Samuel said. "I just ran out of cigarettes. I'm like a locomotive. If I'm not blowing smoke, I don't work."

Frances smiled. "What's a writer without vices?"

"I'll let you know if I ever meet one."

"I think it'll be a long wait," Frances said. Frances found Samuel's contradictions fascinating. She had the wit of a much older, sophisticated woman, yet she was dressed in the striped pullover, jeans, and sneakers of a twelve-year-old boy. Her dark eyes sparked with worldly intelligence, but her little nose was dusted with freckles.

"Hey, I was going to get my smokes at the drugs store," Samuel said. "You want to walk over with me and maybe grab a cup of coffee at the soda fountain?"

Frances flushed with the pleasure of being chosen. "Sure, but I can't stay long. I'm paying a sitter." With half of her mouth still numb from the dentist's novacaine, *sitter* came out as though it started with an *sh*.

Samuel hooted. "You're paying a what?"

"A sssitter. A babysitter," Frances enunciated carefully. "I've been to the dentist to have a cavity filled. That's why my shpeech is shlurred."

Samuel grinned. "And here I was thinking you were a little bit drunk. I thought it was kind of early in the day, but who am I to judge?"

Frances felt an uncharacteristic giggle escape her. "Well, thank you for not judging me." They were walking together toward the drug store.

"Miz Elizabeth would judge you if you were tipsy in the early afternoon," Samuel said. "She says any lady who drinks before five is a dipsomaniac. Don't you love that word—dipsomaniac?"

"I do," Frances said. "I didn't know people still used it."

"They don't. Just Miz Elizabeth. She is a proud anachronism."

"So," Frances said as they approached the drug store, "if any lady who drinks before five is a dipsomaniac, what about men who drink before five? Do they get a free pass?"

"Yep," Samuel said, holding the door open for Frances, "as they do in so many things."

After Samuel purchased her pack of Pall Malls, they wandered over to the soda fountain. The whole area was covered in gleaming white tile and hung with hand-lettered signs advertising malteds and root beer floats and hot fudge sundaes.

They took a seat in a booth, and a bony blond waitress appeared immediately. "Black coffee, Mrs. McAdoo?" she asked. Her red lipstick had bled beyond the margins of her mouth.

"Yes. Thanks, Polly," Samuel said.

"I'll have the same, please," Frances said.

"Well, y'all are easy, ain't you?" Polly said, turning the upside-down coffee cups on the table upright.

"Easy and cheap," Samuel added. "That doesn't sound nice, does it?"

Polly laughed, then looked at Frances. "You've got to watch this one," she said, nodding in Samuel's direction. "I'll be right back with y'all's coffee."

"You know what sounds good?" Frances said. "A banana split. I don't think I've had one since I was in pigtails."

"Hey, Polly!" Samuel called. "We'll also have a banana split. Two spoons."

"Now you're talking," Polly said, grinning. "Might as well live a little, right?"

The banana split arrived in a glass boat with a spoon balanced on either side of the three scoops of ice cream. It looked as perfect as a picture in an advertisement, with a dollop of whipped cream and a maraschino cherry centered on each scoop.

"It's so pretty," Frances said.

"Well, take a good last look because we're about to mess it up real bad." Samuel wielded her spoon and grinned.

Frances spooned up some chocolate ice cream with banana and whipped cream. It was so good she closed her eyes.

“You look like you’re in heaven,” Samuel said.

“This may be the closest I ever get.” Frances sipped her coffee, loving how its hot bitterness contrasted with the cold, sweet ice cream. She loved, too, having Samuel across from her, sharing this small pleasure. Something about it made her remember the soda fountain back in Illinois where girls and their boyfriends would share an ice cream soda with two straws, leaning in so close that their noses almost touched.

“We didn’t have stuff like this much when I was growing up, so it still feels like a special treat,” Samuel said, digging through the scoop of strawberry. “We were too poor to afford sweets. We’d have biscuits with chocolate syrup sometimes. And when blackberries were in season, Ma would send the kids out to pick them, and then she’d make a blackberry cobbler. That was my favorite. Don’t let anybody ever tell you the blackberries you pick out in the woods are free, though. The briar scratches and the ticks and chiggers make you pay plenty.”

Frances wondered if the words flowed from Samuel’s pen as easily as they seemed to flow from her mouth.

“My mother wouldn’t let me have sweets,” Frances said. “She said they’d ruin my figure and my teeth.” She chuckled. “And look at me now, twenty pounds overweight and fresh out of the dentist’s office, stuffing myself full of ice cream.”

Samuel smiled. “Gaining weight was never a worry in my house. My mama worried more about us getting enough to eat. Daddy was bad with money. But good at drinking it up.”

“I’m sorry.” Frances felt suddenly guilty for prattling on about her middle-class upbringing. Worrying about weight gain was such a bourgeois problem, implying that you not only had enough to eat, but too much.

"No need for you to be sorry, you weren't the one pouring the booze down his throat," Samuel said.

"You know what I mean. I'm sorry you had to grow up in that kind of environment."

Samuel licked some chocolate sauce off her spoon, then looked thoughtful. "You know, I'm not sure I'm sorry I grew up that way. If I hadn't, I wouldn't be the person I am. I probably wouldn't even be a writer. I mean, if I grew up thinking everything was hunky dory, what would I have to write about?"

"True."

"Speaking of writing, I suppose I should get back to it, though the temptation to sit here and drink coffee and eat ice cream with you all afternoon is awful tempting."

"It is," Frances said, smiling shyly. "But the babysitter charges by the hour."

Frances reached for the bill Polly had left on the table, but Samuel snatched it up before she could get it.

"Oh, no, you don't!" Samuel said. "My guest, my treat."

Frances hated when people quibbled for a long time over the bill out of a misguided sense of politeness. "Well, thank you. But the next time we do this, I'll get it."

Samuel smiled. "I'll agree to that only because you said there'd be a next time." Samuel looked Frances in the eye for a moment, then quickly looked away.

Frances was relieved at the break of eye contact. Why was it so intense—like Samuel was looking into her instead of at her? "Of course there will be," she said. "And soon."

"Good," Samuel said, pulling a five-dollar bill from her wallet and leaving it on the table. "Because I like you."

Had any woman ever said those words to her before? Since girlhood, she had always had a good sense of who liked her and who didn't, but she couldn't remember anybody announcing their feelings like that. It was nice, though. People should do it more often. And yet she felt nervous about saying the words back. After what seemed like too long a pause, she finally said, "I like you, too."

As soon as Frances saw the luminous smile on Samuel's face, she was glad she'd mustered the courage to say it.

* * *

"WHY IS EVERYTHING SO MUSHY?" DANNY asked, poking at his dinner with a fork. It was indeed a mushy meal: an especially soft meatloaf, mashed potatoes, and applesauce.

"Because," Henry intoned, "today the dentist yanked out every tooth in your mother's head."

"Really? Can I see?" Danny asked, suddenly sounding fascinated.

Frances laughed, then bared her teeth so her children could see that she still had a full set. "No, but I did have a filling, and the dentist told me to stick to soft foods for the next twenty-four hours. So, if I eat mush, you eat mush."

"The Munchkin baby likes mush," Susan said.

Frances was holding Robert on her lap and giving him small tastes of applesauce, which made him smack his lips appreciatively.

"And he is very nearly toothless," Henry said.

"True," Frances said. "Of course, soft food's not all bad. I had ice cream for lunch. At the soda fountain." She stopped short of saying *with Samuel,* but she wasn't sure why she was withholding this piece of information.

"Lucky you!" Danny said.

"Can we have ice cream for dessert?" Susan asked.

Frances remembered there was still some vanilla in the freezer she'd bought to go with the apple pie they'd had a few nights before.

"I think that can be arranged," she said.

Frances scooped ice cream for Susan, Danny, and Henry, whose sweet tooth could not be underestimated. The plain white bowls filled with the plain white mounds looked homely compared with the lavish banana split she had shared this afternoon.

It was funny. She had meant to mention that she had run into Samuel in town, and they had gone for coffee and ice cream together. But somehow that part of the story—the part that *made* it a story, really—hadn't come out of her mouth. She didn't know why she was choosing to keep it a secret. Maybe it was because being a wife and mother was all about giving and sharing, scooping out and dispensing portions of yourself, like filling bowls with ice cream. She loved her family. But it felt good to have one small thing she kept for herself.

CHAPTER 9

A.J. CUT THE LAWN AND PRUNED the shrubbery every Wednesday. On those days, Boots would come home early "for lunch" after his 9:30 a.m. freshman composition class. Boots didn't enter the house right away. Instead, he went around back where A.J. was busily working, sweat drenching his white undershirt so it clung to his muscles, and then disappeared with A.J. into the guest house.

At noon, Boots joined Samuel and Miz Elizabeth at the kitchen table for lunch. His mood was always radiant.

Today, as they did every Wednesday, Boots and Samuel shared a secret smile as he sat down at the table.

"Well, son," Miz Elizabeth said, "I have to say that new gardener is doing a much better job than that last one you hired. I finally feel like I can go to my Garden Club meeting without hanging my head in shame."

"Oh, I'm impressed with him, too, Mama," Boots said, sipping his iced tea. "He is highly skilled."

Samuel suppressed a snicker and gave Boots a playful kick under the table.

Priscilla set down a tray of crustless sandwiches, some filled with homemade egg salad and others with her excellent pimento cheese. Next to the plate of sandwiches she placed the cut-glass relish tray, which was heaped with celery, carrot sticks, olives, and pickles.

"Priscilla," Boots said, passing the sandwich plate to Samuel. "I was wondering if you might set a glass of tea and a sandwich out on the back step for A.J. I think he's really exerted himself this morning."

Samuel didn't meet Boots's eye and feigned a tremendous amount of interest in which sandwich to choose.

"Yes, sir, Mr. Boots," Priscilla said.

Boots flashed Priscilla a winning smile. "So, I was getting my shoes shined outside the barber shop yesterday, and Harold told me that your daughter won the spelling bee over at the colored school. You must be awful proud of her."

Most of the time Priscilla's face was a neutral mask, but at Boots's words, she smiled. "We are proud of Gail. She's a good speller because she reads so much. She's read every book they've got in the school library at least once. Most of them twice. Says she wants to go to college and make something out of herself."

"And if she's smart and hard-working, why shouldn't she?" Miz Elizabeth said, gesturing with a celery stick.

Samuel found it interesting to compare her own family with Boots and Miz Elizabeth when it came to race relations. Samuel's parents held a hatred of Blacks that was so intense Samuel found it difficult to comprehend. As a child, Samuel would listen to her daddy's racist rants and wonder if a Black person had once wronged him in some way. And if so, how could it be so bad that he held a grudge against a whole race of people?

Boots and Miz Elizabeth were different. For all their hatred of them, Samuel's parents hardly ever interacted with Black people, but Boots and Miz Elizabeth interacted with them on a daily basis. These interactions were never purely social, though. It was understood that if a Black woman entered a white lady's house, she was there to clean it. Boots and Miz Elizabeth were never unkind to the Black people who served them, but in polite white society, there were lines you did not cross. You could sound friendly when you talked to your maid or shoe shiner, but you were not friends.

Samuel knew that Miz Elizabeth was more open-minded than most white ladies for opining that Gail deserved to go to college if she was smart and worked hard. But it still seemed unfair that people always had to prove themselves deserving. While white people had nothing to prove.

"Where does Gail want to go to college?" Samuel asked.

"Fisk, Lord willing," Priscilla said, setting an egg salad sandwich and a pimento cheese sandwich on a saucer for A.J.

"Oh, I bet He will be," Samuel said. She wasn't even sure she believed in God, but she wanted to be encouraging.

"Well, she's working hard, and I'm praying hard," Priscilla said, pouring some iced tea in a glass. "I reckon we'll see what comes of it."

Once Priscilla had disappeared out the back door with the food, Boots said, "You know, I was talking to Henry this morning, and we had such a nice chat about *The Odyssey* that

I was wondering if we might want to have him and Frances over for supper on Friday night."

Samuel smiled at the thought of an evening in Frances's company. "Yes, we should." She felt the force of Miz Elizabeth's glare, reminding her that she was not the lady of the house. "I mean, I think it's a good idea. What do you think, Mama Liz?"

"Hmm . . . " Miz Elizabeth said. "This Henry—he's a friend of yours from school?" She sounded like she was grilling the nine-year-old Boots about a friend he wanted to bring home for a sleepover. Samuel wouldn't have been surprised if Miz Elizabeth had asked what Henry's father did for a living.

"Yes, ma'am. He just started this semester. He and his wife are absolutely darling."

"Well, I don't suppose there's any harm in having them over," Miz Elizabeth said. "We'll have to figure out what to serve, of course."

Priscilla came through the back door carrying the empty glass and saucer.

"Priscilla," Miz Elizabeth said, "could you stay late on Friday evening to fix and serve supper for some guests? We'd pay you extra, of course."

"I can do that," Priscilla said. "I don't reckon it'll kill my husband to fix himself a baloney sandwich."

"That genius daughter of yours can come help if she wants to," Boots said. "She could earn herself some college money."

"I'll tell her," Priscilla said.

Samuel couldn't tell if Boots's offer was kind or condescending. She figured Priscilla's daughter would be glad to have the money, but why did she have to wait on white people to earn it?

* * *

"I REFUSE TO PUT ON MY faculty wife party dress to receive visitors in my own damn house," Samuel said. She was standing at the bottom of the stairs, dressed in a plain white blouse and navy blue slacks, and Miz Elizabeth was looking at her like she'd just descended the staircase stark naked.

"You're a McAdoo. You have to have certain standards." Miz Elizabeth was wearing an elegant powder blue sheath with her real pearl necklace. She had gotten her hair done at the beauty shop that morning. "As it is, you look like a little sailor boy going out with the fleet."

"She's Popeye the Sailor Man—" Boots sang. He was wearing his lavender seersucker.

"Cut it out, Boots," Samuel said, thinking but not saying, *Or I'll tell your mama about your proclivity for sailor boys.* "All right. I'll change from pants into a skirt, but that's as far as I'm willing to go."

"That will be some improvement anyway," Miz Elizabeth sighed.

Samuel rolled her eyes and stomped back up the stairs. She knew it must be exhausting for Miz Elizabeth to have a daughter in law who cared so little about her personal appearance. But she also knew it would be even worse if Miz Elizabeth had a beautiful, vain daughter-in-law who rivaled Miz Elizabeth for glamor. The jealousy would be too much for the old lady to bear.

In her room, Samuel changed into a dark blue skirt and tucked her blouse into it. She kept on her white socks but traded her sneakers for penny loafers. She knew this choice would drive Miz Elizabeth crazy, but she was damned if anybody was going to make her wear stockings and heels.

When Samuel came back downstairs Miz Elizabeth looked her over and let out a reserved sigh. "Well, it's a little better, I suppose. But full-grown women have no business wearing bobby socks."

Samuel regarded stockings and garters as the equivalent of a medieval torture device. On the rare occasions she did wear them, the elastic garters stung her thighs like a whip. "You should consider yourself lucky I'm wearing anything on my feet at all. I see no reason for people to wear shoes in their own house."

Miz Elizabeth shook her head, then looked over at Boots. "Son, you married a savage."

"I know!" Boots crowed. "Isn't she glorious? My little barefoot bohemian! She's good for us, Mama. Helps us loosen up."

Miz Elizabeth held up a cigarette for Boots to light. "I thought I always warned you about loose women."

Boots flicked his Zippo. "Not *that* kind of loose."

"Definitely not that kind of loose." Samuel wondered how Miz Elizabeth would react if Samuel spoke the truth: *Actually, I'm still a virgin, Mama Liz.*

There was a soft knock at the back door, and within a minute, Priscilla was standing in the living room with a coltish young girl wearing a beautifully-sewn homemade yellow dress.

"I'm not interrupting an important conversation, am I?" Priscilla asked. She was wearing a floral print dress that was a little fancier than what she usually wore to work, probably a church dress.

"Lord, no," Boots said. "We're just jabbering to hear ourselves talk, like usual."

Priscilla offered no comment on this but said, "Well, I just wanted to introduce y'all to my daughter Gail. She's gonna be helping me serve and clean up tonight."

Miz Elizabeth smiled. "Gail, get over here and let me see how much you've grown! Last time I saw you, you were knee high to a junebug."

Gail gave an embarrassed little smile but approached Miz Elizabeth to be inspected.

"Look how pretty you are with those big brown eyes!" Miz Elizabeth said. "I bet the boys are falling all over each other to get to you."

"Not really, ma'am, but thank you," Gail said, looking down at her patent-leather Mary Janes.

"Give 'em a year or two, and they will be," Miz Elizabeth said. "Boys catch on slow."

"Congratulations on winning the spelling bee," Samuel said, hoping to divert the conversation from beauty and boys.

"Thank you," Gail said, looking less self-conscious.

"Yes," Boots said, "I know your mama's real proud of all your academic achievements and your college plans." He turned toward Samuel. "Sweetheart, we've got a few minutes before our guests arrive. Why don't you take Gail to look at our library?"

"Would you like to?" Samuel asked.

Gail nodded. "Yes, please."

When Samuel flipped on the light switch to reveal the room in which all four walls were lined with brimming bookshelves, she heard Gail suck in her breath.

"I didn't know people could have this many books in their house," Gail said, looking around to take it all in.

"Sure, they can," Samuel said, but she knew the more accurate response would have been sure, they can if they can afford it. Growing up, the only book in her house had been the family Bible. There had been no money for books, and if there had been, books certainly weren't what her daddy would have spent it on.

"I've read all the books in my school library, some of them two or three times," Gail said, running her fingers along the shelved volumes's spines. "But next year I'll ride the bus to the high school in Lexington. I hear there's a bigger library there."

Samuel hated that the public library was off limits to Gail—that it was off limits to any child who wanted to read. "Well, in the meantime, if you want to borrow any books from us, you're more than welcome." Most of the books in "their" collection were really Boots's, and she wasn't sure if Boots would approve of this arrangement. But she also didn't care that much whether he did or didn't.

Gail gave the first real smile Samuel had seen from her. "Really? Are you sure?"

"Abso-tootly," Samuel said. "How about we say you can 'check out' two books at a time, and then when you return them, you can check out two more?"

Gail nodded. "That's how the school library does it. Except the books there are all castoffs from the white school. They've got torn covers and bad words written inside them. These books are so beautiful I'm afraid I'll hurt them."

"I know you'll take good care of them," Samuel said. "I'll leave you to browse, okay?" She sensed that Gail might be self-conscious about picking out books with an adult—and a white adult at that—standing over her.

When Samuel returned to the living room, Priscilla was setting up cocktail fixings on a rolling cart.

"Give us a good hour for cocktails before you call us into dinner, Priscilla," Boots said. "Let us get our gullets good and lubricated."

"Yes, sir," Priscilla said. She looked over at Samuel. "Where has Gail gotten off to?"

Samuel smiled. "She's in the library."

Priscilla shook her head. "Lord, I'll never be able to get her out of there. I guess it won't do any harm for her to stay there while you drink your liquor. She can come help me when it's time to bring the food out."

Samuel sensed, not for the first time, that Priscilla disapproved of their alcohol consumption. Her disapproval was probably even stronger when her child was present.

The doorbell rang. "I'll get it," Samuel said. She felt a little tingle of excitement at the prospect of seeing Frances.

Frances and Henry were framed in the doorway. Frances had a shy smile on her face, but Henry was beaming like Samuel was his favorite person in the world. "Greetings!" he said. "Your home is spectacular. I feel like we should sip mint juleps on the front porch." He surprised Samuel with a hug and a kiss on the cheek.

Boots, who was standing behind Samuel, made a beeline for Frances, took her hand, and kissed it. "Look at this gorgeous creature!" he exclaimed, and Frances blushed.

Many aspects of etiquette were puzzling to Samuel, and this was one of them. Why was it a social expectation for men to slop all over each other's wives?

"Now," Boots said, clapping his hands. "Y'all have to meet the light of my life. My mama."

Apparently, the slopping was just getting started.

Miz Elizabeth was already on her feet. A tall woman, she was imposing in her high heels, but she was also wearing her most charming smile, the one where her eyes twinkled and creased at the corners. The twinkle-crinkle, Samuel called it.

"Mama, may I present to you, Dr. and Mrs. Henry Harmon. Henry and Frances, this is my beautiful mama, Mrs. Elizabeth McAdoo."

"Well, aren't you a big handsome one!" Miz Elizabeth said, offering her hand to Henry, who kissed it.

"I see that where charm is concerned, Boots is just the tip of the iceberg," Henry said.

"Well, he learned at my feet," Miz Elizabeth said.

"It's true," Boots said. "And those feet were always wearing such glorious shoes! Now who wants a drink?"

"I could be persuaded," Henry said.

"It's generally not hard to persuade him to have a drink," Frances said. "As opposed, to say, persuading him to take out the garbage."

"Oh, you're funny," Miz Elizabeth said, looking Frances up and down. "That's good."

Samuel knew what Miz Elizabeth was implying: if you can't be pretty, at least you can be funny. But Samuel thought Frances was very pretty. Her brown hair, when she wore it down loose like tonight, fell in soft waves, and her eyes were a catlike green. Her figure was ripe and voluptuous. The difference between Miz Elizabeth and Frances was that Frances did nothing to accentuate her natural beauty, whereas Miz Elizabeth adorned herself with a beauty-shop hairdo, jewelry, and cosmetics. For Miz Elizabeth, beauty was all about presentation.

Humming to himself, Boots poured a scotch neat for Henry and mixed a scotch and soda for Frances before proceeding to concoct the McAdoo family gin and tonics.

"So, Dr. and Mrs. Harmon," Miz Elizabeth said once she had a drink in her hand, "should I regale you with embarrassing stories about Boots's childhood?"

"Already, Mama? You haven't even had one drink yet," Boots said, but his tone was good-natured. Samuel was aware—even if Frances and Henry were not—that she was watching the beginning of a very well-rehearsed performance.

"Oh, please do," Henry said. "I find it difficult to imagine Boots as a child. I think of him as emerging fully formed, like Athena springing from the head of Zeus."

"Well, he was a child, but he certainly wasn't like other children." Miz Elizabeth took a dainty sip of her drink. "Precocious. That was the word people always used to describe him."

"Well, that was one of them," Boots said. "Obnoxious was another. I'm pretty sure that was what my first-grade teacher wrote on my report card."

"It was," Miz Elizabeth said. "She wasn't from around here. And your daddy and I got her fired, too. There were always some people who were afraid of Boots's intelligence. He started reading when he was just three, and he could read anything you handed to him, from the Sunday paper to *Grey's Anatomy*. His daddy started taking Boots with him to bars. He'd pick Boots up, set him on a barstool and say, 'I'll bet anybody in here five dollars that this baby can read anything you bring to him.' Of course, the fellows in the bar wouldn't believe it. They'd bring him the sports page, the phone book . . . one time some trashy dime novel a fellow had in his pocket."

"In all fairness, I did stumble over the word *voluptuous* in that one," Boots said.

"People always thought there was some kind of trick to it, but of course there wasn't," Miz Elizabeth said. "So, they had to pay up."

"Daddy always gave me one dollar out of every five we made," Boots said. "He bought drinks with his money, and I bought candy and ice cream and Coca-Colas with mine. My early literacy resulted in my becoming an absolute little butterball."

Frances and Henry were laughing so hard they couldn't catch their breath. Their laughter was contagious, and Samuel found herself joining in even though she had heard the story many times. It was an amazing thing, how Miz

Elizabeth and Boots played off each other. Samuel and Boots could be funny together, too, but Samuel knew she wasn't in Mama Liz's league when it came to doing a comic set piece with Boots. Mother and son had been working on their routine since he was in short pants. They were like a comedy duo that had been together since the days of vaudeville.

As soon as their cocktail glasses were empty, Priscilla appeared as if by magic and said, "Dinner is served," which struck Samuel as strangely formal. They always said "supper."

"Wonderful! Thank you, Priscilla," Boots said. "Shall we away to the dining room?"

They never used the dining room except for company or Christmas. Like Priscilla's dinner announcement, it was much more formal than they usually had occasion for. It was a long room with a Queen Anne-style table and chairs, a sideboard on which food could be set, and a glass-doored cabinet which held the McAdoo family china and silver.

Before she married Boots, the only way Samuel knew some families had china and silver patterns was from books. The only treasured food-related item Samuel's mother owned was a well-seasoned cast iron skillet.

The McAdoo china and silver were on full display tonight. The table, which was draped with a white linen tablecloth, was set with it. "It looks like Christmas in here," Samuel said.

Boots pulled out a dining room chair so his mother could sit down. "Yes, we're not always this fancy," Boots said. "But we've got to put on the dog a little when we have company. Gotta spoil y'all a little so you'll come back."

"Well, I certainly feel spoiled," Frances said, smiling in a way that seemed a little nervous.

Priscilla emerged from the kitchen carrying a breadbasket.

"Oh, you've got to try Priscilla's yeast rolls," Boots said. "They're like biting into a cloud."

Priscilla disappeared into the kitchen, then returned with a large platter of roast beef. Gail followed behind her, carrying serving bowls of mashed potatoes and peas.

Frances looked intently at Gail as she set the bowls down on the table. "Do you work here, too?" she asked.

"Not usually, ma'am," Gail said. "Most of the time I'm in school. Tonight, my mama just needed an extra pair of hands."

"Oh, good." Frances sounded relieved. "That's good."

Samuel realized, to her mortification, that Frances had thought they were exploiting a Black child for cheap labor. "Gail just won the spelling bee at the colored school," Samuel said, in hopes of correcting the situation somewhat.

"I'm impressed. I'm a good speller on paper, but spelling bees always made me nervous" Henry said. "Gail, can you spell *antidisestablishmentarianism*? It's the longest word in the dictionary."

Gail smiled. "I can try. Can you run it by me one more time, please?"

Henry said it, slower this time. Gail repeated it, then spelled it correctly.

"Spectacular!" Henry crowed, raising his glass to her.

"Thank you," Gail said, then scurried back to the kitchen.

"Y'all enjoy your meal," Priscilla said. "I'll check back in a few minutes to see if you need anything."

After Priscilla was gone, Henry said, "That's the one thing I can't get used to down here."

"What's that?" Boots asked.

"Segregation," Henry said, spooning up a serving of mashed potatoes. "Like the way you said 'colored school,' Samuel. Where I'm from, we just have schools. No modifiers."

"Well, that's certainly better," Samuel said, thinking of Gail talking about the battered hand-me-down books in her school library. There wasn't even a colored high school in Collinsville. When it was time for Gail to go to high school, she'd have to ride a bus for an hour to Lexington.

"That's not how people want things down here, unfortunately," Miz Elizabeth said.

"You mean that's not how white people want things?" Henry's tone was mild, but he was slicing forcefully into his roast beef.

"Not all white people," Samuel said. She was afraid of what Boots or Miz Elizabeth might say on the subject.

"Surely we can talk about something lighter at the dinner table." Miz Elizabeth flashed a winning smile. "I mean a lighter subject, not lighter skin, of course."

There was laughter, but it was uncomfortable laughter, not like the easy, full-throated kind from when Boots and Miz Elizabeth had been doing their vaudeville schtick in the living room.

"So," Miz Elizabeth said, turning her attention to Frances, "how do you manage with three children at home? I only had Boots to look after, and some days I still had to go lie down with a cold cloth on my head."

"Granted, I still tend to have that effect on people," Boots said, sliding back into their comedy routine.

"Three's not so bad," Frances said. "It's the perfect number for juggling. If we added one more, though, I'd be in trouble."

"Duly noted," Henry said.

Priscilla cleared the dinner dishes, then brought out strawberry shortcake and coffee.

After their dessert plates were cleaned, Boots said, "Would anyone care for a glass of sherry in the living room?"

"Don't mind if I do," Henry said. "I haven't tasted sherry since I used to rob my grandmother's liquor cabinet."

They smoked and sipped sherry and listened to one side of Boots's newest opera album, though Henry confessed himself to be more of a jazz man. Frances seemed to like the music, though. She listened with her eyes closed and a beatific expression on her face, like the Virgin Mary in a painting, if the Virgin Mary had drunk sherry and smoked cigarettes.

Once the album was over, Miz Elizabeth stood up. "Well, this has been lovely, but I'm an old lady and need to retire for the evening. You young folks keep on enjoying yourselves."

After everyone wished Miz Elizabeth a good night, Henry asked Boots if they could have a Scotch in his study, presumably to talk about manly things, though Boots was hardly an expert in the subject. Still, he agreed gamely and said to Samuel, "Maybe you can take Frances outside and show her the rose garden."

Samuel was no more an expert on roses than Boots was on masculinity. But she did like the idea of taking the fresh night air with Frances, walking and talking, just the two of them.

Samuel refilled their sherry glasses, and she and Frances went outside. It was a beautiful night. The sky was clear, and the stars shone.

"Full moon," Frances said, looking up. "Diana is at the height of her powers."

Samuel sipped her sherry and looked at the bright disc in the sky. "The moon goddess, right?"

Frances nodded. "We talk about Greco-Roman mythology a lot in our house. It actually makes more sense to me than Judeo-Christian myth. You've got lots of gods and goddesses in charge of lots of different things, and they have love affairs and jealousies and grudges just like regular people."

Samuel nodded. "So, when something bad happens on earth it's because one of the gods is pissed off about something."

"Exactly," Frances said, smiling. "I mean, I know it's all just a metaphor, but I like it as a way of thinking about things. I guess I have a pagan heart."

"Well, a lot of people around here would call you a heathen, but not me," Samuel said. They were strolling around the yard, and Frances was stopping to admire each rose bush. "You know, the first time I saw the word 'heathens' was in Sunday school when I was a kid. I read it as 'heat hens.' I was so confused—why was the Bible talking about chickens, and why were the chickens hot?"

Frances laughed. "That's what I'll call myself from now on. A heat hen." She reached out to stroke the petals of a pink rose. "So, do you take care of the roses?"

"Lord, no," Samuel said. "About once a month Miz Elizabeth puts on a big straw hat and makes a show of pruning them for about thirty minutes. But we have a gardener who does the real work."

"And a housekeeper, too," Frances said.

Samuel felt embarrassed by her privilege. She knew Frances spent her days cooking, cleaning, and caring for children. "Yeah, we live a lot higher on the hog than the way I was raised. It's taken some getting used to. Not that I'm complaining."

"Of course. I'm still getting used to being in the South," Frances said. "A lot of it still feels strange but being out here tonight under the stars with the air all heavy with the scent of flowers—it feels strange in a good way. Magical, almost."

Samuel felt it, too, but she attributed it to the company more than the foliage and the weather. "Yes" was all she could think of to say.

"You know what I like even more than roses?" Frances said. "That magnolia tree." She wandered over to it and touched one of its huge leaves.

"Yeah, all fine old Southern homes have to have one of those in the yard," Samuel said. "I think it might be a law."

"They look almost tropical. The leaves are so big and shiny, and the flowers are the size of a serving bowl, with that sticky-sweet smell . . . it's almost too much, you know?"

Samuel knew. It was all almost too much. The magnolias and the light from the full moon shining on Frances, making her glow like a goddess herself. Samuel was glowing inside—with the warmth from her second glass of sherry but with another, deeper warmth, too, one that made her say "Frances" and take a step toward her. She leaned forward and brushed her lips lightly against Frances's. They were soft like magnolia petals and tasted of sherry. As soon as she did it, she pulled back, ready to apologize as soon as she saw the look on Frances's face. But Frances was smiling.

CHAPTER 10

HENRY ROLLED OFF HER. "WELL!" HE said. "That was a greater show of enthusiasm that I've seen in a while. Maybe we should get you tipsy on sherry more often."

"Maybe," Frances said. She was still short of breath. "Or maybe it's the full moon."

"It turns you into a she-wolf," Henry said. He tilted his head skyward and howled.

Frances laughed. She grabbed two cigarettes from the pack on the nightstand and passed one to Henry. She handed him a lighter, and he lit hers, then his. Tonight was the first night in years that she had reached for him instead of the other way around. Back before the kids were born, it had been different. She had been so young, her body was her own, and she had been hungry for him all the time.

Tonight, she had been hungry like that again, though she wasn't sure that Henry was the object of her hunger. But he was there, and so she reached for him like a starving person would reach for any food that's close to hand.

She thought only of Samuel's lips on hers, soft as a butterfly's wings.

* * *

Monday mornings were chaotic. Frances stood at the kitchen counter, cracking eggs into a bowl when Henry appeared on one side of her and Danny on the other, Henry saying "Honey, could you—?" at the same time Danny said, "Mom, can you—?"

"One at a time," Frances said. "Henry, you first."

"Would you tie my tie? Every time I do it, looks like it was tied by an incompetent seven-year-old."

Frances wiped her hands on her apron. Henry generally went to work tieless. She often had to remind him to tuck his shirt into his pants. "What's the occasion? Did somebody die?" She evened out the ends of the tie, then started on the knot.

"Meeting with the dean this morning," Henry said. "A funeral would be more cheerful."

"Now, what was it you needed, Danny?" Frances asked.

Danny was nearly vibrating from the hardship of waiting. "I need you to sign this permission slip," he said, waving a sheet of paper in front of her nose.

Frances looked down at the paper, then over at Henry. "It's a permission slip to go to an assembly on gun safety. Do you think that's strange? He's only eight years old."

"Well, the boys in these parts are crazy about their huntin' and fishin'," Henry said. "I guess they try to educate them early so they won't blow themselves to kingdom come."

Frances rested the form on the kitchen counter and scribbled her signature on it. “Okay, you have my permission to go to the assembly, but if you ever touch a gun, the subject of gun safety will be irrelevant because I’ll kill you myself.”

“Thanks, Mom.”

Frances poured a little milk in with the eggs and started whisking them. From his playpen, Robert threw his pacifier across the room and screamed, refusing to be pacified.

“Your bottle’s coming up,” Frances said, eyeing the formula heating on the stove. She poured the beaten eggs into a skillet, then popped some bread into the toaster. She grabbed the bottle and the baby and fed him with one arm while she stirred the eggs with the other. She thought, not for the first time, that mothers should have at least a couple of extra sets of arms like Hindu deities.

Susan came tearing in through the front door, her eyes wide with excitement. “Auntie Em! Auntie Em! There’s a kitty on the front porch! Can we keep her? I want to name her Eureka!”

Of course she did, Frances thought. Eureka was the name of Dorothy’s kitten, who was much less well known than her dog. Toto got all the press.

“Honey, she’s probably somebody else’s kitty who wandered over for a visit.”

Susan looked offended. “That’s not what she told me. She told me she wants to be my kitty because I’ve needed a new kitty ever since Brigid died.”

Brigid was Frances’s beloved calico that she had had since before she and Henry were married. Brigid had died a little over a year ago, and Frances had been too heartbroken to try to replace her. "Well, we'll see if the kitty is telling the truth or if she belongs to one of the neighbors," Frances said. "In the meantime, breakfast is almost ready, so you should go wash your hands."

Finally, miraculously, everyone was settled at the table. The children had their orange juice and milk, Frances and Henry had their orange juice and coffee, and everyone had plates of eggs and toast before them. Robert, his belly full of formula, had peacefully returned to his playpen.

Frances let herself breathe. This was the lull when everybody's needs were temporarily met. Then Danny would run off to catch the school bus, Henry would drive off to work, and she would wash the breakfast dishes and think about what to cook for dinner. But she could think about other things, too. She could think about the story she was writing, which actually seemed to be turning into something. She could think about Samuel.

She could think about the kiss.

Because the fact was, even if she hadn't had the opportunity to think about it without interruption, that kiss had been on her mind all weekend. Sometimes she had found herself pressing her fingers to her lips as if she could find some evidence of it there, physical proof that it had really happened.

She knew it had happened. One cocktail and two sherries weren't enough to make her take leave of her senses. It had happened and it had been good—she felt strangely giddy when she thought about it—but it was confusing, too. What did it mean?

"Frances, come back to us. We miss you." Henry's voice shook her out of her thoughts.

"What?"

"I had asked if you'd refresh my coffee," Henry said.

"He asked you *twice*," Danny added helpfully.

"Oh, sorry. I was lost in thought. I probably need more coffee, too." She got up and retrieved the coffee pot.

After Henry and Danny were out the door and Robert was lying on his back in his playpen, rediscovering the joys of playing with his own feet, Frances plugged up the kitchen sink, turned on the hot water, and proceeded to dump in dishes.

She was scrubbing the egg pan when Susan came running in from outdoors. "Auntie Em! Auntie Em! The kitty's still here! She's on the porch. Come see her!"

"Just a second." France set the still eggy pan on the counter and dried her hands. She knew this was a dangerous proposition. If she "met" the cat, she'd want it as much as Susan did.

"Isn't she beautiful?" Susan asked. The cat was rubbing itself against her skinny little-girl legs.

Frances had never seen a cat she hadn't thought was beautiful. Even the most notch-eared, battle-scarred stray tom had a roguish handsomeness. This cat, though, would've been a beauty in the eyes of all but the most superstitious—sleek, shining black with golden eyes. Frances sat down cross-legged on the porch and held out her hand for the cat to sniff. It did, then licked her fingertips. She stroked its velvety head, and it purred and climbed immediately into her lap. Frances had forgotten how comforting it was to have a warm, furry creature choose you as its armchair.

"Can we keep her?" Susan asked, reaching over to stroke the cat's fur.

"Well, right now we don't know if she's ours to keep. We'll have to see if hangs around and doesn't seem to have any place to go." She petted the kitty under the chin, and it craned its neck so she could reach a larger surface area. "In the meantime, though, I don't suppose it would do any harm to get one of our moving boxes and put an old towel in it, so she'll have a comfortable place to sleep on the porch if she needs one. And I guess it would be all right to set out a saucer of milk in case she's hungry."

"I'll be right back," Susan said and disappeared into the house. She always responded well to being given a project.

In just a couple of minutes, Susan was back with a cardboard box and a towel which wasn't quite as old as Frances would have liked. Then Susan darted back into the house and came back much more slowly, carrying a saucer of milk carefully, so as not to spill.

Susan set the saucer on the porch, and Frances placed the cat in front of it. The cat lapped up the milk ravenously.

"Can we name her Eureka?" Susan asked.

"We can't name her anything until we know she's ours," Frances said. "But I was actually thinking of Hecate."

Susan crinkled her nose. "Why do you want to name her 'Hey Kitty?'"

Frances smiled. "Not 'hey kitty.' Hecate, the goddess of the crossroads and witchcraft. But I like Eureka just fine for a name." In one of the Oz books, Dorothy had named her foundling kitten Eureka because Eureka means "I found it." Frances stood up, remembering the pile of dishes in the sink. She wondered if she should call Samuel after she finished them. "But we can't name her anything for at least a week. And until then, she has to stay outside."

"Yes, Auntie Em," Susan said. But then Frances heard her whisper to the cat, "You have to sleep outside for now, Eureka. But when you can come inside, you can sleep with me in my bed."

Frances had just turned to go inside the house when she heard an adult voice call, "Hey."

She turned back around to see Samuel standing on the sidewalk in her Keds and dungarees. It was as if Frances had conjured her up somehow. Black cats, the person she was just thinking about appearing. Maybe Frances really was a witch.

"Hey," Samuel said, looking down at the sidewalk as if something there interested her.

"Hi." Frances's face felt warm. God, was she blushing?

"Hey," Samuel repeated, still not making eye contact. "I was out walking, trying to work out a scene in my head, and I guess I just happened to walk by here."

"Tip!" Susan said, getting up from petting the cat.

"Dorothy," Samuel said, bowing.

"Can I hug you?" Susan said, trotting down the porch steps. "Tip turns into Ozma, and Ozma and Dorothy always hug when they greet."

"Of course," Samuel said.

Susan threw her arms around Samuel, then took her by the hand. "You have to come up on the porch and see the kitty I found."

Samuel smiled and let herself be led up the steps.

"Black cats are my favorite!" Samuel said. "Unfortunately, Mama Liz won't allow a cat in the house. She says you can't trust them because they steal babies's breath!"

Frances laughed. She had read about this superstition before but had never known anybody who actually believed it. "But you don't have a baby, so what's the problem?"

"Exactly!" Samuel said. "That's what I told her. But she said there might be a baby someday. I told her not to hold her breath."

"Well, at least if she holds her breath, a cat can't steal it," Frances said. She liked to hear Samuel laugh.

"Auntie Em says I can name her Eureka if we keep her," Susan said when Samuel knelt to pet the cat.

"We don't know if it belongs to anybody," Frances said. "It just showed up."

"Well, it is definitely a she," Samuel said. "And she's going to be a mama."

"Kittens!" Susan squealed.

"Are you sure?" Frances asked.

Samuel stood up. "I'm a country girl. I know these things."

Frances shook her head. "I think I will neglect to share this piece of information with Henry. But in for a penny, in for a pound."

Samuel grinned. "In for a critter, in for a litter.'

Frances laughed. "Dorothy, why don't you stay outside and play till lunchtime? Ozma, would you like to come in and have a cup of coffee?" For some reason, this felt like a bold request.

"I'd be delighted," Samuel said.

Once they were inside, a shyness washed over Frances that seemed contagious. They looked everywhere but each other. "I'll . . . uh . . . get the coffee," Frances said stupidly.

"I'll help." Samuel followed her into the kitchen.

"Sit," Frances said. "All I have to do is pour."

They sat silently with their coffee until the tension finally made Frances blurt, "So did you really just *happen* to walk past my house?"

Samuel smiled, looking down into her coffee cup. "No. I walked here completely on purpose. But if you hadn't been out on the porch, I wouldn't have had the courage to knock on the door."

Frances nodded. "Good thing I was out on the porch then. You can thank the cat for that."

"I'll make sure to," Samuel said. She was quiet for a moment. "Frances?"

"Yes?"

"Do I need to apologize to you?"

"What for?"

Samuel was studying her cup again. "The . . . the kiss."

Samuel had said it. More than once over the weekend, Frances had wondered if she'd imagined it. But if Samuel had said it, it was real.

"No, of course not." Frances felt the warmth in her face returning. "It was . . . it was wonderful."

Samuel's face lit up. "Really?"

"Really." Frances reached across the table to touch Samuel's hand. Samuel took her hand and held it.

Frances couldn't remember the last time she had held hands with another adult. How could something so simple, not much different from a handshake, feel so intimate? She was also pretty sure she had never held hands with a woman since childhood. Samuel's skin was soft, and her fingers laced together perfectly with Frances's.

"Listen," Frances said, though she had no doubt that Samuel was listening. "I don't know how many girls Henry has kissed since we've been married. Three I know about for sure, and with one of them it was a lot more than kissing. Before Friday night, I never knew I might like to kiss a girl, too. But I figure if Henry has kissed all these girls, surely I'm entitled to kiss one."

Samuel gave a shy smile. "To kiss one once or to kiss her more than once?"

A little thrill ran through Frances that somehow came out as a giggle. "I guess that's negotiable."

Samuel nodded. "Fair enough. Are you going to tell Henry about us?"

Somehow the two of them had become an *us*. "God, no. He never told me about any of his girls. He just got caught. Are you going to tell Boots? I mean, you're a married woman, too."

Samuel gave Frances's hand a little squeeze, then let it go. "I love holding hands with you, but I'm dying for a cigarette."

"I'll have one with you."

Samuel put two cigarettes in her mouth, lit both, and passed Frances one.

Samuel took a long draw on her cigarette, then exhaled. “You’ve probably already figured this out about Boots and me, but we’re not married in the same way you and Henry are married.”

“I had wondered,” Frances admitted. She had been around homosexual men before and generally enjoyed their company. Boots reminded her a little of the director of the community theatre in her hometown where she used to help with sets and costumes.

“Yeah,” Samuel said. “I figure a lot of people wonder, but as long as we’re putting the effort in, they don’t ask any questions. We got married as a way of protecting each other. And we love each other. But it’s like we’re brother and sister, or uncle and niece. We’re not lovers.”

The word *lover* felt so naked that Frances could only nod and mutter, “Right.”

“I don’t ask what he does in private, he doesn’t ask what I do either. But it’s very important that’s how everything’s kept—private.”

Frances nodded again, increasingly aware that she was entering into an agreement that was as real as if she’d signed a contract.

Samuel ground out her cigarette in the ashtray, then stood. She held out her hand.

Frances took it and let herself be pulled up. They were standing close together.

“Is there a room nearby with a door that closes?”

Frances had a hard time finding her voice. "The pantry," she whispered, pointing to its door.

Samuel opened the pantry door and gently pulled Frances inside, closing the door behind them.

The tiny room was black dark. Still, Samuel's lips found Frances's.

Kissing Henry was always a prickly experience. His thin lips were surrounded by his wiry beard and mustache. But Samuel was soft and smooth, and her lips sealed to Frances's so tightly it felt like it would take an outside force to pull them apart.

Samuel's body pressed into Frances's, pushing Frances's back against the pantry door. For a second, Frances was aware of how Samuel's lean body contrasted with her plumper figure and felt embarrassed, but why would Samuel be kissing her like that if she didn't like the way Frances looked, the way she felt? Frances felt Samuel's fingers in her hair, on her cheek, on her neck, felt Samuel's tongue flick her own, slick and liquid.

Henry's kisses always felt like a box to be checked before moving on to the main event, but here, kissing was the thing itself. There was nothing else but this, no one but them in this tight, dark space that felt like nowhere at all.

A high-pitched wail startled Frances.

Samuel drew back from her. "What the—"

It took a second for Frances to orient herself. "The baby," she said. She was home. On a Monday morning. She had a baby and two other children besides.

"Oh," Samuel said. "You need—to go to him?"

Frances nodded even though it was too dark for Samuel to see her. She pushed open the pantry door and squinted at the daylight. Now she could see the stacks of tuna cans and soup cans in the pantry, the pile of dirty breakfast dishes still in the sink where the water had no doubt gone clammy.

Robert's cries were becoming more insistent. She ran to the playpen and picked him up. The odor emitting from his diaper made the reason for his fussing apparent. She glanced over at Samuel, who looked dazed, like someone just woken from a dream.

"Well—" Frances said, jostling Robert in her arms to comfort him.

"Yeah," Samuel said. "I guess I'd better—" She nodded toward the front door.

"Yeah," Frances said.

Samuel shoved her hands in her pants pockets, looking boyish. "See you soon?"

Frances nodded. "Soon."

CHAPTER 11

"It's really good." Samuel set the manuscript down on the kitchen table where Frances sat across from her.

Frances smiled. "You're just saying that because we—" She blushed and looked down into her coffee cup.

"No, that's not why at all," Samuel said. "I'm not nice about people's writing just because I like them. You should ask Boots how hard I was on the other students when I was in his writing classes." She glanced back down at the manuscript. "It's a truly imaginative and disturbing story, not like anything else I've ever read. In a good way. If you let me show it to Boots, he'd say the same thing."

"You really think so?"

"I know so."

Samuel had been nervous about reading Frances's story. What if she found herself in the awkward position of liking Frances very much but hating her story with an equal intensity? Fortunately, this was not the case. "Welcome to the Neighborhood" was eight tight pages of psychological horror about a housewife who moves to a new town. The other housewives, while outwardly friendly in public, resort to more and more disturbing private methods of letting her know how unwelcome she is. The dark heart of the story gave Samuel a glimpse at the fear and anger that Frances left otherwise unspoken.

"Well, thank you," Frances said, sipping her coffee. "You're the only person I've showed it to."

"That needs to change. Submit it to a magazine. Maybe one of the women's magazines that publishes fiction. Scare the hell out of some housewives."

Frances smiled and shook her head. "You really think so?"

Samuel smiled back. "How many times can you ask me if I really think so?"

Frances laughed. "A lot, apparently."

Samuel and Frances had fallen into a rhythm of spending time together.

Every Tuesday and Thursday, Samuel showed up at Frances's house at nine o'clock, after Henry had left for work and Danny had left for school. They lingered over coffee and cigarettes, talking intensely. Eventually Frances would need to get up to start on the breakfast dishes or tend to the baby, and Samuel would try to help by unpacking and shelving one of the seemingly endless boxes of books. But even as they worked, their conversation continued.

At noon, Susan would come inside from playing and theatrically declare herself to be starving. They'd have a simple lunch—Frances made a mean grilled cheese—and Susan would run back outside, fueled for further play. Frances would give Robert a bottle and put him down for his nap.

Then Samuel and Frances would sneak off into the pantry and kiss till their lips were sore, pressing their bodies together like interlocking puzzle pieces.

Samuel knew the situation wasn't perfect, but who got perfect? Homosexuals never did. This was the only real romance she had ever had, and she had never been happier.

As Frances got up to pour their third cup of coffee, Susan burst in saying, "Auntie Em, Eureka hasn't had her breakfast, and she's starving!" She turned her attention to Samuel. "Oh, hi, Princess Ozma."

"Greetings, Princess Dorothy," Samuel said. She was growing fonder and fonder of this strange, imaginative little girl.

"You can get the kitty a saucer of milk," Frances said.

Susan hurried to the refrigerator and took out a milk bottle. "Princess Ozma," she said, getting a saucer from the rack of dishes drying on the counter, "Auntie Em says that if nobody claims Eureka in three days, then she can be our cat."

"That's great news," Samuel said. "I'll keep my fingers crossed for you."

After Susan was gone with the saucer of milk, Frances sat back down across from Samuel. "I do hope we get to keep the cat. Susan and I have both gotten attached to it."

"You know, I feel kind of like that cat myself," Samuel said. "Hanging around here hoping for some companionship and affection. Hell, you even feed me. If nobody else claims me, will you keep me, too?"

"Well, we'll have to hang up some signs around town," Frances said. "*Found: female writer, brown hair, blue eyes. Smart, good kisser.*"

Samuel laughed. "Lord, I hope nobody else claims me. I don't want to have to kiss anybody but you!"

After they'd had tuna fish sandwiches and Susan had gone back out to play and Robert had lain down for his nap, Frances smiled at Samuel with her eyes downcast. She looked so pretty, so demure. Samuel was sure she had never done anything in her life that could be described as *demure.*

Samuel took Frances's hand. She took a step toward the pantry, then stopped. "I've been thinking about the pantry," she said. "I know it's private, but it's awful uncomfortable. Is there another room we could use—maybe one that's actually a full-fledged room?"

"I've been thinking about that, too," Frances said. "What if we were in the pantry and Susan were to come in needing something? It would look weird if we came out of there together, wouldn't it?"

"Definitely. We'd have to make up some story about inspecting the tuna cans or something."

Frances knitted her brow. The problem is, I don't know where else to go. "We can't use the bedroom because that's where Henry and I—"

"Right," Samuel said quickly. She didn't want to think about Frances in bed with Henry. She knew it happened—those three children had come from somewhere—but she didn't want to picture it.

"The house is so small, and there's no place in it that's just mine."

"There's always the guest house at McAdoo Manor," Samuel said. "Boots certainly makes good use of it."

"But I have to stay here to look after the children."

"Of course." Samuel immediately felt stupid. It was a good thing she wasn't a mother. She would forget about her children and wander off and leave them all the time.

"There is a sofa in the study," Frances said. "But the study door doesn't lock."

"That I can fix. Do you have a table knife?"

"Sure." Frances looked puzzled but went to the silverware drawer to fetch one.

Once they were in the study, Samuel closed the door securely, then shoved the knife blade into the door frame so that the handle made a small bar against the door. "You'd think this wouldn't work, but try to open it now."

Frances turned the knob and pulled on the door. It didn't budge. "Impressive! How'd you learn this trick?"

For a moment Samuel hesitated, trying to decide if she should tell Frances the truth or not. But then, she thought so much of her life was a deception, there should be one person she always told the truth. "Me and my mama used to do this when Daddy got mean drunk. He'd bang on the door and try to kick it open, but he never could."

Frances squeezed Samuel's hand. "I'm sorry you had to go through that."

Samuel shrugged. "Well, it's in the past now. I got the hell out of there. I wish Mama would, too, but she says it's a sin to break up a marriage." She had tried to get her mama to move to Collinsville. Boots had even offered to pay rent on an apartment for her until she found work, but she always refused. "But enough about that. Why don't you show me this couch you've been telling me so much about? Or, as you Northerners call it, a *sofa*."

"It's right here," Frances said. "As you can see, it's old and bumpy and ugly pea green. We bought it used when Henry and I were first married."

Samuel sat down and patted the spot beside her. "Ugly and lumpy or not, it's much more comfortable than standing in a pantry."

Maybe it was because it was more comfortable or because they could see each other when they chose to open their eyes, but their kisses grew deeper and harder, and soon Samuel was lying on top of Frances. Samuel had never felt her own body stretched out over someone else's, had never felt a woman beneath her, wanting her. She kissed Frances's ear, then down her neck. "Can I undo one button of your blouse?" she whispered.

"Yes." The words came out as a breath.

Samuel undid the button and spread the blouse open enough to reveal the deep cleavage of her full breasts over the top of her white lacy bra.

Frances was the opposite of Samuel in every way but her sex. She was soft and rounded where Samuel was lean and angular. Samuel kissed her way down to Frances's collarbone, to the tops of her breasts. Frances gasped and clung to her.

Samuel wanted to undo more buttons, to undo all of Frances's clothes and leave them in a puddle on the floor. But she was afraid, afraid that she'd do something that Frances wasn't ready for, that she'd hear *no* come from Frances's lips and be completely devastated. After that point, there would be no going back. Some things couldn't be undone.

Samuel propped up on an elbow and looked into Frances's eyes. They were wild like a cat's. "We should probably slow down."

"Why?" Frances asked. She was short of breath.

Samuel stroked her hair. "Well, I don't want to pressure you into doing something you're not ready to do. I don't want to do something wrong." Samuel lay down next to Frances and rested her head on Frances's shoulder. It was a tight fit on the couch, but they managed.

"You could never do anything that felt wrong," Frances said.

"Oh, I don't know about that," Samuel said. She figured she might as well be honest. "I've never been with a woman before. Not really."

"And you think I have?" Frances said, laughing. "Honestly, you could do the most ridiculous things imaginable and if you told me that's what women did together, I'd believe you."

"Oh, do you mean the thing with the peanut butter?" Samuel asked.

"What thing with peanut butter?"

"Hell if I know," Samuel said, grinning. "I just made it up."

Samuel walked home feeling like she was walking on a cloud. There was something about being with Frances that softened the world for her, blunted its sharp edges.

When she got home, she found Priscilla in the kitchen rinsing a mess of collard greens.

"Good afternoon, Miz Samuel. There's a piece of mail for you on the table."

"Thanks, Priscilla." She went to the kitchen table expecting junk mail, but when she looked at the envelope she saw the return address was *Fiction Quarterly*, a magazine she'd submitted a story to a couple of months earlier. Her heart hammered as she tore open the envelope and pulled out the folded sheet of paper:

> *Dear Mrs. McAdoo,*
> *We are pleased to inform you that your story "Jump Rope Rhymes" has been accepted for publication in* Fiction Quarterly. *We feel it is exactly the kind of high-quality fiction our readers enjoy. A contract is enclosed stating that you will be compensated with $25 and two complimentary copies of the magazine. Please sign and return if these terms are agreeable, and we will be in touch with further information.*
>
> *Cordially,*
> *Stewart Madison, Editor*

Samuel let out a whoop, which made Priscilla drop the collards.

"Sorry," Samuel said. "I just got a story accepted by a magazine. A national one that pays real money."

"Well, isn't that something?" Priscilla said. "Congratulations." She picked up the dropped bundle of greens. "By the way, I think Gail's gonna stop by after school to bring your books back and pick out some new ones."

"Great," Samuel said. "I'd love to see Gail."

Samuel felt like her heart was full to bursting. She was turning into a real writer, not just a writer because she thought she was one, but a writer because other people—people whose opinions mattered—thought so, too.

And then there was Frances—Frances with whom she could talk for hours and stay utterly fascinated, Frances whom she could kiss for hours and who returned her kisses with equal passion. For the first time ever, Samuel felt like she was finding her way.

There was a light knock on the kitchen door. "I bet that's my baby girl right now," Priscilla said.

Gail's hair was in neat pigtails, and she wore the same kind of plaid dress Samuel's mother had always made her wear to school. What was it about school and plaid? "Hi, Mama. Hi, Mrs. McAdoo. I brought these back." She held out the copies of *Jane Eyre* and *Wuthering Heights* she'd borrowed.

"And what did you think of the Brontës?" Samuel asked, accepting the books.

"I loved them both!" Gail's eyes shone with excitement. "I think I loved *Jane Eyre* a little more, though. I loved *Wuthering Heights,* but I didn't like Cathy very much. Is that okay, to love a book but hate one of the main characters?"

Samuel laughed. "It's perfectly okay. I feel the same way about Cathy. In fact, I'd describe her with a word I'm sure your mama would rather I didn't say to you."

Gail giggled. "Mama read it, too. She said Cathy was a spoiled heifer."

Samuel nodded. "That description works, too. Would you like to go pick out some more books?"

"Yes, ma'am."

Samuel walked with Gail to the library and watched her look around, occasionally stroking the spines of the more handsome volumes.

"It's so hard to choose," Gail said. "What do you think I'd like?"

Samuel scanned the titles. It was hard to choose for someone else, especially a child. And somehow her being a child of another race made it even harder. So many otherwise great books featured crude caricatures and stereotypes of Black characters, and it hurt her to think of Gail reading them, "Well, if you liked those two gothic novels, you'll probably like this one, too." She pulled down *Rebecca,* which Boots called a pot-boiler but admitted that it was a pot-boiler he enjoyed. "It's a lot more recent than *Jane Eyre* and *Wuthering Heights,* but it owes a lot to the Brontës."

Gail studied the cover. "Daphne du Maurier. It's a beautiful name, isn't it?"

"It is," Samuel said. "So feminine and flowery. Hm. Since we've got you on a gothic kick, have you ever read *Frankenstein*?"

Gail shook her head. "No, I've just seen him in some movies. Like *Abbott and Costello Meet Frankenstein.*"

Samuel smiled. "Yeah, that's a far cry from the original novel. Still pretty funny though." She pulled the volume from the shelf. "Why don't you give it a try?"

"Oh, I didn't know a lady wrote it," Gail said. "All the books you've loaned me so far are by ladies."

"That's because ladies are some of the best writers," Samuel said.

Gail smiled. "Well, thank you so much, Mrs. McAdoo. I'll bring these back to you next week."

"Keep them longer if you need to. There's no rush."

"Oh, I'll be done with them by then. Once I start reading, I can't stop."

Boots came home just in time for cocktail hour. He was carrying his seersucker jacket draped over his arm, and had undone his bow tie and unbuttoned his top button. It was a genteel version of disheveled, but by Boots's standards, he looked positively slovenly.

"Somebody better put a glass of gin into my poor, trembling hand!" he said, collapsing onto the couch.

"Of course," Samuel said, dropping ice cubes in a tumbler. "I consider it my wifely duty."

Miz Elizabeth was sitting in her designated chair, also waiting for her cocktail. "What have they done to my Dumpling Boy today?" she asked, her brow knit with concern.

Samuel knew from Boots that this was the same question Miz Elizabeth used to ask when Boots had come home after a hard day at grammar school. But now Dumpling Boy got a gin and tonic to take the edge off instead of milk and cookies.

"Your Dumpling Boy has been rolled flat and cut into collops," Boots said, accepting the drink Samuel held out to him. "And now he's looking forward to being stewed." He looked Samuel over. "But you, my precious wife—you're absolutely radiant! Did you start drinking ahead of me, or did you just have a better day than I did?"

Samuel hadn't known that her happiness was so visible. "I did have a good day. I went over and had lunch with Frances." This wasn't a lie. They did have lunch before they retired to the couch and did things the memory of which made Samuel feel loose-limbed and tingly.

"That's nice." Boots took a long swig of his cocktail. "I was chatting with Henry before the meeting, and he was saying how glad he was you and Frances hit it off. He had been worried about her being too lonesome here."

Samuel felt a rush of emotions she couldn't quite identify. Embarrassment? Guilt? Grateful for the opportunity to change the subject, she reached into the pocket of her dungarees for the letter she had been carrying on her person since she received it. "I also had a good day because I got this." She passed him the letter.

Boots inspected the envelope. "*Fiction Quarterly*, eh? That's some tall cotton." He pulled out the letter and read. "They're taking your story? I thought it might be one of those encouraging rejections—you, know, 'We can't use this one but please send us more.' But they're taking it."

Samuel couldn't figure out his tone, and his facial expression was both unsmiling and unreadable. "You sound kind of shocked."

Boots smiled, but it was small and seemed forced. "Of course I'm not shocked. I've always known how talented you are. It's just . . . this is a big jump in your career. You're on your way, baby. You're really on your way." He gulped down half of his drink. "You know, ladies, I have an absolute splitter of a headache. If you can refresh my cocktail, Samuel,

I think I'll take it to my room and lie down with a cold cloth on my head until suppertime."

"You need me to get you a Percodan?" Miz Elizabeth asked, reaching for her purse.

"That would be lovely, Mama, thank you," Boots said. He sounded tired.

After Boots washed down his pill with gin and disappeared upstairs, Miz Elizabeth lit a cigarette. "You just couldn't resist bragging on yourself, could you?" she said, exhaling a sizable cloud of smoke.

Samuel looked up from lighting her own cigarette. "What?"

"You saw he was feeling down, and you just had to knock him down a couple more pegs." She jabbed the air with her cigarette for emphasis.

Samuel felt as if Mama Liz had slapped her. "It wasn't like that. Boots is my writing mentor. I always show him my work and tell him when I get something accepted for publication. I tell him when my stuff gets rejected, too."

Miz Elizabeth rolled her eyes. "Writing mentor, hell. Boots is your *husband*."

"I never said he wasn't."

"Well, when your husband is feeling down, you build him up. You don't make yourself bigger so he feels smaller."

"That wasn't my intention, Mama Liz. Why would me showing him that letter make him feel small?"

Miz Elizabeth let out an exasperated sigh and looked at Samuel as though she was the stupidest person she had ever encountered. "Honey, do you know how long it's been since Boots has gotten a letter like that?"

CHAPTER 12

FRANCES ALWAYS FELT A LITTLE THRILL when the school bus drove away. There was another when Henry's car pulled out of the driveway. With the boys gone, she knew she had thirty minutes to get Robert settled and to hurry through washing the breakfast dishes, and then Samuel would be there. Samuel with her wry smile, wearing a man's button-down shirt and chinos or a boyish t-shirt and dungarees. Samuel with her Kentucky twang and the wit sharper than the pocketknife she always carried.

As she scrubbed yellow residue from the scrambled egg pan, she tried to remember how she'd felt when she and Henry had first started dating. She had been excited in a girlish, breathless way, happy she had joined the legion of college girls with steady dates with fiancé potential. She had been fascinated by Henry's brilliance, by his encyclopedic knowledge and bon mots.

She was fascinated by Samuel's brilliance too—a brilliance of a kind she had never seen in another woman. But there was something else. Something she couldn't remember having felt so intensely with Henry. That something else was occurring in a place much lower than her brain, in the region Frances's mother had always referred to as "down there." She had felt stirrings with Henry but nothing like this, a pulsing need which broke her concentration and made her mind wander away from household tasks and back to the lumpy green couch where she and Samuel stole an hour or two of bliss, depending on the length of Robert's nap.

Frances remembered that back in college there had been two girls on her hall who were roommates. They were never separate from each other and never went out on dates with boys. All the other girls on the hall whispered that they were lesbians.

Before Samuel, Frances had never felt drawn to another woman in that way. So, was she a lesbian, or did she just like Samuel? Frances fetched a warmed bottle of formula and sat down in the rocking chair with Robert. She laughed at herself. She looked more like Old Mother Hubbard than like anybody's idea of a lesbian.

And yet when Samuel knocked on the door, Frances's heart pounded, and something "down there" fluttered like the wings of a butterfly.

"Hey, I've got an idea," Samuel said as they drank their coffee. It was a white button-down shirt day. She looked handsome.

"It seems you've got a lot of ideas," Frances said, nudging Samuel's foot with hers under the dining room table.

"I do," Samuel said, "particularly where you're concerned. And here's one of 'em." She set down her coffee cup and looked intently at Frances. "On Thursday, Mama Liz has a hair appointment and Garden Club after, so she'll be gone the whole afternoon. We could go to the guesthouse. There's a double bed there, which beats the hell out of that old green couch. Do you think you could get a babysitter?"

Frances felt like she needed to hold onto the table to steady herself. The thought of her and Samuel alone in a bed was almost more than she could imagine. But there was also the guilt of leaving her children under false pretenses. "It's kind of short notice, but I'll try. I . . . I guess I'll have to think up some kind of explanation for why I'll be away."

Samuel leaned across the table and whispered, "You can say you're going to spend the afternoon in bed with your lover."

Frances's face heated up all the way to her scalp.

Samuel smiled. "Or you could say you have a follow-up dentist appointment."

"Yeah," Frances said. "I think I'll go with that one."

* * *

As IT TURNED OUT, KATIE, A college girl who had babysat for them before, was available on Thursday afternoon despite the short notice.

Frances couldn't meet Katie's eyes when she told her, "I should be home no later than four-thirty. I'm not sure how long the . . . uh, procedure will last."

"I feel for you," Katie said. "I hate going to the dentist."

"Thank you," Frances said stupidly. She needed to clear out before she was unable to keep up the charade any longer. She didn't have much practice at lying and was terrible at it. Funny, since she was good at making up stories on paper. The children would be fine for a couple of hours. Katie was already bouncing Robert in her arms and making him giggle while she let Susan brush her long chestnut hair. They were clearly enjoying the novelty of a babysitter.

As soon as Frances walked far enough away that her house was no longer visible, she felt free. It was a lovely day, blue sky with fluffy clouds like marshmallows, the sun warming her face. There was no stroller to push, no little hands to hold. The only person she was taking care of was herself.

She felt a stab of guilt at her elation, but reminded herself it didn't mean she loved her children less if she gave herself a tiny break from them. But she knew this wasn't a little break, like a trip to the beauty shop or bridge with other housewives. She wasn't wholly clear on what she and Samuel would be doing once she arrived at the guesthouse, but she knew they wouldn't be playing bridge.

She walked around the back of McAdoo Manor and across the backyard to the guest house. She knocked so lightly she wondered if it was audible, but Samuel swung the door open immediately.

"Get in here," she said, playfully tugging Frances by the arm, then closing and locking the door behind them.

Frances glanced around the room. The bedspread and curtains were printed with pink roses. "This looks more like an old lady's bedroom than a place for an illicit assignation."

"Oh, is that what we're having? That sounds fun," Samuel said, putting her arms around Frances's waist. "Old ladyish or not, these walls have seen plenty of illicit assignations. Some pretty wild parties, too."

Frances nodded, unable to find her words. She wanted whatever was about to happen to happen, but she was afraid. Afraid she would do something wrong. Afraid Samuel would decide she didn't like Frances that much after all.

Samuel rested her head against Frances's cheek. "Nervous?"

Frances nodded. "A little."

Samuel smiled at her. "There's no need to be nervous. It's just me. It's no different than us on the green couch except it's more comfortable and private. I promise we won't do anything you don't want to do, okay? If you don't like something, just tell me to stop."

"Okay," Frances said. But the truth was, she wanted to do everything even though she didn't know what *everything* entailed. She knew that whatever Samuel did, she wouldn't tell her to stop.

When Frances and Henry made love, she could always map it out in her head as a step-by-step process: "Now, we're at the part where he . . . " But this . . . this was unpredictable, the best kind of chaos. They kissed standing up until they fell onto the bed, and then Samuel's hands and mouth seemed to be everywhere all at once. How many pairs of hands did Samuel have, and where had she been hiding them? And then Frances was naked, though she wasn't sure if it was Samuel who got her that way or if she'd done it herself, and Samuel was wearing just a men's undershirt and boxers, and

Frances wanted to tell her how strangely attractive that was, but she couldn't because Samuel's mouth had found a spot which Henry had ignored during all their years of marriage and suddenly she couldn't speak or think, only feel.

When Samuel lay down on the pillow beside her, Frances gasped, "That was . . . that was . . . I don't have words for what that was."

Samuel laughed. "I'll choose to take that as a compliment."

And then they were kissing again.

* * *

As a little girl, Frances had spent her summer days at the community pool. Most of the other kids there spent as much time out of the water as in it, blatantly disregarding the signs that prohibited running, and whatever "horseplay" was. Frances, though, would stay in the water all day, swimming and floating on her back. In her mind, she was a mermaid. And when the pool closed and she'd walk home. She always felt sun drunk and weak limbed, like her legs were really made for treading water and not for stepping on solid ground.

She felt the same way walking home from Samuel's, like she had been in a freer, floatier place which made the previously familiar one feel alien.

When Frances hit the door, the children descended on her.

"Did it hurt? Were you scared?" Susan asked.

"Was there a lot of blood?" Danny, who was always happy to make things more gruesome, added.

For a couple of seconds, Frances was utterly baffled, then she reminded herself, *The dentist. You told them you were going to the dentist.* "No, of course not," she said.

Katie the babysitter came out of the kitchen carrying a wet-eyed Robert, his lower lip in full pout position. "There's who you've been crying for," Katie said.

A pang of guilt stung Frances as she held out her arms to take the baby. "Did he cry the whole time I was gone?"

"It's fine," Katie said which Frances knew meant yes. She slipped Katie an extra five dollars and sent her away with profound thanks.

Still carrying Robert, who was clinging to her like a baby monkey, she went into the kitchen and opened the refrigerator door in hopes that an idea for dinner would present itself.

"Mom," Danny said, tugging on the hem of her blouse. "Remember I've got to have a clean white shirt for tonight."

"There's one hanging in your closet," Frances said. A sudden wave of apprehension overcame her. "Wait, what's tonight?"

"The fall open house," Danny said, sounding exasperated. "I told you about it last week. You wrote it on the calendar!"

Frances looked at the calendar on the wall near the telephone. SCHOOL OPEN HOUSE, 7:00 P.M. Damned if she hadn't written it down. "Of course. How silly of me."

"You're a very silly mommy sometimes, Auntie Em," Susan said.

"She can't be your mommy and your Auntie Em at the same time," Danny said.

"I know that," Susan said. "She's your mommy and *my* Auntie Em!"

Frances needed to focus. She didn't need to be thinking about how Samuel's hands and mouth had felt on her body. She needed to be thinking about how she could transform some of the contents of the refrigerator into a quick enough dinner that they could make it to the school by seven.

She wanted to think about Samuel's hands and mouth.

Not now. Focus. Hamburger steaks and home fries. While the meat and potatoes cooked, she could throw together a green salad. She plopped Robert into his playpen with a pacifier and started pulling things out of the fridge.

She was cutting up the potatoes when Henry got home. "Hi, dear," she said, without looking up from the cutting board. She felt like if she met his eyes, he'd know what she'd been doing all afternoon, that it wasn't dentistry but adultery. Adultery—where in the back of her brain had that Judeo-Christian word come from? And for a woman, was going to bed with another woman even in the same category as going to bed with another man?

"Uncle Henry!"

"Dad!"

The kids were all over Henry, chattering simultaneously about their days. Danny was fuming over some injustice during a ball game in P.E. class while Susan was rhapsodizing about getting to braid the babysitter's beautiful hair. Henry listened for a minute, patted both children on the head, then asked Frances, "Any chance I could get a Scotch?"

"I'd say a fair to middling one," Frances said, pausing on the potatoes and opening the liquor cabinet.

"God, today was exhausting," Henry said, slumping into a chair at the kitchen table and lighting a cigarette.

Frances poured the Scotch, and Henry poured out the details of his workday: the two classes he had taught, filled with stupid and provincial students, the interminable grading of papers, the insufferable colleagues. Compared to her days of childcare, cooking, dishwashing, and laundry, Henry's days never sounded that difficult to Frances, yet he always described each workday as a litany of horrors, as if he was hard at labor in a poorly regulated coal mine. Part of it, she knew, was just his naturally dramatic personality. As Henry's mother had warned her before they married: *Henry likes to kvetch.*

"Have a drink, but don't get sloshed," Frances said. "We've got that thing at seven."

"What thing is that?" Henry sounded apprehensive.

She wasn't surprised he'd forgotten it, but she was still surprised that she had. "The open house at school."

"At Millwood? No one ever told me about such a function. I can hardly be held responsible if nobody—"

"No, at Danny's school."

Henry heaved a tremendous sigh, then took a big swig of Scotch. "Could you just go? I'm beat."

"Well, Danny is singing a song with his class, and I'm sure he'd like you—"

"But singing isn't really Danny's thing, is it? It would probably mean more if I went to watch him play baseball."

Henry didn't really go to Danny's ball games either, but Frances didn't feel like she could argue with him. Given the way she had spent the afternoon, she was in no position to take the moral high ground. "Okay. I'll just go. We can have some mother and son time."

In a way she was relieved. Her thoughts kept going back to Samuel and though rationally she knew otherwise, she felt like these thoughts were written all over her face and clearly visible to Henry. Also, some one-on-one time with Danny would be nice. He was always running off somewhere these days, and she missed the little boy who used to cling to her skirt.

"You'll take the other kids with you, right?" Henry said.

Frances dumped the cubed potatoes into a pan of sizzling oil. "Well, I was thinking they could—"

"I mean, they'll be going to that school themselves soon enough, right?" Henry said, then took a big swig of Scotch. "Going to an open house there will be fun for them."

Frances knew it might be fun for Susan, depending on her mood, but it wouldn't be fun for Robert, who tended to get overwhelmed and fussy in crowded, unfamiliar settings. But she said sure because what choice was there but to give Henry a relaxing evening with his Scotch and records?

* * *

"And that's the cafeteria where we eat lunch," Danny said as they walked down the hallway of Collinsville Elementary School ("Home of the Badgers," apparently). "But the gym's where we're supposed to be, and it's this way." Danny was clearly enjoying his role as tour guide.

Frances was pushing Robert in his stroller with her right hand and holding Susan's hand with her left. Susan seemed to be held rapt by Danny's lecturing, and Robert, his brow knitted, sucked peevishly on his pacifier, a volcano threatening to erupt any minute.

From the looks of things, Henry wasn't the only dad who'd opted out of this shindig. The place was packed with mothers, elementary school students, and their younger and older siblings. No dads in sight.

The mothers seemed to fall into two categories, the Town Moms and the Country Moms. The Town Moms were wives of professors or local doctors, dentists, druggists, or store owners. They had beauty shop hairdos and wore dresses that had been purchased at the one local "dress shop" or, for the more prosperous ladies, on an out-of-town shopping trip to Lexington or Louisville. They wore lipstick and heels, and many of them sported funny little hats and prim white gloves. The Country Moms wore dresses they had sewn themselves or perhaps ordered from the Sears-Roebuck catalog. They wore sensible flat shoes and had arranged their hair themselves by pinning it up or pulling it back. There was more size variation among the Country Moms than the Town Moms. Some of them were heavy, others were disturbingly gaunt, and still others looked strong enough to perform all manners of hard physical labor. Most of them wore no makeup, but a few wore what the Town Moms, with their lightly powdered noses and soft pink lipstick, would consider too much.

Frances's simply yanked-back hair and flat shoes made her resemble a Country Mom, but her husband's profession put her solidly in the Town Mom category. In reality, though, she was neither. She was Something Else, a combination of characteristics even she couldn't pigeonhole.

She sat in an uncomfortable folding chair in the school gymnasium with Robert on her lap and Susan beside her, and listened to the first graders lisp out a medley of nursery rhymes. She couldn't help but smile at their earnest little faces. Children singing together, even if some of them were out of tune, always sounded sweet. After a round of applause, the first graders shambled off and were replaced by Danny's second grade class. She watched Danny scanning the crowd for her. When he spotted her, he smiled just a little.

"Toto!" Susan whisper-shouted, and Frances shushed her.

The second graders sang a little ditty about the different states, which ended with the unsubstantiated claim that of all the states, Kentucky was the best. Frances figured this song was taught in schools all over the country and that the last line instructed teachers: INSERT THE NAME OF YOUR STATE HERE.

She let her mind wander a bit while the third, fourth, and fifth graders were put through their musical paces. Robert was squirming and whimpering, and she tried to jolly him along by jostling him on her lap. She knew he was getting tired and wanted a bottle and bed just as badly as she wanted a cigarette and a Scotch and soda.

Frances glanced around at the other women sitting nearby, all of them Town Moms. There was a primness to these women that Frances lacked. Their purses matched their shoes. She was sure that their houses were neat and orderly, and that they went to church on Sundays. All of these women had children or they wouldn't be there (surely no childless adult would come to one of these things just because they heard Collinsville Elementary put on a good show), so presumably none of them were virgins.

But had any of these women ever known the kind of ecstasy she'd felt earlier today, lying spread out like a mermaid beneath a lover who seemed to receive pleasure only from the act of giving it? Or had their only sexual experiences been lying dutifully in the marriage bed, planning out grocery lists and dinner menus through all the husbandly huffing and puffing? With a little shiver, Frances remembered the moment when Samuel, still working miracles with her mouth, had reached up to lightly brush her fingertips over Frances's nipples. Surely none of these tight-lipped, tight-thighed church-going ladies had ever lost themselves in pure physical sensation like Frances had today. If they had, they'd be different. Looser, freer. Feeling like that—hell, even knowing it was *possible* to feel like that—changed you.

CHAPTER 13

Samuel hummed to herself as she arranged the ice bucket and glasses on the table. It was, as Boots put it, "that time of the month." In this case, time for a party in the guesthouse where they and their other homo friends could let down their hair. Samuel wished she could've invited Frances but knew there were many reasons why she couldn't.

Boots was arranging chairs but was uncharacteristically silent.

"You're awful quiet tonight," Samuel said. "Usually the idea of a party puts you in a good mood."

Boots sat on the edge of the bed and took out a cigarette without offering one to Samuel. "Well, if you must know, A.J. and I had a little spat earlier. He says he won't be attending tonight."

"What was the spat about?"

Boots rolled his eyes. "It's not important. He'll get over it. He knows what side his bread is buttered on."

Samuel sat down beside him on the bed. "And what side *is* it buttered on? The bottom or the top?"

Boots lip twitched, then he smiled a little. "Dirty girl. Don't ask questions you already know the answers to."

For as long as Samuel had known Boots, his only relationships had been with handsome, masculine, younger working-class men with whom he didn't have a thing in common except, presumably, sex. It was so different from what she had with Frances, where their physical relationship was a complement to their deep friendship.

"Boots, have you ever thought about really dating somebody, like somebody who can talk to you about books or opera?"

"Honey, I don't want them to *talk*. And speaking of talking, what is it with all these questions? I feel like I'm married to Nancy Drew."

"Sorry." She got up off the bed.

Samuel had been saying *sorry* to Boots a lot lately. It seemed like the slightest thing she said or did would send him into a fit of pique. She always apologized even though it seemed like Boots should be the one apologizing for flying off the handle.

She knew the reasons for Boots's moodiness went deeper than just the anger he was capable of feeling at one of his male playthings. Sure, Boots might've been a little jealous of whatever A.J. did when he was not with him, but the real jealousy he was feeling was directed at Samuel. Ever since she had gotten that story accepted by *Fiction Quarterly*, it was like he found her mere presence irritating.

Samuel knew it wasn't just the publication itself. It was something deeper than professional jealousy. Samuel was writing pages and pages every day and Boots wasn't. Or maybe couldn't. She didn't know if he tried to write and was unhappy with it, or if he didn't even try anymore. It was the one thing he wouldn't talk to her about.

There was a gentle knock on the guesthouse door. Carlisle's. Samuel would recognize his knock anywhere. Boots put on his social face and swooped over to open the door.

Carlisle stood in the doorway holding a pretty tin box.

"Carlisle, my heart!" Boots said, all smiles again.

"I made some cheese straws this morning," Carlisle said. "They are not, however, all for you. At the very least share them with your lovely bride. She's getting too skinny. You're clearly not feeding her enough."

Carlisle's cheese straws were legendary. "You've made me a happy woman," Samuel said. "Keep those cheese straws coming, and I won't stay skinny for long. Can I fix you up with a drink?"

"I believe that might be the only thing that could fix me," Carlisle said, sitting down in the chair Boots pulled out for him.

"I'm afraid my play-pretty won't be here tonight," Boots told Carlisle. "We had a little tiff."

"The young ones are temperamental, aren't they?" Carlisle said, letting Boots light his cigarette. "Well, I'll miss the view, but I don't think the conversation will be any poorer for his absence."

Trish and Marj arrived with Marj carrying a plate covered in wax paper. She was wearing a red and white gingham sundress which somehow complemented Trish's jeans and work shirt, making them look like an attractive farmer couple. "Snickerdoodles," Marj said, passing Samuel the plate of cookies.

"*Snickerdoodles* right back atcha," Samuel said, and Marj laughed. "Thank you. I love the cookies and the name."

Trish put her arm around Marj. "I've been calling her my little snickerdoodle all day."

"Yeah," Marj said. "And I hate it." But she was smiling.

They settled in with their drinks and snacks, Boots and Carlisle talking together and Samuel sitting with Trish and Marj.

"You know, you're looking particularly well, Samuel," Marj said. "You look happy. Doesn't she look happy, Trish?"

"She does," Trish said. "But she might not if we keep talking about her like she's not in the room."

"As long as you say good things about me," Samuel said. She was surprised to know her happiness was so visible. "Things have been going well lately."

"Interesting. Any salacious gossip we should know about?" Trish wiggled her eyebrows.

Samuel longed to tell them about Frances, both to share her joy and to gain the insight of lesbians who were older and wiser than she was. But she couldn't. Frances—or at least what she had with Frances—had to stay a secret. "No, nothing like that. I do have a new friend, though. She writes, too."

"A friend or a *friend*?" Marj asked.

Now she had to lie. She shouldn't have said anything about Frances in the first place. "Oh, a friend-friend, not a euphemism friend. She's straight. Married."

Trish drained the last of her gin and tonic. "Well, just make sure you stay nothing but friends. Straight girls will break your heart every time."

"And she ought to know," Marj said, playfully elbowing Trish. "There was a long string of them before I came along."

Marj—probably wisely, Samuel thought—shifted the topic to writing. Marj wrote poems which Samuel suspected were good, but she never showed them to anybody. "It's hard to find enough time to write because I've always got a pile of papers to grade," Marj said. "You're lucky."

"I know it," Samuel said. "It's one of the perks of Boots's and my arrangement. I get almost unlimited writing time, plus an in-house critic."

"And by 'in-house critic' you mean Miz Elizabeth?" Trish said, grinning.

Samuel laughed. "Well, Boots is the in-house critic of my writing, and Mama Liz criticizes everything else about me."

"*Two* in-house critics, then," Marj said.

Samuel busied herself refreshing their drinks. When she sat down, she said, "Did I tell y'all that I got a story accepted by *Fiction Quarterly*?"

"Congratulations! That's the big time!" Marj said, patting Samuel's knee.

"Well, it's not the big time, but it is a big step up for me," Samuel said. She felt a hand on her shoulder and looked up to see Boots, who was holding a drink in his other hand.

"Oh, is she regaling you with tales of her literary triumphs?" Boots said. His speech was a little mushy around the edges. He must have been knocking back the gin and tonics. "Remember it's unbecoming for a lady to brag."

Carlisle appeared beside Boots and put his arm around Boots's shoulders. "Well, it's no crime for a lady to brag if she's got something to brag about. Which Samuel certainly does."

"Seems to me your in-house critic is being a little harsh tonight," Marj said.

Boots took a long draw on his cocktail. "I'm not criticizing her; I'm warning her. Because I know what it's like. I know what it's like to be young and fresh and bright with everyone wanting your words and wanting your body, but then time passes and it all . . . just dries up."

"But Boots," Samuel said, trying to head off his descent into self-pity, "you're still brilliant, and you're still—"

"What?" Boots laughed humorlessly. "Young? Fresh? Baby, I'm as stale as last week's cornbread."

"What you are," Carlisle said, "is drunk and maudlin. Now come over to the bed and smoke a cigarette with me, and we'll gossip."

"You—" Boots poked Carlisle in the chest with his index finger "—are trying to pacify me."

"That's right," Carlisle said. "Because a cigarette is an adult pacifier." He flashed a wicked smile. "You know what else is an adult pacifier?" He leaned over and whispered in Boots's ear.

Boots shrieked and play-slapped Carlisle's arm. "You filthy queen!"

There was another round of cocktails and conversation, but the evening never returned to its easy air of conviviality, and Samuel wasn't surprised when the guests started pleading exhaustion. Everybody cleared out by eleven. They usually carried on till at least midnight.

Boots was lying on the bed propped up on pillows. He looked like if the pillows weren't there, his head would loll like a rag doll's. He fumbled with his cigarette and lighter.

Samuel gathered glasses and set them on a tray to take back to the house. She knew Boots had had a bad day and she knew he was drunk, but she was still mad at him. "You know," she said, "I didn't appreciate the way you talked about me in front of our friends."

Boots looked at her with his eyes narrowed. He exhaled a cloud of smoke. "Well, darlin', there's a lot you don't appreciate." His tone was icy enough to chill gin.

Samuel stopped tidying. "What's that supposed to mean?"

Boots sat up unsteadily. "Well, do you appreciate the fact that I saved you from getting kicked out of school? Do you appreciate that I brought you here to live in comfort and do nothing but write? Most college girls who get married find themselves instantly transformed into housekeepers and brood mares. But you're free of all that."

Samuel thought of all the physical work Frances had to do every day taking care of the children, preparing meals, the endless Sisyphean dishwashing and laundry. "Yes, I am free of all that, and I appreciate it. I appreciate *you*, Boots. You're the least demanding husband on earth."

"I am," Boots said. "But I need to ask you a question, and I'm going to demand an answer."

The effects of the three gin and tonics Samuel had consumed disappeared. She was stone cold sober. She swallowed hard. "All right."

"On Wednesday, when A.J. and I came in here for our usual date, the bed was unmade. It was a rumpled mess, and it didn't look like somebody had been *sleeping* in it, if you know what I mean. There are three people who have a key to the guesthouse—you, me, and Mama. And somehow, I don't think Mama has taken a secret lover." His stare was intense. He looked like a bird of prey in a bow tie. "So . . . have you?"

Samuel knew by the way her face was heating up that Boots could already see the truth. "Yes," she said in a near whisper.

"I knew it!" Boots said. "Of course, I didn't exactly have to be Sam Spade to figure that one out." He looked her up and down. "You little minx! Is it anybody I know?"

"No," she said, too quickly. The lie felt sour on her tongue.

"Oh, so *now* you're choosing to be discreet," Boots said. "Well, at least answer me this. When you and What's Her Name were disporting yourselves in the guesthouse, was Mama home?"

"Lord, no. She was at the beauty shop then Garden Club. And before you ask, Priscilla was out doing the shopping."

"Well, at least you weren't completely stupid about it. But I still must remind you . . . discretion is of the utmost importance. If either one of us gets caught in one of our little peccadilloes, then this whole story we've written ourselves—this collaborative work of fiction that is our marriage—falls apart. As does my job and our shared social status and all the privileges we both enjoy. Do you understand?"

Samuel nodded. "I do." She couldn't believe she had left the bed a mess, but she had been so happy after her and Frances's lovemaking that she was incapable of returning to earthly matters like changing the sheets and making up the bed.

"And part of discretion is cleaning up after yourself, not leaving the bed with twisted sheets that smell of ladies perfume and ladies . . . parts."

Samuel's face burned. "I'm sorry. It's just that it was the first time I had ever really . . . fully . . . you know . . . "

For the first time all evening, Boots's expression softened. "Was it wonderful?"

"It was. Very wonderful."

"Good. Enjoy yourself. I don't expect you to take a vow of chastity, just a vow of silence." He smiled at her for the first time all evening. "You don't have to keep your legs closed, just your mouth."

CHAPTER 14

"THIS TOAST IS BURNT," DANNY SAID with the air of an offended gourmet.

Frances inspected the toast on her own plate. "Well, it's dark. I don't know if I would call it *burnt.*"

"I'd call it burnt," Susan said.

Danny held up his toast and tapped it with his butter knife. "I dub thee . . . *Burnt.*" He collapsed in laughter.

Henry smiled and shook his head. "Kids, don't give your mother a hard time." He took a forkful of scrambled eggs, then said, "But these eggs are a little overdone. Curdy instead of creamy."

"Burnt," Danny said, still laughing.

"I humbly apologize for the lackluster breakfast," Frances said, though she would still make a case for the toast being dark instead of burnt. "I'm a little distracted this morning."

"What does that mean, *distracted?*" Susan asked.

"Distracted means thinking of other things." Frances sipped her coffee. "Like maybe I might not find making toast that interesting, so my mind wanders off to something more exciting which means I'm not paying attention to the toast, so it gets too dark." She was still not willing to concede to "burnt."

"What exciting thing were you thinking about?" Danny asked.

Frances tried to will herself not to blush because of course she had been thinking of Samuel, of her hands and her mouth and her body. "Well," she said, stalling, "actually, I was thinking about a letter I got in the mail yesterday."

"Was it a love letter?" Susan asked.

"Nobody's gonna send Mommy a love letter. She's married!" Danny said.

"It was not a love letter. It was a letter from a magazine I sent a story to. They asked me to make some changes, then send it back to them. They're not promising anything, but they might want to publish it."

"Honey, that's tremendous news!" Henry said. "Why didn't you tell me sooner?"

"Just busy with other things, I guess," Frances said.

But the truth was she had been enjoying keeping the news to be all hers for just a little while. And she had wanted Samuel to be the first person she told.

* * *

AFTER DANNY WAS OFF TO SCHOOL and Henry was off to work, she sat down and gave Robert the bottle that usually launched him into his morning nap—a nap that she knew from previous experience would disappear along with infancy.

Susan came in dressed in her play clothes and carrying a hairbrush. "Auntie Em, would you put my hair in pigtails before I go to Thelma's house?"

"Of course," Frances said. Part of having Dorothy for a daughter was the daily pigtail ritual. Frances brushed Susan's wavy brown hair into a part, then gathered it into two bunches with elastic bands. "Now remember you're staying at Thelma's till after lunch today, right?"

"Right."

Frances had worked out a corrupt bargain with Thelma's mother that Susan would stay there for a couple of hours today in exchange for Frances watching Thelma one day the following week.

Soon the house was empty of children except for the sleeping Robert. Frances decided to take her coffee on the porch and wait for Samuel. She didn't want to risk Samuel knocking at the door and waking the baby. She sipped her coffee and petted the very pregnant Hecate/Eureka, who rubbed against her ankles and purred.

Frances smiled when she saw Samuel ambling down the sidewalk, her hands in the pockets of her mannish gray trousers. The hands that had touched her in ways that made her feel like she had body parts she'd never even been aware of before.

"Hey," Samuel said when she came close enough to be in earshot.

"Hey yourself," Frances said. "I thought I'd wait out here so we can go in quietly. Robert's asleep."

"Well, you know what they say—let sleeping babies lie. Or is that dogs?"

"I'm pretty sure it's dogs," Frances said. "But it's even better advice with babies."

They tiptoed in the house. Frances whispered, "Nobody else is home."

Samuel smiled. "The plot thickens."

"Kiss me." Frances had allowed herself to be kissed many times, but this was her first time demanding a kiss. Samuel pressed her parted lips to hers, and Frances felt so weak in the knees she had to cling to Samuel for balance. When they broke out of the kiss, they were both short of breath. "Listen, I don't want to seem too forward," Frances said.

"I don't mind," Samuel said quickly.

Frances smiled. "Okay, well, Susan's over at her friend's house until after lunch, and I wondered if—well, see, I bought some new sheets for the bed, and I thought you and I could maybe . . . use them . . . and I'd change them afterward."

"So, you're asking me if I want to use your new sheets?"

"On reflection, I could've worded it more seductively, but yes."

"Are you sure you're okay with it? I mean, the bed is yours and—"

Frances touched Samuel's lips to silence her. "I want to be with you again. Like we were in the guesthouse."

Samuel kissed her again, harder this time, and they only stopped kissing long enough to walk hand in hand to the bedroom, where they fell on the bed in a tangle of arms and legs. At Samuel's hands, Frances's clothing fell away like the unwanted peel of a fruit.

"Yours, too," Frances whispered.

"What?" Samuel said.

"Your clothes—can you take them off?"

Samuel visibly stiffened. "I don't know. I mean, I never have . . . in front of somebody. I'm kind of shy."

"You can't kiss me like that and say you're shy," Frances said. "Please. I want to feel your skin against mine." Frances marveled at her own words. Since when had she become so bold in the bedroom?

"Well, when you put it that way," Samuel said. She stood and briskly unbuttoned her shirt and pants. Underneath them, she was wearing a sleeveless undershirt and boxers, no doubt from the boys department. When she stripped off the last layer, though, her body was a woman's, with slim hips and small, shapely pink-nippled breasts. Samuel joined Frances under the fresh new sheets, and time—usually such a solid, inflexible thing—melted into a warm puddle of pleasure.

"Auntie Em!"

Frances was so immersed in feeling Samuel's bare body pressed against hers that it took her a few seconds to make sense of the voice, to register that it was her own child's.

Frances quickly extricated herself out from under Samuel, pulled the sheet up to her neck, and sat up. "Susan, you were supposed to be at Thelma's until after lunch." It was hard to pull off the stern mother persona in this position, but she figured it was her best bet.

"I did stay for lunch at Thelma's. They eat at eleven thirty instead of twelve thirty," Susan explained. "Auntie Em, why are you and Princess Ozma in bed with no clothes on, and why were you kissing when you're both girls?"

Bad, bad, bad was the refrain playing in Frances's mind. This situation was so bad that she couldn't fully comprehend its badness. She had to figure out what to say to Susan. "I'll tell you what, Dorothy," she said, her voice shaking. "Why don't you go to the kitchen and get yourself a glass of juice? I'll be there in just a minute."

Susan's expression was unreadable. Confusion? Judgment? Disgust? But she left the room and closed the door behind her.

Samuel's expression was instantly readable. It was abject terror.

"I'm sorry," Samuel said, gathering up her clothes. "I've been in trouble for this kind of thing before, and I can handle it. But I never wanted to get you in trouble."

Frances was fighting tears—she needed to look calm when she talked to Susan—but she wasn't doing a very good job of it. "It's not your fault. I was careless, and I didn't bank on the fact that Thelma's family eats lunch an hour before we do. I was the one who dragged you into my bed."

"Well, I didn't exactly object," Samuel said.

Frances's hands shook as she buttoned her blouse. "This was too risky. And I'm not usually a big risk taker. It's just that"—she dropped her voice to a whisper— "I've never had these feelings before. I want you all the time."

Samuel took her hand and squeezed it. "I want you all the time, too." She sighed. "But now I'd better get out of here. Maybe I should climb out the bedroom window, so I don't have to face Susan again."

Frances shook her head. She couldn't have somebody climbing out of her bedroom window in the middle of the day, not with nosy neighbors watching. "I'll distract Susan and you leave through the front door like any other guest."

"Okay."

Frances pulled her hair back in a low ponytail, put on her glasses, and went out to face her daughter.

Susan was sitting at the kitchen table with a glass of juice. She had also helped herself to three oatmeal cookies, which was one more than the allowable number, but Frances was hardly in a position to say anything about it.

"Hi," Frances said stupidly.

"Hi," Susan said. Her eyes were cold little beads.

Frances sat at the table across from her. She wanted a cigarette, but she knew her hands would shake too visibly smoking it. "So, I know what you saw was confusing, but what it was—well, it's something friends do sometimes when they want to be close to each other."

"Thelma and me don't do that," Susan said.

"No," Frances said, appalled. "Of course not! I meant grown-up friends."

"Grown-up friends who are both girls?" Susan asked.

Frances felt the heat rising to her face. "Sometimes, yes." She racked her brain for a way to ensure Susan's silence. "But you have to understand, that kind of thing is very private. Nobody else is supposed to see it."

"Like taking a bath?" Susan said, starting in on cookie number three.

"Yes, like taking a bath." It suddenly occurred to her that she would very much like to take a bath with Samuel. Stop it, she told herself. Focus. "But even more private. So, honey, I need you to promise me that you'll never tell anybody what you saw. And that you especially won't tell Daddy."

"Uncle Henry," Susan corrected her.

"Right."

"If Uncle Henry knew, would he be mad?" Susan sounded intrigued by the thought.

He would probably divorce me, Frances thought. And he might not let me take care of you and your brothers anymore. But she couldn't say any of these things, couldn't make it sound like as big a deal as it was. "I just don't think Uncle Henry would understand. Boys don't always understand girls and what they do."

Susan nodded. This explanation seemed to satisfy her. "Boys can be dumb. Especially Danny."

"Your brother isn't dumb," Frances said automatically. "So, you promise you won't say anything to anybody?"

Susan was quiet longer than was comfortable. "I promise."

Frances felt her shoulders relax just a little. "Thank you, Dorothy. We can pretend it's a state secret in Oz. We wouldn't want the information to fall into the wrong hands."

"Okay," Susan said with a little smile. "Could you make chocolate pudding for dessert tonight?"

"Of course," Frances said. She had a feeling she was going to be making Susan a lot of desserts to order.

"Can I go outside and play now?"

"Sure," Frances said. She watched her daughter skip to the front door, her pigtails swinging. She was so tiny—her narrow little shoulders and skinny legs, her dainty feet encased in black patent leather Mary Janes. Frances watched her with fear in her heart. Could someone that small keep a secret that big?

CHAPTER 15

Samuel hadn't heard from Frances since she'd left her house two days ago. She was desperate to know if Frances was okay, but she knew it wouldn't be safe to call Frances's house, even if it was at a time when Henry would be teaching. Not with Susan skulking around and spying. What was it her granny used to say? *Little pitchers have big ears.*

She sat on the front porch with her coffee and cigarettes. She wanted to write, but the words wouldn't come. Her brain was too clogged with worry for her creative juices to flow. The "what if" questions she used when she wrote stories had turned into terrible, real "what ifs."

What if Henry found out? What would he do? He didn't seem like the kind of man who would physically harm his wife, but you could never tell about people.

And what if Henry told Boots? What then? It was one thing for Henry to think she was having a discreet affair with some available dyke, but it was quite another to know she was making love to the wife of his colleague and friend. She and Boots had constructed the playhouse of their marriage carefully. They were like little kids who had a playground wedding and had thrown themselves into acting the roles of husband and wife as only preadolescents would see them. But they weren't preadolescents. They were adults with desires they couldn't fulfill with each other, desires that if acted upon, were illegal. Playhouses weren't like real houses. Their foundations weren't solid. They weren't built to last.

"Morning, Mrs. McAdoo!" their neighbor, Ed, called from the sidewalk. He walked to his law office downtown every day.

"Morning," Samuel answered, though she never got used to being called Mrs. McAdoo. Boots's mother was the real Mrs. McAdoo, even though everybody called her Miz Elizabeth. Samuel was an imposter.

After a second cigarette's time had passed, Priscilla came down the sidewalk and walked up the porch steps. "Well, were you just sitting there waiting to greet me this morning?" Priscilla asked. She was wearing a freshly ironed blue dress, and her hair was in a neat roll at the nape of her neck. She always seemed so put together, so self-contained. Samuel always wondered what path Priscilla's life would have taken if she weren't relegated to working in white women's houses.

"Yup, I'm the one-person welcoming committee," Samuel said. But according to the rules, she couldn't welcome Priscilla into her house as a guest, only as employee. Samuel was tired of the arbitrary rules that governed people's lives. "How are you, Priscilla?" she asked. It was a simple question, but one she really wanted to know the answer to.

Priscilla looked at her strangely for a moment, then said, "I'm just fine, Miz Samuel. How about you?"

"Fine." She felt far from fine, of course, but if Priscilla wasn't going to take her mask off, she'd keep hers on, too.

"Gail wants to come by this afternoon to borrow some books if that's all right," Priscilla said.

"Sure. She's always welcome."

"We appreciate it," Priscilla said. "Well, I reckon I'd better get the laundry started before I fix lunch."

* * *

Samuel was in her study when Gail knocked on the door. She'd been sitting at her desk since lunch, staring at the same blank page, thinking about Frances, thinking about how quickly her bliss had turned to terror when Susan walked in on them. She had never had that experience before, of things feeling absolutely right, then absolutely wrong within a span of seconds.

"Come in," Samuel called.

Gail hesitated at the doorway. She was, as always, immaculate in a hand-sewn school dress and polished Mary Janes. "Sorry," she said softly. "I don't want to interrupt your writing."

"You're not," Samuel said, glancing one last time at the blank sheet of paper. "Come on in."

"I'm bringing back *Frankenstein,*" Gail said, slipping the book back on the shelf with the S's.

"I hope Frankenstein enjoyed his visit," Samuel said.

Gail smiled. "I don't think Frankenstein's monster would make a very good houseguest. But I don't think Dr. Frankenstein would either. I don't like him."

"I don't either," Samuel said. She was on the verge of calling him an arrogant bastard, but then remembered she was talking to a child. "Did you like the book though?"

"I did," Gail said. "But it was different than I thought it'd be. It wasn't scary. It was sad. The monster couldn't help the way he was."

"Yeah," Samuel said. She wondered if there was any member of an outcast group who read *Frankenstein* without thinking, *the monster is me.*

"Do you have *Dracula*?" Gail asked. "I think I'd like to read it next."

Samuel was pretty sure Boots was too much of a snob to own a copy of *Dracula. Frankenstein* was only in his collection because of Mary Shelley's connection to the Romantic poets. "I don't think we have it. But check the S's for Stoker just in case."

Gail looked. "No. Oh, well, maybe they'll have it in the library when I go to high school."

Samuel couldn't stand the thought of Gail having to wait so long to read a book she was interested in. "I'll tell you what. Why don't I check it out of the public library and loan it to you? You can read it and bring it back to me, and then I'll return it for you."

"That's awful nice of you, Mrs. McAdoo."

"It's my pleasure. If you want to walk there now, I can run in and grab it for you." And afterward, Samuel thought, she could walk by Frances's house just to make sure everything looked okay.

It was a short walk to the library, but Samuel felt the judgmental, confused gaze of the white people they passed on the sidewalk. Had it been a colored woman with a white child, nobody would've thought anything of it. They would've just assumed that it was a nanny/housekeeper who had been sent out on an errand with her employer's kid. But apparently if it was a white woman with a colored child, nobody knew what to think.

"People are looking at us like we have two heads," Samuel said.

"Well, we're two people, so we do have two heads," Gail said, smiling.

Samuel laughed. "I meant two heads apiece."

"You get used it," Gail said. "People looking at you funny."

"I am used to it for the most part," Samuel said. "I get funny looks because I dress like a boy."

"If you don't mind me asking, why do you dress like a boy? Mama says you even wear boys undershorts."

"Well, she does my laundry, so she'd know," Samuel said. She knew she couldn't tell Gail about her homosexuality. She was already in dangerous enough territory because of what happened with Frances. "I'm just more comfortable dressed this way. Boys clothes are made for comfort. Girls clothes are made to look nice and feel terrible."

"I know what you mean," Gail said. "But my mama wouldn't hear of me wearing britches out where people could see me."

"Mine wouldn't either," Samuel said. "But once I grew up and left home, she couldn't tell me what to wear anymore." They were across the street from the library. "Why don't you wait here and I'll get the book for you?"

"Yes, ma'am," Gail said.

Inside the library several white children around Gail's age were looking at books. Unlike Gail, they were not subject to laws telling them what public facilities they could and could not use.

Samuel found the book and took it to the elderly librarian at the front desk who stamped it forcefully and said "due back in two weeks" in a tone that implied that an overdue library book was a capital offense.

Samuel caught Gail's eye as she exited the library and held the book up in mock triumph. Gail smiled.

Once she crossed the street, she held out the book to Gail. "This is due back in two weeks. The librarian was very forceful when she told me that."

Gail shoved the book into her schoolbag like it was contraband. "I'll have it back to you sooner than that. Thanks again, Mrs. McAdoo."

"Of course."

As soon as they parted ways, Samuel's mind was once again consumed with thoughts of Frances. It was a short walk to her house. Samuel didn't know what she was expecting to see—perhaps that the house had been razed and was no longer there?

It looked normal. Danny's bicycle was in the front yard. The cat was snoozing on a chair on the porch. Henry's car was not in the driveway. If it had been, she wouldn't have walked up the porch steps and rung the doorbell.

A couple of minutes passed. Samuel was trying to decide whether to ring again or walk away when the door opened.

"Oh!" Frances said. Her expression was surprised but also something else—fearful? "Hello."

"Hello," Samuel said, though it seemed a strangely formal greeting.

Frances stepped out on the porch and closed the front door behind her. "I'm afraid I can't let you in," she said.

"How are things . . . with Susan?" Samuel whispered.

Frances gave a half smile. "Right now, she's blackmailing me for extra desserts. My hope is the novelty of having a secret will wear off soon and she'll think of other things."

"I hope so, too," Samuel said, though she feared it wouldn't be the case. Knowing someone's secrets brought a lot of power. "I miss you," Samuel said, her voice breaking a little.

"I miss you, too," Frances said. A small tear trickled down her cheek. "But I can't have you coming over here anymore. It's not safe."

"I understand," Samuel said. Frances's tears seemed to be contagious. "You know, Miz Elizabeth goes out every Tuesday at lunchtime and doesn't come back till four or so. If you could arrange for babysitting, we could go to the guesthouse—"

"Yes," Frances said, wiping away a tear. "I don't know how I'll pull it off, but I'll do it."

"Okay." This would mean they'd be spending less than half the time they'd spent together previously. But it was better than nothing. "I want to kiss you right now," Samuel whispered.

"Me, too. But you need to go."

Samuel nodded and turned to go down the porch steps. It was ridiculous, but she knew if she had leaned in and kissed Frances out in the open on her front porch, the solid ground of their lives would have dissolved beneath them.

CHAPTER 16

ROBERT HAD GOTTEN GOOD ENOUGH AT sitting up that Frances could put him in the shopping cart's baby seat. He looked around wide-eyed at the aisles of colorful cans and boxes while Susan skipped along beside the cart.

But Susan's eyes were not on the cereal or the soup. Her eyes were on Frances. Or at least that's how Frances felt.

Since The Incident, as Frances had come to think of it, Frances had continually felt that Susan was staring at her, judging her, and perhaps most of all, calculating how she could use the situation to her advantage. As a result, Frances was on edge all the time, terrified of what Susan might say or do.

It was a terrible way to feel around your own child. She loved Susan, of course she did. She just didn't trust her.

"Auntie Em! Auntie Em!" Susan said, jumping up and down frantically. "Can I have some Sugar Crinkles?"

"*May* I have some Sugar Crinkles," Frances said automatically, adding a canister of oatmeal to the cart. What the hell were Sugar Crinkles anyway?

"May I have some Sugar Crinkles?" Susan asked. She had already grabbed the box, which was inexplicably illustrated with a cartoon seal balancing a ball on its nose.

"You know we don't eat sugary cereal for breakfast," Frances said. "We eat nutritious things like eggs and toast and oatmeal and orange juice. Breakfast is the most important meal of the day." It was strange how motherhood caused one to parrot platitudes she would never think of otherwise, let alone say out loud.

"But Auntie Em," Susan whined.

"Okay, okay," Frances said, trying to head off a tantrum. "But you can only eat them for breakfast on weekends."

Susan dropped the box of cereal in the cart. Frances knew the no-sugary-cereal-except-on-weekends edict would be negotiable. Right now, everything with Susan was negotiable, and like a slick politician, Susan always came out on top.

The mother-daughter power dynamic wasn't the only thing that had shifted since Susan had found Frances and Samuel in bed. Frances was constantly on edge. She was prone to crying jags, which she tried to hide from Henry and the children. She missed Samuel terribly. They had gone from spending whole mornings and afternoons together, two or three times a week, to a couple of furtive hours a week in the guest house, provided Frances could find a babysitter.

Frances's emotions seesawed between panic and sorrow. At lunch she had taken to drinking a beer—never more than two—just to get through the afternoon.

After the long march through the grocery store, Frances asked Susan, "Do you want to go to the dimestore and pick out a coloring book?" Maybe if she could get Susan to sit down with crayons and a new coloring book, she could get in an hour or so of writing before it was time to start dinner. If her brain could loosen up enough to write. Her concentration was flagging these days.

"Yes, Auntie Em," Susan said, her big brown eyes widening. "Please and thank you."

The dimestore owner kept a mynah bird in a cage which delighted Susan and terrified Robert. Susan went straight to the bird as soon as they walked in. "Who's a pretty bird?" she asked.

"Joe's a pretty bird," he squawked in a voice that matched the cadence and accent of the store owner's. "Hello" and "Joe's a pretty bird" were pretty much the extent of his conversational efforts, but he was happy to repeat those phrases as long as his audience would listen. And Susan was an appreciative audience. For her, a talking mynah bird was only one step down the yellow brick road from the talking lions and tigers in Oz.

Since Robert seemed to find Joe more of a Lovecraftian abomination, Frances carried him down the toy aisle in hopes of distracting him. The aisle, like every aisle in the store, was so overstuffed it seemed like dislodging one item would cause an avalanche. Frances jostled Robert on her hip and pointed out the brightly colored puzzles and games.

Suddenly he raised his chubby fist, pointed his stubby index finger, and grunted like a piglet. Frances followed the line of his pointer finger to a bin of small red rubber balls. "Ball," she said, taking one out and letting him hold it. It was the perfect size for his two small hands.

"Bah!" he crowed with obvious delight. "Bah!"

"Well," Frances said, smiling at him. "I guess if you can say it, I'd better buy it for you."

Susan appeared in the toy aisle, her conversation with Joe having apparently exhausted itself.

"Bah! Bah!" Robert announced, waving the ball at his sister.

"Yes, it's a ball," she said. "I didn't know you could talk."

"I think he just decided to start," Frances said. "Pick out a coloring book for yourself. Clearly, Robert has chosen a ball."

Susan walked slowly up the aisle, considering every item. Frances glanced at her watch. Five minutes. Five minutes before she would nag her to decide.

It was a long five minutes. Frances's arm was tired from holding Robert, and the anxiety she felt most strongly during idle moments was starting to bubble up to the surface. When exactly five minutes had passed, she said, "Choose a coloring book, Dorothy. We need to get home and put the groceries away and have lunch. I think the book with the circus pictures is nice."

Susan reached for a shelf and pulled down a large box. "I would like this doll, please, Auntie Em."

It was a full-sized baby doll that came with a bottle and two changes of clothes. It cost ten times more than a coloring book.

"That's too expensive," Frances said. "I said you could pick a coloring book, not a toy." Susan's gaze drifted over to Robert, still happily clutching his ball.

"You let him pick a toy," she said.

"I let him pick a toy that costs the same as a coloring book. The toy you chose costs much more." Frances wanted to sound firm, but her voice quivered.

"Linda next door has a doll like this except with blond hair," Susan said, as though she was laying the foundation for a completely rational argument.

Frances set Robert down in his stroller. She was too shaky to safely hold him. She would never do it, but part of her wanted to run, to push the stroller at top speed to get away from Susan, to leave her in the toy aisle holding the doll she couldn't afford. "Susan—" Frances began.

"Dorothy," Susan corrected her.

"Okay, Dorothy," Frances said. She was dangerously close to tears, and she sounded it. "It's very nice that Linda has a doll like that, and you can have one, too, for your birthday. But today you're just getting a coloring book. Now put the doll back on the shelf."

Susan held the box tight. "I don't want a coloring book."

"Fine." Frances was trying not to raise her voice. "Then you put the doll back on the shelf, I'll pay for Robert's ball, and then we'll go home and have lunch." It was definitely going to be a lunch with a beer kind of day.

"No." Susan's tone was firm. She stood still and stubborn, not relinquishing the box.

"You don't get to say no to me!" Frances said, louder than she usually let herself speak in public. "Look, I know you feel like you've got some kind of power over me, but I refused to be blackmailed by someone who hasn't even started first grade yet! Put the doll back on the shelf."

Susan smiled. "Uncle Henry would let me have the doll. Maybe I should talk to him."

Frances knew a threat when she heard one.

"Okay, okay!" she yelled, her voice breaking. "I'll buy the goddamned doll!"

"Thank you, Auntie Em." Susan smiled and walked to the checkout counter.

A familiar woman, decked out in a silly blue hat and white gloves, was at the counter, buying some sewing notions. It took a second for Frances to recognize her as Mrs. Wells, the wife of Henry's department chair.

Frances felt sick. She hoped Mrs. Wells hadn't heard any of the drama that had unfolded about the doll.

Once Mrs. Wells had paid for her purchases, she looked at Frances and said, "Hello, Mrs. Harmon. What cute children. They can be a handful at that age, though, can't they?"

Frances nodded mutely, sure that Mrs. Wells had heard every word.

* * *

"WHERE'S MY BEER?" HENRY ASKED, STANDING in front of the open refrigerator.

"We're out," Frances said. "Maybe this weekend we can drive out to the state line to get more. We can eat at that barbecue place you like."

"It's strange," Henry said. "I could've sworn I only drank two."

"I may have drunk the rest," Frances said. Why did she have to confess like it was some kind of crime? "I guess I thought it was our beer, not just your beer."

"Of course it was!" Henry said, shutting the refrigerator door. "That was one of our marriage vows, wasn't it? That we would join our alcohol resources. I just don't think of you as much of a beer drinker is all."

"I'm not usually," Frances said, busying herself with stirring the pot of vegetable soup which didn't need stirring. "But lately I've been having a beer or two with lunch."

"Lucky girl!" Henry said. "They'd never let me get by with that on our bone-dry campus. Say, could you mix me a Scotch and soda? I want something cold."

"Sure. I'll have one, too." Frances filled two glasses with ice, then poured in three fingers of Scotch and topped it with club soda. When she held Henry's drink out to him, her hand was shaking.

Her nerves were shot, but she needed to ask Henry about securing a steady babysitter for Tuesday afternoons. She couldn't keep impinging on the neighbors's limited supply of good will. And if she couldn't see Samuel alone at least once a week, she was going to lose her mind.

"Good," Henry said after the first sip of his drink. "Why don't we take a load off? It's not like you have to stand over soup and watch it cook."

They settled on the couch. Danny and Susan were playing outside, and Robert hadn't yet awoken from his afternoon nap which he had insisted on taking with his new "bah." The house was strangely quiet. Frances took a long swig of Scotch for courage. "Henry, I need a little break from the kids one afternoon a week. I was thinking Tuesdays might be good." Of course, it was absolutely essential that it was Tuesdays, but she had to sound casual, had to conceal the sense of urgency she felt.

Henry raised an eyebrow. "Is everything all right? Are the kids being little hellions or something?"

In her mind she saw Susan from earlier in the afternoon, refusing to put the doll back on the shelf. "It's nothing like that. It's just . . . you get to be with grown-ups all day . . . well, grown-ups and college students. I spend my days with people who don't have any permanent teeth yet. I love them, but it's not very intellectually stimulating. I'm lonely, Henry." As soon as she heard the truth of this statement, she burst into tears, which was humiliating.

"Oh, dear," Henry said, looking around as if there might be someone else in the room to help him. He finally reached in his pocket, pulled out a handkerchief, and offered it to her.

Frances wiped her eyes. "I'm sorry." Tears were something she always felt she should apologize for. "I just . . . do you think you could find a college girl to come over for a few hours on Tuesday afternoons? That way, I could maybe go to lunch and write in the library for a while . . . maybe run an errand or two without having to watch the children." She knew she wouldn't be doing any of these things. She would be in the guesthouse at McAdoo Manor in Samuel's arms, their clothing scattered on the floor. She took a sip of Scotch to wash down the lie.

"That sounds reasonable. Maybe Katie is available. The children seem to like her," Henry said.

"Thank you."

"I'm sorry you're lonely," Henry said. "Maybe we should have Boots and Samuel over for dinner soon."

At first, Frances's heart leapt at the thought of seeing Samuel. But then she willed herself to think. They couldn't have Samuel over with Susan in the house, not with Susan knowing what she knew. "Or maybe we could drive over to the state line and have steaks and beer at that roadhouse?"

"That would be fun, and no cooking for you," Henry said. "Also, I've been meaning to tell you . . . Dr. Wells mentioned the other day that you'd be welcome at his wife's bridge club. It's all faculty wives."

Frances winced. "Do you really think I'd be less lonely from spending time with those women?"

Henry drained his drink. "No, I suppose not. You're not one to discuss Sunday school and sewing patterns."

"And other women's pregnancies and miscarriages and marital problems," Frances said. She had almost said "affairs" but stopped herself.

"No, you've never been the clucking hen type," Henry said. "I think that's one of the things that drew me to you. Why do educated men want to marry women who can't talk about anything? You can take care of a home and talk about Homer."

Frances felt a sudden wave of tenderness for Henry that increased her guilt at deceiving him. But she didn't feel guilty enough to tell him not to bother finding a sitter. Her entire body, from her teeth to her toes, ached for Samuel.

* * *

As LUCK WOULD HAVE IT, KATIE was available on Tuesday afternoons. Frances couldn't get out of the house fast enough.

As she hurried to meet her lover, the breeze seemed to stroke the exposed skin on her arms and above the neckline of her blouse. Beneath her skirt, she was wearing a pair of filmy pink panties she had bought at the dime store and saved for this occasion. They were so different from the high-waisted white cotton underwear she usually wore, a sexy secret.

When she reached McAdoo Manor, she was short of breath from excitement, not from the exertion of the walk. She crept around the back side of the house, approached the guest house, and knocked lightly.

The door opened immediately. Samuel pulled Frances inside and closed and locked it behind her. Frances's back was pressed against the door, and her front was pressed against Samuel. Their kisses were crushing, ravenous, almost painful. When they pulled apart, Samuel took Frances's face in her hands and said, "God, I've missed you."

"You, too. So much."

And then they were kissing again and peeling off the husks of their clothing and falling into the safe, secret bed where no one would disturb them.

Afterward, as they held each other, Samuel said, "I don't know if I can survive seeing you just once a week."

"I know. I feel the same way," Frances said, tracing her fingers down the soft skin of Samuel's back. "I wish you could still come over to the house."

"She hasn't said anything, has she? About seeing us."

"Not to Henry. It seems like she's always dropping hints to me about how she *could* tell her father, but maybe I'm just being paranoid."

"You probably are," Samuel said. "She's so young she couldn't have possibly understood what she was seeing. She's probably forgotten all about it."

"Probably so," Frances said, though it was her experience that childless adults often underestimated children.

CHAPTER 17

"GIN, GIN, IT RHYMES WITH SIN," Boots sang as he mixed their five o'clock cocktails.

"Well, it's a sin if you're a Baptist," Miz Elizabeth said. "Which is why I'm a Presbyterian. Well, that and because I'm not trashy."

"A Pres-booze-terian," Boots said. Boots took Miz Elizabeth to church once a month, enough for her to show off a new Sunday outfit and to put in an appearance as a dutiful son.

Samuel declined to attend. She would grit her teeth and attend faculty parties and college functions, but she drew the line at church.

"Shall we stand for the Mixology?" Boots said. He sang, "Praise gin from whom all blessings flow . . ."

"Now, you're just blaspheming," Miz Elizabeth said, but she was smiling.

"Not blasphemous, just naughty." Boots handed Samuel her drink. "This town's humor is impaired, especially on the subject of religion." He looked at Samuel, his eyes narrowed.

"You're awful quiet this evening, my darling wife. Have I offended you with my blaspheming?"

Samuel took a long swallow of her cocktail. "Well, you know how delicate my sensibilities are."

Boots's expression turned more approving. "Indeed I do, my fine flower of Southern womanhood."

Samuel understood that Boots was in a playful mood. He wanted repartee and banter along with his cocktails, and Samuel was expected to be his willing partner. Often, she found the boozy banter fun, but this evening she lacked the energy.

The couple of hours a week she spent with Frances were so intense and so real that they made her hyperaware of the artifice of her actions with other people. It was like she was in a play, moving around the set in ways that had been blocked for her, saying her scripted lines on cue. The sound of the doorbell ringing only added to the stagey effect.

"Who lacks the common decency to know that you don't ring the doorbell during cocktail hour?" Boots said.

"It must be a Baptist," Miz Elizabeth said.

"Well, since Priscilla's gone for the day, I'll be the butler." Boots went to the door. When he opened it, he said "oh" in a small, shocked voice.

Samuel turned around to see Gail in the doorway, her face tear-streaked and terrified, flanked on either side by tall, burly police officers.

"Is there a Mrs. McAdoo at this residence?" the older of the police officers asked.

"Yes, sir," Boots said, his voice shaky. "Mama—"

"No," Samuel said, standing up. "I'm who they want." She walked over to the doorway, feeling scared but determined not to show it. "Hello, Gail. Hello, officers. Why don't y'all come in?"

The younger cop, who couldn't have been older than twenty, jerked his head in Gail's direction. "Her, too?"

"Yes, of course," Samuel said. She knew there were white families in town who didn't allow Black people in their homes, and those that did generally made them use the back door.

As soon as they were inside, the older police officer held out the item that Samuel was expecting, the public library's copy of *Dracula.* "The cashier over at the dimestore thought she was shoplifting," the older cop said. "We searched her school bag and there wasn't anything from the store in it, but we did find this stolen library book. It's library property, but it's checked out in your name, Mrs. McAdoo. The girl says she knows you and you can explain." He looked over at Boots and Mama Liz. "I'm sorry to bother y'all about this."

"Of course I know Gail," Samuel said, trying not to sound as angry as she felt. Why did the officer keep referring to Gail as *the girl,* as though everything Gail said, including her name, was a lie? "Her mother works for our family. Gail is an excellent student who loves to read, and I've been loaning her books from our collection now and then. She's already read all the books in her school library."

"Well, this book didn't come from her school library," the older police officer said.

"I'm aware of that." Samuel hated that her voice quivered. "Gail wanted to read *Dracula*, and we didn't have a copy. I checked it out of the public library and loaned it to her. She was going to bring it back to me when she finished it, and I was going to return it."

"Coloreds ain't allowed to check books out of the public library," the younger cop said.

"That kind of makes it less public, doesn't it?" *Careful,* Samuel told herself. *Don't smart off to a cop.* "I mean, I know Negros can't check out books from the library. That's why I checked out the book myself. Now, are there any laws that say if I check out a book from the library, I can't let somebody else read it?"

The older cop didn't meet her eyes. "Not that I know of, ma'am."

"Then are we done here?" Samuel asked. "Can Gail go home? I'm sure her mother is worried."

"We're done," the older cop said. "You take that book back to the library and only check out books for yourself from now on." He pinched the brim of his cap. "You folks have a good evening now."

Once the police were gone, Samuel looked at Gail. She had been so small standing between the two big police officers who were treating her like a hardened criminal. "Gail, I'm sorry that happened. I feel like I got you in trouble."

"You didn't mean to," Gail said, her voice barely loud enough to hear.

"Do you need a ride home?" Samuel asked.

"No, thank you. I can walk." Gail's tone was formal and impersonal, the same tone she would use with any other white lady. She walked to the kitchen and left through the back door.

"Now what I want to know," Mama Liz said, taking out a cigarette for Boots to light, "is why any of that was necessary."

"Exactly," Samuel said, reaching for a cigarette herself. "Do grown men have nothing better to do in their line of duty than to bully and intimidate a little girl?" Looking at her mother-in-law's stony expression, she became aware that Mama Liz's statement had not been one of solidarity.

"Those two weren't the brightest fellows you'll ever meet, but they were doing their jobs as they understand them," Miz Elizabeth said. "You, though, you're supposed to be smart. You should've known better than to put that child in a situation like that."

"All I did was lend her a book she wanted to read."

"It wasn't your book to lend," Miz Elizabeth said, "and you put her in a situation where she was breaking the rules."

"The rules are unfair," Samuel said. She looked over at Boots, but he looked away.

"Yes, they are," Miz Elizabeth said.

"So, are we just supposed to keep on playing by rules we know are wrong?"

Miz Elizabeth exhaled a cloud of smoke. "So, what are you gonna do? Tell the people who make the rules to change them? The rules work for them. They made them that way." She shook her head. "You're too young to understand how things are. But I'm a seventy-five-year-old woman. I've been playing by rules I didn't make for a long time."

Boots had been silently watching the argument between Samuel and Mama Liz like a spectator at a boxing match.

"So, what do you think of all this, my darling husband?" Samuel said, though she knew whose side he'd take.

"I think . . . " Boots cast a glance over at Mama Liz before looking back at Samuel. "I think you made a mistake, but you meant well. You have a soft heart, sweet pea, and that's one of my favorite things about you."

Samuel had heard of people's blood boiling, but until now she had never felt it. "So, I'm some kind of softy because I think a child should be given access to books? Because I think people should be treated like people?"

"Sit down and have another cocktail," Boots said. "You've gotten yourself all worked up."

"I don't want another cocktail. I want to get out of here." Right now, the house felt so much like the set of a play—a play she did not like—that she feared that if she opened the front door, it would just lead backstage.

She went to the front door and opened it anyway and was relieved to step out into the fresh air.

She was halfway down the porch steps when Boots touched her shoulder. "Come back in," he said, his voice soft and coaxing. "It's almost suppertime. Priscilla made chicken and dumplings."

Priscilla. Samuel wondered if Gail would tell her mother about her encounter with the police. Or would she keep it a secret, swallowing the pain and fear so it would fester inside her? "I'm just going for a little walk to clear my head," Samuel said. "I'll be back soon."

Boots let go of her arm. "I know you're upset I didn't intervene more in that situation," he said.

"Intervene *more*? You didn't intervene at all."

Boots held up his hands as if in surrender. "I know. But what you don't understand is that being like I am, I'm in a precarious situation. If I rock the boat, I'll end up in shark-infested waters. Your situation is the same. As long as we go along to get along, nobody will bother us. But if one of us breaks the rules or just speaks out against them, the sharks are waiting for us. We've got to protect ourselves, Samuel."

"Even when it's at somebody else's expense?"

Boots set his jaw. "Unfortunately, yes."

Looking at Boots, Samuel saw the fear he usually kept hidden beneath a well-cultivated surface of jollity and flamboyance. "I have to go," she said.

If she walked any faster, she would have been running. But she knew she couldn't get away from what was gnawing at her. The picture of Gail's terrified face.

Growing up, Samuel had heard every racial slur imaginable coming from her father's lips, especially when he was drinking. But these rants were in the privacy of his own home. None of the members of the race he was casting aspersions upon were present. What Samuel had just witnessed was different. Boots and Mama Liz had been confronted by the suffering of a child—a child they knew who was standing in their own house—and had met this suffering with indifference. What was worse: her drunk, poor daddy ranting about the only group that had less power than he did, or people like Mama Liz and Boots who would never utter a racist slur but would never use their money and power to help a Black person in need?

Samuel walked downtown where all the businesses had closed for the day. She walked past the library where she could check out books, but it was a criminal offense to check out books for Gail. She walked past the drug store with the soda fountain where she could sit down and have a milkshake any time she wanted, but Gail and her family couldn't. She walked past the dimestore where Gail had been falsely accused of shoplifting.

Samuel had always known that the rules of segregation were wrong, but something about seeing Gail's face today made her feel their cruelty.

Samuel walked across the railroad tracks into the colored part of town, past shotgun houses with chipped paint and dirt yards. Men sat on the porches talking, and little girls jumped rope on the crumbling sidewalk.

Samuel watched the girls for a moment, remembering what it had felt like to jump over the rope again and again, counting each jump, feeling the satisfaction of beating your own record. She wondered what would happen if she joined them, if she jumped right in where the little girls were turning the rope. They would probably drop the rope and run away from the crazy white lady who was dressed like a man and thought she could play with little colored girls.

She kept walking, becoming more aware of the looks from people on their porches, from the little boys playing catch. She knew white people in this neighborhood were rare. Maybe occasionally a white lady would give her maid a ride home, but a white lady on foot was probably unheard of.

She kept walking though. She couldn't face going back to the big white house of lies. Not yet.

A woman taking her wash off the line called out, "Hey, miss! You lost?"

Samuel stopped walking. "Yes. Yes, I am."

CHAPTER 18

Frances was sliding a meatloaf and some baking potatoes into the oven when Henry came home. The kids always made a big production of their dad walking through the door. Susan ran to him yelling, "Uncle Henry! Uncle Henry!" and Danny said, "Dad, wanna play catch with me?" before Henry had even set his bag down.

"Later, son," Henry said. "Why don't you and your sister go play outside? I need to talk to your mother."

Usually, Henry was in a pretty good mood when he came home, happy for—if nothing else—the prospect of a stiff drink followed by dinner. But this evening his tone was grim and strangely formal.

He knows, Frances thought, and a wave of panic and nausea washed over her that was so strong she had to grab the kitchen counter to steady herself.

After the children had trooped out, Henry said "sit" as if he were talking to a dog.

"Would you like a drink first?" Frances's voice came out small and shaky.

"Not now." That tone. So unlike the Henry she knew.

"Okay." She sat on the couch. She wanted a cigarette but feared her hands were trembling too much to light one.

"Dr. Wells called me into his office this afternoon," Henry said.

Dr. Wells? Did he have a way of knowing she was having an affair with Samuel? Or was this—she prayed despite her atheism—about something else? But then she felt a different kind of anxiety. Was Henry being fired again?

"It seems Mrs. Wells saw you in the dimestore the other day. She said you were behaving erratically, that you yelled at the children and cursed at them."

"Oh, that," Frances said, waving her hand as if to brush away the accusation. "I was only yelling at Susan. She was demanding an expensive doll I wouldn't let her have. And you know how stubborn she can be."

But as soon as she said it, she wondered if Henry did know. He took two meals a day with the children and sometimes played catch with Danny or a board game with Susan, but Frances did all the many hours of care that were needed between these occasions—the long days that sometimes contained tantrums and misbehavior.

Henry nodded. "We're both stubborn. She comes by it honestly." He looked at Frances's face as if searching for clues. "Did you curse at her?"

"I didn't curse at her," Frances said, feeling far too much like she was being interrogated by her own husband. "I may have said 'Put the goddamn doll back on the shelf' or something to that effect."

Henry grimaced. "Yes, that was the word Dr. Wells mentioned except he wouldn't say it; he just said 'g.d.' . . . and that almost in a whisper. People down here really hate that word. I've learned that from my students. They say it's taking the Lord's name in vain, like you're damning God."

"If I wanted to damn God," Frances said, "and I might, given the day I'm having, I'd say 'damn God' and not 'goddamn.'"

"I know you would," Henry said. "I'd say it too, though since I don't believe in God, it wouldn't carry much weight. People are different down here. Teaching, I'm shocked time and time again at how sheltered the students are, how easily offended."

"But they're not offended by the things that should offend them," Frances said. "They're fine with 'whites only' signs but get the vapors if somebody lets a curse word slip."

"Especially if that somebody is a lady, and that lady is the wife of a professor at the college. You're considered a reflection of me, Frances, so if you do something that damages your reputation, it damages mine, too."

Frances's stomach flip-flopped. If Mrs. Wells swooned into a faint after hearing a curse word, how would she react to the fact that Frances was sleeping with Dr. McAdoo's wife? She'd probably fall into a coma. "It's not fair, though. I don't want to be a reflection of anyone but myself."

"I know, dear, but that's not the way things are, and if I'm going to keep this job a few years so I can claw my way to a better one, we're going to have to play by the rules."

Frances had initially been drawn to Henry because he was a wild-eyed, bearded bohemian who did not play by the rules. What had happened to him, to them? "Well, I certainly don't want to hurt your career," she said, almost in a whisper.

"I know you don't." Henry fished around in his shirt pocket and pulled out a slip of paper. "Dr. Wells told me in confidence that his wife had had some problems with nervousness. Lots of women have those problems from staying home with kids. And then there are also hormones . . . and things," he trailed off, looking helpless. "Anyway, this is the name of the doctor she sees. He says he helped her a lot. And I was thinking you haven't seen a doctor since the obstetrician who delivered Robert."

"Which is a lot more recently than you've seen a doctor," Frances said. Henry hadn't been to a doctor the whole time they'd been married.

"Sure, but look at me. I'm the perfect specimen of health." Henry patted his round belly then searched for a cigarette. "Seriously, though? Will you go see this guy so I can tell the boss man you went?"

She looked at the name on the slip of paper: Dr. Wright. She supposed going to see him would do no harm. She had been a ball of nerves ever since The Incident with Susan. The only time she wasn't nervous or jumpy was when she was alone with Samuel. "Okay. I'll make an appointment," she said.

* * *

THE WAITING ROOM WAS COLD AND smelled of antiseptic. The other patient was a woman a decade or so older than Frances who was placidly leafing through an issue of *Ladies' Home Journal.*

"Mrs. Harmon?" A sturdy, middle-aged nurse stood in the doorway leading to the rest of the medical office. "Dr. Wright will see you now."

Instead of an exam room, the nurse led Frances to an office with a large oak desk and leather-covered chairs. The walls were decorated with stuffed and mounted fish.

"He'll be with you shortly," the nurse said.

Frances stared at the dead fish and let them stare back at her. Most of them were freshwater, trout or large-mouthed bass, but one had giant fins and a pointy snout. An ocean fish—wasn't it called a marlin? Like something out of Hemingway.

"Good morning, Mrs. Harmon." Dr. Wright was a bulky middle-aged man with a salt-and-pepper mustache. He was wearing one of those peculiar short-sleeved smock-type shirts that doctors often favored. His forearms were huge and hairy.

"Good morning," she parroted back at him.

He slid behind the desk and sat down, glancing at the paperwork she'd filled out in the waiting room. "So, you're a mother of three?" he asked. His Southern accent was of the type that is often referred to as genteel.

"That's right," she said.

"What ages?"

"Eight, five, and nine months."

He smiled. "Well, if the youngest is nine months, I don't suppose I need to ask if everything's all right with you and your husband in the bedroom."

She felt her face heat up. "I guess not."

"Good, good," he said, glancing back down at his papers. "But you've been feeling more nervous than usual lately? Maybe having a hard time sleeping?"

"Yes," Frances said, trying to figure out how she was going to explain herself. "I—"

"I see this kind of thing all the time," Dr. Wright said, reaching for his prescription pad. "Fortunately, in our modern age, there are many fine medications which can help young wives and mothers such as yourself." He scribbled something on the pad, tore off the square of paper, and handed it to her. "There you go. You can take this over to the drug store, maybe get a milkshake while you're waiting for them to fill it."

Frances took the square of paper and looked down at the doctor's illegible scrawl. "Uh . . . aren't you going to examine me or something?"

Dr. Wright laughed like she had just made a joke. "I'm not one of those old-timey horse doctors, Mrs. Harmon. I believe in science. In modern medicine. Prescribing the right pill is much more effective than poking and prodding."

"Okay, well, thank you for your time," Frances said. According to her watch, the amount of time he had given her was three minutes and thirty-two seconds.

She felt strange as she left the doctor's office. She was relieved that she didn't have to take her clothes off or have blood drawn, but the whole visit had felt awfully perfunctory.

She walked to the drug store, gave the prescription to the pharmacist, and then proceeded to the soda fountain for a chocolate milkshake—doctor's orders. When the pharmacist called her name and presented her with a small bottle of pills, he said, "Now, honey, you'll want to be real careful about driving a car until you get used to how these hit you."

"I walk most places," Frances said.

The pharmacist smiled. "You might want to be careful about walking, too."

Frances walked home, paid the babysitter, and made lunch for herself and the children. As soon as she finished her last bite of grilled cheese, she swallowed a pill. Less than an hour later, as she was starting a load of laundry, she felt the ball of tension that had been sitting in her stomach for weeks begin to melt like a lump of butter in a hot skillet.

She decided to bake some oatmeal cookies for tonight's dessert, and by the time they were in the oven, she was amazed how loose-limbed and floaty she felt. A soft blanket of calm had enveloped her. Was this how people were supposed to feel and she had never known it?

The screen door slammed, but she felt no startle response at all.

"Auntie Em, it's *raining*," Susan said, shaking her head like a wet dog. "Do you think a storm's a-brewing?"

She fell into the Auntie Em role without a thought. It would be nice if she could be one of the more glamorous characters in the Oz books, but if she had been cast as Auntie Em, she would give it her all. "No, Dorothy, I think it's just a little shower, but you'll have to play inside until it stops."

Susan let out a world-weary sigh.

"It doesn't have to be boring," Frances said. "You could do some drawings of your favorite friends from Oz, and we could cut them out and make paper dolls."

"You know, that's a good idea, Auntie Em," Susan said, sounding shocked that Frances could ever have a good idea.

"Let the kitty in, too," Frances said. "No need for her to get wet either."

Susan brightened even more. "Okay!"

Frances got out construction paper and pencils and set Susan up at the kitchen table. She watched her daughter hunch over her drawing, so absorbed, her child's imagination at play that was somehow also work. It made Frances think of how she felt when she was writing, and thus inspired, she grabbed her notebook and sat down at the table opposite Susan. Hecate/Eureka curled up in Frances's lap to sleep, and the three of them passed a pleasant, productive hour until Robert woke from his nap.

And Robert! Robert was such a joy to her newly tranquil mind. He was soft and cuddly with a talcum powdery, milky smell that was somehow intoxicating. After she changed his diaper, she held him, humming an old ballad, and waltzed around the nursery. Robert seemed puzzled but amused.

Even mundane household tasks took on a more soothing quality. The clothes she pulled out of the dryer were so soft and warm. The suds from the dish soap tickled her wrists and fingers. Even things she didn't like weren't so bad now. She had never cared for the cold, clammy feeling of raw meat, yet when she massaged butter into the pimply flesh of a chicken she was going to roast for dinner, she didn't mind it so much.

That was the thing about these pills. When you took them, you didn't mind things so much anymore. They should call them Nevermind pills. Nevermind reminded her of Neverland, where Peter Pan and the Lost Boys were kept free of the responsibilities of growing up.

But there were no Lost Girls. They had to grow up and become mothers.

The front door slammed, and she calmly turned her head to see who the culprit was.

"Hiya, Ma," Danny said, in that new way he had of talking like he was in a gangster movie. What was it Jimmy Cagney said in that old picture? *Top of the world, Ma!*

"Hi, Pooh Bear," Frances said, so awash in affection that she accidentally used his baby name.

"Aahh, whaddaya gotta call me that for?" he said. "I'm practically grown now. We got any cookies?"

Frances suppressed a smile and opened the refrigerator door to get his milk. "As luck would have it, I just made some oatmeal cookies."

"Okay," he said. "They're not as good as chocolate chip though."

"They're better for you than chocolate chip," Frances said, handing him a glass of milk.

"Yeah," Danny said. "But cookies aren't vegetables. You don't eat 'em cause they're good for you."

She had to concede that he had a point.

When Henry came home, she was taking the roast chicken out of the oven.

"Something smells fantastic," Henry said, setting down his bag and shucking off his jacket. He always dispensed with his tie in the car on the way home from work.

"It's my new cologne, Eau de Poulet," she said.

Henry chuckled. "It smells good enough to eat." He came up behind her and leaned over to kiss her cheek. "You're in a good mood."

"The doctor gave me some pills. They're very soothing."

"I'm glad to hear it," Henry said. "I think I'd find a Scotch on the rocks very soothing."

"By all means," Frances said, reaching for the liquor cabinet. She poured a double for him but a single for herself since she wasn't sure how the Nevermind pills would mix with alcohol.

As it turned out, they mixed very well. Like apple pie with vanilla ice cream. She sipped the Scotch as she busied herself with dinner, heating a can of peas, mashing potatoes. Jazz was wafting from Henry's study, and by the time Frances's glass was empty, she was gliding across the kitchen floor like a lady in a beautiful ball gown. She had never realized how much weight she had been carrying until now when she felt so light and loose and unencumbered.

She set the roast chicken and the bowls of peas and potatoes on the table. "Dinner!" she announced.

* * *

Frances had decided that the one day of the week she would skip the Nevermind pills was Tuesday. The pills made hard things easier and dull things bearable, but being with Samuel was never hard or dull.

As she lay in the guesthouse bed in the afterglow of their lovemaking—a wash of wellbeing that felt like a naturally induced version of the effects of the pills—Samuel laid her head on Frances's shoulder and said, "Why does the best part of my life have to be just a few minutes a week that feel like they're stolen?"

A prickle of anxiety penetrated Frances's calm. "Well, I guess because I have to take care of the children—"

Samuel touched Frances's lips to shush her. "You don't have to answer. I understand the practical reasons. It's just sad how people keep the best parts of themselves locked away because they're afraid of what people think."

"It's not just what people think," Frances said. "It's what they do based on what they think."

"Yeah," Samuel said, rolling over and reaching for her cigarettes on the nightstand. "You've got something there. People's thoughts have consequences. I'm sure any colored person in this town would agree with you." She lit a cigarette for herself and one for Frances.

Frances pictured the dry-cleaning store downtown with the sign on its door reading *Whites Only*—a statement that did not pertain to the colors of clothes they washed. "I'm sure they would," she said, taking the cigarette from the V of Samuel's fingers. She listened to Samuel tell a horrifying story about how their housekeeper's daughter had been accused of stealing a library book. By the time Samuel finished, Frances found herself wishing she had taken one of her pills. "That makes me so mad," Frances said. "As a mother, trying to imagine one of my children being falsely accused of theft, and then to know in this case it was because of the color of the child's skin—insanity, that's what it is."

"It is," Samuel said. "I didn't mean to get her in trouble. In my mind, kids who want to read should get to read, it's as simple as that."

"That's how it should be," Frances said. "But there's a big difference between *should* and *is.*"

"Yes," Samuel said, sitting up in bed. "But just because something is a certain way, does that mean we have to accept it? I mean, I should be able to tell everybody in the world that I love you. It should be safe for me to be able to do that."

Three of Samuel's words stood out in relief. "Tell everybody in the world you love me? You've never even told *me* that."

Samuel's cheeks reddened. "Well, I do. Love you, I mean."

Frances felt herself melting like vanilla ice cream under a blanket of hot fudge. "I love you, too." She was surprised to feel tears well in her eyes.

"You do?" Samuel said, like this was surprising news.

"Yeah, I do," Frances said, and they were both laughing and crying at the same time. It was the kind of emotional display that would send most men running for the hills, or at least for the nearest bar.

"I've never told somebody I love them before," Samuel said. "It feels good."

Frances felt a pang of worry. "But you're not going to tell anybody else how you feel, are you?"

"No, of course not," Samuel said. "I know it's not safe. You've got too much to lose. And I do, too. I could lose you, and that's everything."

CHAPTER 19

SAMUEL CAME INTO THE KITCHEN TO refill her coffee cup. What she really needed was to refuel her brain, which seemed to run on coffee and cigarettes, for more writing. Priscilla was at the counter, rolling out a pie crust. Samuel had felt uncomfortable around Priscilla ever since Gail had been picked up by the police. She didn't even know if Priscilla knew about the incident, and she certainly wasn't going to tell her about it if she didn't.

"Making a pie?" Samuel asked, instantly feeling stupid since it was pretty obvious what Priscilla was doing.

"Yes, ma'am."

"What kind?"

"Apple."

"Boots's favorite." With the topic of the pie exhausted, she decided to take a small risk. "Will Gail be coming over to borrow a book this afternoon?"

"No, ma'am." She still didn't look up. "She won't be doing that anymore."

So, she knew. How could she not? Mothers had their ways

of knowing. "Priscilla, I'm so sorry about what happened. I didn't mean to get her in trouble."

"I know," Priscilla said. She laid the dough in a pie pan and pushed it down flat. "You was just doing what you thought was right. You're a nice white lady. But there's lots of white folks that ain't so nice, and when they saw her with that book, they jumped to their own conclusions."

Samuel nodded grimly. "My good intentions backfired."

"They did . . . because you ain't used to having to think three steps ahead like colored folks have to."

Samuel nodded because what else did she have to say? She couldn't know what Priscilla and her family's life was like, couldn't know how it felt to live every day with that level of caution and fear. "Well, could you tell Gail I said hey?"

Priscilla was peeling the apples now. The skin unspooled in a long, red ribbon. "I'll tell her."

Samuel took her coffee back to her study and sat at her desk. A wave of sadness swept over her. She knew she'd never see Gail again. Oh, she might see her in passing and exchange polite greetings, but Gail would never be a guest in Samuel's house again, would never talk about the books she loved or her hopes for the future. Samuel had tried to poke a small hole in the wall that had been erected between white and Black—a hole just large enough to slip a few books through—but the hole had been bricked back up and sealed with cement.

Her sadness turned to anger. She knew that anger, like coffee and cigarettes, could serve as fuel for writing. She wrote furiously for she didn't know how long, until her shoulder ached, and she heard the front door open and Boots call, "Yoohoo! Girls! I'm home!"

* * *

"I WISH THEY HAD SOMETHING TO drink besides beer," Boots said as they pulled into the gravel parking lot of Opal's, the state line roadhouse where they were meeting Henry and Frances for dinner, a fact which filled Samuel with a complex cocktail of anxiety and excitement.

"I like beer," Samuel said. "It was the first booze I ever drank, so there's something comforting about it."

"Comforting the way all fattening things are," Boots said. "Not that you have to worry. You stay lean as a bean no matter what. I have to suffer for my girlish figure."

Samuel laughed. "Of course, I probably shouldn't find it comforting. I used to steal it from the icebox when Daddy was passed out and hope he wouldn't remember how many he'd had the next morning. If he did remember, I got a whoopin'."

"Was it worth it though?"

Samuel laughed. "Of course it was!"

Opal's was not a fancy establishment. Neon beer signs were the only decorations. The floors were sticky with long-ago spilled beer and crunchy with discarded peanut shells. Samuel and Boots slid into a peeling vinyl booth. A metal bucket of peanuts sat on the middle of the table. Samuel knew the peanuts were one of the classic tricks in the bar-keeper's book. Eating peanuts made you thirsty, so you bought more beer. She knew the trick, but she loved peanuts, so she fell for it every time.

Samuel threw the peanut shells over her shoulder like a feasting medieval lord tossing bones to the dogs. But Boots arranged his shells in a neat little pile on the table. Even though tossing shells was *de rigueur* at Opal's, he could never bring himself to do it.

When Frances and Henry walked through the door, Samuel stifled a gasp. Frances had clearly spent more time on her appearance than usual. Her brown hair fell in soft waves around her shoulders, and her rose lipstick transformed her lips into kissable petals. Samuel hoped that while primping, Frances had been thinking of her.

Boots waved Frances and Henry over to their booth, and they slid in across from them.

"Greetings!" Henry said, grinning broadly and looking around as if he were greeting the whole room.

Frances smiled at Samuel but then blushed and broke eye contact.

A peroxide blond waitress appeared at the table and asked, "Y'all want some beers?"

"Yes, ma'am," Boots answered. "A pitcher of your finest with four mugs, please."

"I reckon that'd be the Schlitz," the waitress said. She squinted at Samuel. "Hey, didn't you used to live way out in Frog Level?"

Samuel felt strangely put on the spot. Most of the time she could pretend she was living more than forty-five minutes away from where she had grown up. "As a kid, yes."

The woman grinned, revealing a smear of lipstick on her front tooth. "Kathy Boatman, right? I was Lovella Simms. I'm

Lovella Millsaps now. You look just the same—ain't changed a bit."

"You, too," Samuel said, but it was a lie. The Lovella she saw before her bore only a scant resemblance to the Lovella she remembered, with her wild mane of brown hair and wide, trusting eyes. The hair was dyed and beaten into submission now, and something in her eyes had hardened.

Lovella grinned. "Well, I knew you wrote stories. I didn't know you told them, too. I'll be right back with y'all's beer."

"My grandmother used to say that," Boots said. "'Telling a story' for telling a lie."

"Mine, too," Samuel said. She was elated to be in Frances's presence but also extremely nervous with both of their husbands there. Maybe the beer would calm her.

"My grandmother always said, 'Henry, that's a damned lie,'" Henry said. "But she was from New Jersey and not one to mince words."

"I don't think we mince our words in the South," Samuel said. "It's more like we grease them up so they go down easier."

"We *season* our words," Boots said. "Just like you season a pot of greens with onion and fatback."

"When we first moved here," Frances said, "I couldn't believe how strangers would ask you such personal questions, like *how long have you been married* and *how many children do you have* and *where do you go to church*."

"We call that being friendly," Boots said. "The police call it interrogation."

Lovella returned with the pitcher and four frosty mugs. Her top was low cut and when she leaned over the table,

Samuel was confronted with an eyeful of her cleavage. It reminded her of Frances's glorious breasts, which she knew she shouldn't be thinking about while sitting across the table from Frances's husband. After Boots filled her mug, she drank down half of it gratefully.

There were two items on the dinner menu at Opal's, T-bone steak and home fries, so that was what they ordered. Samuel and Boots and Frances ordered their steaks medium, but Henry said. "I want mine rare. Still mooing if you can manage it."

Lovella smiled. "I'll bring it out on a leash."

Samuel found that she had more of an appetite for drink than food. Perhaps because of her nerves, the steak felt like a lot of work to cut, chew, and swallow. The beer went down easy, though, cool and refreshing. Soon Lovella brought them a second pitcher.

"Gotta love any woman who has 'love' as part of her name, eh, Boots?" Henry said. He had already polished off half his steak. The rest of it lay in a pool of blood like a murder victim.

Boots gave a little smile. "I hadn't thought of that."

Of course you hadn't, Samuel thought. She knew Boots got uncomfortable when the talk turned to heterosexual innuendo. He and Carlisle could talk outright smut about men they found attractive, but heterosexuality was a language he didn't speak.

"How can you not?" Henry said. "I read somewhere that the average man has a sexual thought every thirty seconds."

Samuel wanted to say stop talking about lusting after other women in front of your wife, but since she was having an affair with his wife, this seemed hypocritical. So instead, she said, "Every thirty seconds? Then how do you get anything done? It makes you wonder how men are running the world."

"It also explains why they're not doing a very good job of it," Frances said, and she and Samuel burst into laughter. Henry and Boots joined in, which a lot of men wouldn't.

Henry had finished his steak, and everyone else had given up on theirs.

"I think I may excuse myself to go to the powder room," Frances said.

Boots laughed. "With all due respect, my dear, I don't think this place has anything resembling a powder room. I think it's a john."

"Well, so much for euphemisms," Frances said, smiling. She must have been a little tipsy; her s's were softening. "Samuel, would you care to join me?"

Samuel would join Frances anywhere, even the john at Opal's. "Sure."

Henry slid out of the booth so Frances could get out. "So, this is the part where the ladies abandon the menfolk to go to the restroom together?"

"That's right." Frances patted his arm. "It'll give you some time to ogle the waitress."

Samuel followed Frances, admiring the subtle sway of her generous hips.

The bathroom was dark and dank but blessedly unoccupied. Samuel looked at Frances, her hazel eyes a little sleepy-looking from the beer, her hair spilling down her shoulders, her full lips. "You're so beautiful I can't stand it," Samuel said.

Frances blushed and reached for Samuel's hand. "Come here, you."

She pulled Samuel into a stall and locked the door behind them. Their lips pressed together as if pulled by a magnetic force. It has hard kissing, with tongue and teeth, their inhibitions lowered by the power of beer. Their hands were all over each other. It wasn't safe and Samuel knew it, but somehow, she also didn't care. Or maybe the danger made her want it more. She slid her hand up Frances's skirt.

"Please," Frances whispered. "Do it."

And then Samuel was inside her, and Frances was biting her shoulder hard enough to leave a mark. They were both panting.

The main door of the restroom opened with a squeak.

Samuel pulled away so suddenly she lost her balance and had to steady herself on the undoubtedly germy stall wall. They stood across from each other as the other restroom patron entered the adjoining stall. Samuel hoped the woman was either so drunk or so oblivious that she wouldn't notice the two pairs of feet in the stall next door. They held their breaths as the stranger peed, then flushed. In a few seconds that felt like minutes, they heard the main door squeak open, then close.

"She didn't wash her hands," Frances whispered, and they both collapsed into giggles.

When she caught her breath Samuel said, "We should probably get back to the table before the boys think we fell in the toilet."

"Kiss me one more time," Frances said.

Samuel knew that someone else could walk in any minute. But Frances was a temptation she couldn't resist.

"We took the liberty of ordering another pitcher," Boots said as they slid back into the booth. "You girls have got some drinking to catch up on."

"I learned long ago not to try to keep up with Henry," Frances said.

"My lovely wife is blessed with a hollow leg," Boots said. "She can drink most men under the table."

"Well, you can certainly hold your own, my dear." Samuel patted Boots on the cheek, then withdrew her hand quickly, remembering where it had been a few moments before.

Was it her imagination that a flicker of recognition passed across his face, that his eyes went from bright and twinkly to flat and lizardlike?

Boots turned to Henry. "So, tell me, which translation of *The Odyssey* do you prefer?"

Instantly, the menfolk were off discussing classic literature, ignoring the womenfolk entirely. It wasn't like Boots to shut Samuel down like this, and she felt a Gordian knot of tension forming in her belly, which she tried to untangle by dousing it with beer. Frances smiled at her from across the table, but she was afraid to smile back.

On the small plywood stage in the corner, a band started to play a twangy song.

"Excellent!" Henry said, clapping his hands. "We should dance."

"The high school I went to was all girls," Frances said, "so when we had dancing class, we had to dance together."

"Well, isn't it fortunate you don't have to resort to that anymore?" Boots said. He reached his hand out to Frances. "May I have the pleasure?"

Frances's eyes widened a little in surprise, but she said, "I'd be delighted."

Samuel watched Boots lead Frances to the tiny dance floor where they commenced a graceful two-step. Like a lot of good dancers, Boots had the ability to make his partner appear better than she was.

"I guess that leaves the two of us," Henry said, grinning. Something about the wideness of his grin beneath his mustache reminded Samuel of Teddy Roosevelt. "Though I fear you'll find me a clumsier partner than my better half."

"I'm a lot clumsier than Boots, too," Samuel said, sliding out of the booth. She didn't want to dance with Henry but didn't know how to avoid it without seeming rude.

He offered his arm as if he were about to march her down the aisle, and they proceeded to the dance floor.

"I'm afraid a box step is all I can manage," Henry said. "Unlike Frances, I didn't go to a school that offered dancing lessons."

"Me neither," Samuel said. Now that she was standing, she realized she was a little drunk. She put one hand on Henry's sweaty back and let him hold her other hand in his giant one.

He ran his other big paw down her back and let it rest at her waist. "Well, you have an actual woman's body underneath those clothes, don't you?"

Samuel felt a flash of embarrassment, as if he were looking through her clothes. “What were you expecting? A chimera? Clearly you read too much mythology.”

Henry laughed. “You and your husband are such a hoot. I can’t imagine how bored we’d be in this town if we hadn’t met you two.” They completed an awkward box with their feet. “Seriously, though,” Henry said, “you’re an attractive woman. Why do you choose to dress so mannishly?”

“Have you ever worn high heels and a panty girdle, Henry?”

“No, I can’t say that I have.”

“Well, try those on for size and then report back to me about which sex gets to wear the more comfortable clothing.”

“Touché,” Henry said, chuckling.

As soon as the song reached its twangy end, Samuel moved away from Henry more quickly than was probably polite. “Thank you for the dance,” she said to offset her rudeness.

“My pleasure.”

When Samuel returned to the booth, Boots was standing beside it.

“I was just saying to Frances,” Boots said, “that’s it’s getting to be past my bedtime.”

“Oh, but it’s the shank of the evening!” Henry said. “It’s only ten o’clock, and we paid the babysitter to stay till eleven-thirty.”

“We parent-types don’t get an evening out that often,” Frances said. “We’ve got to make the most of it.”

“Well, all the better for us to leave you to have some romantic time to yourselves,” Boots said. “Like the old gray mare, I ain't what I used to be. I can't stay out all night yowling like a tomcat—"

"You're mixing your animal metaphors," Samuel said.

"It's a sign of my exhaustion," Boots said. "All the more reason to say good night. Besides, I know when we get home Mama Liz will be waiting up for me the same as she did when I was sixteen years old."

They said their goodnights quickly, but Samuel and Frances locked eyes for a moment in a silent good night to each other, one that meant, at least to Samuel, *I'd kiss you if I could.*

On the way to the car Boots said, "I wish they sold liquor in that place. Beer always makes me feel so slow and burpy and bloated. I always thought beer was for people who couldn't afford anything better to get drunk on."

"I'm sure that's why my daddy drank it," Samuel said, sliding into the passenger seat.

Boots started the car. "It explains so much, that you come from trash."

Samuel felt like she'd been slapped. "Excuse me?"

"The way you were raised," Boots said. He was backing out of the parking space too fast and nearly hit a truck parked behind them. "If you'd come from a better family, you'd know how to act."

"Boots, I have no idea what you're talking about." They were hurtling down the winding country road.

"Did you think I'm such a fool you could cuckold me and I wouldn't even notice?"

Samuel knew he knew, but hearing him say it made her feel like she was going to throw up. "Boots, who since

Geoffrey Chaucer uses the word 'cuckold?' And since when were you and I supposed to be monogamous, given that we've never slept together? It's not like you don't have a certain gardener tending to your . . . bush."

"A.J. is different, and you know it," Boots said, taking his eyes off the road to glare at her. "Our relationship is completely transactional, and he doesn't cross paths with anybody from any other aspect of my life, so everything is one hundred percent discreet. But for you to have an affair with the wife of one of my closest colleagues—"

"What makes you think I'm having an affair with Frances?" If all else fails, she thought, deny it.

"The fact that I've got more than two brain cells to rub together, for one thing." He was gripping the steering wheel with white knuckles. "Samuel, when the two of you came back from your epic journey to the ladies room, there was lipstick on your mouth. You never wear lipstick. And it was the same color Frances was wearing. It hardly took brilliant detective work to figure that one out. And my superior upbringing forbids me to mention the scent that was on your fingers when you touched my cheek. It was all I could do not to pour a pitcher of beer over my head to decontaminate myself."

"Don't talk about Frances like she's unclean—"

"Yes, defend your lady love," Boots said. He had let the car drift too far over to the left and had to swerve to avoid an oncoming vehicle. "That's the problem with women. You can never separate sex from love."

"We were already in love before we had sex," Samuel said. "Boots, you should really drive more carefully."

"And you really should *live* more carefully. Because you know whose professional lives you're in danger of ruining? Mine and Henry's. And what about Frances? If word gets out that she's some kind of Sapphist, do you think anyone will think she's a fit mother to raise her children? I saved you from the consequences of your actions back when you were in college. I can't save you this time, and you're dragging me down with you."

Samuel wiped back tears. "It's not fair. People should be allowed to love each other."

"Goddamn it, Samuel!" Boots slammed a fist on the dashboard. "It's time for you to grow up and realize that this world doesn't operate in shoulds!"

The car lurched to the right. There was a loud explosion that sounded like a gunshot, followed by a long, snaky hiss. The car ran off the road and came to rest at the edge of a cow pasture.

Samuel looked at Boots. His head was resting against the steering wheel. She thought he might be unconscious, but then she saw his shoulders shaking and knew he was crying. She reached out to touch his arm, but he shook it away.

"Jesus," he said. "Jesus, I'm scared."

"It's okay," Samuel said. "We just blew a tire. I'll get out and change it."

"I'm not talking about the goddamn car." He grabbed her wrist a little too hard. "The two of y'all have at least had the sense not to tell anybody, right? Nobody besides me knows."

Once again, a wave of nausea washed over her. No, she and Frances hadn't told anyone they were lovers. But that didn't mean nobody else knew. Her mind flashed to Susan standing beside the bed, staring wide-eyed, unsure of what she was seeing. "No, we haven't told anybody."

Boots nodded and took a deep, shuddering breath.

"I'm gonna get out and change that tire now," Samuel said. She slammed the door behind her, dropped to her knees, and vomited up the beer and the steak dinner. When she stood, she looked up for a source of light, but the moon was a faint, thin scythe, and the sky was starless.

CHAPTER 20

"AUNTIE EM, WILL YOU COLOR WITH me?" Susan asked. She was sitting at the kitchen table with a box of crayons and a small stack of coloring books.

"Sure, why not?" Frances said. She had taken her first pill of the day about forty minutes ago, and already her thoughts and the world around her were starting to soften at the edges. The pills made everything like an Impressionistic painting—a softer, fuzzier version of reality, stripped of its harsh lines and boundaries. Lovely.

She sat down across from her daughter, who was looking quite lovely herself.

"Which coloring book do you want, Auntie Em?" Susan asked. She fanned out the books on the table like a deck of playing cards.

"The fairy tale one," Frances said.

"I'm going to color the zoo animals," Susan said.

"Good choice." Frances admired how Susan made her decisions with such confidence.

Frances found a picture of Snow White's glamorous wicked stepmother and selected a royal-looking shade of purple to color her dress. It was strangely absorbing, watching the whiteness of the page being overtaken by the color of a plum, ripe and succulent, sour on the outside and sweet on the inside, the juice running down her chin when she bit into its flesh. A sensual fruit. Something about it made Frances think of Samuel, of the way women's bodies were also sensual and juicy.

"Auntie Em, you're coloring outside the lines!" Susan said, as if she were reacting to a natural disaster.

Frances looked down at the page. As her mind had wandered, her coloring had also wandered past the picture's boundaries. "You know what?" Frances said. "I get tired of staying inside lines that somebody else drew. Why don't we draw our own pictures instead?"

"Okay," Susan said. "I'll get paper. I'm going to draw Princess Langwidere."

Frances recalled an illustration in *Ozma of Oz* in which the cruel but beautiful princess stood in front of shelves of seemingly severed heads, trying to choose which one she would wear that day. When she decided she was tired of the head she was wearing, she'd simply remove it and put on another one.

Frances felt a bit like Princess Langwidere herself. A lot of the time she wore the Mommy Head, which she had to balance with wearing The Wife Head. There was also the Faculty Wife Head, which she donned when she had to appear with Henry in public. Some of the heads she wore were public, but others were private. The Writer Head was private, at least until her work felt finished enough to show someone else. And the head she wore when she was alone with Samuel—the head she didn't have a name for—was the most private one of all.

Susan brought the drawing paper and set to work drawing the vain princess and her gallery of heads. Susan was definitely demonstrating some drawing ability, but like most young children, she had no sense of proportion. The princess herself was tiny, and the heads were enormous.

Frances, her edges softened by the Nevermind pill, chose soft colors from the crayon box. She drew nothing with lines or edges, just swaths of color she overlapped with other colors.

"Auntie Em, you're not drawing anything!" Susan said.

"Yes, I am. I'm drawing how I feel."

"You can't draw feelings because you can't *see* them," Susan explained in the voice of an exasperated teacher,

"But once you draw them, you can see them," Frances said, amused to be having a debate about the nature of art with a five-year-old. "It's like music." A sudden idea struck her. "Hang on." She stood up—too quickly—and had to steady herself by grabbing onto the back of the chair. That was something she needed to get used to about the pills. You had to move at the pace they dictated.

Frances went into the study and grabbed Charlie Parker's *Bird at the Roost* from Henry's record collection. She put the record on the turntable and turned it up loud enough so they could hear it from the kitchen. "Listen," Frances said. "You can *hear* feelings, too."

They drew and listened. Frances matched the rhythm of the music with her drawing, and the colors and notes merged into one. After they listened a little more, Frances asked, "So how does this music make you feel?"

"Bored," Susan said, not looking up from her drawing. "You know what song I like? 'The Farmer in the Dell.'"

Frances smiled and agreed that "The Farmer in the Dell" was a good song, too.

When the knocking started, she wasn't sure how to process it at first—maybe because it was more of a banging than a knocking, loud and insistent.

"Auntie Em, somebody's at the door!" Susan said, her exasperated teacher's voice returning.

"Yes, of course," Frances said, reminding herself to get up more slowly.

She opened the door to find the old lady who lived across the street and two doors down—Frances had met her but couldn't remember her name for the life of her—holding Robert, whose face was tomato red and streaked with tears.

"Yes?" Frances said, trying to make sense of the tableau. Why was this old woman, dressed in a faded blue housedress and pink house slippers, holding her baby?

"I went out to check the mail," the woman said. "And I heard this here baby screaming to beat the band."

"Oh, I guess I didn't hear him because of the record player," Frances said, not realizing how bad it sounded until she had already said it.

The old lady narrowed her eyes. "So, you leave a baby on the porch by hisself so you can listen to records?"

"It wasn't like that," Frances said, though really, she probably shouldn't have turned the music up so loud that she couldn't hear Robert if he needed something. The pills made her feel better, but she was pretty sure they didn't make her think better. "On nice days, I let Robert take his late morning nap out on the porch. The baby books all say napping outdoors is good for them—the fresh air and Vitamin D."

The old lady shook her head. "Well, there wasn't no such thing as baby books when I was raising mine. We didn't need 'em. We had common sense."

Frances felt the jab of the insult but knew she was in no position to argue. She held out her arms for Robert, fearful for a moment that the old woman wouldn't let her have him.

But she handed him over. "He's soaking wet," she said.

"I'll change him," Frances said. "Thank you."

The old woman looked her up and down. "Well, I don't want to tell nobody their business, but I wouldn't be leaving my baby out on the porch no matter what some book says. If some gypsies was to pass by, they'd steal a pretty little fair-haired baby like that before you could say Jack Robinson."

"Uh . . . " Frances was confused. Why was the woman talking about gypsies? "Thanks for the advice. Goodbye."

"Was that the Wicked Witch of the West?" Susan asked.

"No," Frances said, "but is there a witch who basically means well but is really judgmental and annoying?"

She carried Robert to the bedroom and laid him on his changing table. "I'm sorry you were upset and wet," she said. She repeated "upset and wet," making it into a rhyming game punctuated by tickles, and just like that, Robert was in a good mood again.

That was the great thing about babies. They didn't hold a grudge.

She changed his diaper and put him in a fresh outfit, then deposited him in his playpen in the living room. "Why don't you play for half-an-hour, and then I'll get lunch ready?"

"Auntie Em, the Munchkin Baby doesn't know what 'half-an-hour' means."

"No, he doesn't," Frances said. "But the more words we say to him, the more he'll learn."

Susan crinkled her forehead. "Auntie Em, was that old lady who came to the door mad at you?"

"No," Frances said, not sure if it was true or not. "She was worried about Robert. But I am a little mad at myself. I made a mistake putting that record on so loud I couldn't hear Robert if he started crying."

"You make a lot of mistakes," Susan said.

Frances reached for a cigarette. "Well, I make some. I don't know if I'd say *a lot*."

"You forgot to wash Danny's baseball uniform when he got it all muddy," Susan said. "And yesterday you burned the brownies, and black smoke was coming out of the oven."

Frances looked at her daughter. Her brilliant, difficult daughter. "Thank you for reminding me of my shortcomings, Dorothy. You keep me humble."

"You're welcome."

Frances knew that if it weren't for the Nevermind pills, the events of the morning would have rattled her more. But now the "arrows of outrageous fortune" that used to prick and pain her bounced right off her.

She opened the pantry and located a can of tomato soup. There was bread in the bread box and cheese in the refrigerator, so lunch was decided. She needed to figure out dinner, too, which was always harder because there were more palates to please, and more effort was expected.

But first things first. She got out a saucepan and the can opener. She was getting the top off the soup can when the phone rang.

"Hello?"

"Frances, it's Samuel. Are you alone?"

"No." She was never alone. Not really.

"Well, can you listen for a minute?"

"Yes." Frances knew that whatever the news was, it was not good. Sharp points of anxiety were stabbing through the pillowy softness of the Nevermind pills.

"Boots knows," Samuel said.

"Knows what?" Frances knew the answer, but she felt the need to stall, to deny reality for just a few more seconds.

"About us," Samuel said. "Apparently we weren't as discreet as we could have been at Opal's and well . . . he's no fool."

"Right," Frances said. Her knees felt weak, and she let herself sink into a kitchen chair.

"He's upset . . . not because I'm involved with a woman but because I'm involved with you, and Henry is his colleague. It's messy."

If Samuel said they couldn't see each other anymore, Frances didn't know what she'd do. Her time with Samuel had been the life raft that was keeping her afloat. "You're not—"

"Saying we can't see each other anymore? Of course not. I couldn't stand it. But we've got to be careful, and we can't meet at the guesthouse anymore, not with Boots's radar on the way it is. It's not safe."

Susan pulled on Frances's shirttail. "Who are you talking to, Auntie Em?"

"Um . . . your daddy. I'm talking to your daddy."

"I want to talk to Uncle Henry!"

"Not right now, sweetie. He's busy at work. He just needed to tell me something. Go play. I'll call you when lunch is ready."

"I'd better let you go," Samuel said.

The statement sounded so final. "No, wait! Where—"

"I don't know where we can meet yet. It's not like two women can rent a room at the Stardust Motel in the middle of the afternoon. But I'll figure something out, and when I do, I'll let you know."

Samuel hung up.

Fear and worry stabbed Frances. If Boots had noticed her and Samuel's feelings for each other that night at Opal's, had Henry noticed, too? If Boots found out she and Samuel were still seeing each other, what would he do? There were too many ifs, and she didn't like where any of them led.

She went to the bathroom and opened the medicine cabinet. She shook out one of the Nevermind pills and swallowed it with a mouthful of water from the sink. She generally took only two pills a day, but the label on the bottle said, "Take one pill in the morning and one in the evening or more as needed." This pill was needed.

CHAPTER 21

Boots had been giving Samuel the silent treatment ever since he had figured out about her and Frances. Boots was such a loquacious person—the consummate raconteur—that his silence changed the climate of the whole household.

This evening as they drank their customary cocktails, Mama Liz was chattering nervously. "So, I saw Hazel coming out of the beauty shop and she says to me, 'Why, Elizabeth McAdoo! I can't remember the last time I laid eyes on you. Maybe if you made it to church more often . . . ' I said to her, 'Hazel Scoggins, don't you get holier than thou on me just because you found Jesus after the change of life. I remember when there wasn't a boy in this town who didn't know the color of your panties.'"

Boots hooted with laughter. "I remember one time you saw Hazel walking up the aisle in church and leaned over and whispered, 'If that woman had as many sticking out of her as she's had stuck in her, she'd look like a porcupine.' So of course, I had to fake a coughing fit."

Samuel laughed, and Boots glared at her like she had no right to be listening in on his and Mama Liz's conversation.

"I swear I don't know what's going on between you children," Mama Liz said. "And Lord knows I try to stay out of y'all's business. But having a three-person cocktail hour when two of the people aren't talking to each other is downright dreary." She stood up and grabbed her cigarettes from the end table. "I'm going to finish my cocktail upstairs. You two *talk.* Married people need to act like grown-ups."

Samuel watched Boots watch his mother ascend the stairs.

When they were alone, Samuel said, "I'm willing to talk."

Boots took a cigarette from his silver case with excruciating slowness. He lit it and took a few drags before half whispering, "Have you stopped seeing her?"

"Yes." It was technically true. Samuel and Frances hadn't seen each other since the night at Opal's because they no longer had a place to see each other.

"All right," Boots said, looking at her directly for the first time in days. "Here's an idea. Why don't you try falling for a girl who's actually gay? Marj and Trish could set you up with somebody."

Samuel winced. "The last girl they set me up with wore overalls and chewed tobacco. I was in the passenger's seat, and she said, 'Pass me that spit can out of the floorboard, would you, darlin?'"

"Well, maybe you can tell them you're in the market for someone more . . . delicate."

"A bulldozer would be more delicate than her," Samuel said.

"I think you mean a bull dyke, honey," Boots said, and they both laughed.

It was surprisingly easy, after days of silence, for them to fall back into the rhythm of their usual banter. It felt good to be friends again even if the renewed friendship was based on a lie. Boots's talk of Marj and Trish had given her an idea which was probably the very last idea he had wanted to give her.

* * *

SAMUEL HAD SUGGESTED THAT THEY MEET at the soda fountain, but Marj had said that too many of her students went to the soda fountain after school, and she didn't want them to see her and Samuel together, no offense.

No offense was taken. Samuel understood why an unmarried high school teacher would worry about being seen in public with a boyish woman. She knew that in Marj's profession, she had to be extra careful, lest she be seen as a corrupter of youth. Marj and Trish never did their grocery shopping together, and they only went out to dinner or movies two towns over. Their only local social outlet was the private parties they knew were safe, like the ones Boots held in the guesthouse.

And so, Samuel and Marj met at the little park on the outskirts of town where the only other people present were two little girls taking turns pushing each other on the swings.

Samuel poured Marj a cup of coffee from the thermos she'd brought.

"Thanks," Marj said, accepting the steaming plastic cup. "I was actually kind of surprised when you called me. I mean,

I think of you as a friend, but we usually see each other more in group settings."

"I guess that's true," Samuel said. She worried she had been too transparent. Marj knew Samuel wanted something from her.

Marj gave a mischievous grin. "You haven't developed a crush on me, have you?"

Samuel felt her face heating up, not from the coffee. "No, but I think you're lovely."

"Good answer," Marj said.

"I wanted to talk to you because . . . I'm in love with someone. And she's in love with me."

Marj's face brightened into a genuine smile. "Why, Samuel, that's wonderful!"

"It is. And she's wonderful. But there are . . . complications."

"There always are for gals like us," Marjorie said. "The course of true love doth never run straight . . . especially when you're not straight. What are the complications?"

Samuel took a deep breath. "She's married."

"Oof." Marj reached into her purse and took out her cigarettes. "That's a complication, all right. Not insurmountable but definitely significant."

"There's more," Samuel said, reaching for a cigarette herself. "Her husband is a friend of Boots's. They work together at the college. The four of us were going out as couple-friends before the thing between Frances and me happened."

Marj looked thoughtful. "And Frances's husband—he thinks you and Boots are just an old-fashioned, garden-variety heterosexual married couple?"

"Incredibly, yes."

"Straight people's obliviousness never fails to amaze me," Marj said. "But it works to our advantage for them to stay that way."

"Yeah, but Boots isn't oblivious. He knows. And he's furious. Wouldn't speak to me for days."

"Because a scandal could spill over into the workplace?" Marj said.

Samuel nodded.

"I can understand that. Folks like us are always terrified of losing our jobs. And for good reason. An ex of mine got fired from a good government job because somebody ratted her out. McCarthy hates queers almost as much as he hates commies."

"No, it doesn't pay to be red *or* lavender these days," Samuel said before changing the subject back to the problem at hand. "Boots made me promise we wouldn't see each other anymore." Samuel was embarrassed to feel tears spring to her eyes. "I can't stop seeing her, Marj. I can't do it."

Marj patted Samuel's shoulder. "Oh, honey, you've gotten yourself into a mess, haven't you? I hope you didn't come to me thinking I'd know how to clean it up."

"No, I wanted to ask you a favor."

"Okay." She sounded apprehensive.

"Frances and I have been seeing each other once a week in the guesthouse. But now that Boots knows, it's not safe. Not that it was ever safe in the first place, I guess, but now, if Boots found out, it would be . . . bad."

"When you say you've been seeing each other in the guesthouse, you mean you've been seeing each other, not . . . vertically?"

Samuel felt herself blush again. "We are rarely vertical," she said.

"So, you were hoping I knew a place where y'all could meet?" Marj asked.

Samuel nodded. "I was remembering that party y'all had last year and how you've got that second bedroom you never use so it'll look like you and Trish sleep in separate rooms. 'The stunt bedroom,' I think you called it."

"You have a good memory," Marj said. "So, you're suggesting that I turn my sweet little bungalow into a house of assignation?" She put her well-manicured hand to her bosom in what Samuel hoped was mock horror.

"It would just be one day a week," Samuel said. "And we'd clear out before you get home from school and Trish gets home from work."

"Hmm." Marj stared off into the distance. "Well, if I agree to this—and I'm not saying I am—there would be conditions."

"Let's hear 'em," Samuel said. She was so desperate she knew she'd agree to almost anything.

"First of all, even if Boots puts you in thumbscrews to interrogate you, you can't tell him I agreed to this. Boots has been my friend a long time, but that would change fast if he found out I knowingly went against his wishes."

"I promise not to tell Boots," Samuel said.

"Second," Marj said, "and this is why I should probably have my head examined if I agree to this—I don't want Trish to know about it either. She has a moral code like you wouldn't believe!"

"Really?" Samuel was surprised. At parties, Trish seemed laid back and maybe even a little naughty.

"She doesn't object to women sleeping together, obviously. But she doesn't like anybody sneaking around and she doesn't like anybody sleeping with a married woman."

Samuel felt a pang of guilt. "I never thought I'd be doing that myself, but—" She trailed off, words failing her.

"But life is complicated, right?" Marj said. "And you don't choose who you fall in love with. At least not with your brain."

Samuel smiled, glad to be understood.

"Okay, I'll leave a key under the flowerpot on the front porch. And you leave that bedroom exactly the way you found it. No mussed covers, no panties on the floor."

Samuel smiled wider. "Thank you. I won't forget this."

Marj patted Samuel on the knee. "Be careful, kiddo. The married ones are tricky."

* * *

THE HOUSE WAS A SUNNY LITTLE cottage in a neighborhood of grandmothers whom Marj and Trish had convinced that they lived together to save money. Like Boots said, straight people believed what they wanted to believe.

The key was under the flowerpot right where Marj had said it would be. But Frances hadn't arrived yet, and Samuel wasn't sure what to do. Going into the house alone made her feel like she was breaking and entering, but staying on the front porch made her feel conspicuous.

She was just about to decide on breaking and entering when Frances came up the walk, her face lighting with recognition. "So, this is the place!" she said. "I think I walked past it five times."

"I'm sorry," Samuel said. "I should have escorted you here or something. I was just trying to be discreet."

"Discretion is all," Frances said. She held onto the stair railing as she ascended the porch steps and looked at her feet as she walked.

"Are you okay?" Samuel asked.

"Right as rain," Frances said. "Just watching my step on unfamiliar terrain. Rain, terrain." She giggled.

Samuel unlocked the door. The house was cozy and clean but with signs of daily life. Breakfast dishes stacked in the sink, two cigarette butts in the ashtray on the coffee table. A large orange tabby cat rubbed against Frances's ankles.

"Well, hello!" Frances said, kneeling down to pet him.

"That's Jimmy," Samuel said. "Marj and Trish have had him forever."

"Well, it's nice to meet you, Jimmy," Frances crooned. "You certainly are beautiful."

"Would you like me to leave so you can be alone with Jimmy?" Samuel said.

"Please don't. No offense, Jimmy." Frances stood back up. She leaned against Samuel. They kissed for a long time because it had been a long time since they'd kissed. When they drew apart for air, Samuel said, "Shall I show you where the bedroom is?"

Frances, short of breath, nodded.

They walked hand in hand with Jimmy following them.

The bedroom had a yellow and white checked bedspread and a painting of sunflowers on the wall. As places of assignation went, it didn't look illicit at all.

Samuel kissed Frances while unbuttoning her blouse and unzipping her skirt. Jimmy sat on the floor and stared.

"Do you think the cat is going to watch us the whole time?" Samuel said.

Frances smiled. "I'm pretty sure the cat is a voyeur." She giggled. "A peeping Tom."

In bed, Samuel thought Frances felt loose-limbed and pliant beneath her, receptive but less active than usual. After Frances cried out, Samuel held her, and soon Frances was snoring lightly.

It was okay. Samuel usually took her pleasure while making love to Frances. It wasn't necessary for Frances to reciprocate.

But there was something about Frances falling asleep that did bother her. The two of them got to spend so little time together, it seemed like Frances would at least want to remain conscious.

CHAPTER 22

FRANCES HADN'T MEANT TO FALL ASLEEP, but before she knew what had happened, Samuel was awaking her with kisses—she had never been woken with kisses before—and telling her it was time to get dressed.

Walking home, sleep still clung to her, but so did Samuel's kisses. She felt wrapped in softness, like when as a little girl she used to roll up in the pink blanket on her bed until it encased her like a cocoon.

She felt like she had been inside a cocoon, in the dark and unaware, until Samuel found her and woke her up. And now she was a beautiful butterfly, spreading her wings . . . and her legs. Frances giggled. The combination of the Nevermind pills and making love in a stranger's house certainly unleashed some flights of fancy!

When she reached the house, she was surprised to see Henry's car in the driveway. She wondered if he had become ill and had to leave work early.

Inside the house, it was strangely quiet. Danny was in his room, improbably doing homework because there was a television program he wanted to watch later at a friend's house. Susan was on her bed, engrossed in playing with the paper dolls she had cut out of construction paper.

"Did Uncle Henry come home?" Frances asked her.

"Uh-huh," Susan said.

"Did Katy leave?"

"I think so." Susan didn't look up from her paper dolls.

Frances hoped that Henry at least had the presence of mind to pay Katy. She couldn't find him in their bedroom or the study. In the kitchen, she called, "Henry, where are you?"

The pantry door creaked open, and Henry emerged. "Oh, hello," he said, as though running into a casual acquaintance.

"What were you doing in the pantry?" Frances asked.

"Well, I was . . . uh . . . a little hungry. I was looking for a snack."

Generally, when Henry wanted a snack he went to the refrigerator where he could find sandwich makings or a hunk of cheese and maybe a cold beer, too. "Did Katy leave?" Frances asked.

"Katy?" Henry said, not making eye contact with her. "She's the babysitter, right?" He was standing in front of the pantry door, blocking it.

Frances knew. There was no use continuing this ridiculous conversation. "Move aside, please," she said.

"Frances, don't," Henry said, but she had already squeezed past him and swung open the door.

In the darkness of the pantry, Katy was struggling to button her blouse with trembling hands.

"Get out." The voice that came out of Frances was stronger and more authoritative than Frances herself was used to. "Get out of my pantry and out of my house and don't come back."

Katy stepped out of the pantry. Tears—of guilt? Embarrassment? Both?—were running down her reddened cheeks. She looked like a little girl. Frances wanted to be mad at her, but she couldn't hold Katy responsible.

There was only one adult in the room besides Frances, and he was the one who deserved her anger. "Did he pay you?" Frances asked.

Katy's eyes widened. "For—"

"The babysitting," Frances said.

"Oh! No, ma'am, but it's okay—"

"I'll pay you," Frances said. "It'll be the last time you ever see a cent from me, though." Frances retrieved a five-dollar bill from her purse and handed it to Katy. "You know the way out."

"Yes, ma'am. I'm sorry, ma'am." She scurried away, shutting the front door behind her.

Something about the way Katy kept calling her ma'am made Frances feel old and frumpy compared to Katy's youth and nubility. It was strange. Just an hour before, under Samuel's touch, she had felt beautiful. She sighed and turned to Henry. "So, we're doing this again, are we? The revolving door of coeds?"

"It's not a revolving door, I promise." Henry held his hands up like he was begging for mercy. "It was just a moment of weakness, that's all."

"If you added up all those moments in our marriage, I wonder what you'd get. Days of weakness? Weeks of weakness? Months—"

"Stop," Henry said. "You know I love you. You know you're my girl. This little dalliance—it meant nothing."

Tears were welling in Frances's eyes. She didn't want them to spill. "That's always what you say. Is it supposed to make me feel better that you're willing to hurt me over something meaningless?"

What was bothering her most was that the "dalliance" had taken place in the same pantry where she and Samuel used to touch and kiss. But their touching and kissing hadn't meant nothing. It had meant everything. And now Horny Henry—she knew the girls at his prior school had called him that—had cheapened the space because he couldn't keep his hands off yet another college girl.

Henry had the sad doggy look that she sometimes found charming. Not today.

"What I mean," he said, "is that it has nothing to do with how I feel about you. My appetites are so huge—"

"Well, maybe you should go on a diet! Women do it all the time with food, living on dry toast and grapefruit halves. Maybe you should try it with sex!"

"Auntie Em, Uncle Henry, why are you yelling?"

Frances looked down, and there was Susan, looking back at them with her intelligent brown eyes.

"We're not yelling, honey," Frances said, hearing herself use that voice parents use when they want children to think everything's all right, even though it obviously isn't. "We're just having a grown-up conversation."

"Well, it's a loud conversation," Susan said. It was just like her to run right into the middle of a conflict. Danny had no doubt heard them, too, but chose to stay hidden in his room, probably writing down lists of favorite baseball players.

"Susan, sweetheart, why don't you go out and play with the kitty?" Henry said. "Your mommy and I need to talk."

"My name is Dorothy," Susan reminded him. "Where's Katy?"

"Katy won't be coming here anymore," Henry said.

Frances wished he hadn't said it. But then, she wished a lot of things.

Susan's eyes filled with tears. "But why? I like Katy. We brush each other's hair like mermaids."

"Because your mommy says she can't come over here anymore," Henry said.

Right now, Frances's biggest wish was that Henry would stop talking. "Henry, please don't make this into my fault."

Susan, her face streaked with tears, said, "Are you mad at Uncle Henry because he hugs and kisses Katy naked in bed?"

Henry sputtered, "It was just that one time—"

"But Auntie Em," Susan interrupted her father, "you said that kissing and hugging naked in bed is a way for friends to be together. You said it when I saw you and Princess Ozma—"

Frances had the sensation of being crushed, of the walls and the floor and the ceiling pressing on her till she couldn't breathe.

"Susan, go to your room NOW!" Henry shouted. He never yelled at the children, and Susan ran to her room as if a monster were chasing her.

"What the hell was she talking about?" Henry said. His face was red and drops of sweat beaded on his forehead.

"Well . . . " Frances's voice, like the rest of her, was trembling. "You know what an imagination Susan—" She stopped herself. She couldn't paint her own child as a liar. Susan was imaginative, but she was also honest to a fault. "Susan accidentally walked in on Samuel and me—"

"*Samuel* and you? That little fucking dyke! Did she . . . attack you?"

Incredibly, Frances felt a laugh bubble up in her throat. Samuel was five feet tall and couldn't weigh more than a hundred and ten pounds. She was hardly a threatening presence. "Attack me? No, of course not. I wanted it. Wanted her. I still do." She dissolved into tears.

Henry ran his fingers through his hair. He paced back and forth. "This is insanity! If you were a giggling schoolgirl or a lonely spinster, it would be different. But you're a mature woman with a husband and children. For you to behave that way—"

"Aren't you in kind of a precarious position to take the moral high ground with me?"

"No," Henry said. "I don't think I am. What I did was succumb to a perfectly normal temptation that would've been equally tempting to any other healthy adult male. What you did—" He regarded Frances like something unpleasant he had just discovered on the sole of his shoe. "I can't even look at you right now."

He grabbed his jacket and stomped out the front door. Because if you were a man, leaving was always a choice. You could go out and find a few drinks and a group of sympathetic male friends, or a girl who didn't make any demands.

But the woman had to stay. Frances couldn't leave the children home by themselves. She had to cook dinner, even though she couldn't imagine eating a bite herself. She had to give Robert a bottle and a bath, and make sure Danny finished his homework. She would make sure Danny and Susan had baths, too, and tuck them into bed. She would comfort them and soothe their fears even though she was consumed with fear herself.

She couldn't walk out and get drunk. She couldn't call Samuel even though she longed to because chances were that Boots or Miz Elizabeth would answer the phone. And even if Samuel did answer, she probably wouldn't have the privacy to talk.

But there was one thing she could do. She went to the bedroom and took her pill bottle from her nightstand drawer. She shook out two pills and swallowed them dry. Today was an interesting day to assess the Nevermind pills's ability to induce apathy.

Never mind that your husband knows about your lover. Never mind that your husband knows your lover is a woman. Never mind that your husband is indulging in the same thoughtless promiscuous behavior that got him fired from his last job. Never mind that he thinks his behavior is normal and yours is aberrant.

Maybe the pills would take her to that state of mind, but in the meantime, the children still had to eat.

She stood in the kitchen, feeling as helpless and lost as if she were in a stranger's house. She didn't want to open the door to the pantry. She had such blissful memories of being in that small, dark space with Samuel, and seeing Katy there, fumbling with her blouse, had made the tiny room seem illicit, dirty.

She went to the refrigerator, where she was reasonably sure a half-naked girl wouldn't be hiding. There was a thawed package of ground beef. Hamburgers. The children loved hamburgers.

She took out the meat and put a skillet on the stove. Mindlessly, she pinched and patted the meat into patties, one for Susan and one for Danny. She couldn't even think about eating.

The smell of the frying patties made her queasy. She wondered where Henry had gone. She wondered how she could get a message to Samuel, but there was no safe way.

Nothing felt safe.

She put the cooked meat on buns and fetched the mustard, ketchup, and pickles from the fridge. She poured glasses of milk for the kids and a double Scotch for herself. "Kids!" she yelled. "Dinner!" Now she just had to make a bottle for Robert, and all the children would be fed. As long as she was taking care of the children, she didn't have to be alone with her fears.

Susan and Danny entered the kitchen cautiously, as if expecting some kind of explosion, but Danny brightened when he saw what was for dinner.

"Hamburgers!" he said. "You made something good for a change."

"I'm not sure if I should say thank you or not," Frances said. The Scotch was steadying her a bit, and the pills were starting to make things softer.

After Danny had downed nearly half his hamburger in a few bites, he said, "Where's Dad?"

"He went out," Frances said and took a slug of Scotch.

"He left because he's mad at Auntie Em," Susan said, taking a small, rabbity bite of her sandwich.

"He *left*?" Danny's voice rose in panic. "He's coming back, right?"

"Of course he's coming back," Frances said with a confidence she didn't entirely feel. "He just needed to cool off."

"What's he sore about anyway?" Danny asked.

Susan said, "He's sore because—"

Frances cut her off. "It's a grown-up problem and not something for children to worry about. Now finish your dinner." She knocked back the rest of the Scotch which, she supposed, was her dinner. Robert fussed in his playpen, reminding her of the bottle she had heating on the stove. She was a little wobbly as she went to retrieve it and told herself to be extra careful picking up the baby.

She sat down carefully at the dining room table and fed Robert his bottle. His baby softness and warmth comforted her. She loved her children so much, even Susan who had squealed on her.

Sometimes, though, she worried she didn't love her children the way other mothers did. Other women seemed to regard having a houseful of children as enough to keep them happy, but Frances always needed something else, too. She needed to write. She needed to read. She needed Samuel. Just thinking her name made tears spring to her eyes.

She blinked and swallowed hard. “Take your plates and milk glasses to the sink,” she ordered the children. “Danny, do you have homework?”

“I finished it.”

Usually, she’d ask to look at it and make sure it was truly finished. Tonight, she was going to take his word for it. “All right. You can walk over to Billy’s house but come straight home once your program is over. Susan, you can play for an hour, but then it’s bath time.”

After Robert finished his bottle, she burped him and deposited him back in the playpen so she could wash the few dishes from the simple meal. The urge to cry was still there, so she poured another drink to sip while she worked.

When would Henry come home, and what state would he be in when he arrived? Still mad but also drunk was her guess. Was it better to have him home and mad and drunk than to not know his whereabouts? Frances didn’t know what to wish for.

But that wasn’t exactly true. What she really wished for was that Samuel would walk through the front door and somehow make everything better.

By the time she finished her drink and the dishes, she felt too tipsy to safely give Robert a bath. She settled for undressing him, sponging him all over with a warm wet washcloth, and changing him into a fresh diaper and pajamas. When she laid him in his crib, she had a strange urge to lie down on the floor and stay near him. Right now, she felt safer with Robert than with any other member of the family. He was too young to get mad at her, too young to ask questions.

Once all the children were in bed, she didn't know what to do with herself. She stared at the phone, thinking of calling Samuel but knowing she couldn't. She sat in an armchair and tried to comfort herself with the cat and a novel, but she was too distracted to focus on the story or consistently pet the cat, who got up in a snit and sauntered away.

She poured a third Scotch—her last one, she promised herself—and walked a tad unsteadily down the hall to the bedroom. She stepped out of her shoes, took off her skirt and blouse, and unfastened her bra and girdle. Even in her distressed state, she still sighed in relief when her breasts and belly were released from their restraints. She slipped on her nightgown and crawled into bed.

Under the covers, she thought of the love she and Samuel had made in this bed, in the guesthouse bed, in the bed at Samuel's friend's house. What if they never got to make love again? What if the last time they did it really was the last time? She cried. It was the audible sob kind of crying, so hard her shoulders shook.

She heard the front door open.

Henry stood in the bedroom doorway. His shirttail was hanging out, and his hair was disheveled. "There you are," he said. His speech was slurred.

"Here I am," Frances said, unable to think of anything else to say.

He stumbled toward the bed and pointed to the glass on the nightstand. "You've been drinking."

"Pot, kettle," Frances said. She wondered if he'd driven to one of the state line beer joints or if he'd imbibed at the house of a male friend who commiserated with his bad luck about getting caught.

Henry sat down hard on the foot of the bed. "You've been cheating on me," he said, like he still couldn't believe it.

"Pot, kettle again," Frances said, draining the dregs of her Scotch.

"It's not the same," Henry said, rubbing his face. "You need help."

If she weren't so upset, the absurdity would have made her laugh. "Henry, you're a Classicist! You know good and well that people in ancient Greece had homosexual affairs all the time. It was perfectly normal."

"The ancient Greeks partook in many practices that are unacceptable in modern society, from public nudity to polytheism. One shouldn't model one's behavior on the norms of the ancient world."

"Maybe I'm just an old-fashioned girl," Frances said.

"Not funny."

"I thought it was."

Henry held the bedpost to steady himself, stood, and started unbuttoning his shirt.

"If you think you're getting into this bed with me tonight, you are very much mistaken," Frances said. The thought of him lying beside her, as though nothing had happened, was unimaginable.

"Why? Does my masculinity offend you?"

"No, your infidelity offends me."

"*My* infidelity?" He laughed.

Frances wasn't going to let him equate his dalliances with her feelings for Samuel. "Henry, it's been a pattern for a decade now. You devour coeds like cupcakes, one right after another. And the school is willing to turn a blind eye if you're discreet. But you weren't discreet back in Connecticut, which is what landed us here."

"Are we going to go over that old story again? I thought we had agreed to put it behind us."

"The story's not that old, Henry. And neither is the child that's somewhere out in the world who's a half sibling to our kids."

The girl Henry had knocked up had been expelled from school and shuttled off to a home for unwed mothers until the baby could be delivered and put up for adoption. Frances wondered about the girl and the baby often. She doubted that Henry did.

"That child was probably adopted into a happy family and has no idea how he was brought into the world."

Frances shook her head. "So, no harm done, right?"

"I didn't say that. Don't put words in my mouth." He looked at her appraisingly. "Are you taking your pills? You seem agitated."

"I am taking my pills. Unfortunately, they can't shield me entirely from normal human feelings."

"Given what I've learned today, I'd hardly consider you an expert on normal feelings."

Frances couldn't argue anymore. It was like when one of the children wanted to play Tic-Tac-Toe and they'd play over and over again with nobody winning. "Take your pillow, Henry. There are blankets in the hall closet."

Frances lay awake despite the substances that were supposed to relax her. Her body felt loose and heavy, but there was a buzzing in her brain that wouldn't go away.

If two pills weren't doing the job, would four be better? She grabbed the pill bottle from her nightstand drawer, shook out two pills and then, reconsidering, a third. She swallowed them then lay back and waited for the blackness to fall upon her.

CHAPTER 23

SAMUEL ALWAYS FELT A LIGHTNESS IN her step on her Tuesday afternoon walk to Marj's house. Tuesday always came when she felt like she couldn't wait one minute longer to see Frances, as though sixty additional seconds without her would cause her to blow to bits like some ill-fated cartoon character.

She hummed to herself as she turned the key in the door—a popular song Boots would dismiss as "insipid pablum." She and Frances had developed a ritual when arriving at the house of assignation. Samuel arrived first and left the front door unlocked. When Frances arrived, she would silently enter and find Samuel waiting for her, either on the couch or on the bed.

Today was feeling like an "in the bed" kind of day. Samuel undressed, slid under the sheets, and waited. After a while, Jimmy the cat jumped up on the bed and butted his head against her arm, demanding to be petted.

"Hey, buddy," Samuel said, scratching his head. She felt a little weird petting the cat while she was naked, but she probably shouldn't have. It wasn't like Jimmy was wearing any clothes, either.

When Samuel checked her watch, Frances was thirty minutes late. Five or ten minutes was normal—it was hard for her to extricate herself from her children—but thirty minutes was unusual. Samuel felt a small prickle of worry.

Once thirty more minutes passed, the prickle of worry turned into a bundle of tension in the pit of her stomach. Something had gone wrong—maybe one of the children was sick, or Henry had come home for lunch unexpectedly—and Frances had no way to contact her. Samuel began to feel foolish lying naked in bed, so she got up and dressed and moved to the living room.

She spotted an issue of a trashy movie magazine on the coffee table. By the time she had read it from cover to cover, she knew Frances wasn't coming.

She was tempted to leave a note for Frances on the front door but knew she couldn't. What if Trish came home before Marj and found it?

She decided to walk the route Frances took from her house to Marj's. She wasn't sure what she expected to find. A trail of breadcrumbs that would lead her to Frances? Frances sprawled, injured or unconscious, on the sidewalk? She winced at the thought. Surely, whatever was keeping her away was nothing serious.

Unsurprisingly, she saw no signs of Frances on her route.

She stopped at the phone booth outside the Piggly Wiggly, dropped in a nickel, and dialed, knowing she was taking a big risk.

"Hello," a chirpy female voice that definitely did not belong to Frances answered.

So, Frances had gotten a babysitter for today just like every other Tuesday. "Um . . . I was trying to reach Frances," Samuel stammered.

"She's not available right now, ma'am. Can I take a message?"

"No message, but do you have any idea what time she might be back?"

There was a pause before the girl said, "Are you a friend of hers, ma'am?"

"Yes. A close one." This conversation was making her increasingly nervous.

"Well, then, I don't guess Professor Harmon would mind if I tell you . . . Mrs. Harmon is in the hospital."

Samuel's nervousness transformed into terror. "Oh my God, what happened?"

"I don't know, ma'am. I just know Professor Harmon said she'd had some kind of accident."

Samuel slammed the phone down. She couldn't breathe in the cramped booth, but when she walked out into the fresh air, she couldn't breathe there either.

The hospital, like everything else in town, was in walking distance. Samuel ran.

When she arrived at the squat brick building, she was panting and soaked in sweat, but she didn't stop to catch her breath.

"Yes?" the formidable gray-haired nurse at the front desk said.

“Could you give me the room number for Frances Harmon?”

The nurse frowned down at a clipboard. “There’s no patient here by that name,” she said.

“But—but I was told she was here!” Samuel said. She was on the verge of crying. She couldn’t remember the last time she cried in public. Had she been a child?

The nurse must have seen how upset she was because she said, “Give me a minute and I’ll see what I can find out.”

“Thank you.” As she stood and waited, Samuel wondered what she would do when the nurse found Frances’s room number. Samuel had to go see her, had to find out if she was okay. But what if she walked into the room and Henry was there? She supposed she’d burn that bridge when she came to it.

The nurse returned, walking silently in her white shoes. “I talked to one of the other nurses and found out about your friend,” she said. “She was brought into the emergency room two nights ago. She stayed here one night and then was transferred to another hospital.”

The blood in Samuel’s veins froze. Whatever kind of accident Frances had been in, she was apparently in such bad shape she couldn’t be treated in a small community hospital. “What . . . what hospital was she transferred to?”

The nurse looked down at some papers on her desk and shuffled them pointlessly. “Our Lady of Peace,” she said, without looking up.

Samuel put her hand on the desk to steady herself. “But why—”

“I’m sorry. That’s all the information I can give you,” the nurse said.

Samuel stumbled out of the hospital and into the blinding late afternoon glare. All her life she had heard the name *Our Lady of Peace* used as shorthand, as in, *if he keeps on talking like that, they're gonna send him to Our Lady of Peace,* or *Lord, if these young'uns drive me any crazier, I'm gonna have to go to Our Lady of Peace.* And now Frances was there, and Samuel couldn't help feeling that she was who had put her there.

CHAPTER 24

THE ROOM WAS WHITE. THE SHEETS on the narrow bed, the nightstand, and the chest of drawers. Everything was white except for the black iron bars that covered the window, letting in only narrow stripes of sunlight.

What looked like a ghost floated in, dressed from head to toe in white. But upon closer observation, the face peeking out from all the whiteness was that of a woman about the same age as Frances's mother.

Frances sat up in bed. Her head felt achy and fuzzy at the same time. She was trying, not wholly successfully, to piece together the events of the past seventy-two hours. She remembered waking up in a hospital and a doctor saying her stomach had been pumped and that they were going to keep her overnight to make sure she was okay, then transfer her to a hospital in Louisville that was better equipped to take care of her. She had argued with the doctor and Henry, too, saying she needed to get home to the children, but at some point, she had been sedated. She had only the vaguest recollection of a long ambulance ride.

"I would say good morning, but morning is nearly over," the nun said. "You need to get up and wash and dress. You have therapy at two, right after lunch."

"Okay," Frances said, throwing off the covers. She decided that if someone were asked to draw a picture of the word *brusque*, this nun/nurse would be the result. Frances cast a glance at the other narrow bed in the room, neatly made and unoccupied. "Is there a roommate?"

"No," the nurse said. "It was decided that giving you a roommate would be too dangerous."

Frances was confused. Surely not all the patients here were criminally insane. "Dangerous for me?"

"No," said the nurse. "Dangerous for them."

"Dangerous how?" Frances had been called some things, but *dangerous* wasn't one of them.

"Mrs. Harmon, you have a history of homosexual behavior. If you were to make an inappropriate advance to a patient in a delicate emotional condition, the consequences could be disastrous."

Is that the kind of person Frances seemed like? Someone who would make lewd advances to mental patients? "But I'm . . . not like that."

"Your records indicate that you are. But I'm not here to argue with you, Mrs. Harmon. I'm just one of the many people here who want to help you get better so you can return to your husband and children."

The mention of her children caused a stab of pain. Who was taking care of them—some nubile coed hand-picked by Henry? Were they eating regular meals? As far as Frances knew, Henry didn't even know how to turn the stove on. And what had the children been told about her absence? Were they worried? Scared? "I hope the kids are okay," Frances said, more to herself than to the specter before her.

"I'm sure they miss their mother," the nurse said. "Children need their mothers." She clapped her hands in a getting-down-to-business way. "Now get yourself dressed and down to the dining hall."

Tears sprang to Frances's eyes as she visualized Robert's round face, his trusting blue eyes. Who was changing his diapers, feeding him bottles? Her arms ached to hold him. "Yes, sister," she said.

The corners of the nun's mouth went up into something approximating a smile. "*Yes* is a word we like to hear around here. The more you say *yes* and carry out orders, the closer you are to seeing your children again." She left the room as quietly as she had entered it.

Frances was wearing only an open-backed hospital gown and underpants. She opened a drawer in the white bureau and was surprised to find a stack of four neatly folded blouses and another stack of skirts. She opened the drawer below and found an assortment of stockings and underthings and a nightgown. A pair of flat shoes and her bedroom slippers sat side by side in front of the bureau. She grabbed a blouse and skirt and clean underthings.

A tiny bathroom with just a sink and toilet was tucked into the corner of the room. Her mouth felt mossy, so she used the toothbrush and small tube of toothpaste that had been laid out for her. She found a washcloth and towel—white, of course—and took what her mother used to call a "French bath" in the sink and ran a comb through her hair. She regarded herself in the mirror. *I look reasonably sane. Can I go now?*

But where would she go? She longed for her children but would be just as happy never to see Henry again. She longed for Samuel, but it was this desire that had landed her in the hospital. It didn't make sense. Why was Frances's love for Samuel symptomatic of mental illness while Henry's compulsion to penetrate every college girl he encountered was not?

She left her room and followed the signs pointing in the direction of the dining hall. White walls, white-draped nuns, white-clad nurses who were not nuns with their stiff, white peaked caps. Even the antiseptic in the air somehow smelled white. It was all so hygienic. Excessive cleanliness made Frances nervous. Always had.

She glanced into a patient's room where a young woman lay curled on the bed, staring vacantly. In another room, an older woman paced back and forth, reminding Frances of a caged tiger she'd seen once in a zoo.

The dining hall was as white and bright as everywhere else. Patients, some in street clothes, some in pajamas, sat at long tables. Some hunched over their trays and ate ravenously; others seemed totally oblivious to the food in front of them. Some looked old enough to be grandparents; others looked young enough to be in high school.

Something about the dining hall reminded Frances of high school—of standing in the cafeteria feeling like a pariah, afraid she would be rejected if she tried to join anyone at a table. Right now, though, she didn't have to make a decision about where to sit. She just had to get in line for her tray. Lines at least were refreshingly mindless; no decisions had to be made.

The steam table was staffed by two older women, one white and one Black, who filled the compartments of each patient's tray with assembly line efficiency: one gray disk of some kind of ground meat, covered in gloppy gravy, an ice cream scoop of mashed potatoes, then green peas, canned peaches, and a small carton of milk. Something about the little milk carton felt especially infantilizing. For Frances, one of the joys of adulthood was that no one could make her drink milk anymore. Here was another small freedom she had lost.

She accepted her tray and looked out at the expanse of tables, finally choosing one where the end was unoccupied. There was no risk of rejection if she chose to eat alone.

A woman who looked to be in her twenties with shoulder-length, wavy dark hair approached Frances's end of the table. "Mind if I join you?" she asked.

"Not at all," Frances said. She didn't feel sociable but didn't want to be one of the mean kids who rejected someone looking for a place at the table. She unwrapped the paper napkin from her silverware to find only a spoon. "I seem to be missing some silverware," she said.

"No." The young woman slid onto the bench across from Frances. "We just get spoons. There are some people here you don't want to give forks and knives."

The thought hadn't occurred to Frances, and she rather wished the young woman hadn't told her. "Fair enough," she said. "But I'm not sure how I'm going to eat whatever this meat is supposed to be with a spoon."

"It's Salisbury steak, allegedly," the woman said. "You'll get used to the spoon. You'll also get so hungry, you're grateful for meat no matter what it is. Wait till you see what they feed us on Fridays."

Frances nodded. Catholic hospital meant meatless Fridays. "I'm Frances, by the way," she said.

"Maureen." The young woman unwrapped her spoon. Both of her wrists were heavily bandaged.

"How long have you been here, Maureen?" Frances asked.

"Ten days. My parents put me here because of this." She held up her bandaged wrists.

She said it as casually as someone might say they wanted a cup of coffee or a slice of cake. "Oh," Frances said. She felt like she needed to tell Maureen something about why she was here, but she didn't feel safe talking about Samuel. "I took too many pills," she said.

Maureen smiled like she had found a kindred spirit. "So, you want to die, too."

"No, not really," Frances said, trying to use her spoon to penetrate the Salisbury steak. "I think I just wanted to . . . feel less."

Maureen nodded. She was much better at eating steak with a spoon than Frances. "Yeah, isn't it better just to feel nothing?"

Frances thought of her children's laughter, of the way Robert, fresh out of the tub and sweet-smelling, felt in her arms. Of the electricity that zinged between her and Samuel when they were together. "No."

Frances thought the room where she had therapy would be an office with a desk and a couch like in the movies. She was surprised when she arrived at the appointed room to find an open space furnished with a circle of folding chairs. A few people, all dressed in street clothes instead of pajamas, were already sitting. They seemed to know each other and talked amongst themselves. Frances stood paralyzed in the doorway, unsure if she was in the right place or not.

A blousy, middle-aged woman with bright lipstick yelled, "Hey, hon! You here for therapy with Dr. Crandall?"

Frances nodded.

"Well, come on in," the woman said. "It's group therapy. We sit in a circle and spill our guts. When the hour's over, the janitor comes in and mops up all the guts off the floor." She chuckled, and a couple of other people joined her.

Frances tried to smile, but her jaw was clenched. She couldn't imagine anything more miserable than a bunch of strangers telling each other their secrets which, due to human nature, wouldn't stay secrets for long. She sat where there was an empty chair on either side of her and looked down at her lap to keep from making eye contact with anyone.

A man with salt-and-pepper hair strode into the room. He was wearing a dark suit and tie and carrying a clipboard. Frances knew immediately that he was not a patient.

"Good afternoon, group!" he said, taking a seat in the circle.

A few patients murmured greetings back.

Dr. Crandall looked around the circle and smiled, reminding Frances of an elementary school teacher trying to be encouraging. "We have a new member we're welcoming into the group today," Dr. Crandall said, "so I think it would be good to do some introductions. Why don't we just go around the circle and take turns? When it's your turn, you can tell us your name and a little bit—just a little, remember—about what you're working on."

The middle-aged lady who had greeted Frances went first. "My name is Doris, and I'm here because I had a nervous breakdown after my mama died. She was always my best friend, and after she passed, I got so I couldn't eat or sleep. I cried all the time and couldn't think straight enough to do my job—"

"Thank you, Doris," Dr. Crandall said.

"Oh, but one more thing," Doris said. "I just want to say that since I came here, Dr. Crandall has helped me so much. I think he's just wonderful."

Frances got the feeling that Doris would happily talk all afternoon if Dr. Crandall would let her. She also sensed from the moon-eyed way that Doris looked at Dr. Crandall that her feelings for him weren't entirely professional. Frances had once read that female patients often fell in love, at least temporarily, with their male therapists.

The next patient in the circle was a too-thin young woman with tired, dark-rimmed eyes. "I'm Elizabeth," she said, barely above a whisper. "I tried to give my baby to my sister because I didn't feel like I was good enough to raise him." She blinked away tears.

Frances felt for her. It was scary becoming a mother, especially when you were as young as Elizabeth was. She couldn't have been any older than nineteen.

The next patient, a man around Frances's age, had lost both his job and his wife because of his explosive temper and mood swings. Another, a young woman, had been picked up by the police as she stood on the railing of a bridge, gathering the nerve to jump.

Frances knew she wasn't going to be able to keep track of everybody's names. She was too overwhelmed by the gallery of human suffering on display.

The patient siting nearest to her was a willowy man in his forties, dressed in wine-colored turtleneck and charcoal gray slacks. When it was his turn to talk, he made a big show of taking out a cigarette and lighting it before he said anything. "I'm Nathan," he said finally, his voice full of ennui. He puffed on his cigarette.

"Tell us why you're here, Nathan," Dr. Crandall prompted.

Nathan rolled his eyes. "I'm here because the bar I frequent was busted by the police. I was arrested, and my name was printed in the newspaper. My boss told me if I came here and rehabilitated myself, I wouldn't lose my job."

"And can you tell us what kind of bar you were frequenting?" Dr. Crandall asked.

Nathan smiled. "Why, yes. As a matter of fact, it was a homosexual bar, Dr. Crandall."

Frances felt a sudden solidarity with Nathan but a sudden fear, too. His reason for being locked up made hers feel more real.

"And so," Dr. Crandall said, "you're here because you want to cure your homosexuality."

"I'm here," Nathan said, "because I don't want to lose my job."

"But in order to keep your job, you have to work at curing your mental illness."

"But is it really a mental illness, Doctor?" Nathan crossed his legs and gestured, Bette Davis-like, with his cigarette. "Am I a nut . . . or just a fruit?"

Frances felt herself smile a little, and a few other members of the group laughed.

"We will return to that question later," Dr. Crandall said. "For now, let's all settle down and let our new member introduce herself."

Frances was determined to talk as little as she could get by with. "I'm Frances," she said.

After she offered no more, Dr. Crandall said, "And why are you here, Frances?"

Damn. He was going to make her talk more. "I'm here because I took too many pills."

"Was it a suicide attempt?" Dr. Crandall leaned forward in his chair.

"I didn't mean for it to be."

"The suicide attempt isn't the only reason you're here, is it, Frances?"

Tears sprang to Frances's eyes. She wanted, almost as much as she wanted to be reunited with Samuel and with her children, to just be left alone. But she was in a place where that never was going to happen. "It's my first day in therapy. Do I have to spill everything now?"

"Of course not." Dr. Crandall leaned back in his chair. "Today you can just listen. But after today, the kid gloves will be off. The only way therapy works is if you talk about your problems, and we explore possible solutions."

Frances nodded and was relieved to feel Dr. Crandall's piercing gaze leave her for the time being.

* * *

When Frances returned to her room, a nun—a different one from the brusque one this morning, but still dressed in a white habit—was fussing over her bed. She looked up at Frances and smiled. "Hello," she said. She was younger than the sister from earlier, perhaps in her early forties, though Frances was beginning to notice that nuns had an ageless quality.

"Hello," Frances said because it seemed too rude not to, though after the enforced togetherness of group therapy, she very much wanted to be alone.

"I was just changing your sheets," the nun said. "Clean linens always make me feel better."

"Thank you," Frances said, hoping the nun, however pleasant, would go away.

"You're welcome. I'm Sister Bernadette. I'll be on duty until midnight tonight."

"I'm Frances."

The sister smiled again, this time with a little nose crinkle. "I know. I have your chart. Dr. Phillips is making his afternoon rounds and will be stopping by to see you. You'll need to stay in your room until you see the doctor, and then you'll have leisure time in the rec room until dinner is served at five-thirty."

"Everything here is awfully regimented, isn't it?"

"A predictable schedule helps patients feel more stable."

"What about spontaneity? That can be good for people, too."

Sister Bernadette smiled again. Her face was heart-shaped, and a constellation of tiny moles was scattered on her right cheek. "A lot of our patients don't do well with spontaneity."

A white-coated man with glasses and a bottle-brush mustache appeared in the doorway. "Good afternoon, sister. Mrs. Harmon," he said.

"Good afternoon, Dr. Phillips," Sister Bernadette replied. "I'll leave you two to talk."

Dr. Phillips looked down at the chart he was holding. "You've already seen me once, Mrs. Harmon, but I doubt you remember it. You were heavily sedated when you arrived."

Frances searched her brain for an image of Dr. Phillips. Nothing. "I . . . I don't remember much about how I got here."

"That's not unusual. Many hospitals who send us patients sedate them more than is fully necessary. Now can I ask you to sit on the bed so I can check your heartbeat and pulse?"

She sat and let him slide the cold stethoscope under her blouse, then hold her wrist to feel the blood beating beneath her skin.

"All normal," he said, making a note on her chart. "So . . . my job is to give you the right medicines to get you well so you can return to your husband and children."

"What kinds of medicines?" Frances asked.

"The kind that will calm you down, make you less agitated," the doctor said.

"But isn't taking too many pills part of the reason I'm here?"

Dr. Phillips nodded. "Yes, but clearly you weren't taking the right kind, or you wouldn't have felt the need to take so many. Also, you weren't taking them under strict enough medical supervision."

"So, if I take the new pills I can leave?"

Dr. Phillips smiled without showing any teeth. "In due course of time. We need to make sure you respond to the medication, and you'll need to continue with your therapy. You and I both know that your overdose isn't the only reason you were brought here. Before we release you, we need to be confident that you will not engage in any more harmful behaviors."

"Harmful behaviors?" Frances said. The phrase made her sound dangerous.

"There's no need to be coy, Mrs. Harmon." His tone was stern. "I am of course referring to your inappropriate relations with a member of the same sex. But sorting all that out is your therapist's job, not mine, thank God. I'll give the nurse your new prescription so you can get started taking the pills tonight."

He left without a goodbye.

The recreation room was a large open space furnished with an old brown couch and armchairs and a variety of card tables, at one of which an old man and a young man were engrossed in a game of chess. Cheerful red and white gingham curtains contrasted bizarrely with the bars on the windows.

Frances was glad, though, to lay eyes on a bookcase stocked with books. Reading was an essential activity for her, but whoever packed her belongings had failed to include any books or magazines.

She made a beeline for the bookcase and perused the shelves. Lots of prayer books and devotionals. Three copies of *Ben Hur.* A hand touched her shoulder. She gasped and turned around to see a burly orderly.

"You can take one of them books back to your room," he said. "But you can't read it in here. You're supposed to be socializing."

Frances nodded her understanding but silently resented how every moment of her time was controlled in this place. She continued to scan the shelves and finally found a section of half a dozen Agatha Christie novels. She had read them all, but the prospect of rereading one, of watching the pieces of the plot fall neatly into place, felt comforting.

She grabbed a book. She really wanted to take it back to her room and escape her life by reading, but she figured the strongman orderly had ways of keeping her here.

"Frances!"

She turned to see Maureen sitting at a card table with a colorful box atop it. "Want to help me put together this puzzle?" she asked.

"Sure," Frances said, joining her at the table. According to the box, the puzzle had 500 pieces and depicted a pair of fuzzy yellow kittens in a basket. She had never had the patience for adult-sized jigsaw puzzles—Why obsess over hundreds of tiny pieces when you could be writing or reading?—though she had helped the kids with their simpler puzzles.

"This is the first time I've gotten to do this one," Maureen said. "Someone else always has it when I come in here." She opened the box, dumped the pieces out onto the table, and started turning them over so the colorful sides faced upward. "I like the picture. I like cats. I have one at home."

"Me, too," Frances said, wishing she had the comfort of Eureka/Hecate curled up on her lap.

Maureen smiled as she kept turning over puzzle pieces.

"Where is home for you?" Frances asked.

"Lexington. My parents are loaded . . . in more ways than one, a lot of the time." She didn't look up from the pieces. "I left home and went to college, but then bad things happened, and I ended up here."

"I'm sorry bad things happened," Frances said. She figured that if Maureen wanted her to know more, she'd tell her. Whatever it had been was bad enough that Maureen had thought cutting her wrists was the best option.

"I like to separate all the outside pieces from the inside pieces," Maureen said. "Will you help me?"

"Of course," Frances said. They sorted pieces for a couple of minutes, then Frances asked, "You know how I told you I ended up here because I took too many pills?"

Maureen nodded.

"That was only part of the reason. The rest of the reason is that I fell in love with somebody other than my husband."

This statement made Maureen look up from her puzzle, wide-eyed. "Really? So, your husband had you locked up here?"

"Pretty much, yeah."

"That's positively gothic . . . like something you'd read in a novel!"

"I'd certainly rather be reading it than living it," Frances said.

"I bet." She looked back down at the puzzle and started sorting pieces again. "So, who did you fall in love with?"

Frances felt a prickle of anxiety. Could she trust Maureen? "I fell in love with . . . Samuel."

"I've always liked that name. What's Samuel like?" She was already fitting some of the outside pieces together.

"Smart. Funny. Kind. Also married."

"Uh-oh," Maureen said. "But he sounds wonderful."

"Who does?" Frances was lost all of a sudden.

"Samuel!"

"Oh, yes, of course," Frances said. She had long ago stopped thinking of Samuel as a man's name—it was *her* Samuel's name, that was all. But of course, Maureen would assume that Samuel was male, and correcting that assumption felt like a rockier road than she wanted to negotiate.

"Hey, can you look for all the yellow kitten pieces?" Maureen asked.

"Sure," Frances said.

Until dinnertime, they focused on the puzzle.

* * *

"MRS. HARMON? MRS. HARMON? YOU NEED to wake up."

Frances was dimly aware of someone shaking her shoulder. Her eyes felt sticky as she tried to open them.

"Are you all right?"

After a moment, Frances was able to orient herself and recognize the brusque nun. She really needed to learn her name. "Yes," she managed, though her tongue felt dry and thick. "Those new pills made me sleep so *hard*."

"You didn't have to tell me that. I've been trying to wake you for fifteen minutes!" The nun actually smiled a little as she presented Frances with her breakfast tray: orange juice and coffee, gloppy gray oatmeal, and a piece of toast with one stingy pat of butter.

"Thank you," Frances said. She was used to being the person who served the food, not the person who was brought it. "I just realized I don't know your name."

"Sister Agnes," the nun said.

Frances drank her glass of orange juice in a few quick gulps. She couldn't remember when she'd been so thirsty. "Sister Agnes," she said, "you know I don't belong here, right?"

Sister Agnes raised an eyebrow. "Mrs. Harmon, that's what every patient in this hospital says."

Maureen wasn't at lunch. Frances scanned the dining hall looking for a place to sit. She took a seat at an empty table. She felt like an outcast, but she couldn't muster the energy to make chit-chat with a stranger. She doggedly spooned her way through a piece of meatloaf that was more loaf than meat, mashed potatoes, and the canned green peas that seemed to do vegetable duty at every meal. She wondered if her children were having lunch and, if so, who had made it for them. What stranger was giving Robert his midday bottle? She fought the urge to cry.

As soon as Dr. Crandall got his perfunctory group therapy greetings out of the way, he turned his attention to Frances. "So, Frances," he said, "we gave you a free pass yesterday, but I'm afraid that pass has expired. Now you need to tell the group why you're here."

Frances felt ten pairs of expectant eyes on her. She could barely find her voice. "I'm . . . I'm here because I took too many pills," she said, barely above a whisper.

"And?" Dr. Crandall prompted.

Frances took a deep breath. "And because I fell in love with someone other than my husband."

"You didn't just fall in love. You had an affair, didn't you?"

The members of the group seemed to be listening with great interest, as if her life were a soap opera they'd just tuned in to.

"Yes," Frances whispered.

"And tell us about the person you had the affair with."

"I'm . . . I'm not giving names," Frances said. Was therapy supposed to so closely resemble a cross examination by Perry Mason?

"Tell us the sex of the person you had the affair with," Dr. Crandall said. He made the word *sex* sound particularly distasteful.

"Oh." Frances realized what he was fishing for and suddenly felt in danger of losing the institutional lunch that was sitting heavily on her stomach. But there was no use denying it; he would only keep pressing her. "Female," she said.

"Way to go, sis!" Nathan said, giving her a pantomimed round of applause.

Dr. Crandall pointed a finger at him. "Nathan, the last thing she needs is your encouragement." He turned back to Frances. "Frances, I will leave the moral instruction to the fathers and sisters on the staff. I want to focus on the psychological aspect of the problem, which is the immaturity of your behavior."

Frances's anxiety turned into anger. "If you're saying it was immature of me to be unfaithful to my husband, then my husband must be even more immature than I am. He's constantly unfaithful to me."

Dr. Crandall smirked. "Is he unfaithful to you with other men?"

It was a strange question. "No, of course not. With younger women, generally his students."

Dr. Crandall nodded thoughtfully. "Well, while I certainly do not condone that behavior, it strikes me as understandable. If he's lacking the warmth he needs from a wife, it makes sense that he would seek that warmth elsewhere."

"So, when he does it, it's not immature?" It never failed to amaze her how men got a free pass for everything.

"No," Dr. Crandall said. "Your infidelity is immature because you turned to a member of your own sex—you, a full-grown woman with a husband and three children—should be demonstrating an adult sexual identity, but instead you have regressed to girlhood, seeking a playmate instead of a partner, perhaps because you envied your father's power and never fully embraced your femininity as a child. We can only move forward in life, Frances. We cannot go back. You must accept your role as an adult woman, as a wife and mother."

Frances wanted to get up and leave. But where would she go? She was locked up. Instead, she said to Dr. Crandall, "I read some Freud in college, and you're plagiarizing him badly. This is bullshit."

"Amen, sister!" Nathan said, laughing.

"A typically immature response from both of you," Dr. Crandall said. "And Frances, watch your language."

"There'll be no more language from me today. I'm done talking." Frances crossed her arms in defiance.

"Fine," Dr. Crandall said. "Perhaps your silence will give you time to reflect on what I've said."

Frances felt wobbly walking down the hallway, badly shaken but still burning with anger. When she got back to her room, Sister Bernadette said, "Sit down, Mrs. Harmon. You look like you've just seen a ghost, and I don't mean me; there's a gentleman on the locked ward who's thoroughly convinced that all of us sisters are ghosts."

Frances sat.

Sister Bernadette disappeared into the lavatory and came back with a small paper cup. Just like forks and knives, real glasses were forbidden at Our Lady of Peace.

Frances drank down the water.

"Was group therapy hard today?" Sister Bernadette asked.

Frances nodded.

"It's never easy, especially at first. Being made to take a

long, hard look at ourselves, especially if we don't like what we see. Do you want to talk about it?"

Frances shook her head. She was tired of talking.

"Okay, well, as soon as Dr. Phillips takes a look at you, you can go to the rec room and relax until dinner."

The rec room reminded Frances of Maureen. "Oh, there was one thing I wanted to ask you," she said.

Sister Bernadette gave a benevolent smile. "Of course."

"There's a girl I ate with and talked with yesterday, but she wasn't at lunch today. I don't know her last name, but her first name is Maureen. Do you know if she's all right?"

Sister Bernadette patted Frances's arm. "It's kind of you to be concerned. Miss Hotchkiss—Maureen—is one of my charges. She's perfectly fine, but she had her surgery this morning. She came through it beautifully but needed today to recover. She should be up and about tomorrow."

Maureen hadn't mentioned any kind of surgery when they'd talked. "I didn't know you did surgery here," Frances said. "I didn't think it was that kind of hospital."

Sister Bernadette laughed. "Well, we don't do much surgery. It's not like we're taking out people's appendixes. But some of our patients do need a very simple procedure performed on their brains."

After a perfunctory visit with Dr. Phillips, Frances sat in the rec room at the same card table where she and Maureen had sat the day before. The kitten puzzle was exactly as they'd left it. She didn't feel right about working on it without Maureen who, after all, was the one with the well thought out puzzle-solving method. If Maureen was indeed back tomorrow, they could work on it then. Frances went to the art station, got a piece of paper and a marker, and wrote a note to leave beside the puzzle: Do Not Disturb—Work in Progress.

CHAPTER 25

"NO OFFENSE, DARLIN, BUT YOU LOOK like hell," Marj said. She was sitting next to Samuel on a park bench. She had come straight from work and was wearing a green sheath dress and pumps, looking beautiful and put together. Her polish made Samuel feel even grubbier.

Samuel knew Marj's assessment was accurate. She couldn't sleep, couldn't keep down so much as dry toast. It had been three days since she'd bathed or changed clothes. "I know it," Samuel said. She held her cigarette in a shaky hand. "Listen, I need to borrow your car. Tomorrow, if I can."

Marj narrowed her eyes. "Why can't you take Boots's car?"

"Because Boots wouldn't approve of what I'm doing."

"This is about that woman, isn't it?" Marj asked.

"Frances," Samuel said, finding herself near tears, which happened frequently. "Her name is Frances. Please don't call her 'that woman.'"

"Okay. This is about Frances, then," Marj said, lighting a cigarette of her own.

Samuel nodded. "She's in the hospital. I have to go see her."

"The hospital's a ten-minute walk from where we're sitting."

"She's not in that hospital. She's in a hospital in Louisville."

Marj looked concerned. "So, it's something serious then?" *Going to Louisville* was often code for being gravely ill.

"She's in Our Lady of Peace," Samuel said. "Because of me."

"Oh, Lord. Her husband found out about y'all and put her away, did he?" Marj shook her head. "Poor girl. Poor you, too."

The tears that were always just below the surface bubbled up and spilled over. "I just . . . I have to see her."

Marj took her hand and squeezed it. "They may not *let* you see her. Maybe if you say you're her sister or cousin or something—"

"I'll say whatever it takes. Does this mean you're gonna loan me your car?"

Marj sighed. "You can have it on Saturday. But Louisville's a long drive. You better bring it back with a full tank of gas."

"Thank you, Marj." Samuel felt like her heart would burst with gratitude. She opened her arms to hug her.

Marj held up a hand. "No hugs. You stink. If you're gonna go up there and try to see her, you've got to pull yourself together. Take a bath. Put on some clean clothes. Brush your teeth and comb your hair. The way you are right now, those headshrinkers are gonna lock you up in there with her."

Samuel sniffled. "At least then, we'd be together."

Marj gave her a look that was either pity or contempt. “You’ve got it bad, don’t you?”

Samuel put her head in her hands. “Real bad.”

* * *

SAMUEL HAD LEFT THE HOUSE BEFORE dawn, leaving a note that said her mother was sick, that she had borrowed Marj’s car to go check on her, and that she would be back late. She knew Boots and Mama Liz would think it was strange, but she hoped they’d be wrapped up enough in their own affairs that they wouldn’t question it.

Marj had promised to leave the car keys in the flowerpot, and she kept her word. Samuel knew that her friendship with Marj had been more take than give lately, and she told herself that soon, once she and Frances could be together again, she would do something extra nice for Marj.

Samuel hadn’t driven a long distance in forever. Under normal circumstances, she would have enjoyed it, but she was having a hard time remembering what normal circumstances felt like. All her emotions now cycled between grief and rage. Grief for Frances and worry about how she must be suffering. Rage at Henry for what he had done to Frances. Of course, he had felt angry and betrayed, but how could he feel justified locking her away like Henry the Eighth locking away whichever wife it had been in the Tower of London? If beheading her had been a socially acceptable option, would Henry have done that?

And then there was rage at the larger world as well—rage at the fact that love between two adults could be considered a disease that needed to be cured. Samuel gritted her teeth and gripped the steering wheel tight. The only thing that could comfort her was the thought that each turn of the wheels took her closer to Frances.

It wasn't easy to find the place. She had a road map, but since was alone, she kept having to pull over to look at it. By the time she got the map refolded (never correctly) and the car restarted, she had forgotten what the directions said. She was unused to big city traffic, and the number of drivers on the road intimidated her. What she really needed was a navigator.

She made a wrong turn and drove around the same park twice, then pulled into a filling station to try to get her bearings, teary with frustration.

The attendant pecked on her window, and she rolled it down. "Need some help, ma'am?" he asked.

She knew her eyes were red from crying, and she hated to look weak, even to strangers. "I'm looking for Our Lady of Peace," she said.

The attendant looked at her appraisingly, as if to say *I bet you are.*

"I'm visiting a friend there," she added.

"Yes, ma'am," he said. "It's not far. What you need to do—" He took a slip of paper from his pocket and drew a small map with a ballpoint pen. It was much easier to read than a roadmap of the whole state.

"Thank you," she said, pressing a dollar tip into his hand.

She had expected the hospital to look gothic and foreboding, built from gray stone, perhaps, with looming gargoyles. But it was a modern, pleasant-looking red brick building with a well-tended lawn and flower beds. She parked the car and checked herself in the mirror. The redness and puffiness of her eyes had subsided, and as Marj had ordered, she was recently bathed and wearing clean clothes. She looked sane and presentable.

The front desk in the lobby was presided over by a tiny nun in horn-rimmed glasses and a white habit with a peculiar sort of bonnet. "May I help you?" she asked, her voice expressionless.

"Yes, ma'am," she said, then remembered what you were supposed to call nuns. "I mean, sister. I'm here to visit a patient."

"The patient's name?"

"Frances Harmon."

The nun opened a binder and scanned through a list of names. "Hm," she said. "It says here that she is allowed no visitors."

Samuel felt her heart sink to her shoes. "That can't be right. I drove three hours to get here. Frances is expecting me." That last part wasn't true, but she knew Frances would be happy to see her.

"According to my records here, Mrs. Harmon is allowed no phone calls, no mail, and no visitors at this time, so how could she be expecting you, or anyone else, for that matter?"

Samuel could tell the nun wasn't buying what she was selling, so she decided to change her tactics. "I . . . I just meant that Frances would expect me to come visit her because I'm her sister."

The nun looked down at the binder, frowning. “I see nothing about a sister being an approved visitor. I only see a note saying that all visitors are prohibited, as per the wishes of her husband, Mr. Harmon.” She looked back up at Samuel, her eyes beady behind her glasses. “Now if you like, I could get Mr. Harmon on the phone—”

“No, don’t do that!” Samuel said, too quickly. “Just . . . please. I’ve come all this way. Couldn’t I see her for fifteen minutes? I’d take ten. Or five, even.”

“Oh,” the nun said, furrowing her brow at something in the binder. “I just saw a note placed in Mrs. Harmon’s file saying that if a woman matching your description comes asking to see Mrs. Harmon, she should be escorted off the property immediately.”

The nun made a small hand gesture, and within seconds, a massive man in a security uniform was standing beside Samuel, holding her upper arm firmly in one of his massive paws.

“No!” Samuel cried out. “I have to see her! She’s—she’s my friend!”

“Come along now, miss,” the guard said. He was at least six-foot-four with a thick neck and shoulders as broad as a barn door. If this man wanted Samuel to be somewhere else, he could definitely make her go there. He marched her to the front door, still grasping her arm.

“It’s not fair!” Samuel protested, feeling sick. “My friend is in this building! Why can’t I see her?”

“I don’t know why you can’t. I just know you can’t,” the guard said, pulling her through the door. “They don’t pay me to understand the rules, just to make sure they get followed. Now where did you park? I'll walk you to your car."

He gripped her arm as they walked across the parking lot, then stood close to the car as she slid into the driver's seat, lest she make a run for it. "The exit's that way," he said. "You drive safe now."

Samuel had pictured a tearful reunion with Frances. In her fantasies, she had even let herself imagine rescuing Frances from the hospital and driving away with Frances next to her on the passenger's side with the window down and her glorious, toffee-colored hair blowing in the wind. The problem with this fantasy was that Samuel had no idea where they'd be driving to.

But none of it mattered now. She saw the foolishness of thinking of herself as a knight swooping in to save her lady love. She hadn't even been able to get through the gate. Henry had bested her, and now there was nothing she could do but drive back home and return Marj's car, the whole expedition a miserable failure. She cried as she drove, seeing the road through a blur of tears.

It was late when she pulled into Marj's driveway, but Marj came out on the porch wearing a fluffy pink chenille bathrobe and pink slippers. "Come sit on the porch with me a minute," she called.

Samuel didn't feel like talking, but didn't feel like she had a choice either, given the favor Marj had done for her. Samuel sank into one of the wicker chairs.

"Did you get to see her?" Marj asked.

Samuel shook her head.

Marj sighed. "I was afraid it would be like that. Her husband's probably cut her off from seeing anybody, but especially you. As far as he's concerned, you're Public Enemy Number One."

"I don't understand," Samuel said, weak from sadness.

"That's because you've never had any power in the world," Marj said, taking a pack of cigarettes out of her bathrobe pocket and offering one to Samuel. "Your friend's husband is a white heterosexual man. The world is made for him. He has the power to make problems go away. And you, my dear, are a problem."

"I'm a person, not a problem," Samuel said under her breath.

"Not to him you aren't. And his wife being a big lez? He ships her off to the bin so they can make that problem go away, too."

Samuel looked up at Marj. "I don't think they can, do you? Make it go away?"

"No, it's not an illness. It's a part of a person's nature."

Samuel smoked in silence, then said, "I don't know what to do."

"Well, I guess all you can do right now is wait. They'll have to release her from the hospital eventually. And then it'll be up to her to make her own choices. But you need to understand—" Marj trailed off.

"I need to understand what?"

Marj smiled, but there was nervousness behind it. "Hell, I don't know. I'm tired. Lost my train of thought." She stood up. "I need to get some rest, and I know you do."

Samuel nodded and stood up, too. "Okay. Thank you for letting me use your car."

"You bet."

Samuel shoved her hands in her pockets and began the dark walk home. She knew Marj hadn't really lost her train of thought; she had stopped herself on purpose. And she knew what Marj had been about to say: "*But you have to understand that she might not choose you.*"

* * *

WHEN SAMUEL FINALLY DRAGGED HERSELF DOWN to the kitchen, the breakfast dishes were already cleared and stacked in the sink. Boots was sitting at the table reading the Sunday paper. He looked up at her. "Well, look what the cat dragged in," he said. "Which is strange since we don't have a cat. Mama Liz went to church, but I just couldn't face the Presbydrearians this morning. You want coffee?"

"Mm-hm," Samuel grunted, sinking into a kitchen chair.

"I'm making you toast, too," Boots said. "You need to eat. Your britches are getting baggy."

Samuel didn't want to eat, but she didn't have the energy to fight him. "Okay," she said.

He popped two slices of bread into the toaster and poured coffee. He set the steaming cup in front of her and said, "How's your mama?"

Samuel hadn't slept well, and her brain was foggy. It took her a second to remember her ruse of visiting her ailing mother. "It's nothing serious. She made it sound bad on the phone, but I think she just picked up a little virus."

"Well," Boots said, retrieving the toast from the toaster, "I was worried. I thought she must be terribly ill since you were gone so long. I was afraid you had to take her to the hospital or something."

"No," Samuel said. "I just visited with her a while and picked up a few things for her at the store."

Boots placed a saucer of toast in front of her and pushed the butter dish and jam pot in her direction. He sat down across from her. "Look, sweet pea, I know we lie to the world, letting them think we're a regular married couple. But I don't think we should lie to each other."

Samuel's hand trembled as she buttered her toast. "What do you mean?"

Boots rolled his eyes. "I mean I'm not as easy to fool as heterosexuals. I know you didn't go see your mama yesterday. You went to see that woman, didn't you? At the asylum up in Louisville?"

Samuel wished she'd put more effort into coming up with a credible story. "It's not an asylum; it's a hospital. And if it's any consolation, they didn't let me see her."

"I'm not surprised," Boots said, his tone softening a little. "A friend of mine—well, he was more than a friend, really—got put away back when I was in college. I tried to visit him, but they said they weren't allowing him to see any friends from his past who might be a bad influence on him."

"It's not right," Samuel said, forcing herself to nibble the toast.

"No, baby, it's a mean old world, and we've got to take care of ourselves—and each other. And ever since you met that woman—"

"You know her name."

"All right. Since you met *Frances*, you've been taking too many risks."

Samuel's eyes welled. She set down her toast. "I can't help it if I love her."

"Maybe not. But even if you can't control your feelings, you can control your behavior. You need to stay away from her. You're walking on a tightrope with no net here, and if you fall, you're gonna bring me crashing down with you." He looked Samuel in the eye. "I need to know you hear what I'm saying."

"I hear you," Samuel said.

"All right, we'll change the subject then," Boots said, brightening a little. "Carlisle and I are going to see the new Ava Gardner picture this afternoon. Do you want to go? I know you fancy Miss Ava."

Under normal circumstances, Samuel did love looking at Ava Gardner—her sloe eyes, her adorable chin dimple—but she was too despondent to imagine herself in the cheerful environment of a movie theatre. "No, I'm not up to it. Thanks, though."

Boots raised an eyebrow. "Are you sure? There's nothing more interminable than a Sunday afternoon at home."

"I'll be fine. I may take a nap. I'm pretty tired."

"After the drive you had, no wonder," Boots said, getting up from the table. "Suit yourself, but don't forget what I told you. I want you to be safe, and I want to be safe, too."

* * *

Boots hadn't been wrong about Sunday afternoons. But then, all time felt interminable these days. She lay on the bed, trying to nap, but all she could achieve was an exhausted, depressed stupor that didn't let her fully lose consciousness.

When the doorbell rang, her first thought was that Priscilla would get it, but then she remembered it was Sunday, so Priscilla wasn't working. Resentfully, she hoisted herself into an upright position and dragged herself downstairs, with the doorbell ringing ceaselessly the whole time.

"Who in the Sam Hill is ringing the bell like that?" Miz Elizabeth called from her room.

When Samuel opened the door, A.J. was standing on the porch. He had his usual slicked back hair and blue jeans, accentuating his roughneck good looks, but he seemed agitated.

"Hey, A.J.," Samuel said. "What can I do for you?"

"Is your husband around?" he asked.

From the way he slurred the "s" in "husband," Samuel inferred that he was pretty drunk. "No, he went to the pictures this afternoon, but I'll be glad to tell him you stopped by."

"He owes me twenty bucks," A.J. said.

Samuel wondered if the twenty dollars was for gardening or for other services rendered.

"I'm sure he'll pay you as soon as he sees you. Boots hates owing people money."

"I need it now," A.J. said.

Something about his tone made Samuel nervous. "Oh. Well, I'll tell you what. If you wouldn't mind waiting just a couple of minutes, I can see if we've got some cash somewhere in the house."

"All right." A.J. walked through the open door into the foyer.

She hadn't invited him in, but since he was in now, it seemed rude to tell him to get out. "Why don't you wait in the living room and I'll see what I can find?"

He nodded, and she hurried to the kitchen. There was always some cash in the cookie jar, but all she could find today was eight one-dollar bills. She had exhausted her own supply on her ill-fated trip to Louisville. She went back into the living room, and A.J., who had helped himself to a couple of fingers of bourbon but was still standing, looked at her expectantly.

"Make yourself comfortable," Samuel said. "I'll be right back."

Samuel climbed the stairs and knocked on Mama Liz's door. She had to knock a little loudly to be heard over the radio. Mama Liz listened to opera with Boots, but behind the closed door of her room, she listened to more popular fare. Samuel was pretty sure the voice she was trying to be heard over was Perry Como's.

"Who was at the door?" Mama Liz yelled.

"It's A.J.," Samuel said. "Is it okay if I come in for a minute?"

"Come on in," Mama Liz said.

Mama Liz's room was as feminine as she was, with pastel floral wallpaper and a dresser covered in perfumes and powders. "I'm in a bit of an awkward situation," Samuel said.

"A.J. says Boots owes him twenty dollars and he needs it now. He's also kind of drunk."

Mama Liz sighed. "Hand me my pocketbook. It's hanging on the back of the door."

Samuel grabbed the patent-leather handbag and gave it to Mama Liz.

Mama Liz took out her billfold and pulled out a twenty-dollar bill. "I don't know if Boots truly owes this boy twenty dollars," she said. "But I do know that now Boots owes *me* twenty dollars."

"Yes, ma'am, he does," Samuel said. "Thank you."

She came downstairs to find A.J. refilling his glass. "Here you go," she said, holding out the bill.

He took it, pocketed it, downed the bourbon, and set the empty glass on the end table. Mama Liz would be appalled that he didn't use a coaster. "So," A.J. said, "the old professor, does he treat you good?"

Discomfort squiggled inside her like a nest of worms. "Yes," she said. "Boots is a good man. I'm sure he'll be mortified that he owed you money—"

"I mean," A.J. said, "does he treat you good, like a woman needs a man to do?"

Her discomfort was turning into something worse. "A.J., that's a very personal question, and when you sober up, I'm sure you'll be embarrassed that you asked it. I think you'd better leave."

"'Cause you see," A.J. went on as if Samuel hadn't said anything at all, "it seems to me that when it comes to women, the old professor don't have no lead in his pencil if you know what I mean. And it's a shame 'cause you're a good-looking gal. Put on a dress and some lipstick, and you'd be a real good-looking gal. But I reckon the old professor makes you dress like a boy on accounta that's what *he* likes—"

"A.J., I need you to leave now." Her voice trembled.

He grinned. "I'll leave, but how about a little goodbye kiss?"

He grabbed her before she could get away. He held her tight, like a captive, not a lover, and crushed his mouth to hers. She could feel his teeth, taste the bourbon and cigarettes. She tried to push him away, but he was holding her so tight she couldn't have much impact. Still pressing his lips to hers, he reached down and tore her shirt open. He was pushing her toward the couch, no doubt so he could get on top of her and . . . She tried to think of an object she could grab to hit him with. A vase? A decanter?

And then he let go. Samuel stepped backward, not knowing what had happened. But then she saw Mama Liz standing behind A.J., holding a mother-of-pearl-handled revolver between his shoulder blades.

"Now you move away from the lady," Mama Liz said. Her voice was soft but somehow more commanding for it. "I'm gonna walk you to the front door, and once you step off this property, you're never coming back here again."

"We'll see what your son has to say about that," A.J. mumbled, though he was moving to the front door with Mama Liz still holding the gun on him.

"I'm the sole owner of this house, so I get to say who is welcome and who isn't. And if you try to come into my house again, I'll shoot you and tell the sheriff I caught you assaulting my daughter-in-law."

"I'm going, I'm going," A.J. said, his hands in the air. "At least now I won't have your faggot son pawing me every chance he gets."

Samuel winced. The truth was out, in the ugliest way possible.

Mama Liz didn't flinch. "I'm still holding a gun, you know. If I was you, I believe I'd move a little faster."

Once she got him out of the door, she locked it behind him.

Samuel collapsed on the couch, shaking. Mama Liz set the gun down on the coffee table, picked up her cigarettes, and lit one. It was the first time Samuel had ever seen Mama Liz light a cigarette for herself. "You saved me," Samuel said.

Mama Liz shrugged. "I never liked that boy. Always thought he was trashy. And he clipped my rosebushes too close. You know, a gal's gotta know how to take care of herself, but sometimes you need a little help."

"Yes, ma'am," Samuel said, too rattled to say anything more.

"It's four o'clock," Mama Liz said. "Do you think the Lord would forgive us if we had our cocktails an hour early?"

"Under the circumstances, I think he would," Samuel said.

"Well," Mama Liz said. "I don't know that there's anything in the Bible that says cocktail hour has to be at five. I kind of wish there was, though . . . it would drive the Baptists crazy. Don't get up. I'll get us some ice."

It was strange being waited on by Mama Liz, but everything in Samuel's life felt strange right now. When Mama Liz handed her a gin and tonic, she gratefully accepted it.

"I mixed it strong," Mama Liz said. "I figured you needed it."

"I do." Samuel drank down three big gulps. The evergreen taste demonstrated that it was heavy on the gin. Samuel tried to calm herself with a deep breath. "Honestly, Mama Liz, if you hadn't showed up, I believe he would've—"

"Oh, we both know what he would've done, unless you'd managed to poke his eyes out or kick him where it counts." Mama Liz sat down in her chair and sipped from her own cocktail. "It must've been petrifying for you, as big and strong as he is, and you not used to being with a man that way."

It took a few seconds for what Mama Liz said to sink in, for Samuel to realize she needed to protest. "But Boots and me—"

"Are married?" Mama Liz said. "Sure you are, honey, but it's not like he's making any late-night visits to your boudoir, is it?"

Samuel felt her face heat up. "Mama Liz, what are you getting at?"

"You know what I'm getting at. I've known what Boots was since he was four years old. It wasn't hard to tell. When his daddy was alive, he was always wanting to make Boots play baseball and fish and hunt, to toughen him up, you know. But it was like trying to toughen up a marshmallow. I finally got his daddy to back off. I knew nothing was gonna change Boots's ways. You can't make people change. You've got to learn to love them the way they are."

"Yes, ma'am," Samuel said, still in shock. "So, you've always known that Boots's and my marriage was—"

"Play acting?" Miz Elizabeth said. "Of course."

Samuel shook her head in disbelief like a wet dog trying to shake off water. "So why did you just go along without saying anything?"

"Huh," Mama Liz said like she had never really thought about it before. "I suppose it's because I wanted to protect Boots. I know life's always been hard for him, and I think there's something about being married to you that made him feel safe. All his life, all I've wanted is for Boots to be safe. And so, I've protected him however I could, whether it's with money and our family name, or with a sham marriage if that's what he wanted. I guess I figured if y'all were putting on a show of being married, I had a part to play, too."

"So, when you criticized my clothes or hair, you were just pretending to be a critical mother-in-law?"

"Lord, no. That was real. I was trying to help you. You do look godawful most of the time. Just because you're a lesbian's no reason to go around dressed like a street urchin out of Charles Dickens."

Samuel could find no words to respond to the absurdity of it all.

"You've been looking worse than usual lately," Mama Liz said.

"Gee, thanks."

"You've been moping all the time, too. I don't know for sure what's happened to you, but if I had to guess, I'd say somebody's broken your heart."

"Something like that," Samuel said, looking at Mama Liz. "How did you get so smart?"

Mama Liz drained the dregs of her gin and tonic. "I got old. If I got my choice, though, I'd go back to being younger, prettier, and dumber."

"Yeah, but then you'd do dumb stuff like get your heart broken."

Mama Liz got a faraway look in her eye. "You know, I may have broken a few hearts when I was a girl, but I never once got my heart broken. I don't think I ever really loved anybody enough to give them the power to hurt me."

"Not until you met Boots's daddy?" Samuel asked.

"Oh, I was including Boots's daddy. He was a good man, mostly, but I never loved him the way he loved me. I'm not even sure I can love that way." She lit another cigarette. "The only love I've ever felt—the kind where you're willing to sacrifice yourself for somebody else—is for Boots. And I felt that from the moment he was born."

"He loves you like that, too," Samuel said.

"I know it." Mama Liz's eyes glittered. It was the closest Samuel had ever seen her come to crying.

"You know," Mama Liz said, "I don't usually overindulge, but it's been a trying day. Maybe we should have just one more cocktail before your husband gets home."

CHAPTER 26

"You can't get better if you don't talk." Dr. Crandall aimed his penetrating gaze at Frances.

She could feel the eyes of the rest of the therapy group on her as well, waiting for her to make some kind of confession or apology. "I don't need to get better. I'm not sick."

Looking irritated, Dr. Crandall shifted in his seat. "If you're not sick, Mrs. Harmon, then why are you in a hospital?"

"My husband put me here."

Dr. Crandall shook his head and smiled. "But that's not the *reason*, is it? If husbands could hospitalize their wives just because they felt like it, this institution would be filled beyond capacity."

"Everybody in this room knows why I'm here," Frances said. "I don't have anything else to say about it."

Dr. Crandall sighed. "Well, if Mrs. Harmon isn't willing to share with us this afternoon, is there anyone who is?"

The blousy middle-aged woman with the obvious crush on Dr. Crandall was more than willing to share. She was so willing, in fact, that eventually Dr. Crandall had to cut her off so somebody else could have a turn.

"How are we today, Mrs. Harmon?" Sister Bernadette asked once Frances had returned to her room.

"Tired," Frances said. It was the only straightforward answer she had given all day.

"Oh, dear," Sister Bernadette said. "Have you not been sleeping well?"

"With all the pills you're giving me, how can I not sleep?" Approximately an hour after swallowing her nighttime pills, she lost consciousness as though she'd been bludgeoned. The morning pills slowed her down, too, but didn't knock her out—they just made her wander through the day in an apathetic haze.

"Well, that's a good point," Sister Bernadette said, patting her on the arm. "You're homesick, I imagine. You miss your children, don't you?"

Frances nodded and felt tears pool in her eyes. Her children's absence was a physical ache.

"And your husband?" Sister Bernadette asked, sounding a little less certain.

At the thought of Henry, Frances's sadness mixed with anger. "Well, he's the reason I'm here and not with my children."

"Then you should be grateful to him for getting you the help you need so you can resume your duties as a wife and mother. Oh, look, here's Dr. Phillips!"

Dr. Phillips stood in the doorway. "Mind if I break up this hen party?"

Sister Bernadette laughed politely. "Not at all, Doctor. If you don't need anything from me, I'll get out of the way so you can talk to Mrs. Harmon."

"Thank you, Sister," Dr. Phillips said. Frances wondered if he called all the nuns "Sister" so he didn't have to learn their names.

After Sister Bernadette left, Frances sat on the edge of the bed as Dr. Phillips performed the ritual of checking her heartbeat, pulse, and blood pressure. When he was done, he asked, "And how are you tolerating the medication?"

"It makes me tired."

Dr. Phillips nodded. "Well, the nighttime pills are supposed to make you tired, of course. The tiredness you feel from the daytime medication should lessen the longer you take it. The goal is for you to be calm and free of erratic impulses."

"What kind of erratic impulses?" Frances asked.

"Oh, I think you know very well what I mean—the kind that took you on a dark path leading away from marriage and motherhood." He picked up her chart and studied it. "Dr. Crandall says you're being uncooperative in group therapy."

Frances felt like the child victim of a tattletale. "How am I uncooperative? I show up for therapy every day."

"Well, according to Dr. Crandall, you show up physically, but that's all. He says that you don't participate, that you meet his questions with either silence or cutting remarks. Don't you want to get better, Mrs. Harmon?"

"I want to get out of here if that's what you mean," Frances said.

"Getting out is the effect. Getting better is the cause," Dr. Phillips said. "If you want to go home, you have to put in some effort. You get out of this experience what you put into it. Do you understand?"

"I understand," Frances said. She was too tired to come up with a cutting remark.

Dr. Phillips patted her knee. "Good. Understanding is a start."

Maureen was sitting on the couch in the day room. Frances felt surprisingly glad to see her—she supposed Maureen was the closest thing she had to a friend in this place. When she approached her, she was shocked to see that the skin around her right eye was bruised, as if someone had punched her.

"Hi, Maureen. I missed you yesterday," Frances said.

Maureen looked up at her, blinking, like someone who's been sitting in the dark and is surprised when the lights come back on. "You know my name?"

Uneasiness washed over Frances. "Yes, and you know mine. I'm Frances."

Maureen smiled a little. "Yes. Of course. Frances."

"May I sit down?"

Maureen nodded.

Frances sat next to her on the lumpy couch. "You had an operation yesterday?"

Maureen nodded. "Yes. On my brain. So I won't feel sad all the time."

"Do you feel sad now?"

"No," Maureen said, her answer sounding like it was coming from far away.

"Well, that's good," Frances said, though she had an increasing feeling of dread. "Do you feel . . . happy?"

"No."

Frances had only known Maureen for a brief time, but she couldn't help feeling that something about her had fundamentally changed. Before, she had gestured with her hands, and her face had conveyed all sorts of expressions. Now her hands lay idle in her lap, and her face was as blank as a hard-boiled egg. "Do you want to work on our puzzle?" Frances said. "I waited because I thought it would be more fun to do together."

"Okay." Maureen stood a little unsteadily and followed Frances to the card table, sitting after Frances sat.

Frances was glad to see that her "Do Not Disturb" instructions had been followed. The pieces they had sorted were still in neat piles.

"What's it supposed to be a picture of?" Maureen asked.

Could she not remember working on the puzzle just two days before? Frances held up the box lid so she could see the picture. "Kittens," she said.

Maureen showed the faintest shadow of a smile. "I like kittens," she said. "Sweet little things."

"Yes, they are," Frances said, feeling more like she was talking to a child than to an adult.

Maureen looked down at the puzzle on the table but didn't make a move to pick up a piece. She looked up at Frances, her eyes vacant. "Will you help me?"

* * *

In her room after dinner, Frances tried to concentrate on reading another Agatha Christie novel, but her mind kept turning back to Maureen, to how hollow she seemed. Frances had seen the bandaged wrists that marked Maureen as a danger to herself. She had no doubt that Maureen "belonged" in a place like this until she recovered enough to be left to her own devices. But was what the doctors had done to her the help she needed?

Sister Bernadette appeared—nuns never seemed to walk into a room, they appeared—beside her bed. "Good evening, Mrs. Harmon. Ready for your nighttime pills?"

"Do I have a choice?" Frances asked.

"Not really," Sister Bernadette said, smiling brightly. She held out a tiny paper cup of pills, a larger paper cup of water.

Frances swallowed everything. "There," she said.

Sister Bernadette looked at her with a crinkled brow. "Something's troubling you. Something different than usual. Is there anything I can do to help?"

"I don't know if anybody here is capable of helping anybody." Frances knew this was a harsh thing to say to Sister Bernadette, who had never been anything but kind to her. But who knew if the kindness was a façade?

"Well, we certainly try to help people," Sister Bernadette said. "But I know the process can feel frustratingly slow. Real change takes time."

"It didn't seem to take much time for Maureen." The words burst out before Frances had time to think about them.

"What do you mean?"

"I saw her today. She wasn't the same person she was two days ago. Not even recognizable."

"Ah." Sister Bernadette nodded. "What you were seeing is typical of a patient who has just been lobotomized. There's often some confusion . . . or slowness. But there's a new peace within as well. The hope is that over time, the slowness and confusion will subside, but the peace will remain."

"Hope," the way Sister Bernadette had used it, didn't sound hopeful at all. "But when you're cutting around on someone's brain, isn't there a risk that you'll cut out the good parts along with the bad?"

"Medical procedures always come with some risks, but Dr. Phillips is very highly trained and very careful."

"Dr. Phillips is who did that to her?" Frances said. A sudden fear gripped her. "Does he want to do that to me, too?"

"Mrs. Harmon, there are institutions in this country—even in this state—which, in my opinion, are too eager to perform prefrontal lobotomies. Here the procedure is only performed if the patient has proven to be unresponsive to other treatments. In these cases, the procedure can be a miracle of modern medicine."

"Am I considered unresponsive?" Frances asked, her fear growing.

Sister Bernadette crossed the room and shut the door. "I'm going to give us some privacy for a moment. If anyone asks why the door was closed, I'll say I was giving you a shot in the bottom. Do you mind if I sit down for a moment?"

"Be my guest," Frances said.

Sister Bernadette pulled the one chair in the room close to the bed and sat down. "I'm going to be frank with you, Mrs. Harmon . . . Frances. You don't have the reputation of being unresponsive . . . at least not yet. But you are getting the reputation of being uncooperative. You don't talk in therapy, you complain about taking your medication, and you won't admit that there's anything wrong with the behavior that brought you here."

"There's plenty wrong with me. I have flaws like everybody else, but that's no reason to lock me away."

Sister Bernadette sighed. "Frances. I know why you're here. I don't condone your behavior. You and your friend deceived your husbands, and deceit is always wrong. But you and your friend's feelings for each other . . . I understand why a woman would want to spend her life in the company of other women. Or even one woman in particular."

"You don't think it's wrong?"

"That's not for me to say. It's God's job to decide what's right and wrong, not mine. For me, growing up in a big Catholic family and looking at my mother's life, I knew I didn't want to produce a big Catholic family of my own. And I did know I wanted an education. The convent was a clear choice for me. Of the choices I had, it was a good one. I love my sisters, and I love being of service. But you . . . your situation is different. You made different choices, and now more choices lie ahead of you. Difficult ones, I fear. But before you face those choices, there's another one you must make, and that's the choice to get out of here."

Frances felt like a prisoner being told it was her choice when to be released. It made no sense. "How is that my choice?"

Sister Bernadette smiled. "Well, as is so often the case in life, there's a game to be played. It's a matter of strategy. No one ever got out of here faster for being uncooperative. Look at Nathan in your group—no release date in sight, and now he's scheduled for a course of electroshock therapy in hopes that it will make him calmer and more compliant. Frances, even if you feel confident that there's nothing wrong with you, you must act as if you feel differently. In therapy, talk about how sorry you are to have hurt your husband, how much you love him, and how anxious you are to return to being the kind of wife he deserves."

"You're a nun, and you're telling me to lie?"

Sister Bernadette laughed. "Well, it does sound bad when you put it that way, doesn't it? I'll say a few extra Hail Marys for penance. But really, what I'm saying is this: I don't think you belong here, but the only way to convince those in authority that you don't belong here is through compliance and obedience. If you want to win the prize, it's the game you must play."

* * *

FRANCES LEARNED TO PLAY THE GAME. When Sister Agnes brought her morning pills, Frances greeted her cheerfully and swallowed what she was given without complaint. In group therapy, she expressed guilt and regret for the way her infidelity had hurt her husband, though he had never been required to express guilt and regret for the way his numerous infidelities had hurt her.

The more dishonest she was, the more the hospital staff seemed to like it. One afternoon, when she was sure she couldn't keep up the façade anymore, she noticed that Nathan was absent from group therapy. She remembered what Sister Bernadette had said about him being scheduled for electroshock treatment and suddenly felt remotivated to resume her disingenuous ways.

Maureen was a daily reminder as well. She spent time with her in the recreation room, but there were no more puzzles. Maureen was too vague, too foggy, to concentrate. Instead, Frances played with her like she was one of her children. She would select two coloring sheets and a box of crayons from the art station, and they'd sit and color together. Coloring carefully within the lines struck Frances as an apt metaphor for the game she was playing. What she really wanted to do was scribble wildly all over the coloring sheet, tear it up, then get a fresh sheet and draw her own picture. She wasn't sure what it would be, but she knew it would be hers.

After a week of total dishonesty, Frances was called in to see Dr. Phillips in his office. He sat behind a huge, polished oak desk. Stuffed and mounted bass and trout hung on the walls. What was it with doctors and fish?

"Good morning, Mrs. Harmon," he said. "Please sit down."

Frances felt nervous, like a child called to the principal's office. But hadn't she been on her best behavior? She sat.

"I thought it was appropriate to see you in a less medical setting," Dr. Phillips said, "since soon you won't be a patient anymore."

It had been so long since Frances had really smiled that it felt almost unnatural. "I won't?"

Dr. Phillips smiled back at her. "You won't. We—Dr. Crandall, the nursing staff, and I—have been impressed with the progress you've made over the past week. I've talked with your husband and have arranged for you to be released on Monday. You'll still need to take your medications, of course, and keep regular appointments with your family doctor."

"Of course." Frances pictured her children's faces and couldn't stop smiling.

"You're a success story, Mrs. Harmon," Dr. Phillips said, standing up. "You have cast off your depravity and are ready to resume a normal life as a wife and mother. We're all very proud of you."

"Thank you, Dr. Phillips."

When Sister Bernadette had told her there was a game to be played, Frances had thought it would take lots of strategy and concentration, like chess, which she had never had the patience for. But it had been easy like Candyland or Chutes and Ladders, one of the simple, colorful board games she played with the children.

All she'd had to do was tell the doctors and nurses what they wanted to hear. It reminded her of a conversation she'd had with Samuel once after they'd made love. Frances had asked Samuel how anyone could look at her and Boots together and think they were a regular married couple. Samuel had shrugged and said, "People see what makes them comfortable."

It was that simple.

When Sister Bernadette came into Frances's room with her nighttime medication, she leaned close to Frances and whispered, "I hear you won."

"I did," Frances said, feeling another smile coming on. "And it was partly because you're an excellent coach."

"Well, thank you," Sister Bernadette said. "I'm glad I could help. I don't think you'll be getting much help on the outside."

Frances felt a twinge of anxiety. "What do you mean?"

Sister Bernadette crossed the room and closed the door. "I mean that you have a difficult path ahead of you. Well, really, there are two paths ahead of you, but you can choose only one. One is a life with your husband, and the other is a life with your lady friend. You can't have both."

"What I want"—Frances paused, feeling the enormity of saying what she wanted out loud for the first time—"is to be with Samuel and the children, to make a home with them."

Sister Bernadette placed her hand on Frances's. "But you know that can't happen. That's not the way the world works. If Henry took you to court, they'd drag out everything they could about you and your friend's relationship, making it sound as sordid as possible. You'd be branded an unfit mother, Henry would get full custody, and you'd be lucky to ever see your children again."

Frances felt a tear leak from her eye. "How does loving Samuel make me an unfit mother?"

Sister Bernadette squeezed Frances's hand. "In my opinion, it doesn't. But my opinion is not the law of the land. It's hard being women—the choices we have are so limited.

The best you can hope for is to have some of what you want, but not all of it."

More tears were sliding down Frances's cheeks. "So, you chose to be a nun so you could have some of what you wanted?"

"That's right."

"But not all of it?"

For a second, Sister Bernadette seemed far away, but then she blinked and was present again. "No, not all of it."

When Dr. Phillips told her she was being released, all Frances had felt was joy. But now when she thought about the future, she felt like the Fool in a deck of Tarot cards, whose next step was going to send him over a cliff. How far would the fall be? What kind of terrain would be at the bottom? Frances hoped for a soft landing.

* * *

FRANCES'S SUITCASE HAD BEEN PACKED SINCE the night before. It had been a four-week stay, but it felt much longer. After she woke, she made the bed like a polite houseguest even though she knew they'd strip it and put on clean linens for the next patient.

Sister Agnes stood in the doorway. She was smiling, a phenomenon Frances had never witnessed. "Who's ready to go home?" she asked.

Frances was a riot of emotions. She couldn't wait to see the children, but Henry was the obstacle she would have to overcome to get to them. And how would she see Samuel? And how soon? "I am," she said, picking up her suitcase.

She followed Sister Agnes down the long white hall to the living room-like space of the visitor area, where Henry sat on the mint green sofa. He stood up as soon as he saw her.

"There she is!" he said, his voice brimming with cheer. He came over to her, took the suitcase from her hand, and kissed her cheek. "Don't you look well!"

"Do I?" Frances asked.

"The picture of health!" he said, beaming at her. There was a theatricality to his cheer—his smile was manically wide, reminding her of old caricatures of Teddy Roosevelt. He was also disheveled, even by her liberal standards. His shirt and trousers were unironed, and his shirt bore the stains of several meals past. She wondered how many days he'd been wearing it.

"Yes," Frances said. Sister Agnes was still standing there, so Frances said goodbye.

The nun nodded at her. "You'll be in my prayers, Mrs. Harmon."

"Thank you," Frances said, not because she was grateful but because she didn't know what else to say.

Outside the sun was so bright it made her squint. Henry tossed her suitcase in the trunk of the car. "I thought I might take you to lunch to celebrate."

Part of Frances wanted to decline anything he offered, but her growling stomach, tired of subsisting on institutional mush, was louder than her conscience. "That would be nice," she said.

They sat at a table for two in an elegant, oak-paneled restaurant in a downtown hotel, feasting on rare steak, baked potatoes, and creamed spinach. Henry had ordered a bottle of red wine for them to split, and Frances was surprised to feel a little tipsy after just one glass, maybe because of the pills she was taking.

"After the food in that place, I can't believe how good this all is." She was having to pace herself not to gobble everything too fast.

"I would've thought the food would've been better, as expensive as it was," Henry said. "The doctors said it was much nicer than the state hospital."

"Nothing but the best for your girl, eh?" Frances said, cutting into her steak.

Henry looked around as if he was afraid someone was eavesdropping. "I wouldn't put it like that, exactly. By the way," he said, lowering his voice, "the children . . . I told them you were in the hospital with pneumonia. I thought it was best."

It was interesting how under most circumstances, lying was considered a moral failing, but when it came to protecting children from reality, it was "best." Danny might have bought the pneumonia story, but she was sure Susan knew better. Frances didn't want to start an argument with Henry over his parenting choices, so she just said, "Can we order dessert?"

Henry flashed that Bullmoose grin. "Of course!"

* * *

"MOMMY! MOMMY! MOMMY!" AS SOON AS she walked to the front door, Danny and Susan ran to her and flung their arms around her. Robert, who was being carried by a gray-haired, square-shaped woman in a faded housedress, reached out his stubby little arms to Frances. Frances held out her arms, and the sitter handed him over. Frances breathed in his sweet and sour baby scent.

"Mommy, why are you crying?" Susan asked. "Are you still sick?"

"No, honey. I'm crying because I'm so happy to see all of you."

"So, you're all better?" Danny asked.

"That's right. No pneumonia," Frances said, shooting Henry a look.

"If you're all better, could you make us some macaroni and cheese?" Susan asked.

Frances laughed. "I'd be delighted to, Dorothy."

Henry paid the babysitter, and soon Frances was in the kitchen, putting on a pot of water to boil and finding some butter, milk, and cheddar cheese in the poorly stocked refrigerator. Danny and Susan sat at the kitchen table and watched her like a TV show. After her lengthy absence, maybe they were nervous about letting her out of their sight.

"You should've seen the macaroni and cheese that babysitter made," Danny said. "She just boiled noodles and threw cheese on top of them. It was disgusting."

"*She* was disgusting!" Susan said.

"Now, now, that's not nice," Frances said, dumping elbow macaroni into the boiling water.

"But she dipped snuff and spat it into a coffee can!" Susan said.

Frances didn't feel like judging anybody. "Well, to each his own, I guess."

After she had tucked all the children into bed, Frances ran herself a bath. Ablutions at the hospital had been short showers, so it felt good to sink into a tub of hot water for a long soak. A leisurely bath was also an effective way to procrastinate what was going to happen next. She pushed Henry from her brain and thought of Samuel instead. She wanted so desperately to call her, to see her, to feel her touch.

Lying in the tub, she tried to touch herself the way Samuel had touched her. It wasn't as good, but the more she imagined Samuel, the better it got until she was able to reach that destination where Samuel had so often taken her.

She wore her oldest nightgown to bed, her hair wet and stringy from the bath. Henry was waiting for her in his undershirt and boxers.

"I hope you noticed," he said, "that the babysitter I hired was of the matronly variety. I figure if you have to behave yourself, then I should, too."

"I appreciate the gesture," Frances said, though she refused to equate Henry's satyr-like qualities with her love for Samuel. She slid into bed, lying as far from Henry as possible.

He scooted closer. "God, I've missed you," he said.

"Maybe you should've thought about that before you sent me away."

Henry put his arm around her in the protective way she used to like. "Don't be like that. I had to do it. I had to save face to keep my job and keep our family together. These small-town rubes don't take kindly to sordid matters like lesbian affairs and drug overdoses."

"There are plenty more sordid things that go on in this town," Frances said.

"Sure, but not where other people find out about them. You have to know your part and how to act it." He touched her cheek. "God, I've missed you."

Before Frances could process what was happening, her nightgown was up around her waist, and he was on her, then in her. She closed her eyes and tried to act her part.

* * *

"MOMMY! MOMMY!"

Frances opened her eyes to the sound of Susan's voice. For one groggy moment, she feared she was reliving the moment when Susan had walked in on her and Samuel in bed. But no, she was in bed next to her snoring husband, where she was supposed to be. The first light of morning was leaking through the bedroom window. "What is it, Dorothy?" she asked. "Is everything all right?"

"Mommy, Eureka had her kittens! Come and see!" Susan reached out her hand to lead her mother to the site of the birth.

Frances allowed herself to be led, letting go of Susan's hand only long enough to put on her bathrobe. She let Susan pull her down the stairs and out onto the front porch where, in a cardboard box lined with an old blanket, Eureka/Hecate lay nursing four tiny fuzzballs that at this point, looked more like mice than cats. Two were solid black like their mama; the other two were tabbies who presumably resembled their absentee father.

"Aren't they beautiful, Auntie Em?" Susan whispered, her tone reverent.

"They are," Frances said, meaning it. She reached down and stroked Eureka/Hecate's head and said, "What a good mama."

"She loves her babies," Susan said.

"Yes, she does." Frances felt her eyes get misty.

Frances loved her babies, too. So why was it that when she looked down at the mama cat, boxed in with her helpless young sucking nourishment from her body, she felt like both of them were trapped?

CHAPTER 27

Samuel sat on the front porch of Marj's house just as she had sat there for the previous three Tuesdays, hoping to see Frances come up the sidewalk.

She was running out of hope.

There was no way for her to reach Frances, no way to know when she was going to be released from the hospital. It was possible that Boots knew something if he talked to Henry at work, but she couldn't ask Boots about Frances, not when their romance was supposed to be over. The only thing she knew to do was to show up at her and Frances's usual meeting place at the usual time like a dog waiting patiently for its deceased master.

But then she saw her. Frances—a little thinner, tired-looking—but still, her Frances.

A smile spread over Frances's face, over her whole body, really, and Samuel stood up. "You're here!" she said, stating the obvious.

"Yes," Frances said, climbing the porch steps. "Despite many people's efforts to the contrary, I'm here."

Samuel hugged her, clung to her, breathing in her scent,

which always reminded her of apples in autumn. Frances hugged her back with equal force but whispered, “We should go inside.”

“Yes, of course,” Samuel said. She fumbled with the key in her eagerness.

Once they were inside, Samuel took Frances in her arms and kissed her hard. No matter how tight she pressed against her, she couldn’t get close enough. Clothes were an especially frustrating barrier, so she unbuttoned Frances’s blouse and unzipped her skirt and was surprised when Frances’s fingers found the button and zipper of her trousers. Leaving a trail of discarded clothing in their wake, they made their way to the bedroom.

Sometimes their lovemaking was soft and slow, but today it was forceful and ravenous. They had been deprived of each other for too long.

When it was over, their bodies were glazed in sweat. Frances laid her head on Samuel’s shoulder and cried.

“Oh, honey,” Samuel said, overcome by tenderness, “Are you okay?”

“No, I’m not,” Frances said, between sobs. “Because I love you so much and I want you so much, but I know this has to be the last time.”

Samuel stopped stroking Frances’s hair. Her insides turned cold. “What do you mean?”

Frances sat up and used the sheet to cover her breasts. “We can’t . . . do this anymore. It’s too dangerous.”

“Dangerous? Is this some idea the nuns at the hospital put in your head?”

"No. I know there's nothing wrong with how we feel about each other, but hardly anybody in this town would agree with me."

"So?" Samuel said, clasping Frances's hand. "Let's leave this town, then. To hell with it. We'll go someplace where there are more people like us, New York, or San Francisco." She pictured herself in a nightclub slow dancing with Frances, surrounded by other girl-girl couples.

Frances shook her head. "I have children."

"We'll take them with us! You know I love Danny and Robert and Susan, even though she snitched on us. We'll be a family."

Frances let out a short, bitter bark of laughter. "Do you think Henry would ever let that happen? And what about when he'd take me to court? Do you think a judge would be sympathetic to a wife and mother who turned out to be a practicing homosexual? I'd be lucky if I ever got to see my kids again."

In her heart, Samuel knew what Frances said was the truth. "So what? We just give up on the best thing that ever happened to us because other people say it's wrong?"

"If it was just you and me, I wouldn't give a good goddamn about what people say. But the kids are still little. They need me."

Samuel knew it was awful, but part of her wanted to say to hell with the children. Henry would make sure they were fed and clothed and educated, wouldn't he? And if Frances left him, he'd remarry soon, and his new young wife could take care of the kids. But even if Samuel felt this way, she knew Frances didn't. And Frances wouldn't be the person Samuel loved if she did. All she could think of to say was "I need you, too."

Frances touched Frances's cheek. "And I need you. But we don't always get what we need."

Frances made a move to get out of bed, but Samuel grabbed her arm. "Please," she said, "kiss me goodbye." When their lips met, Samuel tasted the salt of Frances's tears mixed with her own.

Frances started dressing while Samuel lay in bed, soaking the pillow with her tears. She had never hurt like this before. She would rather be beaten up or physically injured so that she could look at the cuts and bruises on her body and remember the source of her pain. Instead, she had to look at the only person she had ever loved and know she was the source.

"I can't let you go." Samuel's voice was weak and choked.

Frances's eyes were red from crying, but when she looked at Samuel, her gaze was steady. "You have to."

Samuel looked at the way Frances's girdle held in her lush curves. Why did she have to make choices that constrained her? "What . . . what are you going to do?"

Frances retrieved her skirt and blouse from the floor. "I'm going to go home and pay the babysitter, and I'll be there when Robert wakes up from his nap and when Danny gets home from school. I'll start some laundry, and I'll make a meatloaf and mashed potatoes and string beans for dinner—"

"And that's what your life will be like from now on?"

Frances buttoned her blouse. "No, that's what my life will be like until my children are old enough that they don't need me so much anymore."

But how long would that be? Robert wasn't even a year old yet. "What about Henry?" Samuel tried. "You don't love him. You love me."

Frances nodded. "It's true. But no matter what scenario I imagine, he still has all the power."

Samuel wanted to say that this couldn't possibly be right. But just because she wanted Frances's words to be false didn't mean they were. If Frances stayed with Henry, he was her husband whom she had to pamper, pleasure, and privilege. If she left him, his power remained intact because he could convince a judge to deprive her of her children.

Maybe it wasn't that women made choices that constrained them. Maybe it was that women weren't given any real choices at all.

"I'll wait for you," Samuel said.

"No." Frances's tone was firm, as if she were correcting a child. "That's not fair to you. You can't know what's going to happen to you or to me. Don't wait. Live your life. Write your books."

Samuel couldn't imagine living or writing right now. "Books? I haven't even written one."

"But you will. I love you. I'm going to go now."

Samuel sat up in bed, determined to put her arms around her one last time, feeling a little dot of hope that if she did put her arms around her, it wouldn't be for the last time.

"Please stay there," Frances said. "If you touch me, I may not be able to do this."

"That just makes me want to touch you even more." But she stayed where she was. No matter how much she wanted to beg Frances to stay, she couldn't ask her to leave her children. "I love you," Samuel said, then collapsed sobbing into her pillow as she listened to Frances walk out of the bedroom, across the living room floor, and out the front door.

She didn't know how long she lay there crying. At some point the cat jumped onto the bed and curled up beside her, though she wasn't sure if it was for her comfort or his own. Samuel had felt sad countless times before, but she had never felt this level of despair, this certainty that nothing was good and never would be again.

When she glanced at the alarm clock on the nightstand, it was 2:35. Marj would be home in less than an hour. Whatever Marj had signed on for when she agreed to Samuel and Frances meeting at her house, Samuel was pretty sure it didn't include coming home to find a naked weeping lesbian in her bed. Samuel sniffed loudly, wiped her eyes, and got up to find her scattered clothing.

She left the house key on the porch under the flowerpot. She wouldn't need it anymore.

The walk home felt like a slog through knee-deep mud. Kids walking home from school stared out her, maybe because of her masculine clothes or her tears or both.

When she reached the front porch, she hoped fervently that she wouldn't have to see or talk to anyone. But she had no such luck. Priscilla was setting out clean cocktail glasses in the living room. "You all right, Mrs. McAdoo?" she asked in the tone people use when they know you aren't all right.

"Yes, I've just caught a little cold is all." Her voice was pinched and strange. "I'm going up to my room."

"You want me to bring you up a cup of tea or anything?" Priscilla asked.

Samuel had a feeling Priscilla wasn't buying the cold story at all. "No, thank you. I think I just need to rest."

In her room, she kicked off her shoes and collapsed on her bed. She buried her face in her pillow and sobbed. At least it was her own pillow she was now soaking with tears and snot.

At first, she thought the worst thing she could imagine was never seeing Frances again, but then she realized there was something worse.

It was a small town. Boots and Henry worked together. Sooner or later—at the drug store, at an event on campus—Samuel would see Frances again, and when she did, the two of them would be expected to act like nothing more than cordial acquaintances.

Samuel wouldn't be able to do it. The mere thought made her want to scream. Clearly, the only solution was to stay in this room in this bed and never leave. She lay on her side and curled up like a roly-poly, as if making herself as small as possible would make her pain smaller, too.

It didn't.

There was a gentle knock on her door. "Honey?" Boots called. "It's five o'clock. Will you be coming down for cocktails?"

It took Samuel a few seconds to find her voice. What wanted to come out of her were distressed animal sounds. "No. I'm . . . unwell."

"May I come in?"

"I can't stop you." It was his and Mama Liz's house. She was only there by their sufferance.

The door creaked open. Boots came to her bed, sat down, and looked at her. "Oh my stars and garters, you look wretched."

"Thank you," Samuel mumbled, turning her face into her pillow.

Boots touched her shoulder. "She's back, isn't she?"

It was pointless to pretend she didn't know what he was talking about. "Uh-huh."

"And you saw her, didn't you?"

She nodded.

"Bless your heart. Well, is it over now? Really and truly over?"

Samuel wiped her eyes with her shirtsleeves. "Oh, yes."

Boots produced a white monogrammed handkerchief from his jacket pocket and handed it to her. "Good. It's good that it's over. I know it doesn't feel good right now, but it's like when you get a shot at the doctor's. It hurts, but it's for the best."

"This hurts a hell of a lot more than a shot," Samuel said.

"I know it does, baby."

"Boots!" Mama Liz yelled from the bottom of the stairs.

"I'll be right down, Mama!" Boots called, then he turned back to Samuel. "I'll tell you what, I'm gonna get you a glass of water to replenish all those tears. Drink it and get yourself pulled together to come down to dinner."

A couple of hours later, Boots's voice called "Yoo-hoo!" outside the bedroom door. Samuel couldn't muster the energy to answer.

"All right, I'm coming in," Boots said. "I hope you're not nekkid."

Boots was carrying a tray, somewhat unsteadily. "I told Mama Liz you were feeling poorly, and she suggested I fix you a tray. If you can sit up in the bed, I'll put it in your lap."

"I'm not hungry," Samuel said.

"Well, sit up anyway so I can put the damned thing down."

Samuel propped herself up with pillows, and Boots put the tray over her lap. "Try to eat something. You need your strength."

Samuel glanced disinterestedly at the pimento cheese sandwich and cup of hot tea on her tray. "Why do I need to be strong?"

"Because life requires it," Boots said, sitting down in the armchair next to the bed.

"Maybe I'm tired of life."

"Well, you are right now, but that'll get better. You just went and got your heart broke, that's all."

Samuel shook her head. "That's like saying you just got your arms and legs chopped off, but that's okay . . . they'll grow back."

Boots took out a cigarette. "Well, if your arms got chopped off, I wouldn't say what I'm about to say, which is I want to see you pick up that sandwich and eat it." He took out his silver lighter.

"Oh!" Samuel said. "I do want a cigarette. I left my pack at the place where I met Frances." Saying her name caused a sharp pain in her chest.

"Eat, and drink your tea, then I'll give you a cigarette."

Samuel sighed. "You drive a hard bargain." She picked up a sandwich half and took a tiny nibble. The lump that had formed in her throat from hours of crying made it hard to swallow.

"There you go," Boots said. "See if you can eat at least half."

Samuel forced down lumps of bread and cheese with gulps of tea.

Boots smiled, lit her a cigarette with his own, and passed it to her.

"Thank God," she said.

"Thank your loving husband. God doesn't hand out cigarettes; he's notoriously stingy with them."

Normally blasphemy from Boots would've made her laugh, but right now she couldn't even remember what laughter felt like. The cigarette was good though. Good and needed. She'd been so sad she'd forgotten to smoke.

"All right," Boots said. "Time for some straight talk. Well, maybe 'straight' isn't the right word."

Samuel didn't manage even half a smile.

"You're a terrible audience today, you know that? All right. I figure you can get by with this kind of behavior for two more days. After that, Mama Liz will decide you're so sick she needs to call the doctor. Or more likely, she'll figure out you're not sick and will want to know what's going on. She's no fool, you know."

"I never said she was." Samuel ashed her cigarette on her sandwich plate.

"Right," Boots said. "So, by day after tomorrow, you need to get yourself cleaned up and come downstairs for meals and cocktail hour—start playing the game again."

"The game?"

Boots rolled his eyes. "You know," he whispered though no one else was in earshot. "The game where we pretend to be a regular husband and wife."

She had already lost so much. Would she lose anything else by telling him the truth? "Boots, we don't have to play that game anymore when it's just us in the house. Mama Liz knows."

Boots's hand flew to his chest. His mouth formed an *O*. "You . . . you told her?"

"I didn't tell her diddly-squat, Boots. She told me. Like you said, she's no fool. Maybe we should stop trying to play her for one."

"So, she knows I'm—"

"She's known from the time you were a little bitty boy. She said she never said anything about it to you because she didn't want to make you uncomfortable."

"And I was the same way with her." Boots's eyes glittered with unshed tears. "I didn't want to make her uncomfortable. Lord, I don't know what to do with myself!"

"Well, I guess you could start by relaxing in your own damn house," Samuel said.

"I could, couldn't I?" Boots said, sounding both nervous and excited. "Of course, outside the house it has to stay the same with us as man and wife. And I would never want Mama to know about A.J.—it's just too tawdry. Of course, I've not seen A.J. for a couple of weeks. If he doesn't show up on Wednesday, I'm going to call his boarding house to make sure he's still there."

Samuel shuddered thinking of A.J.'s hands and mouth on her. "Don't," she said.

Boots looked confused. "Don't what?'

"Don't call his boarding house. Mama Liz told him to never come back here. It was that Sunday you went to the pictures with Carlisle. A.J. came over asking for money. He was rude and . . . inappropriate with me."

Boots was up on his feet and pacing. "For God's sake, why didn't you tell me this? What did he do?"

Samuel didn't want to relive the experience, especially when she was already so upset. To keep things as simple as possible, she said, "He kissed me. I was trying to push him away, then Mama Liz came in and made him leave."

"And she didn't say anything to me either!"

Samuel shrugged. "I think she put it in the category of girls looking out for each other."

Boots sank back down into his chair. "I can't believe you didn't tell me."

Samuel could scarcely believe she was still capable of producing tears, but here they were. "I thought about telling you. But you were already so mad at me about Frances, I was afraid you'd tell me to get out."

"You think I'd kick you out of your home because that hairy ape tried to force himself on you?"

Samuel wiped her eyes. "That hairy ape is your lover. I thought if it was between him and me, you'd choose him."

Boots snorted. "A.J. is not and has never been my lover. Lovers love each other. He was a hustler I employed for my own gratification, and he clearly forgot his place. But he won't hustle in this town again. I'll ruin him."

"You don't have to do that," Samuel said, surprised by his vehemence.

"But I will, and I'll enjoy it." He rose from his chair and sat on the edge of Samuel's bed. "Honey, I would always take your word over A.J.'s. I may not love you like a husband loves a wife, but I do love you."

Samuel covered Boots's hand with her own. "I love you, too."

"You're gonna make me cry, too, if you're not careful. But you and I are something A.J. and I never were. We're friends. And friends keep each other safe." He gave her hand a squeeze and rose from the bed. "All right. It is my official decree that you get three days to wallow in misery over this Frances business, and then you get downstairs to your desk and get back to writing. Nothing wakes the Muse like a good, old-fashioned broken heart."

* * *

It took Samuel a full week to get back to her writing desk, but when she did, she found that Boots wasn't wrong. Heartbreak was apparently the Muse's close companion. The words, sentences, and paragraphs poured out onto page after page. She became her characters, forgetting for a time about herself, about Frances, about life's daily miseries and indignities. Regardless of how little she slept, she got out of bed each morning at seven, made coffee and toast, and wrote nonstop until five o'clock cocktail hour. Any interruption, such as a ringing phone or a full bladder, was infuriating. After losing Frances, writing was all she had left, and she resented anything that took her away from it.

By five o'clock, though, she was exhausted and hungry and ready for a gin and tonic and whatever meal Priscilla had prepared and left for them. She had taken to washing the dishes after supper, in part because its repetitive nature soothed her troubled mind. Both Boots and Mama Liz chided her, saying that Priscilla could do them in the morning, that that's what they paid her for. But Priscilla already did so much for them, cooking for them and cleaning up after them like they were helpless babies. Surely Samuel could give her a break by completing one small daily task.

The dynamic in the house was different since Boots learned that Mama Liz had never been fooled by their playing house. There was a lightness, a lack of guardedness, and many nights after the post-supper opera record, the three of them would sit at the kitchen table and play Chinese checkers or Scrabble. Mama Liz usually won.

After keeping herself busy all day Samuel would close the door of her room and cry as hard as she had the day Frances had left her. If sleep came, it was because she had cried herself into exhaustion.

* * *

SHE KNEW SHE WAS GETTING CLOSE to the end, but when she found herself writing the last sentence of the last paragraph, she felt instantly bereaved. Without this story to sustain her, what did she have left?

Part of her wanted to start all over from the beginning so she'd have something to absorb her once again. Instead, she got up, stacked the manuscript's pages, and tied it together with twine. Boots was still at work, so she entered his bedroom, with its crimson velvet canopied bed and tapestry of a fox hunting scene on the wall, though Boots had never hunted—foxes, possums, or otherwise. She laid the manuscript on his bed where he'd be sure to find it.

Suddenly, she felt more exhausted than she could ever remember feeling. She crossed the hall to her room, lay down on her bed on top of the covers and fell into a deep, black sleep.

When she opened her eyes, the light outside was gray, and Boots was sitting on the edge of her bed in his burgundy robe and blue satin pajamas. "I'm sorry to wake you," he said, "but I wanted you to know I stayed up all night reading this." He held up the manuscript.

"You did?" she said, her voice thick and dull with sleep.

"I did. And Samuel, it's beautiful and luminous and transcendent. I almost hate you for writing something so good. It beats the hell out of my first book. Or, I suppose I should just say 'my book.'"

"Don't be silly," Samuel said. "My little scribblings can't hold up next to your flawless prose. And when your next book comes out, you're going to put all the literary lions to shame."

Boots shook his head. "You don't understand, precious. The next book isn't coming out, ever. You know how much of that so-called book exists? Thirty-seven pages. I haven't written a word of it in over twenty years."

"But you've written other stuff, right?" Surely, when Boots locked himself away in his study, he was creating the beautiful sentences that made up his evocative stories.

"No, my darlin, in the past two decades I haven't written anything more than comments on a student paper or the occasional letter or dirty limerick. My much-lauded slim novel was born from the exuberance of youth, and now that both the youth and exuberance are gone, all I can do is rest uncomfortably on my rotting laurels at a third-rate teachers's college."

Samuel felt pity but fear, too. Creative power was so mysterious and unpredictable. "Do you think it'll be the same with me? That I won't be able to write anything else?"

"No, baby, you're the genuine article. You're possessed by writing, mad with it. I had the talent but not the dedication. Sitting down and writing every day is too much like work. I'd rather drink gin and chase boys."

"Well, I've given up on chasing girls." She would never feel for someone else what she'd felt for Frances. She wasn't even sure she would want to.

Boots laughed. "Given up? Baby, you've not even gotten started yet!"

"I can't hurt like this again."

"And you won't. Every new love will be a new kind of pleasure, every heartbreak a new kind of pain. But—" he touched her nose with his index finger "—I didn't come in here to discuss your personal life. I came to discuss this stroke of genius right here and how we're going to get it out into the world."

Despite her previous ambitions, Samuel hadn't really thought about the future of the novel after finishing it. She had used its writing as a way not to think about Frances, and once that was over, she hadn't thought beyond leaving the manuscript on Boots's bed.

"I was thinking we should make a copy of this and send it to my agent, along with my letter of recommendation. He's sure as hell not getting a novel from me, so he might as well get one from somebody else."

"You'd do that?" Samuel asked, overcome by his generosity.

"If the work is worthy, you bet your boots I would. And this work is worthy. To tell the truth, I'm as jealous as hell. If I could bump you off and pass the book off as my own, I'd do it."

"But since you're squeamish about that kind of thing, you'll help me instead?"

Boots shrugged and smiled. "If you can't beat 'em, join 'em," he said.

* * *

THE ACCEPTANCE FROM THE AGENT CAME two weeks after she mailed the manuscript with Boots's letter (which she feared laid the praise on a little too thick). The acceptance letter from Kestrel Books, a well-respected medium-sized publisher, had come six weeks after that. Boots scoffed at the amount of the advance and called it stingy, but Samuel couldn't complain. It was more money than she'd ever seen in one place before.

They celebrated by driving to Lexington for steaks and martinis at a restaurant for the horsey set. Carlisle joined them—he had been spending more time with them at the house since Boots and Samuel had dropped their pretense of heterosexuality with Mama Liz. Mama Liz seemed to like him and had declared him "festive."

At the restaurant, Mama Liz positively shimmered. She wore a scoop-necked midnight blue sheath with a string of pearls Boots's daddy had given her for their thirtieth anniversary. Waiters danced attendance on her like she was Hollywood royalty.

"Now if your publisher is gonna send you out on a book tour, you've got to get yourself some new dresses," Mama Liz said to Samuel. "That dowdy little black number needs to be put out to pasture."

Samuel looked down at the "faculty wife dress" she had donned when she had heard the preposterous news that the restaurant required ladies to wear dresses or skirts. "Maybe I don't want to wear dresses on tour. Maybe I want to wear trousers and shirts."

"Well, then get yourself some nice ones. Go to the boys department of a good department store and get them altered to fit."

Samuel sipped her martini. It was cold and strong. "You know, you used to criticize the way I look so much I thought you hated me."

Mama Liz was holding a martini in one hand and a cigarette in the other. "I never hated you. I hated your clothes."

Samuel let herself join in Boots's and Carlisle's laughter. It should've been a lovely night. The steaks were thick and juicy, and the drinks were potent. She was surrounded by people who loved her in their way, the closest thing to a happy family she'd ever known.

But she felt Frances's absence stronger than she felt anyone else's presence.

It was even worse at home. If she caught a glimpse of the guest house out back, her mind filled with images of the blissful hours she and Frances had spent there. The big house had been a place for her to write, a place for her and Boots to perform the lie of their marriage for Mama Liz. But now both of those stories were over, and there was nothing left.

After she drank a cup of coffee and played with a piece of toast, she walked downtown. She was at the door of the dimestore as the cashier was flipping the sign from "closed" to "open."

The cashier opened the door for her. "You're out awful early this morning. You looking for something special?"

For a moment it seemed like a deep question, one she could only answer, yes, but I don't know what. But then she reminded herself that she had come here on a simple errand. "Do you sell suitcases?" Samuel had never owned a suitcase. When she had arrived at college, she had carried her two changes of clothes in a brown paper grocery sack. When she had moved in with Boots, she had brought a paper sack of clothes and a cardboard box of paperback books.

"You mean luggage sets?" the woman said. She wore cat's eyeglasses, but her short curly hair reminded Samuel of a poodle.

"Yes, I guess that is what I mean," Samuel said.

"Well, we don't have a big selection, but there are a couple in the back."

Samuel followed her through an aisle filled with soaps, shampoos, and lotions to a shelf against the store's back wall which was apparently used to house larger items—wagons and tricycles, lamps and end tables.

"We've just got the two luggage sets," the woman said. "They both come with a big suitcase and a smaller overnight bag. There's this powder blue one with gold clasps which is real pretty for ladies, and then there's this plain black one."

"I'll take the plain black one."

"All right," the lady said, sounding puzzled by Samuel's choice. "You need anything else?"

"No, thank you," Samuel said, reaching for the suitcases.

"Oh, those are the floor models," the lady said. "I'll go get you a pair from the back that hasn't been handled. I'll meet you up at the cash register."

The lady disappeared behind a door marked Employees Only, and Samuel walked down the toy aisle toward the front of the store, pausing to glance at jacks and marbles and jump ropes. Her parents had refused to "waste good money" on toys when she was a kid, so she still had a fascination for them.

"I'm sorry I kept you waiting," the cashier's voice said from the front of the store. "I had to help a lady looking for some suitcases."

"Oh, a trip! I don't even know her, and I'm jealous of her."

Samuel would've recognized Frances's voice anywhere. Her heart pounding, she knelt behind a display of play balls and willed herself invisible.

"I'm buying lemon drops for me and jellybeans for my brother because they're his favorite. My big brother, I mean. My little brother can't eat candy because he's just a baby."

It was Susan. Or should she say Dorothy? And what was it she had called Samuel? Princess Ozma. "Dorothy" was a piece of work, and then there was sporty, fun Danny and little Robert with his big, blue, innocent eyes. Samuel wondered what it would've been like in some other kind of world, where she and Frances and the children could've made a home together, and Samuel could have been a lover and partner to Frances and not a father to the children, but something else.

But such a world was as imaginary as Oz. Samuel stayed hidden, waiting for Frances and the children to leave.

Once she was sure they were gone, she stood and walked up to the cash register.

"Are you all right, honey?" the cashier asked.

Samuel hadn't even thought about wiping the tears that streaked her face. "Oh, yes. Just sad. I'm leaving town for a funeral." Lies made people so much more comfortable than truth.

"I'm real sorry to hear that, honey. You travel safe, all right?"

She couldn't bring the suitcases into the house because it would give away her plan. She hid them behind some rose bushes and decided she would get them when Priscilla was busy in the kitchen and Mama Liz had lain down for her afternoon nap.

Once Samuel was inside the house, Priscilla called, "Mrs. McAdoo, is that you?"

This, too, seemed a difficult question, but Samuel said yes.

Priscilla came out of the kitchen, drying her hands on a dish towel. Samuel thought about the different world she had imagined earlier and wondered what kind of world Priscilla might imagine for herself.

"I was gonna ask," Priscilla said, "was it you that signed Gail up for the Young People's Book of the Month Club?"

"It was," Samuel said. She had seen an ad for it in a magazine a month ago, and it had occurred to her that if she wrote a check for the appropriate amount, this company would send Gail a book every month without knowing or caring what color her skin was.

"That was very kind of you," Priscilla said. "I'll get her to write you a thank-you note."

"That would be nice," Samuel said, though she knew she wouldn't be around to get it.

Once she sneaked the suitcases into her room, she packed the large one with a week's worth of underwear and socks, her three least ratty pairs of pants, six shirts, and the pajamas Boots had given her for Christmas which were probably the nicest clothing she owned. In the smaller bag, she packed a comb, a toothbrush, the manuscript of her novel and all the paperback books she had brought with her plus half a dozen more.

She went through the motions of a normal evening at home: cocktail hour, supper, the playing of an opera record. She was quiet, but Boots and Mama Liz knew she was sad, so they didn't seem to find her behavior odd. Boots suggested a game of Scrabble after the record was done, but Samuel said she was tired and had a headache and thought she would turn in early.

Waiting was agony. She knew sleeping would be the best thing to do—if it were even possible—but she would have to set her alarm clock to wake up, and Boots or Mama Liz would surely hear its deafening, spine-shaking bells. And she couldn't read because all her books were packed.

She probably should be planning what was going to come next, but when she thought of the future, it was a blank page that she had no idea how to fill.

There was a soft knock on the door.

Samuel wiped her perpetually leaky eyes and took a deep breath. "Come in."

"Hey," Boots said, standing just inside the doorway. The light of the hallway made his white and yellow seersucker suit glow like the raiment of an angel. "I saw your light on and wanted to make sure you were all right. You need some aspirins or something?"

"No, thank you."

Boots nodded. "I kind of figured you were suffering more from heartache than headache."

"Yeah."

"You want to smoke a cigarette?"

"Sure." It seemed rude to say no.

Boots sat down in the armchair next to the bed, took out his monogrammed silver lighter, and lit them each a cigarette. "You're not going to believe this because people never do, but it'll get easier."

Samuel blew out some smoke and watched the cloud dissipate. "You're right. I don't believe it."

"It's true, though," Boots said. "It's like getting over a sickness. You'll get a tiny bit better every day. At first the improvement will be so slight you won't even notice. But then one day you'll realize that hours have passed and you've not even thought of her once."

"I'd settle for minutes."

Boots smiled. "I know you would."

She teared up again. "I just miss her. Do you miss A.J.?"

"I miss things about A.J. One thing in particular. But it wasn't like you and Frances. It was transactional and therefore transitory. But that one thing I miss? It was transcendental."

Samuel wasn't up to laughing, but she still managed a smile. She would miss Boots.

"Well, I'd better retire to my chambers," Boots said. "Got to roll out early to teach the little mediocrities. Which, I suppose, makes me a mediocrity as well."

Samuel's heart overflowed with fondness for Boots who had taught her so much so well. "You could never be a mediocrity."

Boots rose from his chair. "It's kind of you to say so. Goodnight, sweet pea."

She was the only person in the room who knew that goodnight was also goodbye.

She knew she should leave before dawn, though she didn't relish the idea of having to sit in the bus station for hours waiting for the first departures. When she heard the first birds chirping, she knew it was time to go. She pulled the suitcases out from under the bed and put on her Keds, her quietest shoes.

She tiptoed down the stairs, a suitcase in each hand like a milkmaid trying to balance two full buckets. She crossed the foyer and set down the heavier suitcase so she could open the front door.

"Thought you'd sneak out in the middle of the night, did you?"

Samuel turned toward the source of the voice. Mama Liz's face was partially visible from the glow of her cigarette. She was sitting in her customary chair.

"Uh . . . what are you doing up?" Samuel wondered if her voice could be heard over the pounding of her heart.

"You have to answer my question before I answer yours," Mama Liz said.

There was no plausible lie that Samuel could think up. Besides, she was tired of lies. "Yes, I was sneaking out in the middle of the night," she said.

"And I'm up because I couldn't sleep," Mama Liz said.

Part of Samuel wanted to slink back to her room like she was a teenager who had been caught violating curfew. But she wasn't a teenager. She was an adult woman who could make her own choices.

"Decided there was nothing for you here?" Mama Liz said. "You're probably right. You're young and full of gumption. I always liked that about you. There wasn't much out there for a girl with gumption when I was coming up. I wanted to go to college, but Daddy said I didn't need a college degree to change diapers. So, I got married and had Boots, and Daddy was right—I changed diapers just fine without a college degree." She took a drag of her cigarette, then exhaled a cloud into the semidarkness. "But look at you. College educated, with a book coming out. You don't need to be hanging around here with dinosaurs like Boots and me."

Even though she hadn't walked out the door yet, Samuel felt a pang of nostalgia for the time she had spent with Boots and Mama Liz—the cocktails, the meals, the games, the laughs. "Well, you're very fun dinosaurs."

"That's good to hear," Mama Liz said. "Were you gonna walk to the bus station?"

"Yes, ma'am."

"You want me to drive you?"

It would be easier, Samuel thought, not just because if would save her a half-mile walk with two suitcases, but because it meant that for the very first part of her journey, she wouldn't be alone. "Please."

Eighteen Years Later

THE LINE WAS LONG, PLENTY LONG enough to give Samuel time to consider the fact that she probably shouldn't even be here. But she had seen the ad in the paper then had convinced herself she was just going out for a walk and then ended up standing in a line that snaked around the corner of the bookstore. No one seemed as restless as she was. But New Yorkers were used to waiting in line for things.

Right now, she was living in New York, but as a guest. She was doing one in a seemingly endless chain of writer-in-residence gigs that her status as an author of four well-received, introspective, Southern-set novels gave her. A "writer's writer," she didn't make enough on the books to live, but the one-year residencies at different colleges and universities provided a fairly steady income. They also provided her with a free college-owned apartment or cottage for the time of her stay. She could even opt to eat for free in the school's cafeteria if she chose (she usually didn't). She liked the lightness of this way of life. She had plenty of time to write and no roots to tie her to one spot. By the time she was getting tired of one place, it was time for her to move on to another.

When the line moved forward enough that Samuel was inside the store, she found herself standing next to an easel holding a sign reading:

FRANCES HARMON

SIGNING

WITCHES'S SABBATH

TODAY, 6:00-7:30 P.M.

Seeing her name—and knowing that the woman herself was sitting just a few feet away—increased Samuel's urge to turn and run. But she had come this far.

She comforted herself with the thought that Frances probably wouldn't recognize her anyway. All the faces she saw at events like this had to blend into some kind of indistinct blur. Plus, Samuel had changed markedly since Frances had last seen her. There were crow's feet and a slight turkey wattle, and why were so many signs of aging bird-related, anyway? She had become leaner in middle age and wore her hair mannishly short and parted on the side. Sometimes she got called "sir" by strangers.

"Ma'am?"

Samuel realized that a young, curly-haired woman had been talking to her. "I beg your pardon?"

"I said, will you be purchasing a copy of *Witches's Sabbath*?"

"Yes, sorry."

The young woman handed her a pen and an index card. "Please write down who you'd like Ms. Harmon to inscribe it to."

She wrote down *Samuel* and handed the card and the pen back.

Samuel had seen pictures of Frances in magazines and accompanying articles proclaiming her the Queen of Suspense. But seeing her in person—even from the distance she was from her right now—made her feel weak-limbed and fearful that she would be incapable of speech. Frances's hair was long past her shoulder blades with shining streaks of silver. She wore a black tunic with a loose purple velvet jacket and a long black skirt. Silver bangles clanked on her wrists, and silver earrings dangled low enough to brush her shoulders. She looked radically different from the '50s housewife she had been trying to be when Samuel knew her, but really, she hadn't changed. It was like the person Samuel had always known Frances was had emerged so everyone else could see her.

Samuel watched Frances's well-practiced booksigning ritual. A store employee would hand her a copy of *Witches's Sabbath* with an index card marking the title page. Frances would open the book, glance down at the index card, then look up at the customer and exchange brief pleasantries before signing their book and moving on to the next person.

When Samuel's book reached Frances's hands, she opened it like all the others and looked down at the index card, but something passed across her face—a memory? A feeling? She looked up and then stood up from her chair so fast she knocked it over. Her face was flushed, and she looked equally on the verge of laughing or crying. She took a deep, shuddering breath and finally said, "It's you!"

"Yeah. Hi." Samuel's face burned at the sound of Frances's voice, and she wished she had rehearsed something not stupid to say.

"Wow," Frances said, righting her chair and sitting back down. "I've read all your books and they're wonderful, and I've thought so many times about—" She trailed off, looking at the line of people behind Samuel. "There's no way I can have the conversation I want to have with you like this. I'm done at seven-thirty. Could you maybe . . . wait for me?"

It was better than anything Samuel had let herself hope for.

* * *

NEITHER OF THEM DRANK MUCH ANYMORE, so they ended up at the automat across the street from the bookstore where they sat in the bright dining area over cups of coffee and slices of lemon pie they had selected from little compartments. Everything about the place smacked of an earlier era's idea of modernity.

"Maybe we should've gone to a bar," Frances said. "The lighting would've been more flattering."

"You look great," Samuel said.

"You look great, too."

They did the thing where they both started talking at the same time, then laughed and apologized. After a pause, Samuel said, "You first."

"I don't know where to start! It's been almost two decades."

Samuel sipped her coffee. Somehow its pleasing bitterness seemed to give her courage. "Okay, I'll prompt you. Boots told me y'all moved about a year after I left—that Henry got into some kind of trouble."

"I'm sure you know what kind of trouble it was," Frances said. "But this time the girl complained both to the dean and her daddy who it turned out was a major donor to the school, so—"

"So, bye-bye, Professor Harmon."

"Yes. But then he landed a job at a Jesuit college in Cincinnati—all male students, so that solved a lot of problems. Plus, it got Danny a free college education, and Robert started there last year."

Samuel tried and failed to think of Robert as anything but a chubby infant. "What about Susan?"

"She went to Ohio State. Full academic scholarship. She raised all kinds of hell there—she's a big feminist. She's working on her master's in social work now."

"I'd expect nothing less of her. Even at four she was a force of nature."

Frances smiled the same smile Samuel remembered. "Yeah, she was. And is."

They were silent for a moment, Samuel thinking of how Susan had been a force of nature who, however innocently, had torn the two of them apart. Finally, she mustered up the nerve to say, "So you and Henry—"

"Are no more," Frances finished for her. "We split up right after Robert started college. Once the kids were raised, there was nothing left that we shared. He's in Ohio. I've got a little bungalow in Connecticut about an hour's train ride from the city. But you haven't told me anything about you. I don't even know where you're living."

"Here, for the next academic year anyway. After that, who knows?" Samuel told her about her writer-in-residence gigs at different schools around the country. She told her she was still in touch with Boots, who had retired to Key West with Carlisle after Mama Liz passed. Boots had found her dead in her chair, with her legs crossed and an unlit cigarette in one hand and a glass of sherry in the other. She died, Boots said, without spilling a drop.

Samuel told all she could think of to tell, but there was still something she was trying to get up her nerve to ask. Stalling, she scooped up a forkful of her untouched lemon pie and tasted it. It was remarkable—somehow sweet and sour and creamy all at the same time. It was lovely and complicated, like life. "So," Samuel asked, "since you and Henry split, have you been seeing anyone?"

"No," Frances said. "I just write all the time, which is wonderful. I talk to the kids on the phone a lot. And of course, I have the cats for company."

Samuel smiled. "And how many cats do you have without Henry to rein you in?"

Frances pursed her lips. "Less than a dozen."

"So . . . eleven, then?"

She laughed. "Okay, you're right. I have eleven cats!" When their laughter quieted, Frances said, "How about you? I'm sure there have been a slew of women since me."

"I'd say a few, not a slew." Girlfriends-in-residence, Samuel had taken to calling them. Single women—Samuel was done with the married ones—who were usually on the faculty of the school Samuel was visiting. These relationships generally ended as Samuel's residency ended, as though she had been assigned a girlfriend for the exact duration of her stay. It made sense, though. Most relationships were based on proximity and little more. But that had never been true of her feelings for Frances. "The thing is, though, I've never felt about anyone else the way I feel about you."

Frances's expression was soft but also searching. "Felt?" she said. "Past tense."

"Feel," Samuel said. "Present tense."

"I'm in the present tense, too," Frances said.

And they were, in this bright cafeteria, with its shining white and metallic surfaces. Samuel wasn't sure who reached out first or if they both reached at the same time and met in the middle, but they were holding hands across the table, out in the open. They didn't care who saw.

ABOUT THE AUTHOR

JULIA WATTS IS THE AUTHOR OF fourteen novels and several short story collections in the genres of young adult fiction and adult lesbian fiction/erotica. Her books, set in Appalachia, often depict the lives of LGBTQ people in the Bible Belt. Her most recent novel, *Needlework* (Three Rooms Press), was selected as Tennessee's youth selection for the "Great Reads from Great Places" list for the 2022 National Book Festival of the Library of Congress, and won Honorable Mention for Best YA novel of the year in the *Foreword* Indies awards. Her novel, *Quiver* (Three Rooms Press), set in rural Tennessee, was selected for the American Library Association's Rainbow List. Her novel *Secret City* (Bella Books) was a finalist for the Lambda Literary Award and a winner of a Golden Crown Literary Award. Her novel *Finding H.F.* (Alyson Press) won the Lambda Literary Award in the children/young adult category. In 2020 Watts was given the Tennessee Library Association's Intellectual Freedom Award. She lives in Knoxville, TN.

RECENT AND FORTHCOMING BOOKS FROM THREE ROOMS PRESS

FICTION

Lucy Jane Bledsoe
No Stopping Us Now

Rishab Borah
The Door to Inferna

Meagan Brothers
Weird Girl and What's His Name

Christopher Chambers
Scavenger
Standalone

Ebele Chizea
Aquarian Dawn

Ron Dakron
Hello Devilfish!

Robert Duncan
Loudmouth

Michael T. Fournier
Hidden Wheel
Swing State

Aaron Hamburger
Nirvana Is Here

William Least Heat-Moon
Celestial Mechanics

Aimee Herman
Everything Grows

Kelly Ann Jacobson
Tink and Wendy
Robin and Her Misfits

Jethro K. Lieberman
Everything Is Jake

Eamon Loingsigh
Light of the Diddicoy
Exile on Bridge Street

John Marshall
The Greenfather

Alvin Orloff
Vulgarian Rhapsody

Micki Ravizee
Of Blood and Lightning

Aram Saroyan
Still Night in L.A.

Robert Silverberg
The Face of the Waters

Stephen Spotte
Animal Wrongs

Richard Vetere
The Writers Afterlife
Champagne and Cocaine

Jessamyn Violet
Secret Rules to Being a Rockstar

Julia Watts
Quiver
Needlework
Lovesick Blossoms

Gina Yates
Narcissus Nobody

MEMOIR & BIOGRAPHY

Nassrine Azimi and Michel Wasserman
Last Boat to Yokohama: The Life and Legacy of Beate Sirota Gordon

William S. Burroughs & Allen Ginsberg
Don't Hide the Madness: William S. Burroughs in Conversation with Allen Ginsberg edited by Steven Taylor

James Carr
BAD: The Autobiography of James Carr

Judy Gumbo
Yippie Girl: Exploits in Protest and Defeating the FBI

Judith Malina
Full Moon Stages: Personal Notes from 50 Years of The Living Theatre

Phil Marcade
Punk Avenue: Inside the New York City Underground, 1972–1982

Jillian Marshall
Japanthem: Counter-Cultural Experiences; Cross-Cultural Remixes

Alvin Orloff
Disasterama! Adventures in the Queer Underground 1977–1997

Nicca Ray
Ray by Ray: A Daughter's Take on the Legend of Nicholas Ray

Stephen Spotte
My Watery Self: Memoirs of a Marine Scientist

PHOTOGRAPHY-MEMOIR

Mike Watt
On & Off Bass

SHORT STORY ANTHOLOGIES

SINGLE AUTHOR

Alien Archives: Stories
by Robert Silverberg

First-Person Singularities: Stories
by Robert Silverberg
with an introduction by John Scalzi

Tales from the Eternal Café: Stories
by Janet Hamill, with an introduction by Patti Smith

Time and Time Again: Sixteen Trips in Time
by Robert Silverberg

The Unvarnished Gary Phillips: A Mondo Pulp Collection
by Gary Phillips

Voyagers: Twelve Journeys in Space and Time
by Robert Silverberg

MULTI-AUTHOR

Crime + Music: Twenty Stories of Music-Themed Noir
edited by Jim Fusilli

Dark City Lights: New York Stories
edited by Lawrence Block

The Faking of the President: Twenty Stories of White House Noir
edited by Peter Carlaftes

Florida Happens: Bouchercon 2018 Anthology
edited by Greg Herren

Have a NYC I, II & III: New York Short Stories;
edited by Peter Carlaftes & Kat Georges

No Body, No Crime: Twenty-two Tales of Taylor Swift-Inspired Noir
edited by Alex Segura & Joe Clifford

Songs of My Selfie: An Anthology of Millennial Stories
edited by Constance Renfrow

The Obama Inheritance: 15 Stories of Conspiracy Noir
edited by Gary Phillips

This Way to the End Times: Classic and New Stories of the Apocalypse
edited by Robert Silverberg

MIXED MEDIA

John S. Paul
Sign Language: A Painter's Notebook (photography, poetry and prose)

DADA

Maintenant: A Journal of Contemporary Dada Writing & Art (annual, since 2008)

HUMOR

Peter Carlaftes
A Year on Facebook

FILM & PLAYS

Israel Horovitz
My Old Lady: Complete Stage Play and Screenplay with an Essay on Adaptation

Peter Carlaftes
Triumph For Rent (3 Plays)
Teatrophy (3 More Plays)

Kat Georges
Three Somebodies: Plays about Notorious Dissidents

TRANSLATIONS

Thomas Bernhard
On Earth and in Hell
(poems of Thomas Bernhard with English translations by Peter Waugh)

Patrizia Gattaceca
Isula d'Anima / Soul Island

César Vallejo | Gerard Malanga
Malanga Chasing Vallejo
(selected poems of César Vallejo with English translations and additional notes by Gerard Malanga)

George Wallace
EOS: Abductor of Men
(selected poems in Greek & English)

ESSAYS

Richard Katrovas
Raising Girls in Bohemia: Meditations of an American Father

Far Away From Close to Home
Vanessa Baden Kelly

Womentality: Thirteen Empowering Stories by Everyday Women Who Said Goodbye to the Workplace and Hello to Their Lives
edited by Erin Wildermuth

POETRY COLLECTIONS

Hala Alyan
Atrium

Peter Carlaftes
DrunkYard Dog
I Fold with the Hand I Was Dealt
Life in the Past Lane

Thomas Fucaloro
It Starts from the Belly and Blooms

Kat Georges
Our Lady of the Hunger
Awe and Other Words Like Wow

Robert Gibbons
Close to the Tree

Israel Horovitz
Heaven and Other Poems

David Lawton
Sharp Blue Stream

Jane LeCroy
Signature Play

Philip Meersman
This Is Belgian Chocolate

Jane Ormerod
Recreational Vehicles on Fire
Welcome to the Museum of Cattle

Lisa Panepinto
On This Borrowed Bike

George Wallace
Poppin' Johnny

Three Rooms Press | New York, NY | Current Catalog: www.threeroomspress.com
Three Rooms Press books are distributed by Publishers Group West: www.pgw.com